Heroes of Urowen

Gamebook

David Velasco

Contact the author

Website and social networks:

www.david-velasco.net/english

E-mail: info@david-velasco.net
WhatsApp: +34 654 890 508
Skype: david-velasco-morales

ISBN: 9781520810881

These are tough times we are living in; times of change, of uncertainty, of deep regret... No doubt many are really suffering, but in Chinese, the word 'crisis' also means 'opportunity'.

This gamebook is the result of a great dream, the crowning moment for two years of hard work to create its basis and storyline. It is a book that intends to find that 'opportunity' by providing enjoyment to those who decide to go deep into its pages.

I therefore want to dedicate this book to Maria, for always being there, for maintaining a clear mind in the worst moments of crisis, for having answers and solutions for any question or situation, even when this would seem impossible. For her words of encouragement when there was little comfort left, for showing a smile and finding a kind face for everything, for supporting me in what seemed impossible, and for helping me, come hell or high water, to keep on searching my 'opportunity'.

One phrase joined us and, despite the time that has passed, I can still remember it clearly as if then was now. I will copy it hereafter as a token of our union, and may that phrase be, as well, my tribute to the great master:

«Elen síla lúmenn' omentielvo».
«A star shines in the hour of our meeting».

Heroes of Urowen

Name: .... Race: ....
Kingdom: .... Career: ....

Base life points (LP)

Power points (PP)

Experience points (EP)

Strength (STR) ....

Skill (SK) ....

Magic (MAG) ....

Perception (PER) ....

Skills

Armor   Helmet (H) ....
Chestguard (C) ....
Armbands (A) ....
Greaves (G) ....

Damage location roll

1	Legs	-1
2/3/4	Trunk	0
5	Arms	+1
6	Head	+3

Weapons

Miscellanea   Leather bag: you can only carry 6 objects

Zaifas ....

Magical and special items   They don't fill a slot in your leather bag

Base camp: ....

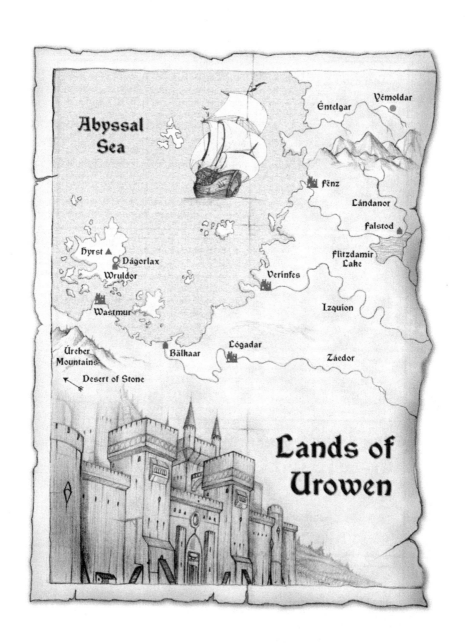

Abyssal Sea

Éntelgar

Vémoldar

Fénz

Lándanor

falstod

Hyrst

Dágorlax

Wruldor

Verínfes

flitzdamír Lake

Izquíon

Wastmur

Üreber Mountains

Bälkaar

Lógadar

Záedor

Desert of Stone

Lands of Urowen

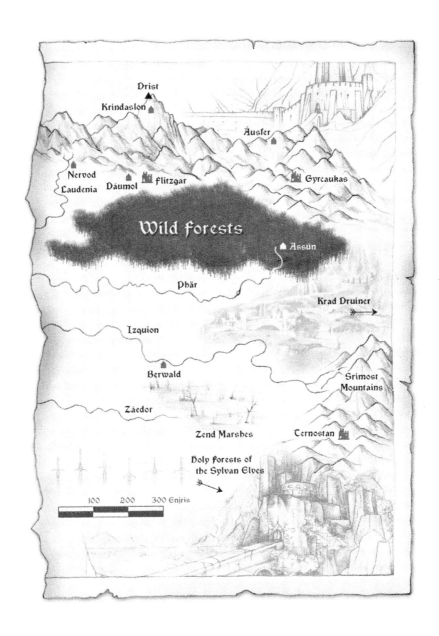

HEROES OF UROWEN

Gamebook

Rules

Prepare your character file, make decisions, roll dice, fight, use magical powers, equip an endless number of weapons... because now, you are the hero.

This work has been specially conceived for reading enjoyment, making you the central part of an unfolding history. This interactive adventure is based upon the trilogy 'The Manuscripts of Neithel', a series of novels by David Velasco. It can be read and played independent of that written saga, and with over twenty endings at your disposal, its pages will transport you to the mythical Lands of Urowen; an amazing fantasy world full of magic and deadly creatures that populate an extraordinary continent still to be explored.

Cast powerful spells, fight dangerous creatures, use your wits, purchase goods at the market, find magical objects, weapons and potions... Meet new characters and skilfully use steel to survive the multiple challenges you will have to face. To do so, you do not read this book in the usual way, instead you will have to follow the instructions within these pages. You can restart the book as many times as you want – choosing a different character each time – to discover the multiple quests you will have to complete. This adventure holds a great number of choices that you will have to make, requiring intuition or even on the power of your magic... But be extremely careful, as not all of the paths lead to the desired ending, and danger may await whenever you turn the page.

Continue reading the numbered section until you face a new challenge. Don't forget that you are the hero of this story, and that its development depends on your wits and skill, together with your luck at rolling dice.

The material that you will need to begin your first adventure is detailed hereafter, along with an explanation of the few simple rules you must follow to create your hero and to move on the story.

Material

First things first: your character file, which you must have already found on the previous pages. As you will have to repeatedly amend this file with changing data and corrections, you should photocopy or otherwise copy it so that you can record your adventures as many times as needed in different games.

The character file is also available for download from the author's webpage (www.david-velasco.net/english) so that you can print it quickly and easily as many times as you want.

Apart from that, you will only need a sheet of paper to write down annotations, a pencil and an eraser, and two six-sided dice (the usual type found in board games, preferably different in size or colour). Once you have these items, you're ready to start.

Character file

Before you start your adventure, you must complete your character file. As in any other roleplaying game, this sheet is very important, as it describes all the attributes and characteristics of your hero, which you will then repeatedly modify during the game. Gain experience points, magical objects, armor and a myriad of devices to improve your character file. Remember that you can download the template from the author's website.

Character information

For a start, let's go through the basic information of your hero. First of all, name your character, and add this in the space provided at the top of the file. Then, you will have to choose their race. There are three basic races that are then divided in nationalities or kingdoms. This decision will affect your hero's attributes as follows:

Attributes

There are four main attributes that will affect the fate of your hero: Strength (STR), Skill (SK), Magic (MAG) and Perception (PER).

1. Strength (STR): this is the stoutness of your hero, seen in the power of their muscles. Some weapons can only be employed by characters using this attribute.

2. Skill (SK): this includes both agility and the ability of your hero to perform certain activities. Some weapons can only be employed using this attribute.

3. Magic (MAG): this is the arcane power and concentration of your hero. Thanks to this attribute, your hero is capable of mastering the magical energies of Urowen.

4. Perception (PER): this represents the sensory capacity of your hero – how heightened their senses are. In certain occasions, it can be very useful to detect details that would otherwise go unnoticed.

These four attributes start from 0, i.e., they have no given points. They will only be modified at the beginning of the game, depending on the race and the job chosen for your hero. During the game, the maximum value these attributes can reach thanks to experience points is 6, and at the beginning of the game no attribute can have a value over 1.

Races: elf, dwarf and human

Elves

If you decide to play as an elf, you can choose between two nationalities: sylvan elves or snow elves.

Sylvan elves are usually blonde, very tall, slender and nimble. They are in constant contact with nature. They are good magicians, although there are also great warriors among their kind. Most of them live in the Holy Forests of the Sylvan Elves situated in the southeast region of Urowen.

Snow elves have white hair, with pale, delicate skin. Their appearance usually conceals great levels of endurance. They are extremely nimble and are great fighters on the battlefield. Snow elves live in the Ice City of Krindaslon, which is located in Drist Mountain, the highest peak of the Kandrist mountain range, to the north of Urowen.

If you choose to be a sylvan elf, add 1 point to the Magic (MAG) attribute on your character file. If you choose to be a snow elf, add 1 point to your Skill (SK) attribute.

Dwarves

The two main dwarf people of Urowen are both very similar regarding their physical attributes and personality traits. They are both bulky, sturdy and feisty. They are great friends and companions, loyal until death, extremely stubborn and orderly. As they are very strong, they are powerful fighters, specialised in the use of the battleaxe. Their two main towns, both dug deep out of the mountains, are Gyrcaukas, located in the Kandrist mountain range to the northwest of Urowen, and Ternostan, located in the Srimost Mountains, to the east.

If you choose to play as a dwarf of any kingdom, add 1 point to your Strength (STR) attribute.

Humans

Humans are the most populous race living in Urowen Lands. Although there are many human kingdoms, in this particular chapter we have made a selection of the most important and interesting ones. You should choose one of the following for your hero.

1. Kingdom of Flitzgar: one of the oldest and most respected peoples of Urowen. Most men of this kingdom are soldiers, although there are also many farmers and breeders because of the wide-open plains in its territory. They are honorable people, and their given word makes an oath. The

Kingdom of Flitzgar spreads all over the North of Urowen, and has several important cities. Its capital is Flitzgar.

If you choose to be a human from the Kingdom of Flitzgar, add 1 point to the Skill (SK) attribute on your character file.

2. Kingdom of Verinfes: they are extremely loyal and passionate. For a long time they have been dealing with Zorbrak adepts, the followers of the Dragon God, who try to reach the mainland from the Abyssal Sea. This kingdom has a powerful army of well-trained and well-equipped soldiers, although they have suffered many casualties because of continued fighting against their enemies. Their main city and capital is Verinfes, to the West of Urowen.

If you choose to be a human from the Kingdom of Verinfes, add 1 point to your Strength (STR) attribute.

3. Berwald: as their main characteristic, we can say that these people are divided into family clans. They are mostly humble and ordinary people involved in breeding and growing the fertile croplands that they live in. They occupy vast grasslands located to the North of the Zend Marshes, in the vicinity of Izquion River, to the East of Urowen.

If you choose to be a human from the Berwald Lands, add 1 point to your Skill (SK) attribute.

Careers

The job you choose for your hero will determine their future abilities, as well as their ease in learning how to handle certain weapons or to master certain spells, etc. There are seven main careers, each described below. Before choosing a career and writing down the extra points that specific job allows you to add on your character file, you should keep in mind that at the beginning of the game the maximum value you can start with in any attribute (Strength, Skill, Magic or Perception) is 1 – you cannot start a game with a value of 2 for any attribute. That's why, if the career chosen adds a point to an attribute that already has a point, it will instead be added to Perception. For instance, if you are a sylvan elf and you choose to be a sorcerer, you will begin your game with 1 point in Magic (MAG) and 1 point in Perception (PER) instead of 2 points in Magic. Thus, it is recommended (and usual) to start your game with 1 point in PER (you will find that very useful in certain moments) and another point in a different statistic. Nevertheless, this will change very soon, as you gain experience points, as you will discover. Regarding these instructions, when building your character file, you should consider that, to face the combats properly, it is wise to specialize in either STR, SK or MAG (only one of these attributes) – points may be wasted if distributed among these attributes, although you are free to play as you wish and to experiment if you decide so. Once you have chosen your job, add the points to your character file (following the rules described above) and the special ability granted for each character.

1. Sorcerer: your objective is to maximize control over the arcane energies in Urowen. A sorcerer's magic is based on their mental power, although to cast the charms properly it is essential that the sorcerer perfectly understands the right words and hand movements that will unleash their magical energies. If you choose to be a sorcerer, add 1 point to the Magic (MAG) attribute on your character file.

Special ability: when you make a damage roll, the sorcerer cannot roll 1 as a result. When this happens, it will 'magically' become a 3.

2. Hunter: skilled in bow and sword, the hunter is accustomed to outdoor life, to the forests, and is able to survive on the resources they can locate. If you choose to be a hunter, add 1 point to your Perception (PER) attribute.

Special ability: if the hunter has a bow, whenever attempting to fight hand-to-hand, their skill allows them to shoot a single arrow before beginning battle with a sword or similar weapon. In order to succeed with that shot, you need to attain the appropriate result for each bow. For instance, for a bow with difficulty 7, you'll need to roll a 7 to hit your enemy. To do so, you roll a dice and then add to that the points of your Skill (SK) attribute. If you succeed, you have hit your target and you'll then roll for damage location and damage incurred – these rolls will be explained further on in the Combat section. After this single shot that you are entitled to because you are a hunter, the first round of the combat will start, and you'll have to make the first opposed attack roll, which will be explained further on.

Example: Melnar is going to fight a frightening Servant of Neucen in hand-to-hand combat; a ruthless enemy from the dangerous Éntelgar Valley. His enemy runs towards him holding a two-handed battleaxe, but Melnar coolly seizes his bow and shoots before his enemy reaches him and is then forced to grab his sword to make an opposed attack roll. Melnar has a longbow with a difficulty of 8. He rolls a dice and gets a 6, and then adds the 2 points he has in his Skill (SK) attribute, so he achieves the 8 point total he needed. Luckily, his arrow hits his opponent and he now rolls for damage. If he had rolled a 5, even after adding his 2 Skill points, he would only have had a total of 7 points, and thus, his shot would have missed its target.

3. Warrior: the ultimate fighter. Trained since their youth in the use of weapons, with continued training they will become someone to fear on the battlefield. If you choose to be a warrior, add 1 point in the Strength (STR) attribute on your character file.

Special ability: given their expertise with weapons, when the warrior rolls for damage they add 2 additional points when they roll a 6, inflicting 8 damage points.

4. Thief: a 'go-getter' who tries to survive in a hostile world by using all of the means at their disposal. With clever hands and skilled with weapons, the thief won't hesitate to fill their pockets with their neighbour's goods. If you choose to be a thief, add 1 point to the Skill (SK) attribute on your character file.

Special ability: throughout your adventures, your clever hands will help you to obtain objects and treasures where others would have to pay, or find nothing. Additionally, you carry a larger leather bag, allowing you to carry 7 objects, whereas other characters will only be able to carry 6.

5. Minstrel: a citizen of the world well-versed in many arts, you know the roads, the different traditions in Urowen, the legends of the past. Because of your many journeys, you move easily in town and in the countryside. If you choose to be a minstrel, add 1 point to your Skill (SK) attribute.

Special ability: when you lose an opposed attack roll and are about to take a damage roll, as a minstrel, you can try to avoid the blow. To do so, roll a dice, and if you get 6 as a result, you completely avoid your enemy's attack.

6. Sàgrast Knight Monk: although usually human, members from any race and sex can join this order. They are cultivated people who can read and write. These monks have many properties all over Urowen, and they bow down to the god Sàgrast, the main enemy of Zorbrak, the Dragon God. Their main attribute consists of being good healers. Many of them have medical expertise, and some of them control magic. If you choose to be a Sàgrast Knight Monk, add 1 point to the Magic (MAG) attribute on your character file.

Special ability: this ability can be used just once per combat. When you win an opposed attack roll and you are going to make a damage roll, as a Sàgrast Knight Monk, you can choose between hurting your enemy (damage roll) or healing yourself to receive as many life points from the roll of a dice. If you roll a 6, it is considered a complete success and you will be healed an additional 2 life points, making a total of 8.

7. Alchemist: unlike the sorcerer, their mastery of magic focuses on chemical compounds and the use of potions. An alchemist is quite a cultivated person, what you could call a scholar of his time. The great passion of an alchemist is to broaden their knowledge and to become more powerful in magic. If you choose to be an alchemist, add 1 point to the Magic (MAG) attribute on your character file.

Special ability: all of the potions used to gain life points will have an extra effect on an alchemist. As a result, they will recover the usual life points granted by the potion, plus the extra points from rolling a dice for each potion they take.

Life points (LP)

As its name implies, life points indicate the health of the character (it measures both a resistance to illness and venoms, and to physical injuries). At the beginning of the game, your character's base life points are 20 (write this down on your character file). If your character's life points drop to 0, your hero dies. For the purposes of the game, that 'death' means that your hero has simply been knocked out and you'll be allowed to keep on playing after recovering. You will then resume your game from one of the cities that have been marked on the map during your visit, from one of the base camps you have written down on your character file, or you'll have to follow the instructions given in the book (this will be the most usual procedure). In that case, you will regain your 20 base life points (or more, if you have augmented them), but you will be penalised in a way that will be indicated in each case.

You fully recover your life points after every combat. This means that if you win a fight, you'll have your 20 base life points again (or more). If you recover LP during a combat, for instance, by taking a potion, you cannot then gain more life points than your base amount.

Just like yourself, your enemies recover their life points after each combat. That is why, if you are defeated and the book tells you to fight an opponent again, this opponent will also have their original life points restored, regardless of how many life points were lost during your previous fight.

* **Special note:** due to some events occurring during combat, both you and your opponent may reach 0 life points at the same time. This is a quite unlikely event, but it may happen. If this occurs, the combat continues on in the usual way, but now in negative numbers: the combatant with the lowest result after each round will be the loser (0 wins over -1). If there is a draw, even when in negative numbers (for instance, if you both reach -1 at the same time), keep on playing combat rounds until the tie is broken.

Power points (PP)

They indicate your powers of concentration and control over magical energies. Only sorcerers, Sàgrast Knight Monks and alchemists have power points.

Write down on your character file the power points as follows:

- **Sorcerer:** 3
- **Sàgrast Knight Monk:** 1
- **Alchemist:** 2

These are your initial points, but during the game you will have the chance to exceed these figures. Power points are not wasted in simple magical attacks – this will be explained further on in the combat section. They are only wasted if you cast really powerful charms that require your character's full concentration. However, at the beginning of the game you don't know any of these charms. You'll have to learn them during your adventures, and when you learn them you'll know their effects, and the power points necessary to cast them.

If you waste all your power points, or if you need more of them to cast a charm, you can earn them thanks to experience points, which will be explained in the following section.

Experience points (EP)

Experience points indicate the practice and expertise that your hero acquires during their adventure, as you face powerful enemies and your character completes more difficult quests. When you complete a mission you'll be informed about exactly how many experience points you have won, and you'll then add them to your current experience point total on your character file. At the beginning of the game, all characters start with 0 experience points. When you have gained enough experience points, you'll be allowed to spend them at any time to improve your character file and make your hero more powerful. Experience points are spent as follows:

- If you decide to increase 1 point in STR, SK or MAG, you'll need to spend 8 experience points (and deduct this amount from your character file). Remember that the limit of these attributes is 6.

- If you decide to increase 1 point in Perception (PER), you'll need to spend 2 experience points (and deduct this amount from your character file). Remember that the limit of this attribute is 6.

- Power points increase automatically. That means that, unlike in the previous cases, you don't need to spend experience points to increase your power points. For the purposes of the game, you automatically receive 1 power point whenever you have gained 4 experience points. You won't need to spend them and you'll be allowed to keep on stacking them in order to increase one of the other attributes (STR, SK, MAG or PER). To do so, every time you gain 1 experience point, write it down on your character file by marking one of the four checkboxes in the power points section. Once you have filled those 4 boxes, you'll get one power point with no need to spend experience points. Remember to erase all marks in the checkboxes once you've gained a power point, and then get ready to mark them again as you gain further experience points.

- Base life points also increase automatically. As in the case of power points, this means that, unlike what happens with the attributes STR, SK, MAG or PER, you don't need to spend experience points to increase them. For the purposes of the game, you receive a base life point automatically whenever you gain 10 experience points. You won't have to spend them and you'll be allowed to keep on stacking them in order to increase one of the other attributes (STR, SK, MAG or PER). To do so, every time you gain 1 experience point, write it down on your character file by marking one of the 10 checkboxes in the base life points section. Once you have filled these 10 boxes, you'll get 1 base life point with no need to spend experience points.

Remember to erase all marks in the checkboxes once you've gained a base life point, and then get ready to mark them again as you gain further experience points.

- When you lose experience points during the game, you only lose that point, and you won't have to erase any box that you have marked to automatically increase power points or base life points.

Skills

Skills are abilities and special techniques that you will learn during the game. You will find many different skills that will make your hero more and more powerful. When you learn a new skill, you will know how to use it, and its effects. Don't forget to write it down on your character file to keep it in mind when you face new challenges.

Combat

At this point, you must have almost chosen your desired hero, so you'd better understand how hand-to-hand combat functions before choosing weapons and armor.

For starters, you must know that every combat round will have two phases:

Phase 1. Opposed attack roll: as its name implies, you'll have to compare the value obtained in your roll with the result obtained by your enemy. The combatant who obtains the higher result wins this phase and has the chance to wound their opponent. In real combat this would mean that, after crossing swords with your enemy, you have overcome their defense and are attempting to injure them. To complete this roll, take one of the following attributes as a base: STR, SK or MAG. To do so, we'll have to consider which kind of weapon the character is using (when you gain a new weapon, you'll know which attribute it uses as a base, and you will record this on your character file). You then roll a single dice and add that result to the value you have in that specific attribute. The total result will be your opposed attack roll.

Example: Melnar is facing a bandit with his sword, which uses SK as a base attribute. He then rolls a dice, with 4 as the result. As Melnar has 2 points in his SK attribute, the total of his opposed attack roll is 6. We then compare this result to your opponent's result.

The bandit he is fighting against is holding an axe with STR as a base attribute. The bandit rolls a single dice, with 2 as the result. He then adds 1 point, as he has only 1 point in his STR attribute. His total is 3. As Melnar's total was 6, he is the winner of this phase and will be the one to make a damage roll.

If there is a tie, both rolls are cancelled out and you'll have to make new rolls. In real combat this would mean that both weapons have hit in the air, blocking each other, and a new attack will be attempted. If one of the combatants is currently losing life points in each round (due to a venom or because of a serious injury, for instance), a tie in the opposed attack roll stands for a whole combat round and that combatant will then lose the indicated life points before making a new opposed attack roll.

Characters with the required knowledge of magic can fight with their magical energies. To do so, they'll need a weapon using MAG as a base attribute, or they'll have to know an attack charm. These simple magical attacks don't spend power points. You use MAG the same way as explained in the previous paragraph, that is to say, the character rolls a dice and you add the points in their MAG attribute.

Phase 2. Damage location roll + Damage roll: the winner of Phase 1 makes these rolls, as only they now have the opportunity to wound their opponent. To do so, firstly determine the damage location. You will find a small table within your character file, so that you can easily refer to it at any time. The damage location table is as follows:

Damage location:
1. Legs: -1
2/3/4. Trunk: 0
5. Arms: +1
6. Head: +3

In order to determine the damage location, roll a dice and compare the result obtained with this small table. If you rolled a 1, it means that you will wound your enemy on the legs, and are required to deduct 1 point from the total damage of your weapon. This process will be further explained hereafter. If you wound them in the trunk, the result is not modified and remains the same. If you hit them on the arms, you'll add 1 damage point; and if you hit them in the head, you'll add 3 damage points.

Once you know the damage location, the moment has come to determine the damage inflicted (damage roll). To do so, check the weapon that you are using on your character file for its dice value of damage, or the damage of your enemy's weapon when they have won the opposed attack roll. You'll be given this information when you gain a new weapon, which must be written down on your character file, in the Weapons section.

Example: after having won an opposed attack roll, Melnar rolls a dice to determine the damage location, with 5 as the result. This means that he hits his enemy on one of his arms, and therefore wins an extra damage point. Melnar now rolls to determine the damage inflicted by his weapon. He is using a sword with damage of 1 dice (1d6). He rolls a 1, and adds the extra point for the damage location. Thus, the total damage inflicted on his opponent is 2.

Now it is time to check the kind of armor your opponent is wearing on the body part that you have hit. We will have to check how many points that piece of armor protects, then we will deduct this from the damage delivered as a result of the damage roll.

Example: as Melnar has hit his enemy on the arms, we must check what kind of armor his opponent wears in that location. If no protective gear is worn on the arms he would lose 2 life points, as the result of the damage roll was 2. However, if the bandit is wearing armbands – granting him 1 protection point – then this point is deducted from the result of the damage roll (2-1=1), and the enemy loses only 1 life point, as the other damage point is cancelled out by the armbands.

Once this result has been calculated, write down how many life points have been lost by either combatant. In the above example, Melnar has taken 1 life point from his opponent's 20 life points, so he now has only 19 life points remaining. You can write down these changing combat calculations on a separate sheet of paper, as suggested at the beginning of the Material section.

Next, as both opponents are still alive, another round of combat would begin with another opposed attack roll – repeat this process until one of the combatants reaches 0 life points. Note that hunters can only shoot 1 arrow with their bow in the first round.

Armor

You do not wear any type of protective gear at the beginning of the game. As your adventure unfolds you'll gain new pieces of armor that will then protect your hero, making them far more powerful.

Armor consists of different items: Helmet (H), Chestguard (C), Armband (A) and Greaves (G). Armor worn does not fill a slot in your leather bag.

- Helmet (H): a helmet only protects the head, preventing injury when your enemy rolls a 6 in a damage location roll.

- Chestguard (C): if the description given doesn't indicate otherwise, the chestguard protects just the trunk. Its protection is only applicable when your enemy rolls a 2, 3 or 4 in a damage location roll.

- Armbands (A): armbands protect just the arms, preventing injury when your enemy rolls a 5 in a damage location roll.

- Greaves (G): greaves protect just the legs, applicable only when your enemy rolls a 1 in a damage location roll.

Whenever you gain one of these armor items, write down its attributes and the protection points it grants in the appropriate place of the Armor section on your character file.

Weapons

At the beginning of the game, you only have the use of a small blunt knife. Write this down on your character file in the Weapons section as follows:

- Knife (SK). Damage: 1d6-3

* Note: in short, dice will be abbreviated as follows: 6-sided dice = 1d6.

So, 1d6-3 means that the knife inflicts damage equal to the value obtained when rolling a single dice and then deducting 3 points. That is to say, when you roll a dice, if you get a 4, you will only inflict 1 damage point, as you have to deduct 3 points from the result obtained. If you roll a 2, the result will be -1, but you will still be able to inflict damage to your opponent. Don't forget that you can get additional damage points from the damage location roll, and if you roll a 6 for damage location (and thus get 3 additional damage points for striking your opponent on their head), you would inflict a total of 2 damage points. If a storyteller was describing your attack, they may say that at the eleventh hour you finally cut your opponent's forehead, making their blood run into their eyes to obstruct their vision.

As you progress through the game, you'll gain more powerful and lethal weapons. Add these new items to your character file, discarding old weapons no longer required, as every weapon but the one you have at your waist (the one you usually use for combat), fills a slot in your leather bag, and it can only contain a maximum of 6 objects at any time.

Miscellanea

Every item that you gain during your adventures (except for magical and special items, which will be explained in the next section) fills a slot in your leather bag. Consider which items are important for you to carry during your adventure (for instance, potions, which can be used at any time), and which items should be discarded, as you can only carry a maximum of 6 items in your leather bag (unless you are a thief, then you can carry 7 items). Write down all required details of any new item in your character file, and delete all used or discarded items.

At the beginning of your game your leather bag is empty (all 6 slots), as you are only carrying a knife and, as it is your main weapon, it does not fill a slot. For hunters, a bow and arrows (when you gain them) don't fill a slot either, as they are also considered as a main weapon, complementary to a sword, for instance.

This category also includes zaifas (the name of the most common coin in Urowen). Carrying any amount of zaifas will NOT fill a slot in your leather bag. As far as money is concerned, you start your game with 15 zaifas. Add this amount to your character file.

* **Note:** for reality's sake, it is highly recommended that you use some coins to purchase some food. For the purposes of the game, food will never fill a slot in your leather bag. Write down this fact on your character file so that you don't forget it during the game.

Magical and special items

The first characteristic of these items is that they don't fill a slot in your leather bag. However, some of them are limited and you will only be allowed to carry a limited number of them, but you will discover that during your adventures. These items have magical powers or special attributes that you will be allowed to use to meet the challenges you will face along the way. As you find them, you will discover their attributes, their effects, etc. Explore the limits of Urowen to find the most powerful items.

Map

In the first few pages of this book you will have found a map of the Lands of Urowen (you can also download it from the author's website). This is the world where your adventures will take place. Get familiar with it, so that you can keep in mind the mainland you journey within, with its many different towns, rivers, etc.

Base camp

This is an important section for the purpose of playing the game. You will see that there is a space on your character file to add the different base camps you will find during your adventures. When you begin your journey some sections of the book will lead you to different sections, telling you the number of the section that you must turn to. You will have to be attentive to these numbers, as some of them will be followed by the words 'Base camp'.

When you find one of these numbers, write it down on your character file, as this is an important fact. These marked numbers are the exact place that you must return to when resuming an adventure after finding yourself unable to overcome an enemy. If you lose a combat and have no other option but to move back, then you must resume your game from the last number written down on your base camp list. That section number will be the most advanced location that you have found so far, and you will have to complete the penalty that you will be told about for having lost a fight.

Therefore, it is much like a videogame. The base camps are similar to places in which the system allows you to save a game – a safe point where you reappear in case you lose a life. Remember, whenever you come back to a base camp, you'll get back all of your life points.

These sections are also important if you ever lose track of your place within the adventure and can no longer correctly follow your story. Thanks to the base camps, you'll have a handy reference point available to easily find the section that you were reading before losing track.

Penalties

If you lose a fight or fail a specific roll, etc., you may be given some form of penalty that you will have to complete. If the text indicates that you are to lose an experience point and you don't have any at that moment (because you recently used them to upgrade your STR, SK or MAG), you don't lose an attribute. On the other hand, when you lose an experience point as a penalty, you only lose that, one of the experience points (EP) that you have stacked. You do not lose any marks of the checkboxes filled to automatically upgrade your base life points or your power points, so you won't have to delete any of these boxes.

How to read this book

It's very simple. As you've been told previously, you don't read this book straight from front to back, as per a traditional novel. Within its pages you will find endless indications that will guide you through the interactive reading process. These text indications will tell you the exact number of the section you must read next, or they will give you options to choose the next section, as in the following example:

- If you decide to enter the cave: 51
- If you'd rather continue on your way: 63

These options provide the number of the section you must read next to continue your adventure according to what you have just decided. That number doesn't tell you the number of the page, but the number of one of the many sections in which this text is divided – you will have to keep on reading from that specific section.

* Note: for those who have read the trilogy 'The Manuscripts of Neithel' (you don't need to have read these novels to play this adventure), the plot of this gamebook happens right between volumes II and III.

Difficulty levels

In some sections, especially in big cities where you have many options to choose from, you will be told of the difficulty level of some of the adventures. By taking note of these levels you can guess which challenges you should meet first in order to get ready for the more difficult challenges yet to come.

Game levels

According to the liking of different players, as if this was a videogame, you can use some simple rules to change the book's difficulty level.

If you read the book and follow all instructions as it is written, you will be playing the game at a 'standard' level. This is the default option and the most recommended level for starting players, as it can be too easy or incredibly difficult otherwise. However, you may want to play a second game or, if you enjoy really hard challenges, you may want to change its difficulty level. To do so, you only need to follow these simple rules, which will accordingly affect your character file.

1. Destroyer level: if you are really unlucky with the dice, or you just like to play as a real 'skull breaker', now you can play 'Heroes of Urowen' at a difficulty level that will undoubtedly help you to easily sweep away everything that stands in your way. Whenever you gain zaifas (coins) – except for bets – you will always receive 20 more zaifas than what is stated in the book, if the stated amount is under 100. You will get 40 more zaifas if the amount is 100 or more. Additionally, you will be allowed to increase your STR, SK or MAG attributes by using just 6 experience points instead of 8. The same benefit is also applied to the checkboxes that automatically increase power points or base life points, as you can now fill two less boxes than in standard mode.

2. Easy level: you will need only 6 experience points to increase your STR, SK or MAG attributes, instead of 8.

3. Standard level: you won't need to make any change to play at this level, as the book is already written for this level of difficulty.

4. Difficult level: whenever you gain zaifas (coins) – except for bets – you will receive 20 less coins than what is stated in the book if the amount is under 100. If the amount is 100 or more, you will get 40 less coins.

5. Heroic level: whenever you gain zaifas (coins) – except for bets – you will receive 20 less coins than what is stated in the book if the amount is under 100. If the amount is 100 or more, you will get 40 less coins. Additionally, to increase any attribute you will need 1 extra experience point. It is also the same for checkboxes to automatically increase power points and base life points.

Aside from these levels, your game may be made easier or more difficult depending on the race and job chosen for your character. These attributes and special abilities can have different impacts during the game, but that's something you will have to discover on your own.

Website and social networks

Remember, you will find additional information, downloadable content and more at the author's website. Plus, you can keep informed about David Velasco's books and all of the latest developments by following and interacting with his social networks. Be sure to visit them!

www.david-velasco.net/english

Contact the author:

If you have any queries about this gamebook's rules, or you want to ask a question or make a suggestion, you will find further information on David Velasco's website, otherwise you can contact the author directly:

E-mail: info@david-velasco.net
WhatsApp: +34 654 890 508
Skype: david-velasco-morales

*Now you are ready to meet the many
dangers that are waiting for you in
the unknown Lands of Urowen.
Do you dare to begin?*

*If you are willing to do so,
you only need to read the next page.*

Good luck, and welcome to Urowen!

Let the adventure begin...

«The life of every hero can become legend and make him immortal».

Famous proverb written by Neithel of Flitzgar in the
'Sinqua Çalendor' or 'Desolation Codex'.

The startling, powerful sound of a crowing rooster wakes you just after dawn. You lift your head a little from the pallet that you lie upon and, within the dim light that now filters through the cracks of a rickety window, you see a small room that appears strange to your bleary eyes. At that very moment all of the memories of the last estrios (in Urowen, days are called estrios) come back to you, as you are no longer at home.

→ If you are a sorcerer, a Sàgrast Knight Monk or an alchemist, 15.
→ If you are a hunter, a warrior, a minstrel or a thief, go to 20.

1

"I don't want to hurt you!" you shout loudly to be clearly heard. "Furthermore, I'm not carrying anything valuable."

"You liar!" he answers, enraged. "I saw you at the inn! Sure you're not carrying some zaifas! Give them to me!"

The strange bandit's nervousness increases rapidly, and almost seems to be out of control.

"I repeat, I don't want any trouble!" you insist again. "Let me be on my way!"

"You'll go when I say so! Give me what you're carrying first!"

You attempt to retreat to avoid this unwanted confrontation, but when he sees that you're trying to escape, the stranger immediately leaps on you, advancing with his fists, his face contorted with rage.

→ Go to 9.

2

You know that you won't be able to return to sleep, so you decide to get up and open the window. Light from Estrion, the shining star that illuminates Urowen, is barely seen on the horizon. Despite it being so early, you hear voices from downstairs, in the main room of the inn. You have nothing else to do here, so you pick up your meagre belongings and head downstairs, your stomach rumbling from hunger. When you enter the main room you see the innkeeper standing at the bar, talking to another man you have never seen before.

→ If you decide to approach: 22
→ If nothing holds you here and you leave the inn: 28

3

You chase after the bandit and almost without realising it, find yourself amid a dense sea of greenery. Trees stand all around you, hiding Estrion's light with their many leaves. You continue to inch forward, attempting to track of your enemy. You inspect the ground, but there are no visible footsteps, no broken branches in the bushes... nothing. Your attacker seems to have vanished without a trace. At that very moment you hear a distant crack.

■ Roll a dice for Perception (PER) with a difficulty of 6, adding your Perception points to the rolled result. If the total obtained is 6 or more, you have succeeded.

→ If you succeeded: 29
→ If you failed: 10

4

"Thanks for your help! You have chosen wisely, as this war in which we are currently engaged becomes increasingly complicated every estrio, and is about to extend to other regions of Urowen. Zorbrak's followers spread like a plague and we are too few to face them... But I have gone on for too long and darkness is coming. Come, let's get this place ready for the night!"

Laurmod immediately resumes his digging, helped by a thick branch, as he aims to light a small fire hidden from direct view of any passing enemies. You decide to help him, and working together you set the fire in short time, at the bottom of a big hole surrounded by a low wall of rocks. By this time, night has fully descended upon Urowen lands and you decide to share your food with him, while you continue talking animatedly of the facts that have led you here.

The woods seem to be in a state of total calm, so, tired as you are, you decide that the moment has come to sleep for a while. However, you do not do so without setting a lookout rotation, as according to Laurmod, it is very likely that bandits are near. After having seen the exhausted face of your companion, you volunteer to take the first shift and are soon surrounded by a terrible silence, broken only by weak crackles in the small bonfire, essential to keep yourselves warm during the cold night.

Time passes slowly while the dying fire continuess to burn with the few branches with which you feed it. At that moment, late at night, a sound grabs your attention...

■ Roll for Perception (PER) with a difficulty of 6. If the total is 6 or more, you have been successful.

→ If you succeeded: 17
→ If you failed: 21

5

"Who are you?" a voice suddenly asks, momentarily taking your breath away.

When you turn and focus on the speaker, you see a very old woman with a pockmarked face. Her long white hair is tied up in a thick braid on the left side of her head, falling down upon her chest. This stranger's body is bent, leaning on a wooden staff a little taller than herself, and she is dressed entirely in black, with cloth covering her head, contrasting with her snow-white hair.

"Who are you and what are you doing in my woods?" the woman asks again.

Without reason to hide the truth, you tell her your name and briefly describe the recent events that led you here. After hearing you out without interruption, the old lady, downhearted, seems to collapse, as she now leans her full weight on the staff.

"I sincerely regret what has happened to you," she says after taking a deep breath, "and I apologise on behalf of my son, as he would likely be the one who attacked you. I just beg of you to forgive him, as he suffers a disease that has no cure. He has suffered hallucinations since he was a little child... he feels that someone's chasing him so he attacks people, robs people, and he sees things that don't really exist. I have never separated from him because of this condition, but yesterday, I don't know how, I lost sight of him on the road and I had to venture into the wilderness to find him. Please, help me find him! If what you say is true, he must be seriously ill... He needs me..."

→ If you help the old lady to find her son: 25
→ If you think that it is better to forget about this issue and head back to the road: 32

6

You walk through a woodland full of ferns. Their twisted trunks are very thick and the gnarled shapes are fully covered with moss, lichens and an endless number of different climbing plants, many of them full of thorns. You quickly realise that it's going to be very difficult to find a suitable place to spend the night. These thoughts occupy your mind when you suddenly see something in the distance. You are not sure of what it is, but you believed that you saw something, or someone, moving nimbly between the trees. Extremely watchful and with your body completely tense, you head in that direction, hopefully remaining unnoticed.

Very slowly and silently, you reach a group of rocks where you hear a clear sound: somebody seems to be digging in the earth, possibly attempting to light a fire. You continue to approach, intrigued by this strange situation, until you finally see who it is that shares the wood. Then, after looking attentively at its clothing, you decide to show yourself.

↑ You gain 1 experience point (EP).

→ Go to 19.

7

"I am in your debt, but I have no zaifas to pay you," she says sadly. "Nevertheless, I have felt a great power within you," she adds as she approaches, now resting a hand upon your chest. "Yes, yes... there is magic in you; there is no doubt about that. What I am going to do next is something unusual for me, but you have earned it by far. If you wish so, I will teach you a powerful spell to master fire..."

* **Fireball.** Power Points (PP) needed to cast it: 2. Effects: after casting the spell, a fireball rises from the palm of your left hand and shoots out at the enemy. Directions for use: in order to cast this spell correctly, you have to win an opposed attack roll, making this with your character's MAG, and thereupon you have to spend the needed PP. Example: a sorcerer with MAG 2 rolls against a bandit. If the sorcerer wins the dice roll (the usual roll for combat), adding the 2 MAG points, you can choose to spend PP to cast the spell. Damage: 1d6+5 (this spell also has a dice roll for the location of damage to determine where the fireball hits). Notice: neither a magic object nor a magic weapon is needed to cast the spell. You just roll the dice on the MAG of the character, on their arcane energy. Write down this basic data of the fireball on your character file, in the skills box, on the back of the page or on another sheet of paper (as you prefer). Together with the name of the spell, you can also write down the number of this section, so that you can always come back here to check these instructions. As an example, so that you can take this into consideration throughout your adventure, you can note this down as follows:

- **Fireball (7).** PP: 2. You have to firstly win an opposed attack roll (MAG). Damage: 1d6+5.

After your meeting with the old lady, who insistently checks that you have learnt the spell correctly before letting you go, you head back to the road to resume the journey you started after leaving the inn. → Go to 32.

8

With your last attack you succeed in severely cutting open his stomach, so that his guts spill out while the bandit writhes on the ground in a pool of blood.

↑ You win 1 experience point (EP). Write it down in your character file and remember to check one of the boxes of your Base Life Points and Power Points.

You turn your gaze to your companion, who has also defeated his own opponent, but right at that very moment a volley of arrows falls on you. Roll a dice: if you roll a 1 or 6 you will be hit by an arrow. You have regained your 20 Life Points again, but take 2 away if you have been hit by the arrow, which injures your side. Another bandit comes out of the woods and immediately attacks with his sword. Get ready to fight, because this enemy seems to be much fiercer than those previous...

◻ **Bandit:** Regular sword (SK). Damage: 1d6 / SK 1 / LP: 20 / Armor: Leather chest (C). Action area: trunk (Points 2, 3 and 4). Protection: 2 LP. Remember that when inflicting damage points, if your attack aims against points 2, 3 or 4, you should deduct 2 points from your damage roll, corresponding to the 2 protection points that the chest armor awards. Keep on reading:

→ If you succeed in taking 12 LP away and reduce his LP to 8: 23
→ If you are defeated: 30

9

You quickly move your hand to your belt and grip your knife, hardly having enough time to do anything else before the strange assailant is already upon you, screaming unceasingly and attacking you by force:

◻ **Bandit:** Fists (SK). Damage: 1d6-4 / SK 0 / LP: 15 / Armor: None (From now on, unless it is noted otherwise, this means that this character has no armor at all) / Special Ability: Coward. If the bandit loses 5 LP, he will flee from battle, terrified.

→ If you succeed in making the bandit flee: 18
→ If the bandit defeats you: 24

10

You try to sharpen your senses to locate the origin of this sound, but you remain unsure of its source. You finally decide to make your way towards what you think is north, where you thought you saw a clearing in the thicket. You move very slowly, trying to make as little noise as possible, but your heavy steps seem to have betrayed you, as with your heart racing, you feel somebody now touch your back... → Go to 5.

11

You cross the large square in front of the market and enter the crowded tavern. It's named 'The Blue Fire' according to a wooden sign hanging over the door. As you enter the room, you immediately notice that the tavern is crowded with many different kinds of people. Due to the lateness of the estrio and the constant rumbling of your stomach, you choose to approach the bar, where a young maid moves towards you to assist. She offers the following:

- **Wine jar:** 1 zaifa.
- **Beer jar:** 1 zaifa.
- **Pork stew:** 3 zaifas.
- **Meat pie:** 3 zaifas.
- **Onion soup:** 1 zaifa.
- **Great journey bread; two estrios:** 4 zaifas.

While you are enjoying a well-earned rest, a man begins playing the lute, while another starts singing a rather lively, funny song that raises much laughter from the assembled audience. While this is happening a burly man, apparently the innkeeper, approaches with a massive six-candled candelabra that lights up the room. After pouring the content of a small leather bag onto the palm of his hand, the innkeeper blows on it with all of his might. Then, you look on with surprise as a white powder darts towards the thick candles, inexplicably enlarging their flames into a striking shade of vibrant blue as the crowd responds with enthusiastic applause and cheering.

Temporarily mesmerized by the intense azure glow of the flickering flames, you now hear somebody nearby shouting the word 'dogfight'. Not knowing what this means, you approach a group of people huddled around a table, seemingly placing bets.

"What is that for?" you ask one of the regulars, a man with grey hair and a bulging belly.

"In a moment a dogfight is going to start. People place their bets and you may win large profits – although you can also lose everything if luck is against you."

"Where will the fight be held?" you ask, interested.

"Just over there, in the backyard... Two legendary beasts will fight today. Hurg and Gränkot are their names, two bloodhounds as fierce and as burly as a mountain lion. In addition, their masters are old enemies, so a great show is guaranteed. If you have some zaifas, I suggest that you should consider a bet... It will make you feel alive!"

→ If you decide to place a bet: 56
→ If you forget about this contest and head back to the bar: 64

12

The skillful bandit has been too powerful for you. ↓ As a penalty for having been defeated, you lose all of your zaifas, if you have any.

→ Go back to 27 and fight him again.

13

You walk through a woodland full of ferns. Their twisted trunks are very thick and the gnarled shapes are fully covered with moss, lichens and an endless number of different climbing plants, many of them full of thorns. You quickly realise that it's going to be very difficult to find a suitable place to spend the night. These thoughts occupy your mind when somebody at your back suddenly speaks.
"Stop! Who are you? You don't look like a bandit."

→ Go to 19.

14

This battle was closely fought, but you lacked the skill required for such an intimidating opponent.

↑ You win 1 experience point (EP). Write this down on your file. You can only win this point once, no matter how many times you come back here.

↓ Your wounds are very serious, so although you can repeat the fight at section 25, you will restart with 17 life points instead of 20 (once you defeat your enemy, you will get your 20 life points back). Note that if you return here again, you will repeat the fight against the wolf with one life point less after each defeat, that is to say, 16, 15... and so on.

15

You sit up in your bunk, remembering your master's last words, which won't stop turning over and over in your mind: «Your time here is over, young apprentice. You can no longer learn anything new from me. The time to leave has come. Seek new masters, search old grimoires and then study their spells. Increase your powers and learn to control magic. Travel as much as you can, explore incessantly, as that is the path that leads to becoming a great magician. I know you are a restless spirit, and that will help you in your quest. I wish you luck, young apprentice. But now, strike out and don't look back». → Go to section 2.

16

"I am in your debt, but I have no zaifas to pay you," she says sadly. "Nevertheless, I have felt a great power within you," she adds as she approaches, now resting a hand upon your chest. "Yes, yes... there is magic in you; there is no doubt about that. What I am going to do next is something unusual for me, but you have earned it by far. I know it's valueless compared to what you have done for me, but please accept this present as a token of my gratitude..."

The old lady gives you a small wineskin containing a powerful mixture:

- **Healing potion.** How to use it: in battle, after rolling dice for an opposed attack, if you have won the right to injure your enemy, you can choose to drink this potion instead. There is potion enough for 1 dose. When you drink it, you will recover 1d6+4 life points. Write it down on your character file in your leather bag, as this potion fills one of its slots. Once used, erase it from your file. Together with its name, you can also write down this section number, so that you can always come back here to check these instructions. As an example, so that you can take this into consideration throughout your adventure, you can note this down as follows:

- **Healing potion (16).** Win opposed attack roll first. Recover: 1d6+4 LP.

After your meeting with the old lady, who finally recovered her son, you head back to the road to resume the journey you started after leaving the inn. → Go to 32.

17

Startled by the sound, you rise from the fire and take a couple of steps towards its source. After focusing your gaze on the surrounding darkness, you spot a distinctive shadow in the distance that appears to be aiming directly towards you with something in its hands. Then, you hear the sound of a bowstring and you immediately jump aside, shouting at your sleeping companion to rise. An arrow passes right by you, lightly touching your head, and hits the nearby tree trunk, hard. Get ready for the imminent battle, as the shouts of several assailants now spread throughout the nearby forest... ↑ You win 1 experience point. → Go to 27.

18

After inflicting a couple of cuts on your opponent, the bandit understandably feels terribly inferior in both strength and skill, and realises that his life is in grave danger if he continues his attack. So without further reflection, he suddenly flees to the side of the road and jumps into the thicket.

↑ You win 1 experience point (EP). Write it down on your file.
→ If you are a sorcerer, an alchemist or a Sàgrast Knight Monk: 26

Otherwise, keep on reading:

→ If you decide to chase the strange character into the thicket: 3
→ If you prefer to forget about him and resume following the road: 32

19

"Excuse me, sir, I didn't mean to bother you," you say in a calm voice. "I am just a lone traveller looking for a safe place to spend the night."

The stranger then, surprised, looks at you curiously, as if he is trying to discover whether you are telling the truth. You take these few moments to further study his appearance, as it powerfully draws your attention. He's a man getting on in liznars (years are called this in Urowen), with a respectable face and a poorly trimmed beard. Despite his dishevelled appearance, he's wearing an opulent uniform of the Flitzgar Guard. You recognize the uniform because of the emblem on his leather cuirass, the Golden Key, the emblem of the kingdom. To complete his outfit, he's wearing a thick, sturdy coat, riding boots and a trimmed silver helmet. He's also carrying a sword in its sheath and a knife on the opposite side of his waist.

"Where are you headed, traveller?" he asks as his hand moves to the grip of his sword.

"Verinfes is my destination," you quickly answer.

"In that case, we walk down the same path. But tell me... What is your name and what are you doing in these lands?"

After telling him a little of your history and the reason for your journey, the stranger seems to relax and decides to tell you his story:

"My name is Laurmod, and I come from the distant city of Flitzgar, carrying an important message that I must deliver as soon as possible in Verinfes. The war intensifies towards the North..." After a short pause, he resumes his story, thoughtful and with his gaze lost within the thicket. "I have been wandering through the forest for two estrios. I was riding my horse at good pace towards the city when a group of bandits took me by surprise. They were undoubtedly Zorbrak spies; there are many of them operating unimpeded through our kingdoms. They took me by surprise, as I was saying, and my horse was hit by three arrows, so it collapsed, seriously injured. I was forced to escape, leaving the animal behind, and in order to gain some advantage, I went deep into the wood. I have been constantly running from these swines, but they are always breathing down my neck. I have killed two of them so far... but they are still after me. I thought you were one of those bastards, but with your appearance I would bet that you aren't. I wish that I am right, and that Sàgrast has set you on my path to help me reach my destination, as I am very weak and still have a long way to go. Tell me... will you help? As I have told you, it is of great importance that I deliver the message I'm carrying. If you help me, I am positive that you will be amply rewarded by the Court of Verinfes."

→ If you help the soldier of Flitzgar: 4

→ If you decide to move away and resume your walk to Verinfes alone: 50

43

20

You sit up in your bunk, remembering the last words your father told you, which won't stop turning over and over in your mind: «Your time here is over, my son. You can't learn anything else from me. The time to leave has come to look for a better life, as I don't want you to follow my footsteps. If you stay, you will only have the plow and an infertile plot of land that produces just enough to survive. I don't want that for you, my son. I know destiny has chosen you to do great things and I have taught you all that I know. Go now and travel as far as you can, you have the whole world to discover. Maybe fortune will smile on you... I wish you luck. But now, strike out and don't look back. Maybe we will meet again one estrio or another».

→ Go to section 2.

21

You thought that you had heard a light sound of movement nearby, but after listening attentively and focusing your gaze in the darkness for a long time, you decide that it must have been a mouse or some other nocturnal animal. You look back at the fire and throw on another small branch. A that very moment, you clearly hear a distinctive whirring, the unmistakable sound of a bowstring breaking the silence of the night. Unfortunately, it is too late to react, as your enemy has shot at you from close range. Without being able to do anything to avoid it, you feel a terrible pain in your left arm: an arrow has struck your shoulder. Luckily, although the arrow has inflicted a deep cut that begins to bleed profusely, it hasn't permanently stuck in your unprotected flesh.

By now though, shouts are spreading in the forest. Get ready for the imminent battle...

↓ Lose 2 life points, as you have been injured by an arrow.
→ Go to 27.

22

"Good estrio!" the innkeeper says exuberantly when you approach, instantly dismissing the other man. "Did you have a good night? I do hope so. Do you want something for breakfast or some supplies for the road?"

If you want, you can buy one of the following foods:

- **Milk jug:** 1 zaifa.
- **Piece of bread:** 1 zaifa.
- **Block of cheese:** 1 zaifa.
- **Trip food rations for two estrios (days):** 5 zaifas.

* Note: in order to bring some realism to the game and provide a suitable background, it is highly recommended that you adequately supply your character by spending some zaifas on food. For the purposes of the game, food will never fill slots in your leather bag. Write this fact down on your character file so that you don't forget it throughout the game.

After your short encounter with the innkeeper, you notice the stranger by your side, who apparently hasn't yet noticed you. You can't think of anything else of interest to hold you here, so you resume your trip to the West, towards the Abyssal Sea and the city of Verinfes, where you have decided to start your quest. → Go to 28.

23

After your last attack, your enemy staggers and takes a step back, seriously injured. But something you hadn't expected happens just then, as your companion, Laurmod, who has killed another bandit, launches a devastating attack on your enemy's back, striking him on the neck. In less than a second your enemy's head is cleanly chopped off and now rolls towards you.

"Hurry!" says Laurmod, trying to put out the fire with his feet. "We don't have much time to waste!" he adds.

Before fleeing, you crouch by your enemy's corpse and tear off a small leather bag that was hanging from his belt.

Covered by the shadows of the night, you run desperately through the forest. Shouts are heard, and when you turn your head to check behind you, you clearly see the flickering light of several torches coming towards you.

You shadow Laurmod in complete silence. He moves skillfully in the thicket, like an expert scout. You keep on moving like this for a long time, gaining a significant advantage over your pursuers. Then, you reach a sharp, dangerous slope, but it is apparently the only way forward. That's why you don't hesitate to follow the soldier of Flitzgar, who has already started the descent. Fortunately for you, the small ravine is not as treacherous as it seemed in the darkness, as it had many rocks and trees you could grab on to. As a result, both of you arrive at your destination safely and you finally have a few moments to catch your breath. You now examine what's inside the bag taken from the bandit, and are pleasantly surprised when you discover 30 zaifas (if you are a thief, you will get 20 more zaifas, as you also searched one of his pockets). But there is no time for anything else, as Laurmod is extremely worried and nervous, believing that it's best to resume the journey to Verinfes without waiting for dawn to arrive.

→ If you decide to stick with him: 40

→ If you have had enough and you think it best to turn away from him, and allegedly from danger: 50

24

Although you were more powerful than your enemy, and were better equipped, the bandit has unfortunately been more skillful on this occasion and has defeated you. After having being knocked unconscious, you wake up with a terrible dizziness, and soon discover that the bandit has stolen all of your zaifas, your supplies and the knife. From now on, you will have to fight with your fists: (SK). Damage: 1d6-4.

The black eye and terrible bump on your forehead, given to you by your mad assailant, should teach you a good lesson.

↑ You win 1 experience point (EP). Write it down on your file.

→ Applying the noted penalties (erase all lost items from your file), go back to section 9 and try again to defeat him.

25

"Thank you for helping a fragile old woman!" she says with tears in her eyes. "May Sàgrast bless you!"

"Do you have any clue as to where your son may be?" you ask, pointing towards the forest's thick blanket of vegetation. "I couldn't follow his tracks."

"Unfortunately, I also lost his trail, but have been following a small trail of blood for a while. I have also seen footprints, I think wolf footprints... I do hope that I am wrong, although I fear the worst. Everything suggests that my son is injured and that wolves are stalking him. We have to hurry – come, let's follow the track."

Without speaking further, the woman sets off with her gaze focused on the surrounding vegetation. She stops suddenly, moving her hand to a great green leaf where you can see a couple of blood drops.

"We're on the right track. Let's hurry!" she says, resuming the trail.

You walk for a long while and, suddenly, after traversing a slope, you hear a distant yell.

"Sàgrast, it's my son! And he needs help!"

You focus your gaze on a distant thicket, where you now see the strange bandit who attacked you earlier – he's being attacked by three massive black wolves.

"Take this!" shouts the old lady, her hand unexpectedly holding a sword. "You're going to need it!"

You immediately grasp the offered weapon, deeply puzzled as to how she concealed it, but knowing that this is not the best moment to think further about it. You quickly follow her, as the old woman is already running towards the wolves at an unnatural pace for her age. Write down the following details on your character file:

- Regular sword (1 hand, SK or STR). Damage: 1d6

After a short but frantic run, you arrive at a small clearing where her son is lying on bloodied ground. You see that his clothes are stained with blood, his arm injured. Nevertheless, he is adequately defending himself from the ground with a long branch, which he is handling with ease. But there is no time for further thought, as while the woman bravely leaps on one of the wolves, the third one – the largest of the trio – turns to face you and races directly towards its intended prey.

◘ **Black wolf:** Fangs (SK). Damage: 1d6-1 / SK 1 / LP: 11 / Special Ability: Biting power. If the wolf rolls a 6 in a damage roll, it has achieved a perfect bite with its powerful jaws, biting with all of its considerable might: add 2 to its damage. Thus, as its damage is 1d6-1, if it rolls a 6, 1 point will be deducted, but 2 points will be added due to this perfect bite, resulting in 7 damage points.

→ If you kill the wolf: 36
→ If the wolf knocks you out: 14

26

Your magical powers cause you to feel a strange arcane energy from somewhere close to where you are standing. It seems to be coming from under your feet, just a few steps away. You approach slowly, closely monitoring the ground ahead, from where you suddenly spot a small silver ring, faintly glowing upon the earth. It appears that the bandit dropped this item during your confrontation. Attracted and intrigued by the magical vibration that the ring casts, you pick it up and, when you sense that its energy isn't harmful, you decide to place it on your finger.

- **Voldar ring** (magical object that does not fill a slot in your leather bag). It is a plain, untarnished silver ring. It allows you to fight with your fists using your magical power. The attacks you make by doing so do not use power points (PP).

- **Voldar ring**, attack with bare fists (MAG). Damage: 1d6-1

→ Go back to 18 and keep on reading.

27

You look over at Laurmod, who is already standing ready for battle, but you don't have the time to see anything else, as another bandit, different from the one that fired the shot, comes out of the thicket and leaps on you, grasping what seems to be a massive, rusted sickle...

▫ **Bandit:** Sickle (SK). Damage: 1d6 / SK 0 / LP: 19 / Armor: Leather armbands and greaves (A) (G), Protection: 1. Remember that, when inflicting damage points, if your attack aims at his arms or legs, you should adjust the total of your roll corresponding to the protection point awarded by armbands and greaves. For example, an attack aiming at his legs would require you to deduct 2 points, one for the damage location (legs, -1), and another corresponding to the protection awarded by the bandit's greaves.

→ If you defeat him: 8
→ If he beats you: 12

28

You resume your trip, quickly leaving the inn behind, a cool breeze following you through this forlorn environment. You are, after all, in the vicinity of the Izquion River, which assists many trees and bushes to grow lushly, so the many greens of copious varieties of plants is the prevailing colour here. You walk silently, lost in your own thoughts, listening to the sound of a nearby bird. But then a loud crack makes you turn your head to the left where you see the stranger from the inn coming out of the thicket.

"Give me all your belongings! Hurry up! Don't make me say it twice!" he says quickly, clearly nervous.

The man appears to be unarmed, and he doesn't look like a very fierce or powerful enemy. Actually, he's a rather skinny individual, and quite unconfident, judging by his visible lip tremors.

→ If you try to avoid this robbery by talking to him: 1

→ If you think that this wretch deserves to be punished, you grasp your knife and determinedly face him: 9

29

You focus on your hearing, and after the first crack you keep on listening to a very faint sound you believe to be footsteps. You take several steps through the thicket tracking this sound and now you are positive: somebody is walking slowly through the forest, shuffling as they walk. You decide to hide at once, as everything you sense suggests that the stranger is coming directly towards you. Without any further hesitation, you crouch among some nearby bushes until you are partially hidden. From your hiding place, vigilant and in complete silence, you hear the steps coming closer and closer, until you finally see the stranger approaching...

→ Go to 5.

30

Although you fought bravely, this enemy was far too powerful for you. ↓ During the battle you have lost an item from your leather bag – if you were carrying any. Now take a deep breath and gather your strength, as you will have to give your best to beat him.

→ Go back to 8 and show him what you're made of. Fight the bandit directly with your 20 LP now restored.

31

When you hurriedly move closer, you see that Laurmod now lies on the ground. He can hardly breath and responds with great difficulty.

"I won't be... able... I won't get to... Verinfes..."

"What's wrong?" you ask, extremely nervous at this news.

"I was injured in the... side," he says as he moves his cloak to show an injury apparently not too serious. "I thought I could... get ahead... but now I'm sure... The weapon I was injured with was... poisoned."

"Come on, me must go on! I will help you get to Verinfes!"

"It's useless... Listen to me carefully... because I have no time left." He hastily searches through his clothes and produces a small, carefully folded parchment. "You must go to Verinfes, and deliver this... Ask for Brádoc in... the stronghold... He'll know what to do."

"But why would they listen to me? They wouldn't believe me!"

"Don't worry about that... The parchment is sealed... and it carries the intact seal of King Xon Lorker... Tell them what happened..."

At that very moment, Laurmod collapses backwards while a black foam begins to dribble out of his mouth. You try desperately to revive him, and he seems to regain consciousness somewhat, so he speaks again:

"Now... run... run... don't stop."

After that, he collapses again, unconscious, until you see that his breath steadily fades little by little. Distraught, you struggle between trying to help him, which seems now to be totally impossible, and quickly running away. In the end, with no hope to save him, you decide to obey Laurmod's last words and quickly continue on to the city of Verinfes, now travelling alone.

It is not too long before you locate the Izquion River and, as expected, the imposing image of Verinfes soon appears in the distance. Reassured by the idea of reaching your destination, you walk faster, until you finally stand before one of the gates of the city, well guarded by a large group of soldiers. Hastily, you move closer to them, knowing that they'll be able to help you in your quest.

"I have a message for Brádoc! It's extremely urgent!"

At the beginning all of the soldiers look at you suspiciously, but after you briefly explain what has happened, and show them the sealed parchment, they decide to escort you to the city stronghold. There they keep you waiting in a small room, sitting before a wooden table. Then, the door opens and a strange man walks in.

"I am Brádoc, Senior Soldier of Verinfes! I've been told that you have something important for me!"

Brádoc is a man getting on in liznars, who limps slightly on his left leg. His long, grayish hair is drawn back in a ponytail, and a dark eye patch that covers his right eye – lost after a serious battle against dreknars, the bloodthirsty inhabitants of Éntelgar Valley – stands out on his stern face. He wears a simple black tunic with the badge of the Bear Skull embroidered on its chest – the original symbol used by the founders of Verinfes, and a coat of arms that fell into disuse dozens of liznars ago. On one side of his waist hangs a stunning double-edged sword, featuring a long hilt of the same dark colour as his clothes.

After being momentarily surprised because of his magnificent appearance, you report to him fully, telling him all about Laurmod and of your trip, and hand him the parchment.

"King Xon Lorker's seal is certainly authentic," he says with great interest before breaking the wax seal and unrolling the parchment. A tense silence hangs over the room while Brádoc carefully reads the parchment. "You have rendered a great service to the Kingdom of Verinfes, my friend! Wait here and you will be rewarded. Thanks again for your help!"

After saying these few words, Brádoc quickly leaves. After having waited for several moments, a soldier enters the room and hands you a small bag containing 60 zaifas.

→ Write this amount on your character file, and go to 45.

32
Base camp
(write this number down on your character file)

You resume making your way to Verinfes, the city you expect to reach sometime soon. You are looking forward to discovering all that this wonderful city has to offer. People say that you can find almost anything in its great market, as hundreds of merchants come and go following the trading routes of Urowen, covering the whole of the mainland.

Eagerly, you keep on walking, but nightfall has descended before you have reached your desired destination, as Estrion is beginning to set on the far horizon. Darkness will soon have taken over everything. You look around, but you see only the plants and vegetation of the thick forest. It appears that you will have to spend the night in the open air, so you decide to head into the thicket, where you will be more secure, to look for a place to rest.

■ Roll a dice for PER with a difficulty of 4. Remember, roll a dice and add your PER. → If the final value is 4 or higher, go to 6. Otherwise, go to 13.

33

While you walk nonchalantly across the main square of Verinfes, you notice odd movement nearby... a hooded stranger moves a little too close to a man who appears to be a rich and successful merchant. Then, you see a knife moving extremely fast through the air, expertly cutting the belt that holds the bulging bag of coins at the merchant's waist.

"Thief!" you shout at the top of your lungs, while the startled merchant begins screaming, desperately looking for the person responsible for the robbery, who seems to have instantly vanished.

You look all about you, attempting to spot the fleeing thief, but the crowd restricts your vision, assisting the shadowy figure to escape.

■ Roll a dice for PER with a difficulty of 6.

→ If the total is 6 or higher: 49
→ Otherwise: 59

34

This extraordinary and powerful creature has proved to be too tough for you. ↓ As a consequence for having been defeated, you lose 1 experience point (EP). This loss of points is only applicable once. That is to say, if you fight her again and you are defeated, you won't lose any more points. Now you have two options:

→ If you decide to fight this strange monstrosity again, go back to 70 and attempt to defeat her.
→ If you prefer to now leave and resume looking for the cave: 52

35

"Well said, my young friend! I see that you are as brave and as bold as I've been told, as I'm sure that it must have been really difficult to reach Verinfes carrying that message... Well, as I see that you are determined to go on, I'm going to unravel the secrets behind this mission. What I need you to do is to go into a cave half an estrio away from here, north of the city, situated very close to the coast, to bring back a chest buried there. I will provide all of the required directions so that you can locate the cave and the hidden chest."

"Is that all?" you ask with a worried frown, as it seems somewhat too easy. "What is the catch?"

"The trap you must overcome, my friend, is the nocthilius who has made that cave her home."

A harsh shiver runs down your spine as you hear that name, as there are many legends in Urowen about this ominous being. Few have seen one and then survived to tell their story, as it is a night creature, flesh-eating and extremely ferocious. It is said that nocthilius have powerful bat-like wings and four legs ending in retractile claws. Regarding the rest of her body, the available descriptions are contradictory, as very little is known for sure about this dark and dangerous creature.

"Tell me, are you determined to continue?" the old man asks suddenly, interrupting your thoughts.

"What will I receive if I accept this task?"

"That's a good question! You see, as far as I know, in the chest I have told you about you will find a small bottle containing a black liquid, weapons, a bucket full of zaifas, and probably some powerful items. I only want the bottle, you can keep the rest. I can assure you that the reward will be worth the danger. Regarding the bottle, its contents are mine, and I do not wish to be questioned further about it. So, tell me, are you interested?"

→ If you would prefer to go back to the main square of Verinfes at this point to better equip yourself or to look for other challenges in order to become mightier, go to 45. In this case, write the number 35 on your character file together with the word 'nocthilius', so that you can return to this section whilst still in Verinfes to begin the search for the hidden chest.

→ If you decide to accept this mission: 58

36

After a long, bloody combat, with one mighty blow you finally and fatally pierce the black wolf's body with your blade. After shaking violently, your defeated opponent now lies on the ground, lifeless, in a pool of blood. At that very moment, you look up from the deceased wolf to see how the strange old lady, after tearing her own enemy apart, now dashes for the remaining wolf that still attacks her son. Then, before your astonished eyes, the long staff that the old woman grasps firmly begins to shine with such a shimmering brightness that you are forced to cover your eyes.

When the intense light has subsided and a calmness finally returns to the clearing, you see the corpse of the third wolf lying on the ground, completely burnt, still smoking intensely. The old woman is kneeling by her son, hugging him tightly, reciting in a low voice what seems to you to be some sort of invocation.

↑ If you killed the wolf at your first try, you win 1 experience point (EP). Write this down on your character file.

"Thank you very much for your help!" the old lady says again when she perceives you standing nearby. "Without you... I couldn't have made it. My powers are becoming weaker and weaker... I would've only barely been able to overcome the wolf that you fought. I will be eternally grateful..."

→ If you are a sorcerer, a Sàgrast Knight Monk or an alchemist: 7
→ If you are a hunter, a warrior, a minstrel or a thief: 16

37

◻ **Nocthilius:** Claws and fangs (SK). Damage: 1d6+1 / SK 2 / LP: 20 / Armor: none / Special Ability: Poison. When the nocthilius injures you, if it rolls a 1 in its damage roll, not only has it inflicted 2 damage points, but it has also inoculated the poison within its fangs. From this point forward, at the beginning of each round, you will lose 1 life point due to the venom's lethal effect. You lose this life point just before rolling dice to attack.

→ If you are defeated by the beast: 62
→ If you have already become a hero, having victoriously crushed this abominable creature: 55

38

"I see that not all of what's been said about you is simply loose talk," the girl adds when she realises your interest in knowing what it is she wishes to propose. "You are brave, and daring... I like that. We could put you to good use in the mission we are about to begin. We have been chasing our objective for a long time, and we've finally located him... Oh, but I think that I wasn't fair to you before."

↑ If she actually stole some zaifas from you, she now gives them back with an impish smile.

↑ You also win 1 experience point (EP) because of your bravery and for having come this far.

"And now tell me..." the girl speaks again. "Do you understand anything of what I'm telling you?" → Go to 51.

39

"Excuse me, sir! Do you have any zaifa for me?"
"What do you want it for?"
"It's for my mum... She's ill. Well, not exactly."
"What do you mean?"
"Many people don't believe me; they think that I'll cheat them, but my mother is the victim of an incantation by a mighty wizard. These days she can't even rise from her bed... She feels pain everywhere, and that man asks for a lot of zaifas from us to set her free from the incantation."
"A wizard? Who is this man?"
"I don't know much about him. He lives on the outskirts of the city, in a small hut by the river. One estrio he came to my house and told my mother that, if she didn't give him 500 zaifas, he would curse her. Since my father died, we barely have enough to eat. We told this man that, but he didn't care and cruelly cast his curse on my mother. Now he is asking for that amount from us again to set her free, and she becomes worse and worse every estrio. I have tried to talk to the soldiers, but nobody believes me. They think that I am crazy and now I don't know what else to do..."

You watch, astonished, as the little girl starts crying uncontrollably. Touched by what you see, you kneel by her side and try to calm her.

"Will you help me, please? I have 30 zaifas so far. I will give them to you if you agree to help my mother..."

→ If you want to know more about this strange issue: 61
→ If you think that this is a waste of time that doesn't deserve your attention: 45

40

Quickly, and in complete silence, you travel for an extended time, until dawn arrives introducing a new estrio. You are exhausted, but you keep on walking and walking without stopping to rest, as the city must be very close. Nothing seems to stand in your way now, as there is no trace of the bandits that attacked you. Then, when your hope is rising, you see that Laurmod, who walks by your left side, suddenly collapses amid the branches of a great bush.

↑ You win 1 experience point (EP) for standing firm, for sticking to your word, and for not leaving a companion on his own. → Go to 31.

41

"What is this Cult of the Golden Light?" you ask with interest, having never heard of that name before.

"They're one of the worst sects on the face of Urowen! They worship Neucen, the God of Death, and to our misfortune they have become more and more powerful within Verinfes. They are fanatics who perform macabre rituals in the city's necropolis – desecrating it some times. But their actions go far beyond this, as their main objective involves children; they gut them and use their entrails as sacrifices in dark ceremonies to their god. It's a shame that Braucos had to leave the city, as he would have been able to put an end to this madness... Now his father, Brádoc, the current Senior Soldier of Verinfes, tries to do his best to stop them, but the ongoing war against Zorbrak's adept forces most of his attention outside our walls. So that's how the Thornless Rose was born, although I hate that name. All who form part of it have been victims of the Cult of the Golden Light at some point in one way or another, so now we devote our lives to eradicating them."

"But I saw you stealing from that merchant..."

"That swine is an adept of the Cult! He has built great wealth thanks to trade, and is therefore more use to us alive than dead. I would have already cut his filthy throat with my sword, yet we need zaifas to continue our fight... food, weapons... We have little help and we have many mouths to feed. I don't always like what I do, nor do I feel proud of it, but this is the life that I have to live. They took my family, and my innocence with it, and now I'll take their zaifas and their lives. It's a more than fair exchange in a terribly unfair and cruel world."

"How did you get here? What happened?"

"I really don't like talking about that, but I will tell you. I had two daughters, a family... You can imagine the rest."

"And what about your appearance? Why do you look like a young girl?"

"I do so for protection. I've become very popular among the adepts of the Cult of the Golden Light. There's a huge price on my head – all those outside do their best to protect me. We have a sorcerer with us, and he changes my appearance on a regular basis. I look like this right now; tomorrow, who knows?"

"You told me about an important mission, and that you needed somebody prepared to risk their life for their beliefs... Is your offer still valid?" you ask, seriously interested in this task after all that you have heard.

"It is, and as I told you, the risk will be high – but we could gain a huge profit. I think that you could be a great associate. We are not many as you have seen and time is against us. Tell me... are you willing to help? I will understand if you prefer not to risk your life for our cause, and it will be as if we had never met. But I have seen something inside you that made me trust in you, maybe a bit too much, although I'm not usually wrong about people. If you decide to do this for us, there will be no turning back, as I will tell you all that I know. I need your answer now, as I've already told you that time is against us..."

→ If you choose to help the Thornless Rose: 71
→ If you prefer to forget about her mission and head back to the square of Verinfes: 45

42

You descend the narrow track until you finally reach the beach. After walking for a short stretch you find a bonfire far bigger than you had initially thought. You look closely at the sand surrounding the fire and quickly realise that you cannot see a single footprint. This circumstance is rather perplexing, as somebody must have lit the fire and, if the sea had then encroached and covered their tracks, it would have also doused the flames. Then, while you are experiencing an odd, unsettling feeling, a sweet voice greets you.

"Good estrio, traveller!" you hear, the speaker uncomfortably close.

You immediately raise your eyes and see that a beautiful young woman, dressed fully in white, sits upon a nearby rock by the fire. You would swear that she wasn't there just seconds before, but your senses may have tricked you.

→ If you talk to the young woman: 70
→ If you choose to leave and keep on searching for the cave: 52

In a corner inside the chest you discover a pair of black fur gloves. Despite their rather unexceptionable appearance, you immediately feel that they hold a great power, so you take them without delay. Write this down on your character file:

- **Gloves of power:** while you are wearing them, you will receive 1 extra protection point in your arms as if you held a shield. During the game they will protect 1 extra life point in location number 5 (aside from the extra protection of any armbands). That is to say, they will only have effect when an enemy obtains a 5 when rolling dice for the damage location. (Magical object; it does not fill a slot in your leather bag).

Also, after rummaging around the inside of the chest, you find an old carefully folded parchment, from which you learn a new spell:

* **Poppy.** Power points (PP) needed to cast it: 3. Effects: after casting the appropriate spell, a thick mist suddenly appears from nowhere and immediately surrounds your enemy, making them feel terribly tired. How to use it: in order to cast this spell correctly you have to win an opposed attack roll, making this dice roll on the MAG of your character and thereupon you have to spend the needed PP. Example: a sorcerer with 2 MAG rolls against an enemy soldier. If the sorcerer wins (rolling the dice and adding his 2 Magic Points to the obtained value), he can choose to spend the needed PP to cast this spell. Effects: your enemy, now comprehensively exhausted, will lose much of his fierceness for the fight. Whenever he tries to hurt you for the rest of the combat, deduct 3 points from the total value of his damage roll. For example, if his damage is 1d6+1 and he rolls a 4, his damage would be (4+1-3) = 2 points. In addition, for the rest of the combat, he will also deduct 1 point from all of his opposed attack rolls.

- **Poppy (43).** PP: 3. First win an opposed attack roll (MAG). Effects: -1 in all opposed attack rolls of your enemy / -3 in all their damage rolls.

→ Go to 80.

44

You quickly hide behind a bush, and from there you clearly hear the cracking sound of a branch splitting. You look in that direction and discover a sentinel crouching at the foot of a tree. With your target now detected, you circle him and attack from the rear. Thanks to the element of surprise, you obtain 3 additional points in your first opposed attack roll.

→ Go to 77.

45

Base camp
(write this number down on your character file)

City of Verinfes: you finally reach your destination, the big city where you will be able to begin your quest and your learning for real. The walled city of Verinfes, in the mouth of the Izquion River, at the western end of the Plain of the Three Rivers, was founded well before the beginning of the First Age by the first settlers of the Known Lands, and has lived great moments of glory and splendor. Dozen of rulers from the most reputable families have controlled their destiny here throughout history. Respected and feared by their enemies, the armies of this kingdom are powerful, and they have a great number of well-trained and well-equipped soldiers. In the present day, Verinfes is one of the richest cities of Urowen thanks to its volume of trade. The harbour is occupied by a hive of people coming from all corners of the mainland, and countless vessels, loaded with a wide range of goods, depart to the coastal cities of the Abyssal Sea or inland along the Izquion River. Consequently, Verinfes has the largest market in Urowen; a huge building built in the middle of the city, with a massive blue-marble dome that is visible from almost any place within the city.

It is approximately mid-estrio and you stand in the big square before the bustling market. You have many options, and will now be able to move freely throughout the city. For example, you may visit the market as many times as you wish to purchase equipment, or attempt to complete missions previously deferred because you didn't feel ready to attempt them.

→ If you go shopping at the market: 54 (Difficulty: Low)

→ A girl comes to you to beg. If you want to hear what she has to say: 39 (Difficulty: Medium)

→ You hear about an 'inn' where you can give free rein to your instincts (games of chance, betting, alcohol, sex...): 60 (Difficulty: Medium)

→ You see a tavern called 'The Blue Fire'. If you decide to enter: 11 (Difficulty: Hard)

→ You discover a hooded man stealing a bulky coin bag from a merchant. If you decide to chase him: 33 (Difficulty: Hard)

→ You hear a merchant offering a job as an escort to another city. (It is possible that this duty will take you far from Verinfes, and for a long time, so it is not recommended to take this assignment if you want to stay in the surrounding area of the city, which will allow you to come back to section 45 whenever you want to. If you choose this option now, you won't be able to come back to this section to play the previous options): 66 (Difficulty: Very hard)

* Remember that as you are in the city of Verinfes for the first time, you will be able to come back here during your adventures (to section 45) whenever you want to, provided you are still in the surrounding area of the city.

46

When you are about to begin, a loud strike is heard upon the door. A man armed with a two-handed axe bursts into the room and immediately attacks you, shouting that your partner is his, and his only. His sudden charge completely surprises you, so all of your clothing and gear remains scattered across the floor. Although you have grabbed your weapon, you wear no armor in this fight. Additionally, the archer won't be able to shoot his bow, nor will you be able to use any potions, or any other object from your bag. Get ready to fight...

◻ **Jealous enemy:** Two-handed axe (STR). Damage: 1d6+2 / STR 1 / LP: 20 / Armor: Leather chest (C). Action area: trunk (points 2, 3 and 4). Protection: 2 LP.

→ If you defeat him: 67
→ If you are defeated: 98

47

Your last attack is devastating, so your enemy collapses on the sand, where her body now begins to waste away in a column of thick black smoke. The horrendous smell of burnt flesh, and a pile of ashes, is all that remains of the dangerous creature.

↑ You win 1 experience point (EP). Write this down on your character file.

↑ While you are trying to regain your breath after the fight, the rays of Estrion reflect something within the ashes that catches your eye: you carefully remove a thin silver chain. Write it down on your character file:

- **Life necklace:** whilst you wear it, your base life points are increased by one: +1 LP. (Magical object; it does not fill a slot of your leather bag).

→ Go to 52 to keep on searching for the nocthilius' cave.

48

Realising that this angry, violent enemy is thoroughly drunk, you decide that it is best not to involve yourself in such ugly business. You discreetly step away from the scene and escape from danger, ignoring Dösser, who's writhing in pain on the floor. You may have avoided a good kicking, but you begin to feel like a real coward. → Go back to 60.

49

You immediately put all your senses to work, and off in the distance you thankfully locate the retreating hood of the loathsome thief. You chase after him without hesitation, shouting constantly to bring this incident to the attention of any soldier of Verinfes. Desperate to catch the thief, your urgent pursuit soon finds you running alone along a narrow alleyway. At the end of this narrow alley you spot the athletic thief disappearing round a corner, supple as the wind. You turn to look back for a moment, downheartedly realising that nobody has followed to help. Regardless, you have no time to waste, as stopping here any longer would almost gaurantee the thief's escape. You keep on running until you finally reach the corner where you had lost sight of the thief.

To your surprise, the thief is standing just a few steps ahead, leaning on the wall and trying to regain his breath. You are not able to discern his face within the deep shadow of the hood, yet you feel that you exchange brief eye contact.

Without a word spoken, the stranger turns and runs again, even faster now than before. You quickly follow his steps with a racing heart and sweat dripping from your brow; this has now become something personal, and you have no intention of letting him go. However, you suddenly stop running when you see that your quarry enters an old, multi-storey house, whose rickety door remains ajar.

→ If you decide to follow the thief inside the building: 75

→ If you believe that it is too risky to enter the building, go back to the market place of Verinfes: 45 (Author's note: Coward!)

50

After quickly saying goodbye to Laurmod, you decide to make a detour, ceasing further travel towards Verinfes for the moment, as you believe it most likely that the bandits will continue to follow his path to the city. Whilst you walk on, you remember the brave soldier asking you not to leave him alone, but you had decided it was best to do so and nothing he could have said would have changed your mind. Now, alone in the darkness of the night, you are not so sure of having made the right decision.

You keep on walking until you reach a rocky wall offering some protection. You begin to search along its length, and immediately locate a ledge you can safely shelter under. You settle down as best you can under cover of the rocks, as you are now exhausted after such a tough day. You finally sit, leaning your back on the rock wall, and wrap your cloak around your body to generate some warmth and comfort. Very sleepy, you soon nod off, despite the fact that you want to keep watch.

When you wake up, Estrion is already peeking above the horizon, so a new estrio has been born in Urowen. You rise and soon resume your direction of travel towards Verinfes, which must now be quite close. You quickly leave behind the safe place where you spent the night and, after walking a good distance, find an unmistakable trail of blood. Alerted by the sight of blood, you decide to follow this trail, and shortly thereafter hear a weak voice calling your name. → Go to 31.

51

"I don't know what you are talking about, and..." You don't even finish your sentence before another man runs into the building and hurriedly stops by the two men standing at the bottom of the stairs.

"Jhaddïyä, you've been followed!" the newcomer exclaims, clearly nervous and looking up at the girl. "I don't know if they've followed you or that one," he adds pointing directly at you, "but they're here!"

"Damn it!" the girl says. "Up, quick! And you," she shouts, pointing at you with her finger, "you'd better come with us if you don't want to die. Come on!"

Overwhelmed by the situation, you quickly follow Jhaddïyä's retreating steps, with the three strangers close on your heels. Not knowing where you're headed, you hurry along a dark corridor without delay, suddenly walking through a wall that's been torn down and that was apparently connected to another building.

At that very moment you hear a startling noise, and look ahead to see someone hanging from a rope swing into the room, smashing through a large window that explosively shatters into a thousand shards of glass. Without delay Jhaddïyä grasps a sword that had been hidden by her cloak, and she immediately launches a fierce attack against the intruder. Her companions rush forward to help, but four more strangers swing through the shattered window, following the first. There's now no possibility to avoid a confrontation, as one of these men advances towards you, a long rapier in his hand.

◘ **Hooded enemy:** Rapier (SK). Damage: 1d6+1 / SK 1 / LP: 20 / Armor: Leather chest (C). Action area: trunk (values 2, 3 and 4). Protection: 2 LP. Remember that when inflicting damage, if your attack aims at value 2, 3 or 4, you will have to deduct 2 points from your damage roll, corresponding to the two extra protection points granted by their chest armor.

→ If you defeat your enemy: 69
→ If you are defeated: 81

52

You scan your memory, searching for the exact words that Gwenzor spoke. You leave behind the path that has led you here and keep on walking northwards along a narrow beach full of dangerous sharp-edged rocks.

Despite this fact, you maintain a decent pace, so after a period of intense walking, you reach the area where the cave should be. Now your full attention is focused on finding the wreckage of an ancient watchtower, now abandoned and mostly ruined. Finally, from the top of a cliff overlooking the sea, you spot the weathered remains of an old watchtower – it is undoubtedly the sign that you were looking for. You follow the cliff to where you think you will find the den of the nocthilius, discovering that the old man was right, as his directions have been very accurate. You now see the entrance of a spacious cave before you, heading deep into the earth through a darkened tunnel.

The moment of truth has arrived, as Estrion is at its highest point in the sky: the best moment to take your enemy by surprise, according to Gwenzor. So you use the tinder and the flint to set a fire with which to light one of the torches you've brought with you from Verinfes.

When everything is ready, you look into the sky, instilling the courage necessary to face the hard test awaiting you. Then, your heart beating rapidly in your chest, you enter into that barren and ominous tunnel.

As soon as you enter, you feel a dramatic drop in temperature, undoubtedly due to the high humidity in the air. Large water droplets fall from the ceiling, landing on stinking mud that prevents you from walking normally. You slowly proceed for only a short distance before arriving at a fork in the tunnel. You clearly remember the old man telling you to turn to the left, so, following his instructions, you take the left passage, looking for the sign that will pinpoint the exact location to dig: a rune engraved in the stone wall.

You keep on walking normally, paying full attention to all that surrounds you, as you know that the nocthilius could jump on you at a moment's notice. But unexpectedly, the attack doesn't take place, so you safely reach a bend where you find a beautiful rune carved into the stone. Below the rune, hidden underground, is where your objective lies, so you prepare to dig immediately, aiming to leave this darkened place as soon as possible.

Terribly anxious, you place your torch among nearby rocks and begin your hard task, although fortunately you do not need to dig too deep. As you were told by the old man, the chest lies just a couple of hands below the surface. A wide smile spreads across your face when the shovel suddenly strikes what is undoubtedly its wooden lid. But your joy dies immediately, as an ominous roar, coming from deeper within the cave, reaches your ears, making you shake in terror. Without delay, you grasp your torch again and get ready for combat. You hardly have time to do much else before a scuttling noise makes you turn towards the ceiling. Raising the torch high to light the area, you immediately spot a massive beast creeping deviously above you; it turns its horrible head towards you and stares purposefully, roaring with wide jaws as its expansive wings, similar to bat wings, spread fully across the tunnel. The nocthilius now drops to the ground in front of you; it is quite near and you can clearly see most of its horrible shape within your flickering light. As the old man had told you, the creature has four muscled legs covered by a thick black fur, ending in powerful, retractile claws. A massive head, where you can see four entirely black eyes, stands out from the rest of its body, with horrible jaws full of fangs as long as knives and a deformed nose whose two nostrils sink deeply into its skull. With another alarming roar, the nocthilius attacks...

→ Go to 37.

53

You approach a table where a knife throwing contest is being organised, and prompted by what you have seen, you decide to take part. The game is rather simple. You will face a single opponent and each one of you will throw their knives against a wooden dartboard. The one who gets closest to the center of the board will be declared the winner. You can bet as many zaifas as you want with a maximum bet of 15. Your opponent will bet the same amount of zaifas as you. That is to say, if you bet 15 zaifas and you win, you get your 15 zaifas back and you'll get 15 zaifas from your opponent. If you lose, say goodbye to all of the zaifas that you have bet. This game can be rather addictive, but if you want to play it again you will only find two other people who are interested, so you can compete three times at most.

- The playing system of this game is as follows: you will roll 1d6 for yourself to represent each knife thrown, and another 1d6 to represent your opponent's throws. The value 1 corresponds to the bullseye, while 6 corresponds to the farthest area of the dartboard. Roll the dice in turns, comparing the values obtained after each round (1 wins over 2, 2 over 3, etc.). The player whose throw is nearest the bullseye wins a point. The first to win 5 points wins the game and the zaifas. If there is a tie in any round, simply roll the dice again.

→ When you have finished betting, you once again look around the main room of 'The Scarlet Goddess': 60

You see the impressively large market building and head directly for it. A massive blue-marble dome roofs the building, which you now enter via one of the countless archways that circle its perimeter. Inside there are four clearly distinguished floors circling above you, each accessed thanks to stairs that connect one corridor to another. These floors are actually just narrow walkways attached to the walls. There are many shops set against these walls, and before them is a corridor ending in a rail which is beautifully forged, simulating branches of different trees. Because of these delightful patterns, the center of the building is open. You can see the massive blue dome, with its beautifully painted frescos created dozens of liznars ago, from the ground floor where you now stand.

The entire building is lit by bright, natural light due to its great stained-glass windows, which were placed in specific positions so that the rays of Estrion shine through one window and then on to another. Additionally, there are hundreds of oil lamps at every corner of the market, providing further warm light. From the ground floor you are amazed by what you are seeing, as the building is full of shops all over. You begin walking the different streets that divide this large, busy space, and although there are countless different products being offered, you only keep an eye on those items that you believe will be useful, and are affordable. Remember to write down on your character file any items that you purchase, and to deduct the zaifas that you spend.

Weapons:

- **Shortbow (only for hunters):** 8 zaifas (SK). Damage: 1d6. Difficulty: 5.

- **Arrows:** 5 arrows cost 1 zaifa (Note for hunters: neither the bow or the arrows fill a slot in your bag. In order to shoot you need to have arrows and you should keep track of how many arrows you have at the time. If you are a hunter, write this down on your character file so that you won't forget it during the game).

- **Rapier:** 45 zaifas (1 hand, SK). Damage: 1d6+1

- **Axe:** 43 zaifas (1 hand, STR). Damage: 1d6+1

- **Kandrist ring:** 37 zaifas (fist attack, MAG). Damage: 1d6

Armor:

- **Iron hull:** 45 zaifas. Action area: head. Protection: 2 LP.

- **Leather chest:** 55 zaifas. Action area: trunk (values 2, 3 and 4). Protection: 2 LP.

Other items:

- **Chemical products (only for alchemists):** 5 zaifas. With the components purchased, the alchemist will be able to make 1 healing potion that can heal 1d6 LP (added to his extra points for special ability of the alchemist, that is to say, 2d6). You use it the usual way as with potions: during combat, after winning an attack roll, instead of hurting your enemy you can drink this potion. Each potion of this kind fills a slot in your leather bag. Once used, delete it from your character file.

- **Healing potion:** 15 zaifas. During a combat, after winning an attack roll, instead of hurting your enemy, you can drink this potion. There is only potion enough for 1 dose. When you drink it, you recover 1d6 life points. Write it down on your character file, filling one slot of your leather bag. Once used, delete it from your character file.

→ When you have finished shopping, go back to 45.

55

With a loud cry full of unrestrained rage, you wound the beast mortally; it collapses to the ground with a huge gash spilling the bloodied contents of its belly. This large quantity of blood, as thick and as black as the darkest night, has splashed everything nearby: your clothes, your face, the walls of the cave... a foul smell coming from the nocthilius' spilled guts fills the entire cave, making you hold your breath because of its terrible reek. You quickly escape from the cave to catch your breath, and only when your breathing has returned to normal, and your heart has slowed, do you feel ready to come back to the inside of the cave, to where your reward awaits you. You grasp the spade again and dig a little further to release the chest, which is secured with an old and rusted lock. Fortunately, the lock is so damaged that you have no problem in detaching it from the chest. Then, now extremely anxious, you drag it to the entrance of the cave to look at the secrets it conceals within under the light of Estrion.

↑ Contents of the chest (Write these down on your character file, keeping in mind that if you exceed the 6 item limit of your leather bag you will have to get rid of something else. Remember that your main weapon and items such as armor do not fill a slot in your bag):

↑ Small crystal bottle, beautifully sculpted, containing some sort of black liquid.

↑ You find 80 zaifas wrapped in a scarf.

→ If you are a sorcerer, a Sàgrast Knight Monk or an alchemist: 43
→ If you are a hunter, a warrior, a minstrel or a thief: 68

56

You now stand at the end of a queue waiting your turn to bet on the dog fight. In the meanwhile, it is explained to you how the betting process works:

- You can only bet an even number of zaifas, and the limit is 20. No bet is allowed over that amount.

- If you bet on Hurg, and it wins, you will receive 1 zaifa for each zaifa that you bet. So, if you bet 10 zaifas and Hurg wins the fight, you will receive your 10 zaifas back plus an additional 10 zaifas, resulting in a total amount of 20 zaifas. If Hurg is defeated, you lose your 10 zaifas.

- If you bet on Gränkot, and it wins, you will receive 1 zaifa for every two zaifas that you bet. So, if you bet 10 zaifas and Gränkot wins the fight, you will receive your 10 zaifas back plus an additional 5 zaifas, resulting in a total amount of 15 zaifas. If Gränkot is defeated, you lose your 10 zaifas.

After placing your bet by handing your zaifas to an old sailor who seems to be in charge of the accounts, you head for the courtyard where the fight will take place. People carrying numerous wine and beer mugs jostle around a small wooden fighting pit where the confrontation will take place. The two masters of the animals now appear, holding their eager animals with sturdy chains. Everything is soon ready, and after a signal from the old man responsible for the bidding, both men set their animals free, who spring forward at each other with open jaws. The fight has just begun...

- To determine the result of the fight, you will have to roll dice for both dogs, as in a normal combat, according to the characteristics that are stated below.

- In Verinfes, unlike other places of Urowen, dog fights do not continue to the death. Therefore, the animal whose life points are first reduced to 3 will lose the contest.

◘ **Hurg:** Fangs (SK). Damage: 1d6-1 / SK 1 / LP: 18

◘ **Gränkot:** Fangs (SK). Damage: 1d6 / SK 1 / LP: 20

When the winner is announced, a few men quickly jump into the fold to separate the animals, who are exhausted and bloody after this brutal and cruel confrontation. After all, these are dark and terrible times all over Urowen, with a war that has caused countless deaths, and that threaten to plunge all of the enemies of Zorbrak, the Dragon God, into slavery. That, inevitably, reflects on the type of recreation favoured by people touched by the degradations of the war.

If you haven't been lucky this time, you have lost any zaifas bet. On the contrary, if you have been lucky, you now happily collect your winnings. If you are a thief, regardless of whether you have won or lost your bet, you collect 5 extra zaifas that you snatched from the crowd when they were trying to collect their winnings.

→ After this unique experience, you decide to go back to the bar: 64

57

You think that you hear something nearby, so you quickly hide within some bushes, but after a while you no longer feel that anything is amiss. However, that's because you are no longer the hunter, but the prey, and then suddenly an unexpected attack is launched from behind your back. As the element of surprise is against you, you'll have to deduct 3 points from your first opposed attack roll.

→ Go to 77.

58

"Wonderful!" says the old man, smiling. "I see that you are as tough as the best steel, and that is good, very good, as the creature you will face is an extraordinary enemy... As it is already late," he adds after a pause, "I hope that you will accept my hospitality for the remainder of the evening. I will meet the cost of your dinner and I will pay for a room where you can spend the night. We will meet here again at dawn tomorrow, when I will give you the details of your mission. Do you find that acceptable?"

You have no objection, so you accept what the old man proposes. After he speaks with the innkeeper and provides him with several coins, he says goodbye until the following estrio.

You spend your night comfortably lodged in one of the tavern's warm, comfortable rooms on the upper floor. But you find that your visit here is too short, for when a new dawn enlightens Urowen and you make your way downstairs, the old man is already waiting for you with a broad smile.

"Good estrio, my dear friend!" he says coming closer, carrying a spade. He immediately hands you this tool (write it down on your character file. It fills one slot of your leather bag). "Take this, you'll need it to dig. But come, I'll walk with you until we reach the gates of the city."

Therefore, you leave the inn together, heading for one of the gates. The old man buys some fruit on the way and he offers it to you as breakfast while he explains the different steps you will have to take to reach the cave. Furthermore, the old man buys what seem to be three torches, as well as tinder and flint to create a fire. He gives these items to you (write them down on your character file: together the torches, tinder and flint fill one slot in your leather bag).

"You'll certainly need these items," he says with an extremely serious expression. "Believe me when I say so, because these are the clues to defeat the beast. Don't dare to fight it at night as nothing will be effective against it, but with Estrion in the sky you can enter the cave to fight her. Try to catch her while she is resting, and always keep a lighted torch with you, not only to see in the darkness, but also to gain an advantage, as it is said that nocthilius really fear fire. Besides, by carrying a lit torch, the beast won't see you clearly, as the light will blind it. These are the tips that I can give you – I hope that they prove to be useful."

Now, after having walked for some time following a lonely path north of Verinfes, you recall the last words you told the old man before saying goodbye:

"I will bring you the bottle you need, as promised. But I have realised that I do not know your name. I would like to know it."

"Gwenzor, everybody calls me Gwenzor! Now, off you go... and remember, when you come back, look for me at 'The Blue Fire'! I wish you the best of luck."

So, highly motivated but with a heavy heart, you have walked alone for some distance according to the old man's instructions. Initially, you left an old mill behind, and you then reached the location of a great cliff from where you could see two jagged rocks rising out of the sea. You should go north from here, in parallel with the beach, until you locate a narrow pathway that will lead you down to the seashore. You are standing there now, at the top of another cliff, with the immense Abyssal Sea before you, and the path descending at your feet. According to the information Gwenzor provided, you still have a distance to travel, so you decide to delay. But then, when you look south along the beach, you notice a thin column of smoke rising from a fire, although it appears that nobody is around.

→ If you explore this bonfire: 42
→ If you choose to continue on: 52

59

Disoriented, you look around trying to locate the thief, thinking that it is impossible for anyone to have vanished so quickly. Just a moment ago you had him within sight, and then suddenly there is no trace. Then you feel somebody putting their hand upon your bag; you look back instantly and there you find the strange figure, a dark hood hiding their face. You turn away to avoid the theft, but you are too slow.

↓ If you have any zaifas, roll 6 dice. The total sum of the values obtained is the amount that the thief has stolen from you.

Without further delay you grasp your weapon, but the thief has vanished before your very eyes, once again aided by the crowd.

→ Go to 49.

60

Base camp
(write this number down on your character file)

After hearing a few men speaking about bets, you decide to ask them about the best place to indulge in some betting. They tell you that, if you want to gamble and experience some powerful emotions, you should make your way to 'The Scarlet Goddess', a disreputable inn located in the underworld of Verinfes, in the southern area; a rather dangerous place according to some of the many merchants here. Nevertheless, your thirst for exploring the city and your curiosity to know more about 'The Scarlet Goddess' inexorably drags you there all too soon. After walking for a long while, asking others of the exact location of this exotic destination, you finally end up in a filthy, foul-smelling street.

The rich sound of kettledrums reaches your ears; the music coming from inside the building now before you. This plain, three-storey brick building features only two closed windows and a single door, yet above you hangs a golden-lettered signboard with the name of the 'inn' that you seek. After pausing for just a moment, you feel attracted to the hue and cry coming from inside, but then a strange voice to your left whispers a query from the darkness.

"Hey, you! Yes, you! You're new here, aren't you? Come here, come...!"

"What do you want from me?" you ask this hooded stranger.

"Are you going to enter 'The Scarlet Goddess'? You'll need zaifas there, and by your appearance you wouldn't have many of them. Do you want to earn a bucket full? Tell me... do you?"

"And how am I supposed to earn these zaifas?"

"Oh, I see you like the idea! Zaifas! Zaifas! Come, come with me... Let's move away from the door of this den and I'll tell you as I don't want to be seen by The Golden One, a bloke that's inside. I want to take revenge on him. Come... Let's go!"

Interested in what he has to tell you, you closely follow this stranger whilst keeping an eye on everything around you, as you don't yet trust him.

"Oh, come on! I'm not going to hurt you. I'm harmless," he says when he notices your suspicion. "My name is Rashtan and all I want is revenge. As I've already told you, there's a bloke inside called The Golden One. He's called that because of his four golden teeth. He is rather stout, with long black hair and a thick beard. Now, I want you to beat him up. If you can send him off with his tail between his legs, making him stay in his hole while recovering from his wounds, I'll be satisfied. I'll pay you 50 zaifas for that simple job. Will you do it? Eh? Will you?"

"What did he do to you to deserve this?"

"That's my business, but if you have a bad conscience, I'll tell you that the bloke is of the worst kind. He enjoys abusing women and things of that kind... Many girls in the inn are marked permanently because of his wrongdoing... And I don't mean just punching or kicking, no... I mean nasty burns, knife cuts, rope marks and things of that sort. He's just a damned coward who needs to be humiliated in a way similar to how he has acted himself. What do you say? Will you help me? Are you interested in 50 zaifas?"

"I'll think about it!"

After giving your reply, you move away from Rashtan and enter 'The Scarlet Goddess'. As you do so, you are surprised at the amount of hustle and bustle, the smoky air, and the combined odours of sweat and spew mixed with the smell of beer, wine and mead. Many scantily clad girls walk around the room, while young lads serve trays full of jugs. Three dancers liven up the evening to the sound of the kettledrums, while people laugh and boast here and there, cheering on those who, heavily inebriated, take part in various competitions and games of chance throughout the room.

→ If you want to take part in a knife throwing competition: 53

→ If you want to play dice: 72

→ If you want to go up to a bedroom with a girl or a boy, paying for their services (for practical reasons this book is written in the masculine, however, depending on your preference or if you are playing as a female character, you can choose whichever gender you wish to meet): 83

→ If you feel like taking part in a drinking contest: 96

→ If you head to the bar to have a drink and avoid troubles: 108

→ In a corner, sitting at a table with two other men, you see a bloke who matches The Golden One's description. If you decide to fulfill Rashtan's assignment: 119

→ When you are ready to return to the market square of Verinfes: 45

61

Intrigued by what the girl has just spoken of, you let her lead you to her nearby house, as she wants you to see her mother so that you will believe her story. You walk along very narrow streets until she finally stops before a door that she opens immediately. A candle lit inside a small room is the first thing that draws your attention, although suddenly you can only think of the nauseating smell coming out of this room.

"Who is it? Daughter... is that you?" asks a very faint voice.

"Yes, mother! It's me, Naira! I've brought somebody who will help us."

"Who are you? Please, come in, though I'm afraid I've got nothing to offer you... Is it true what my daughter says? Will you help us?"

"I mean to do so," you say with conviction, after checking in horror the parlous state of this poor woman. "Is it true what your daughter told me? Are you under a spell?"

"Naira, my dear, fetch water from the fountain. I've got to talk to this gentleman alone."

"Very well. I'll be back soon," the girl answers as she takes a jar just before leaving the small room.

So you are left alone with the woman, who asks you to close the door and have a seat on a small stool.

"I can talk to you sincerely now," Naira's mother says finally. "What my daughter has told you is true, but she doesn't know the whole truth. That damn bastard was a friend of my late husband, and he promised he would take care of me. But when my husband died from a bad fever, all that he did was to abuse me again and again. He threatened me saying he would do the same with Naira if I resisted, and that's why I tried to endure it, but there came a moment when I couldn't stand it anymore, even for my child. One night, while he was sleeping, I took a knife and I tried to kill him. I don't know how, but he awoke and I... I missed in my assault. Unfortunately, I could only strike one of his eyes and, although the injury wasn't fatal, he had to flee looking for help. He went through that very door squealing like a pig, bleeding profusely because of the cut I inflicted upon him... I didn't see him again for a long time. I prayed to Sàgrast for his death, but my prayers were never listened to, as Korindor returned when he was least expected. Yes, yes, that was his name... Korindor, who wore an eye patch then as he had lost the wounded eye. I remember that I feared for Naira's life, but his revenge was very different, as he cast the spell that's slowly killing me. Look what it has already done to me!" When she speaks these words she casts aside the blanket covering her legs, revealing their repulsive condition.

Horrified, and sick to your stomach, you realise that the foul stench that spreads throughout the room emanates from her rotting legs. Overcoming the vomit that attempts to force its way into your mouth, you step a little closer to better view her decaying legs. You can see flesh detaching from bones, which is covered by some sort of greyish pus, and as you look on, now completely repulsed, a small worm makes its way out of this oozing mess.

"This is what that bastard did to me. If nobody aids me, I will die in a very short time. Please, you have to be merciful and help me. I'm not begging for me, but for my daughter. The estrio when I'm no longer here,

I'm sure Korindor will come back looking for Naira. He is aware that I know it, and that is why he has caused me this agony, as I will be helpless to protect myself or to protect her, and I will die knowing what my daughter will have to endure. All I have is 30 zaifas. I will give them to you if you kill him. If he dies, the charm will disappear and I will slowly heal. That is the only way I can rid myself of this illness – killing him – as he won't give in otherwise. Please, help me, help my daughter..."

"Mother, here's the water!" says Naira, who has just opened the door, returning with a full jar.

"Leave it there, Naira. What do you say? Will you help us?" Naira's mother asks again, looking you in the eye...

→ If you wish to help Naira and her mother: 78

→ If you prefer to go back to the market square and forget about them: 45

62

Despite all of your efforts, the nocthilius has proven to be an enemy impossible to beat. Not only have you been unable to unearth the secrets lying in the hidden chest, but the weapon you fought with has been damaged during the fight, which is subsequently reduced by 1 point. If, for instance, you fought with a regular sword with damage of 1d6, its damage is now 1d6-1. This represents that the sword has been nicked during the fight or, if it was a magical item, that it has lost part of its power.

You have now two possible choices. You can go back to Verinfes and try to get better equipped, thus becoming more powerful before facing this quest again: in that case, go back to 45, your last base camp. Write down section number 37 on your character file, together with the word 'nocthilius'. By doing so, as you already know the way to the cave, you will be able to return to section 37 at any time, when you feel ready to face your enemy and resume the chest hunt where you left it, fighting against the beast.

If you feel bold enough and desire to challenge the nocthilius right away, go to 37. Remember that, if you are defeated again, your weapon will loose 1 damage point each time this occurs. If your weapon is reduced to 0 damage (1d6-6), it will become completely useless.

63

Despite all your efforts against this fierce enemy, the wild dog has proven to be far more powerful than it had first seemed: you have been defeated. ↓ Lose a third of your coins (rounding up any fraction). When you regain consciousness you can try to track the animal to fight it again.

→ If you want to fight the wild dog again: 135
→ If you choose to forget about the animal and keep on hunting for Korindor: 141.

64

Still thinking deeply about the startling blue-flamed candles, you head back to the bar. From here you inspect the room's picturesque decorations, intrigued by two massive, stuffed boar heads, that hang on the wall over a great chimney. Lost in your own thoughts for a minute, an old man quietly makes his way over to where you stand, and now speaks to you in a low voice.

"Are you the messenger who delivered a message to Brádoc?" he asks.

As you can't think of a reason to hide the truth from him, you decide to answer sincerely. The old man smiles at you in response, revealing multiple dark spaces between his black teeth.

"In that case, let me buy you a drink," he says, raising a hand to call on the maid behind the bar.

He purchases two great jars of wine and then moves to a nearby table set apart in a corner, where you now sit by candlelight.

"Mmmm, this is surely the nectar of the gods," he exclaims after taking a long drink from his glass. "But let's stick to the deal that I wish to speak of. As you can possibly guess, I have contacts in the court, and thanks to them I have known of you and of the quest that has brought you here. You have done the Kingdom of Verinfes a great favour by delivering this important message – great marvels are now spoken of you. That is why I have decided to seek you out, as I am in need of somebody of your capability to embark on a dangerous errand as soon as possible. I must warn you that the danger you'll face is considerable, however, the treasures that you will be rewarded with are impressive. What do you say, will you consider this offer?"

→ If you decide to listen to the old man: 35

→ If you choose to drain your drink and forget about this strange old man, you now return to the main square: 45

65

With a final blow of your axe, you finally defeat the toughest of enemies – a proud fighter who boldly defied you. ↑ You win 1 experience point for reaching this point. Write it down on your character file.

While you try to regain your breath after these hard fought victories, you look around to see nothing but further enemies. They seem to come from everywhere, so you are suddenly alone and circled. Apparently, many Verinfes soldiers have now come to avenge the death of their captain, and they all have a clear target to attack: you. Suddenly possessed by an extreme fury, you begin roaring with rage, thumping your chest with a fist, aggressively defying anything that your enemies can throw at you. Their response doesn't take long to arrive, as many now grab their weapons, ready to fight... → Go to 105.

66

"Who are you?" the fat merchant asks as you approach him. "I'm in need of somebody just like you to be by my side for the dangerous journey that I'm about to embark on! If zaifas are what you're looking for, let me assure you that you'll have them – plenty of them – but you will be at my service in return, and that means that your life will be in danger."

"Which town are you heading to?" you ask, rather interested in what this man offers.

"I see that you like to get down to brass tacks! That's fine... really fine! My destination is the great city of Bälkaar, home of the feared amazons, to whom I must bring a valuable cargo. What do you say? Are you up for joining my caravan?"

"Tell me about the wage?"

"I am willing to offer you 300 zaifas to come with me all the way to Bälkaar! – plus food and lodging whenever we can find an inn! I'll pay you 50 zaifas in advance, and the rest when we reach to our destination. Is that okay with you?"

"Fair enough," you reply, knowing that you no longer have anything else to do with your time in the city. The mythical Kingdom of Bälkaar, home of the brave amazons of Queen Zarkända, is a truly exotic place, according to all travellers. It is also a place that you have always desired to visit one day, attracted by what it may bring to your apprenticeship.

"Actually, there's something I would like to know," you now tell the fat merchant. "Which route will we follow to Bälkaar?"

"We'll travel overland, along the coast; there are several villages we'll pass where I must stop to conduct business. Besides, nowadays it is the safest route. A sea journey would be much faster, if that's what you're thinking, but the waters around Verinfes are infested with pirates who wouldn't hesitate to cut your throat. It's madness to take a sea journey to Bälkaar, and I don't want to lose my valuable goods – nor my life – to some wretched buccaneer. So, what do you say? Will you join me?"

Satisfied with the deal, you accept his conditions. He smiles broadly in response, more than happy with the newest member of his caravan.

"We'll meet tomorrow with the first beam of Estrion! Meet me at the Eastern gate of the city. You'd better enjoy your estrio, as from tomorrow it will certainly be rough."

At that moment, the merchant reaches out his hand to shake yours, but then he seems to remember something, and speaks again. "By the way, I'm Hormäz!"

↑ You can write down on your character file the 50 zaifas that Hormäz has paid you in advance before leaving, thus trusting your word and proving his. → Go to 85.

67

Despite the initial surprise, and the compromising situation in which you found yourself, you finally gain the advantage over your mad opponent and knock them out. ↑ You win 1 experience point and also get back the zaifas you paid to come up to the room, although you return to the main room a bit frustrated, as you couldn't finish what you craved for. → Go to 60.

68

Tucked in a corner inside the chest you find a kind of brown leather belt. Despite the fact that its appearance is rather unexceptional, you feel that it has a great power in it, so you put it on immediately.

↑ Write it down on your character file. While you're wearing it, it does not fill a slot in your leather bag.

- **Resilience belt:** as long as you're wearing it, you will add 1 extra protection point to the trunk area, as if you held a shield. In the game, it will protect 1 extra life point in the damage location area number 3 (and will be added to any breastplate that you are wearing). That is to say, it will only have an effect if an enemy rolls a 3 when locating damage (Magical object; it does not fill a slot in your leather bag).

Furthermore, after having searched the inside of the chest thoroughly, you find an old fur wrapped around a beautifully decorated scimitar, its blade carved with elvish characters.

- **Elvish scimitar:** (1 hand, SK or STR). Damage: 1d6+3

→ If you are a thief, go to 90; otherwise, go to 80.

69

Under the watchful eye of Jhaddïyä, who has beaten her opponent easily, you deal with your enemy without too much inconvenience, and leave him wallowing in a pool of blood while his life slips away. Just as the girl has, her companions have also easily despatched their opponents, so you resume your flight through the inside of the old mansion.

↑ You win 1 experience point (EP).
→ Go to 92.

70

"Who are you?" you ask, walking around the fire to talk to her. "What are you doing here on your own?" She seems to be harmless but you remain somewhat wary.

"My name is Ainära and I come to this beach every estrio to wait for my love to return. I know that he will never come back, but his memory is all that I have left."

"Why do you say so?"

"Because he drowned at this very beach. He had gone fishing with three others when a terrible storm caught them out on the high seas. They rowed their best to reach the shore here, but before doing so a huge wave overturned their small vessel. None... none of the three crewmen could save his life," she says with a broken voice, just before painful tears start to flow.

Concerned by her deep sorrow, you approach and try to soothe her while she covers her face with both hands, crying inconsolably. As you stand by the girl offering her comfort, she raises her eyes to you, and you are instantly shocked and astounded by what you see. Where before there were white and perfect teeth, there are now just greenish sharp fangs, and what was previously fair and silky hair is now tangled and dirty. But worst of all are her eyes, now completely white, without a trace of life within them. Then, jumping an inhuman distance, she suddenly perches upon the rock where she had been sitting, issuing a terrifying roar that extends the length of the beach. Huge, sharp claws now replace her once delicate fingers, and with a sinister grin, she opens her mouth and speaks with a hoarse and powerful voice:

"Come with me, traveller! You will never leave me!"

Without further ado, she flexes her knees and jumps powerfully towards you. Get ready to fight if you don't want to die...

◘ **Ainära (unknown being):** Claws (SK). Damage: 1d6 / SK 1 / LP: 20 / Armor: Energy field protecting her full body (locations from 1 to 6). Protection: 1 / Special ability: Dodging. This being is supremely agile. Every time you try to wound her (that is to say, before a damage roll), she will attempt to dodge. Roll a dice: if you roll a 6 your enemy has dodged your blow, and consequently she won't be harmed.

→ If you defeat her: 47
→ If you succumb to her attack: 34

71

"Well said!" she happily exclaims, "I knew that I was right about you!" Now, I will tell you what we have in mind. Tomorrow is a sacred estrio for members of the Cult of the Golden Light, as Émacel and Émandel (the two shining stars that light Urowen's nights) will cross in the sky, pointing the way to the presence of Neucen in the firmament. As I say, it will be a great estrio for them, and thanks to one of our spies, we know that they will be celebrating a great rite before an old menhir south of the city. They will do so at night, and some of the more important members of the Cult will be there, but our main objective will be Dëvian, a young, skilled thief, trained in the arts of stalking and discretion: they use her to kidnap the children for their gruesome rites. As far as we know she arrived in town recently, and that the Cult pay her lavishly to fulfill her duty. She is good, too good... Until now, she has always outrun or outsmarted us, but tomorrow we can't fail. We must kill her promptly, as the lives of many innocent children depend on this act. Besides, we believe that the fat man you saw at the market, the same one that I stole the coins from, will be there too. Taking advantage of the fact that we will be out of town, our plan is to hijack him to obtain a good ransom, although we are certain that he will be escorted. They will all be well protected, and that is why we need people of your kind. Now come, I'll introduce to the rest of the group."

You both leave the room and Jhaddïyä approaches each of her companions. You then discuss with them their plans for the following estrio. Later, you finally have some respite, so you spend the night there and get to know the members of the Thornless Rose, hearing the horrible stories that have lead them here: babies stolen from their beds, crippled bodies, whole families killed by the Cult... There's no doubt that the thirst for revenge runs through the veins of these men and women who offer you food and show you great respect and admiration for volunteering to help them.

Time slowly passes while the group continues to receive reports from their spies; soon everybody gets ready to move. The time for action finally arrives as Estrion now hides on the horizon, so you leave the town along many different streets, avoiding notice and suspicion. You walk in the company of Jhaddïyä, who now shows a different face; this one far more mature.

↑ As a token of thanks for your help, before leaving, Jhaddïyä has given you as a present; simple but effective leather greaves:

- **Simple leather greaves (G).** Action area: legs. Protection: 1 LP.

→ Go to 86.

72

You approach a group of men playing a dice game. If you wish to participate, you will face just one opponent, rolling your dice in turn. You can bet up to 15 zaifas. Your opponent will bet the same amount, and the winner will take his opponent's coins. That is to say, if you bet 15 zaifas and win, you will get your 15 coins back and you'll take the 15 coins that belonged to your opponent. If you lose, say goodbye to all of the zaifas that you have bet. There are only two men willing to play against you, so you can play this game twice.

- This game called 'Nine' is played as follows: you will roll 2d6 for yourself, and two different d6 for your opponent. The player who rolls closest to but not exceeding 9 (adding together the value of their 2d6), wins the round. Both rolls are simultaneous. To determine the winner, total the value rolled for each opponent. For instance, 9 beats 8, 8 beats 7, and so on. 10, however, has exceeded 9, so won't beat a measly 2. If you tie, simply roll again. The opponent who rolls closest to 9 without exceeding it wins a point. The first player to get 5 points wins the game and the zaifas.

→ When you've finish betting, you turn back to the main room seeking a new challenge: 60

73

"It's been a genuine pleasure to know you," you say, approaching Jhaddïyä with your hand out to shake hers, "but I'm afraid that other important issues now require my attention."

"Equally, it's been my pleasure, as well," Jhaddïyä answers. "We would never have achieved so much without your help. The zaifas I have given you don't adequately reward the bravery you've shown. I hope our paths meet again very soon. As far as the Thornless Rose are concerned, you will always be warmly welcomed."

You finish saying goodbye to Jhaddïyä, and then head off again for the main square of Verinfes, where you will surely find new challenges.

→ Go to 45.

74

Fear of the unknown has defeated you this time, so you step away and run, alarmed and troubled by such a strange sorcerer. On this occasion, your flight has saved your life, for when you finally look back, Korindor apparently hasn't followed. Nevertheless, you'll have trouble sleeping for a long time, as you feel that you have been a coward, sealing the fates of the unfortunate Landanar and her little daughter.

→ Return to the market square of Verinfes: 45

Absolutely determined to stop the thief, you slowly push open the door to reveal a darkened room. Only the dim light coming from outside lets you distinguish an abandoned room, completely unfurnished, with another door situated at the back and a flight of stairs leading to an upper floor. Without a second thought, you enter the room and right then you hear steps on the upper floor. Slowly, with your back against the wall, you start ascending step by step, but your pursuit is halted by a question that breaks the silence...

"Do you value your own life so lowly that you dare to follow me for just a handful of coins?"

With a lump in your throat, you quickly try to digest the information that you have at hand. There's no doubt that this voice came from upstairs, but the person who spoke seemed to be a girl of no more than fifteen or sixteen liznars (remember that in Urowen, years are called this). You take in air preparing your response, but when you open your mouth to talk, two dark shapes surprise you from below. At that moment, you are midway up the stairs, and at their foot, two very stout strangers, hooded and cloaked, block any escape. They both hold swords and they seem to be very fierce opponents. At that moment, you hear steps coming from above, and when you turn your head to look in that direction, you see the thief standing there. He pulls the hood back slowly from his face, revealing the delicate features of a beautiful girl.

"Lay your weapons down," she says, waving vigorously to the two guys at the foot of the stairs. "I don't think our friend here wishes for this to go any further. Do you?"

"It would be a rather unequal fight," you answer trying to keep your voice calm, as you know that your life hangs on a very thin thread.

"You're not from here, if I am not wrong. Where do you come from? What are you doing in town?" the girl asks, exhibiting great authority.

Knowing that you are at the mercy of her two henchmen, you decide to tell the truth, so you tell her your story and of some of the experiences that have brought you to Verinfes.

"So you are the stranger who delivered the message for the Chief Soldier," the girl interrupts, apparently surprised. "In that case you are our ally. Why did you chase me then?"

"You were stealing..." you answer, rather lost in the conversation.

"Oh, so that was why!" she exclaims with a cheeky grin. "A small detail, no doubt... As I can see, you know very little of what's happening in town."

"I don't know a thing. I've only just arrived."

"And tell me... would you like to know? From what I know about you, I am inclined to believe that you are a man of honor. Not only have you aided Verinfes by bringing the message to Brádoc, but you risk your life chasing a petty thief. We need people of your kind to help us in our daily struggle. Tell me, would you like to help us? We are engaged in an important mission and we need brave, capable people willing to risk their life in pursuit of their beliefs."

"Beliefs and principles are okay," you reply, "but is this mission profitable? I have seen that you are unwilling to let go of a thick bag of coins."

"As I've told you, we are animated by a grand cause, but I won't deny the fact that you could gain great reward. What do you say? Do you wish to hear what I have to tell you?"

→ If you want to keep on talking to the girl: 38
→ If you prefer to forget about her proposition and ask her to let you go: 51

76

That was good, really good! With a wide, satisfied smile, you stand over the body of the defeated bastard now lying at your feet. He shouts and writhes in pain until his body begins to waste away, melting as if he was made of ice. A bluish smoke now rises from his body, and soon there's only a damp stain to mark where he once lay upon the ground. Satisfied with your achievement, you decide to enter the sorcerer's hut to look for anything useful.

Korindor's hut is full of strange glass bottles containing different mysterious products. In a corner you see a small wooden cage where you find a couple pigeons that you decide to set free. You continue searching the dwelling, hoping to find something useful:

↑ You win 1 experience point. Write it down on your character file.

↑ You find 20 zaifas on a little shelf.

↑ **Healing potion.** Instructions: during combat, after winning an opposed attack roll, instead of wounding your opponent, you may choose to drink this potion. There is potion enough for 1 dose. When you drink it, you recover 1d6+3 life points. Write it down on your character file, as this potion fills one slot in your leather bag. If you are a thief, you get an extra healing potion, less effective than the other one: you recover 1d6+1.

→ Keep on reading. Go to 146.

77

◘ **Guard of the Cult of the Golden Light:** Rapier (SK). Damage: 1d6+1 / SK 1 / LP: 19 / Armor: Leather breastplate. Action area: trunk (values 2, 3 and 4). Protection: 1 LP.

↓ If you are defeated, you lose 1 experience point and return to your last base camp.

→ If you defeat him: 94

78
Base camp
(write this number down on your character file)

After leaving their humble home, you recall the agonized face of the poor woman, Landanar, and her young, hopeful daughter. Fortunately, they can now count on your aid. Landanar has informed you of where to locate the abusive wizard Korindor, as he goes to the market of Verinfes every estrio – although you will likely find him in the small hut he uses to perform his rituals, located beside the southern riverside.

With that valuable information, you head off to the outskirts of the city, ready to keep your promise. You walk purposefully until you have left the gates of Verinfes behind and, once at the southern bank of the Izquion, you push through thick vegetation to where the sorcerer has his hiding place, not far from the city.

■ Roll for PER with a difficulty of 5 as you try to perceive something.

→ If you are successful and the result is 5 or above: 100
→ If you are absent-minded and you roll under 5: 112

79

Unable to stand by and witness this violent attack, and no longer able to hold your tongue, you astonish everybody by raising your voice in protest.

"Leave him alone! Can't you see that he's drunk? He's had enough."

"And who the hell are you? Shut up if you don't want to get your own share!"

"I don't think you understood me..." you reply.

"You're the one who didn't get me, bastard! Now I'm going to make you shut your mouth!"

Without saying another word, the stranger pounces on you with his fists poised to strike. Get ready for battle. As in any tavern fight, weapons are superfluous, as the only thing at stake here is the manliness of each opponent. In this fight you won't be able to use weapons, nor spells or potions. Both of you will fight with bare fists: the damage they do is 1d6-1. In your case, you can choose to roll on STR, SK or MAG.

□ **Drunken opponent:** Fists (SK). Damage: 1d6-1 / SK 1 / LP: 17 / Armor: Leather breastplate. Action area: trunk (values 2, 3 and 4). Protection: 2 LP.

- Special ability for both opponents: in this combat both combatants can try to grab objects from the bar or nearby tables to strike their opponent with – jars, bottles, a chair... These objects will add extra damage to your blow. You'll know if you or your opponent have managed to grab one of these objects when one of you roll for damage. If a 6 is rolled, an object has been used, so in that turn (and only in that turn), the damage is automatically 1d6+1. That's to say, the damage is 7, as you can only pick up an object when you roll a 6.

→ If you defeat your opponent: 125
→ If you are defeated: 138

80

Once you have finished searching through the chest, you decide that it would be best to return to Verinfes as soon as possible. There's still some time left for Estrion to hide behind the horizon, so if you walk briskly you know that you'll make it back to the city before night falls. So you start walking quickly, feeling satisfied with yourself for having fulfilled the mission Gwenzor entrusted you with. Finally, in the distance, you see the lights of Verinfes welcoming you back with their warm glow. You quickly head to 'The Blue Fire', where you expect to find the old man.

"Did you find it?" Gwenzor says excitedly, coming towards you as you enter the room.

"As promised, here's the bottle," you answer, revealing the precious object recovered from the chest.

Extremely nervous, the old man takes it with a broad smile. He immediately invites you to a sumptuous dinner, offering to pay for another night at the tavern.

↑ You win 2 experience points. Write them down on your character file.

After spending a very pleasant evening with Gwenzor, who asks you to tell him every detail of your fight against the nocthilius, you finally leave for your room to get some much needed rest. After sleeping soundly throughout the whole of the night, you wake the next morning fully recovered, willing and able to begin a new adventure. → Go to the main square of Verinfes and make your next choice: 45

81

Despite your skill, dedication and courage, you have not been able to match the bravery and swiftness of the hooded enemy.

↓ You lose an item during the fight. Erase 1 item, of your choice, from your leather bag.

You fall to the ground stunned and badly bruised, but when you think that your opponent is going to deliver a fatal strike with his rapier, you see in surprise how Jhaddïyä crosses his throat with her sword. Without delay, her companions, who have also killed their own opponents, help you to your feet, so you resume your flight through the old mansion. → Go to 92.

82

Determined to keep your promise to Landanar, you try to dodge the bolt of energy to then attack your enemy, but suddenly, without being able to avoid it, you are surrounded by a strong white light that blinds your sight. Then, plunged into an unexplainable calming peace, you feel yourself floating and your eyes close as you fall into a deep dream...

When you regain consciousness you are surprised to find yourself upon a wide beach of white sand, with a troubled sea at your back and a powerful storm rolling over the land. Rain falls heavy on you, drenching the thick beard that covers your chest. At that moment you realise that this is not your body. Frightened, you look down at tattooed hands which are not your own, hands that grasp a massive double-edged axe; your arms, supremely strong and powerful, are also tattooed with tribal symbols. You wear only leather trousers and a pair of boots – your sturdy chest is naked.

Two hundred Servants of Neucen stand nearby, fanatic dreknar disciples of the King Tarkarod who live in the Éntelgar Valley. They shout a battle cry, as before you, facing the sea, is a full detachment of soldiers of Verinfes, ready for combat. At that moment, one of the savages shouts something that you can't understand, but you find yourself running in response regardless, together with the rest of the Servants of Neucen, facing the men of Verinfes who are already charging towards you at the beginning of a terrible battle. Get ready to fight...

- For the time being, forget about your character file. You are now under Korindor's spell and you'll have to give your best effort to survive. Although you are held within the body of a dreknar, a disciple of Zorbrak, enemy of the free peoples, now fighting against your allies, you'll have to fight to remain alive. From this moment on, these are the statistics of your character (write them down on a separate sheet of paper, without modifying any part of your character file):

* **Servant of Neucen:** Two-edged axe (STR). Damage: 1d6+2 / STR 3 / LP: 30 / Armor: None / Special ability 1: Extreme fierceness. If your life points fall below 10, your savagery grants you extraordinary strength. For the purpose of the game, your STR 3 becomes STR 4 / Special ability 2: Limb amputating axe. When you roll a 6 for damage, aside from the 8 damage points you inflict on your enemy (1d6+2), you'll also amputate the extremity to which the blow was aimed. If the blow was aimed at a leg (damage location 1), you'll amputate that leg and your enemy will now lose 5 life points at the beginning of every subsequent combat round. If the blow was aiming for their trunk (damage location 2/3/4), you practically cleave your enemy in half, killing him immediately. If the blow was aimed at an arm (damage location 5), you'll amputate that extremity, and your enemy will now lose 5 life points at the beginning of every subsequent combat round. Finally, if your blow was aiming for their head (damage location 6), you'll behead them, causing immediate death.

Now, when you are familiar with your new character, face your first enemy, one of the many men of Verinfes running into battle.

◻ **Soldier of Verinfes:** Sword (SK). Damage: 1d6+1 / SK 2 / LP: 21 / Armor: Leather breastplate (C). Action area: trunk (values 2, 3 and 4). Protection: 1 LP.

→ If you defeat him: 115
→ If you are defeated: 105

83

With your base instincts close to the surface, you focus on all the waiting girls and boys. Finally deciding to approach one of them, you engage in a short but intense conversation, and then the haggle begins – as is usual in 'The Scarlet Goddess'.

- There are three possible prices: 5, 10 or 20 zaifas. If you spend 10 zaifas, you'll add 1 point in your 'Ambiance table' roll; if you spend 20 zaifas, you'll add 2 points. If you spend 5 zaifas, your roll will not be modified.

Once you have agreed upon the price, you go upstairs, where your partner leads you into a small room that, even if it is far from luxurious, is still much better than what you would have expected when looking at the building from the outside.

- You now roll 2d6. If you have purchased a modifier, add it to the result and check your total on the 'Ambiance table'. Follow the instructions listed there and, if you are instructed to do so, roll 2d6 again. You'll have to check the result of this second roll on the 'Pleasure table':

Ambiance table:

- **2:** Bad luck! → Go to 46.
- **3:** When the action is about to begin, your partner asks you to double the zaifas agreed. If you accept, make your second roll and check the 'Pleasure table'. → If you don't agree, go back to the common room: 60.
- **4:** Your partner brings along a bottle of wine and you drink it all, ending up with a hangover: deduct 1 point from your second roll.
- **5:** The 'battlefield' is not as neat and clean as it should have been, giving you an infection that will trouble you for some estrios to come. Start your next combat by reducing your life points by 3. Write this down on your character file and then make your second roll.
- **6:** A loud creak in your neck means that it will now hurt for several estrios. Start your next combat by reducing your life points by 2. Write this down on your character file and then make your second roll.
- **7:** One of the legs of the bed breaks, resulting in a bad bump against the wall. The 'battlefield' is now tilted, making for a far more interesting situation. Make your second roll.

- 8: Your partner asks to move to the balcony and, despite the cold air, it adds significant interest: add 1 point to your second roll.

- 9: Your partner draws a deck of cards and then plays funny and impudent games depending on your chosen card: add 1 point to your second roll.

- 10: Your partner is really accommodating and a real expert in these arts: add 2 points to your second roll.

- 11: Your partner coats your body with honey: add 3 points to your second roll.

- 12: Both of you have a perfect understanding, making the evening an experience beyond words: add 4 points to your second roll.

Pleasure table:

- 2: It ends before it has really started, disappointing both of you. Lose 1 experience point (EP).

- 3: A lack of masculine motivation makes it an impossible task. Lose 1 experience point (EP).

- 4: An awkward position causes you injure a wrist. You gain 1 experience point (EP), but you'll have to deduct 1 point from all opposed attack rolls during your next combat.

- 5: You are really disappointed when your partner undresses. Strange memories of what you have seen will come back to you for estrios, making you absent-minded when you shouldn't be. You win 1 experience point (EP), but you'll have to deduct 1 point from all damage rolls during your next combat.

- 6: It's been a short but intense experience, so it has been satisfactory, but nothing worth remembering. You'll try to do better next time.

- 7: After having a short rest, you enter into action again. Roll 2d6 again, deducting 1 point from the result and checking this table again. If you rolled a 2, the final result is 2.

- 8: It's been great, so you feel a real hero, now energised to cope with your adventures. You win 1 experience point (EP), and can add 1 point to all of your damage rolls during your next combat.

- 9: You feel really proud and very high in confidence: that was just what you needed to cope with your adventures. You win 1 experience point (EP), and can add 1 point to all of your attack rolls during your next combat.

- 10: It's been so wonderful for your partner that you are given 10 zaifas back. You win 1 experience point (EP).

- 11: Simply sublime. Your satisfied smile betrays you. You win 2 experience points (EP).

- 12: Minstrels will sing songs about you and your performance, there is no doubt about that. You win 2 experience points (EP).

→ When you have finished here, go back downstairs to the common room: 60.

84

Jhaddïyä leads you to the northern area of the city, where you travel along narrow lanes that finally take you to your destination: an old mansion that seems to be abandoned. Despite this, Jhaddïyä knocks on the door and, after a while, the door is opened by an old woman who had peered through a small window to verify her visitors. The woman, whose white hair is gathered in a complicated braid, smiles at your companion, but she looks at you with deep suspicion in her eyes.

"Who is he?" she asks, frowning.

"Easy, Lizzider, he's a trusted friend. I vouch for him!"

"Mmm, if you say so," replies the old woman, contorting her wrinkled face. "All right, come in... And you, girl, tell me how you are doing..."

You head into a room dimly lit by an oil lamp that the woman has set on the floor. Before going any farther, Lizzider checks that she has shut the door, firstly locking it and then barring it with a thick wooden beam. Then, while Jhaddïyä tells her everything about your encounter with the disciples of the Cult, you go down a narrow spiral staircase that leads you to an underground chamber.

"Have a look around and see if you find anything to your liking," says the old woman as she starts to light some candles with the flame of her oil lamp.

As the light in the room grows brighter you are increasingly stunned by what you see all around you. There is a real armory down here, and an endless variety of bottles containing many strange products.

- Here is a short list of those objects you are most interested in, and that you can afford:

Weapons:

- **Elvish bow** (for hunters): 9 zaifas (SK). Damage: 1d6+1. Difficulty: 6.

- **Arrows:** 5 arrows, cost 1 zaifa (they do not fill a slot in your leather bag).

- **Double-edged combat axe:** 100 zaifas (two-handed, STR). Damage: 1d6+2. Special ability: Critical damage. When you wound an opponent, if you roll a 6 in your damage roll (1d6+2), it not only means that you have inflicted 8 damage points, but you have also seriously wounded your opponent. At the beginning of each subsequent combat round, your enemy will lose 1 life point due to excessive bleeding. This life point is lost just before the opposed attack roll.

- **Flail** (description: weapon consisting of a wooden shaft with two chains, each ending in an iron ball covered in spikes): 100 zaifas (two-handed, SK). Damage: 1d6+2. Special ability: Critical damage. See the description under double-edged combat axe, above.

- **Dragon bone ring:** 100 zaifas (fist attack, MAG). Damage: 1d6+2. Special ability: Power concentration. This valuable magical ring assists with channelling arcane energies. Thanks to this characteristic, while you are wearing it, you only need 3 experience points (instead of 4) to gain a power point. Keep in mind that, as it is a ring, you can wear it whilst in battle, gaining power over your concentration.

Armor:

- **Elf-made leather breastplate (C):** 75 zaifas. Action area: trunk (values 2, 3 and 4). Protection: 3 LP.

- **Leather armbands (A):** 30 zaifas. Action area: arms. Protection: 1 LP.

Miscellany:

- **Sylvan healing potion:** 20 zaifas. Instructions: during combat, after winning an opposed attack roll, instead of wounding your enemy, you can choose to drink this potion. There is potion enough for 1 dose. When you drink it, you recover 1d6+2 life points. Write it down in your leather bag, as this potion fills one of its slots. Once used, erase it from your character file.

- If you are a thief, one of these potions will inexplicably end up in your leather bag without you paying for it.

When you have finished your shopping, you leave the building with Jhaddïyä by your side.

→ Go to 73.

Now keen to look for better equipment for use on the tough journey that awaits, you decide to visit the market to see what you can find to spend your zaifas on.

- You can visit the shops that you already know of: 54 (Note that you are at section 85 so that you can easily return here, as you will find other interesting items here, as detailed below, and you will also find instructions to advance your quest).

Miscellany:

- **Poison:** 25 zaifas. Instructions: spread along the blade of your chosen weapon just before combat (or on your magic ring if you are fighting with MAG). There is poison enough for 1 use. During the following combat, when you wound your enemy for the first time, you will inflict not only the corresponding damage, but you will also inoculate the poison on your weapon. Therefore, at the beginning of each subsequent round, your enemy will lose 1 life point due to the lethal effects of the venom. This life point is lost just before an opposed attack roll. Add this poison bottle to your leather bag, as it fills one of its slots. Once you have used it, erase it.

- **Net:** 21 zaifas. Instructions: throw the net on an enemy just before combat. The net will be damaged as soon as you throw it, as they will attempt to free themselves using their weapon. Therefore, you will only be able to use the net once. To throw it, roll a dice before the first opposed attack roll. If you roll a 5 or 6, you have successfully captured your opponent. If you roll a value from 1 to 4, your throw has failed, but you retain the net for use in a future combat. If you successfully capture your enemy, you will limit their movement during the combat. For the purposes of the game, your enemy will deduct 3 points from the value rolled in any opposed attack. Write the net down in your leather bag, as it fills one of its slots. Once you have used it, erase it.

→ Once you have finished shopping, keep on reading; go to 107.

86

Base camp
(write this number down on your character file)

After leaving the city, you walk together with Jhaddïyä through a wood near the coast. Your mission is rather clear. Undoubtedly, the Cult of the Golden Light has hidden watchmen in the thicket, protecting the area where the old menhir is, where they will celebrate their rite. You must find and kill as many enemies as possible, while trying to remain unnoticed. So as you walk on in complete silence, you seek the faintest trace of any concealed enemies.

■ Roll a dice for PER with a difficulty of 4.

    → If the value you rolled is 4 or higher: 44
    → Otherwise: 57

87

After being beaten and stunned, you attempt to keep up with the quick steps of the soldiers as best you can. You finally reach the doors of the fortress of Verinfes, where you are immediately taken to a small dungeon and, after handing over your arms, locked up alone. Exhausted, you sit on a filthy straw bed, trying to recover from your wounds. You don't have long to wait, as shortly thereafter a group of soldiers reappear, unlock the door and lead you to Brádoc.

    → Go to 95.

88

Despite having given your best, your enemy is a real beast, a titan that is extremely hard to beat. When you regain consciousness, you realise that you are lying in a corner of 'The Scarlet Goddess', in what seems to be someone else's spew. Bruised and bloodied, and now sick to your stomach, you quickly rise from the soiled floor, disgusted by the foul smell all around you. Apparently, after proving to be an opponent who wasn't his match, all those present made fun of you, and The Golden One returned to his table. If you're brave or foolish enough, you can measure your ability against him once again.

↓ Horrified, you discover that half of your coins have been stolen. Deduct this amount from your character file.

→ Go to 60.

89
Base camp
(write this number down on your character file)

After leaving the fortress of Verinfes with a somewhat strange feeling after all that you have experienced, you locate a humble, quiet inn in which to spend the night. As your bag of coins is rather heavy, you decide to lighten it a bit by having a good dinner and a well deserved rest, as everything suggests that your life is going to change very soon.

- **Wine jar:** 1 zaifa.
- **Beer jar:** 1 zaifa.
- **Veal stew:** 4 zaifas.
- **Meat pie:** 3 zaifas.
- **Roast chicken:** 2 zaifas.
- **Grilled fish:** 2 zaifas.
- **Bread:** 1 zaifa.

- **Single room:** 12 zaifas.
- **Sleep in the common room:** 4 zaifas.
- **Stable and food for your horse:** 2 zaifas.

After a peaceful night of deep, restful sleep, you wake up full of enthusiasm and energy, willing to embark on the path that will lead you to the city of the amazons. However, your joy quickly fades when you look outside to see that the sky is completely black, with a heavy rain falling all over the city.

'That's a really good start! This is the ideal estrio to start a journey like mine!' you think, now gathering your equipment to leave the inn and meet Hormäz at the eastern gates of Verinfes, as agreed.

You head outside and are soon riding Nëmster, who snorts due to the inclement weather, to your destination. As the streets are almost empty because of the severe storm, you reach Hormäz in good time; when you arrive he's sitting on the seat of a huge carriage, protected from the rain by a small awning.

"Oh, here you are, the last to arrive. We're all here now, so let's move on immediately! It doesn't seem like it will be raining for long," he adds, looking at the sky, "so we'll delay any introductions. Let's get moving, as complying with strict delivery times is vital for my business. You're going last," he says, pointing directly at you, "in the rearguard! And keep your eyes open wide. Let's go!"

Acting by Hormäz's orders, you take the road leading south from Verinfes. You haven't been long on the road when the rain begins to subside, now only drizzling. Meanwhile, you have closely observed your companions in this caravan. Two skilled and feisty horsemen, mercenaries like you with a mission to protect the merchant and the merchandise, lead the way. Two massive carriages, each being pulled by four horses, ride after them. Upon the seat of one of these carriages sits Hormäz, accompanied by a dwarf now getting on in liznars who holds the reins and is surely someone that Hormäz trusts. The second carriage, which brings up the rear, is lead by another dwarf, this one looking even fiercer than the one riding on the first carriage. Finally, at the rearguard, you ride Nëmster, looking over the caravan as the wheels of the heavy carriages sink their way deep into the muddy trail.

Despite the difficulties of this wet ground, you ride on until mid estrio, when Hormäz calls a stop at a crossroads.

"We must wait here," he tells the crew of the caravan. "Someone else will join us. Here he comes now, if I'm not mistaken."

You immediately look in the direction that the merchant indicates, and there you see a horseman riding out of a group of trees. The rider's horse is of a beautiful chestnut colour, with a white mane that contrasts with the rich colour of its coat. This stranger is wrapped in a brown hooded cloak, which prevents you from seeing any part of their body. When the rider finally arrives and stops by the merchant's carriage, you are amazed, as when you hear their voice, you have no doubt it is a woman who speaks.

"You've finally arrived!" she says to Hormäz with an authoritarian voice.

"I sincerely regret the delay, but the rain made us move more slowly than we had anticipated."

"I do hope you've brought the merchandise, at least!"

"Of course! I gave my word."

"All of the merchandise?"

"All!"

"I'm glad to hear it... In that case, let's move along!"

So, after a mere minutes pause, you resume your way along the windswept path. It is not until lunch that you benefit from any real rest, when Hormäz distributes bread, cheese and wine among the tired crew. At this time the merchant makes some brief introductions.

"You should know that we enjoy the great pleasure of travelling with one of Bälkaar's amazons!" he exclaims. "Her name is Mhändara, and she belongs to one of the most important families of her kingdom. I've been doing business with her family for a long time. She will guide us to her city, and thanks to her we will enter Bälkaar free of any trouble."

Surprised by Hormäz's words, you look carefully at the beautiful blonde amazon, who sits on a rock, chewing a chunk of bread.

"As for the two horsemen that have led the caravan until now, they're both friends, skilled warriors, born in a small village near Lógadar. Their names are Tarúk and Jurköm, and they really are as fierce as they look. This is not my first journey with them and I'm always happy to have them by my side..." Hormäz pauses briefly before continuing. "Then we have the dwarves of the group. Nödrik-Nígodar is the first of them (he says, pointing at one of the dwarves with a thick, black beard and a bulging belly, who seems to always have his massive battle axe at hand). He was born in a mine near Ternostan, and we have known each other for a long time... As with Süod-Helbórian, my most trusted companion, who was born north of the Srimost range; the best blacksmith I've ever known."

Smiling broadly, Hormäz pats the second dwarf on his shoulder, a truly horrible being with brown braided hair, a deformed nose (undoubtedly due to an old injury), and a mouth showing many gaps where teeth are no longer found. "And finally (the merchant says, waving a hand towards you), we have our new friend, who I don't really know anything about. That's why, if you don't mind, I think you should introduce yourself. We're all wanting to know more about you..."

So, following Hormäz's instructions, you briefly, and discreetly, introduce yourself, avoiding as many details as possible after checking the strange and rather motley group that you have become a member of.

Finally, Hormäz leaves you to enjoy a few more minutes of rest before the journey resumes. You know that you don't have much time, but you try to gain a little more information about the caravan and its crew before you depart.

→ If you decide to approach the amazon to talk to her: 99
→ If you'd rather talk to the brothers Tarúk and Jurköm: 109

90

When the chest seems to now be empty, your great skill as a thief encourages you to look more closely at the lid, as it is significantly thicker than would be expected. After knocking on its boards and pushing on the wooden strips, you agreeably discover that your senses haven't been fooled, as everything suggests that there is indeed a secret compartment hiding within. Thus, using your weapon, you pull off one of the strips, exposing the compartment, where you find a new object:

- **Speed potion.** Instructions: drink it just before starting combat. There is potion enough for 1 dose. After drinking it, during that combat, you will add 1 additional point to all of your opposed attack rolls. Add it to the leather bag on your character file, as this potion fills one of its slots. Once you have used it, erase it.

- **Speed potion (90).** Drink before combat. Effects: +1 to all of your opposed attack rolls during that combat.

    → Go to 80.

91

You seem to have already become quickly accustomed to your new horse, as you fight masterfully upon Nëmster's back. However, there's no time to enjoy your victory, as a new enemy immediately faces you. Remember that you have all the advantages of fighting on horseback, but you won't be able to charge again. Keep on reading. → Go to 137.

92

Almost without realizing it, you proceed down a flight of stairs, but instead of descending just the one story you had already risen, you now descend two, most likely into a basement. Then, one of the men lowers himself to his hands and knees and begins crawling along a low, narrow tunnel dug out of the rock. You do the same with Jhaddïyä following you, and when all of your group have entered this cold and damp passageway, you hear a heavy metallic door closing behind you.

After crawling in the dark for a long while, you finally reach a new door, which is knocked on three times by the leading man.

"Verinfes and the Thornless Rose! Désmokay!" he says as a watchword. In response this new barrier is quickly opened, letting light slip through to the narrow tunnel.

"Vikord, I didn't expect to find you here! Did something go wrong?" you hear somebody ask from the other side. "Is Jhaddïyä with you?"

"We're all fine, but we were followed to the mansion. Come on, let us in!"

You crawl out of the passageway into what seems to be a spacious cellar where ten other people, both men and women, are waiting, fully armed and equipped. A hundred unanswered questions buzz about in your mind, however, you feel that you are in no danger, as after some words of introduction Jhaddïyä speaks to the group; they all seem to have heard about you, and the important message you delivered to Brádoc. You are invited to sit at a table where you are offered a bowl of hot broth that quickly warms you after the cold of the narrow passageway. Once you have finished your meal, a new surprise is now waiting, as the lad named Vikord comes to you and asks you to follow him.

"Come with me! Jhaddïyä wants to see you – just the two of you."

You follow him into another room where Jhaddïyä is already waiting. The door is quietly closed at your back as Vikord departs, leaving you and the girl alone. It's a tiny, simple room, with just a couple of chests and a wooden table, where Jhaddïyä sits and eats.

"Come, take a seat! Do you fancy a drink? Wine?" she says kindly, pouring a glass for you without waiting for an answer.

"What am I doing here? Exactly who are you?"

"I guess you have many similar questions, and I have answers for them all. But let me start at the beginning... As you already know, my name is Jhaddïyä, and I'm the leader of the Thornless Rose, a group of elite warriors that work outside the law and whose only purpose is to end the nefarious activities of the Cult of the Golden Light. I know you're thinking that I'm too young to hold this honor, but my appearance is simply the result of an enchantment..." → Go to 41.

93

Despite all your efforts, this sorcerer has simply been too tough for you. ↓ You lose 1 experience point because of this defeat (this point is only lost once, no matter how many times you come back here), but you can fight him again after deducting 1 life point. For instance, if you had 20 life points, you'll start the next combat against the sorcerer with 19 life points. → Go back to 105 and deliver justice. Remember you can go back to the main square of Verinfes (45) whenever you want.

94

↑ You win 1 experience point after killing your enemy. After finishing him you see a new opponent running towards you. If you roll for SK with a difficulty 5, you'll be able to make a surprise attack, adding 2 points to your first opposed attack roll.

◘ **Second watchman of the Cult of the Golden Light:** Rapier (SK). Damage: 1d6+2 / SK 1 / LP: 22 / Armor: Leather breastplate (C). Action area: trunk (values 2, 3 and 4). Protection: 2 LP.

→ If defeated, you lose 1 item from your leather bag, and if you want to, you can fight him again with your life points restored. If you don't feel ready, you can head back to the city of Verinfes (45) to find better equipment or to complete other missions to make yourself more powerful before attempting this quest again. Write section number 94 on your character file so that you come here directly when ready.

→ If you defeat him: 110

95

Brádoc waits in an underground chamber located deep in the fortress of Verinfes, where you find him sitting before a huge wooden table full of documents and maps representing the different areas of Urowen.

"Leave us and guard the door," he instructs the two soldiers. "Don't bother us until I come out!"

"By your order, my lord," one of the men answers before leaving the room and closing the door, leaving you alone with the intimidating First Soldier of Verinfes.

"Have a seat!" Brádoc says in his strong voice, pointing to a chair by his table. "We have things to discuss... As I guess you'll know by now, I have eyes and ears throughout Verinfes, and that's why I'm well informed of your wanderings. You are a tough man who does not beat about the bush, and I like that! In these dark times, we need people of your kind... I've heard that you've wasted little time since your arrival in gaining a few friends, and some dangerous enemies, too. You must be careful from now on, as there are many vengeful people who you have offended... Regardless, what has surprised me the most is that I've heard you're soon embarking on a journey to Bälkaar – a road that involves some dangers, especially if you're guarding Hormäz... That greedy merchant! Be careful about him, as he would sell his own mother if there was a profit to be made, no matter how small..."

You listen carefully to Brádoc words, surprised by all that he knows about you and your adventures.

"I must confess that I like you, and that's far more than I can say about many of the people around me. You're brave, bold and determined... and there's a grain of folly within you that reminds me of my youth, and even my son... Well, I'll get down to business! I've brought you here to entrust you with a mission of vital importance that I hope you'll accept. This has come about due of your sudden journey to Bälkaar... ah, Bälkaar, such good memories! Have you ever been there?"

"I've never had the chance," you answer, slightly intimidated by Brádoc's impressive appearance.

"As I've told you, I'm certain that there is a grain of folly in you if you're willing to go there. What do you know about the amazons and Queen Zarkända?"

"Not much, truth be told. It's said that they're really beautiful women, and that their queen is the most beautiful of them all."

"Oh yes, beautiful and terribly dangerous. And they hate men – every man. If you've never been to Bälkaar, nor know anything about these warrior women, then listen to me carefully, as my words could save your life. Amazons are skilled warriors, experts in the use of the bow. Most of them don't have a right breast. Shortly after birth, their own mothers burn it with a red-hot iron to stop it from growing. This then allows them to use their bow in a highly skilled way, which they do so masterfully, even on the back of their horses, the legendary bälkian thoroughbred, impressive animals that mean far more to the amazons than just a mere mount. Since early childhood, they train endlessly in the arts of war... and you are heading directly to their capital, Bälkaar, located at the mouth of the Záedor River. Since time immemorial, these lands have been ruled by women. The matriarchs of important families decide the destinies of their men in a council that advises the queen... But I don't want to frighten you. I have good memories of that place despite all that I have said, so I may not be the best person to warn you."

After a few moments of silence in which Brádoc's blank face seems to be lost in thought, he speaks again.

"Returning to the issue at hand, as I've told you, I have an important mission to entrust you with. But I firstly require your word that what's spoken inside this room will never be repeated outside these walls."

Intimidated by Brádoc's inquisitorial look, you immediately nod in agreement, thus accepting his terms, fully aware of the consequences if you were to break your promise.

"Great, I didn't expect any less from you," Brádoc says. "Now I can talk to you frankly... All of the reports from our explorers and spies indicate that the amazons from Bälkaar will join the disciples of Zorbrak in the war against the free peoples. We no longer have any doubt that they will enter into battle, and that's why I ask you to kill Marok-häi, one of the most influential amazons in town. Marok-häi is their most skillful warrior, the leader of the armies of Queen Zarkända, the woman that will undoubtedly lead their army when they ultimately face us. Killing her would be a severe blow that would force the queen to leave the city, as if Marok-häi is not leading their army, it will be the only other woman capable of doing so: Zarkända herself. I know it is an extremely difficult mission, but I trust that you will be able to fulfill it. Of course, if you accept, I will give you all of the information we have on Marok-häi, and you will earn pride of place within our ranks. Likewise, your reward will be large, consistent with the difficult task imposed on you. What do you say – will you accept this challenge?"

"Before making up my mind, I'd like to hear a little more about the mentioned reward. What do you have in mind?"

"If you accept this risky mission, I'll give you a bag full of zaifas, armor, and one of the best horses in Verinfes to take you to your destination. And all of these rewards I will give to you in advance, on your word of honor that you'll do your best to kill Marok-häi. And, if you fulfill your mission and then come back to Verinfes alive, I can assure you that there will be another substantial reward waiting. So, do you now accept my mission?"

→ If you decide to reject Brádoc's mission: 121
→ If you accept the deal and thus accept the mission: 140

96

Letting out shrieks of laughter and shouts of joy, an enthusiastic crowd of onlookers cheers on both of the participants betting their zaifas in a drinking competition. If you want to test your own resistance to alcohol you'll have the chance to do so in the next round, as the hunt for further brave competitors is already in full swing. If you do decide to take your chance, you'll face a single opponent, each of you drinking wine jar after wine jar until one of you gives up. You can bet as many zaifas as you want, up to a maximum amount of 30. Your opponent will bet the same amount as you, and the winner will take their opponent's zaifas. So, if you bet 30 zaifas and win, you'll get your 30 zaifas back, and you'll keep the 30 zaifas bet by your opponent. If you lose, say farewell to all of your money. For obvious reasons, you will only be able to take part in this competition once, as you'll hardly be able to stand once you've finished!

- The game is played as follows: double your base life points (if you have 20 you'll start the competition with 40). Your opponent, having 21 base life points, starts with 42. Roll two dice – one for you and one for your opponent: this represents the drinking of the first wine jar. The values rolled indicate the life points that each of you now lose. You then drink the second wine jar, and so on, deducting further life points from those remaining. The first participant to reach 0 life points loses the competition.

If both of you reach 0 life points in the same roll, keep on deducting life points to get a negative result: the one who gets the lowest score loses. For instance, -1 wins over -3. If there is still a tie, continue rolling dice until one competitor has reached a lower score.

→ When you're finally able to refocus your eyes, you dizzily rise from the gaming table, looking for new adventures: 60

97

Despite all of your efforts, you've been unable to finish off your enemy. Unfortunately, a harsh blow also knocks you down (if you were riding your horse, you now fall from it). Stunned and knowing that you are at your enemy's mercy, you look up in horror to see the bandit raising his weapon to deliver the coup de grâce. Just when you believe that your end is near, your enemy suddenly staggers with an arrow through his neck, collapsing to the ground while drowning in his own blood. Not believing what you have just witnessed, you quickly turn your head to see the impressive amazon in her saddle, holding the bow that has delivered the life-saving shot. Keep on reading.

→ Go to 127.

98

When you finally regain consciousness, you see that you're lying on your own on the floor, a terrible headache causing you great pain. ↓ Not only you have lost the zaifas invested to go up to the room without obtaining anything in exchange, but you also lose 1 experience point. With wounded pride and your morale at rock bottom, you return to the common room to recover from the humiliation.

→ Go to 60.

99

The amazon woman is rather intimidating, so you approach her with some trepidation.

"So you're going to be our guide," you say, keenly watching her reaction and demeanour.

"So it seems!" With these three words, Mhändara instantly terminates the conversation, as she turns her face away to look over the surrounding landscape.

"Have you come from Bälkaar?" you insist, courageously attempting to extract some information. The amazon doesn't even bother to answer your question as she simply stares at you without responding, slowly looking up and down at you until you begin to feel uncomfortable.

Hormäz walks over to you, a knowing smile on his face. "She's not especially good at talking, as you've discovered. I'm afraid that you'll have to ask your questions again some other time, as we must get moving," he states, now also talking to the rest of the group.

Keep on reading. → Go to 123.

100

You proceed slowly through the thicket, and with the noise of running water nearby, you suddenly hear something else moving in front of you. Immediately standing motionless, attempting to blend in with your surroundings, you distinguish the dark shape of a massive dog running directly towards you through the underbrush. You have no doubt that this dangerous animal has noticed you, as it begins to bark incessantly. As it moves closer you also notice a frothing about its jaws – it is going to attack! Get ready for the impending fight. → Go to 135.

101
Base camp
(write this number down on your character file)

Just before engaging in combat, you quickly drink the potion Jhaddïyä has given you, and immediately feel far more powerful:

- **Resilience potion.** Instructions: drink just before entering into battle. There is potion enough for just 1 dose. After drinking it, you will begin combat with 50 life points. Unfortunately, its effects only last for a short period. Your objective will be to beat your next three enemies, Dëvian included, using just those 50 life points: you will not recover life points between battles. So, if you are victorious in the first fight, you will start the second with your remaining life points. If you finally beat all three enemies, the effects of the potion will disappear, and you will once again have your usual life points for your next combat.

◘ **First bodyguard of the Cult of the Golden Light:** Two-handed sword (SK). Damage: 1d6 / SK 1 / LP: 20 / Armor: Leather breastplate (C). Action area: trunk (values 2, 3 and 4). Protection: 1 LP

◘ **Second bodyguard of the Cult of the Golden Light:** Two-handed sword (SK). Damage: 1d6 / SK 2 / LP: 21 / Armor: Leather breastplate (C). Action area: trunk (values 2, 3 and 4). Protection: 2 LP. Helmet (H). Action area: head. Protection: 2 LP

◘ **Dëvian:** Rapier (SK). Damage: 1d6+2 / SK 3 / LP: 20 / Armor: Leather breastplate (C). Action area: trunk (values 2, 3 and 4). Protection: 2 LP / Special ability: Critical damage. When Dëvian wounds you, if she rolls a 6 in her damage roll (1d6+2), not only has she totalled 8 damage points, but she has also inflicted a serious injury. Therefore, at the beginning of each subsequent combat round, you lose 1 life point due to blood loss. You lose this life point just before the opposed attack roll.

→ If you are defeated by any of these three enemies, you must lose 1 item. You can choose a weapon, a piece of armor, something you are wearing, a magical item, an item from your leather bag... and then you can try again. If you are defeated for the second time, for the third, the forth... you lose 1 experience point each time. Remember that you can head back to Verinfes (45) to find better equipment or to attempt to become more powerful and then return here when you feel ready.

→ If you defeat your enemies: 132

102

It seems that you're not yet accustomed to your new mount, subsequently falling ungracefully from your horse. Get ready to face a new enemy, this time on foot. Begin combat having lost 1d6 life points due to your fall.

→ Keep on reading on 137.

103

Being aware of the difficulties that Landanar and her daughter Naira still face, you refuse to take the offered zaifas. Despite the woman's insistence, you finally convince her to keep the coins, as they will surely need them far more than you. Deeply grateful for your help with Korindor and for declining the zaifas, Landanar leads you to a corner of the room, where she locates an object that she offers to you at once.

"Please," she says tearfully, "accept this small present! It's the least I can do, and I don't need it at all..."

When you happily accept the offered item, you are surprised to discover that you hold a small wineskin that, according to Landanar, contains a powerful potion:

- **Dwarf power elixir.** Instructions: drink just before combat. There is elixir enough for 1 dose. After drinking, add 1 additional point to all of your damage rolls during this combat. Write it down on your file as it fills a slot in your leather bag. Once you've used it, erase it from your file.

→ After having said goodbye to Landanar and her daughter, you return to the market square of Verinfes, where you will be able to resume your adventures: 45

104

Tired of bearing the dwarf's reproaches and insults for an entire estrio, you can no longer hold back your growing rage.

"A good beating? Just you and me? I'd like to see that because I'll make you swallow your words!"

A stony silence descends while everybody looks on; the faces of your startled companions giving little away. Do they now see you as someone capable of meeting the challenge of such a ferocious dwarf, or do they simply think of you as a madman.

"Well, very well!" answers Nödrik-Nígodar as he comes closer. "I see that you haven't run out of courage. That's something!"

"What are you doing? Are you crazy?" Hormäz says to you, visibly upset. "I know I won't be able to stop this madness! Nígodar, in all the God's names, don't leave me without one of my men! We've just left Verinfes! If there's a thread of sanity left in you, remember that we still have a long journey ahead to reach Bälkaar."

"Don't worry about your merchandise," Nígodar responds, grabbing his imposing axe. "I'm just going to give our new friend a couple of gentle strokes!"

"It's like talking to a brick wall. Be as the Gods want. I don't want to know anything else about this issue!" the merchant says giving up, aware that the dwarf is beyond control.

"All right, my friend," the dwarf says to you. "Get ready, because I'm going to teach you how to fight!"

Now that he is standing very close, ready for combat, you begin to realise that it was likely not a good idea to have provoked the dwarf. As although Nödrik-Nígodar is still limping due his leg injury, he remains a remarkable, dangerous enemy. Get ready for a tough fight as you endeavour to defend your honor before all of your companions...

◻ **Nödrik-Nígodar:** Battle Axe (STR). Damage: 1d6+3 / STR 4 / LP: 30 / Armor: Dwarf-leather breastplate (C). Action area: trunk (values 2, 3 and 4). Protection: 4 LP. Helmet (H). Action area: head. Protection: 3 LP. Dwarf-leather armbands and greaves (A) (G). Action area: arms and legs. Protection 2 LP / Special ability: Dwarf rage. If Nödrik-Nígodar's life points fall below 10, his dwarf rage will rise; a savage warrior fury that will raise his strength value from 4 to 5.

→ If you defeat Nödrik-Nígodar: 118
→ If the dwarf defeats you: 134

105

You suddenly experience a strong dizziness in your head and a powerful buzzing that rings in your ears. You can hardly endure the tormenting pain that is now taking control of your mind, just as if a thousand worms were eating through your brain. Unable to stand, you drop your weapon and collapse to the ground, holding your forehead with both hands; you think that your head will soon explode, such is your suffering. Just when you have begun writhing in pain on the ground, fighting to maintain consciousness, you see the corpse of a soldier lying next to you. When you look at his face, you realise in horror that it is you (your usual character) who is lying there with a blank face, rain falling heavily on your corpse. Unable to withstand this insane situation any longer, you shout out in rage and pain, trying to escape this nightmare... You can't do much more than shout though, as right then several enemies fall on you, plunging their weapons deep into your body...

You close your eyes at this terrible suffering, and are surprised to hear a grim laughter from above. Quickly reopening your eyes, you see the figure of Korindor standing in front of you, laughing heartily. You are in your usual body again, and are back before the sorcerer's hut, by the Izquion River. Your usual character file is now in operation again, with everything as it was.

"What do you think of what I've shown you?" Korindor asks with an annoying, mocking voice. "That may be the grim ending awaiting you... Only Gods really know, but that can only happen if you manage to leave this place alive. Now, get ready to die, you defiant bastard! Landanar and her daughter are mine, and I'll make what I desire out of them! Neither you, nor anybody else can prevent that!"

Get ready to fight Korindor. Author's note: Crush this bastard – he deserves no mercy.

◻ **Korindor:** Ice attack with his wand (MAG). Damage: 1d6 (no armor can protect to you from these frigid attacks) / MAG 1 / LP: 20 / Armor: none / Special ability: Freeze. When Korindor wounds you, if he rolls a 6 for damage location and the attack strikes your head, it will have a lethal effect on you. That's why (beside of the usual damage of that attack), at the beginning of each subsequent combat round you'll lose 1 life point because of the freezing sensation that now spreads throughout your body. You lose this life point just before rolling each opposed attack roll.

→ If you defeat Korindor: 76
→ If you can't defeat the bastard: 93

106

A couple of men now enter the room, carrying small wooden boxes. As they do so another man speaks loudly, addressing the entire room.

"Come all and participate – don't hesitate to double your zaifas for a single moment! There are no wild dogs competing tonight, no bears or saber-tooths! Instead, we have something really special. Maybe not so spectacular at first glance, but undoubtedly much more exciting and unpredictable... Tonight we'll see the unique confrontation of a tarantula and a scorpion! Yes, my friends, yes! You heard right. A Lógadar tarantula will gauge its strength against an Izquion riverbank scorpion! You've never seen anything like this in your life! Come and bet – the fight will start soon!"

Attracted by these words, the vast majority of the people here move towards where the wagers are taken, looking to increase their zaifas.

At that time, Tarúk, who had gone to the bar, comes back to your table with news.

"Listen to me, this might be interesting for us! One of the girls has told me that the man sitting alone at that table in the corner is a well known local alchemist who sells several kinds of potions. The maid suggests that his wares may be useful to the likes of us. It might be a good idea to go and ask."

→ If you decide to place a bet: 129

→ If you approach the alchemist: 170

→ If nothing here appeals to you, or if you have already played both options, keep on reading. Go to 160.

107

Base camp
(write this number down on your character file)

When you move away from the market, looking for a place to spend the night, two armed men from the city guard suddenly stop in front of you.

"Are you the foreigner who delivered the message to Brádoc?"

After acknowledging your identity, both men seem to relax, as they have finally located their objective.

"Brádoc wishes to speak with you as soon as possible, as he has something important to tell you. We are to bring you to him immediately. Will you accompany us to the fortress?"

→ If you agree and then follow the soldiers to Brádoc: 95

→ If you refuse their request: 128

108

Somewhat tired from all of your exertions up until this point, you decide to relax at the bar. You make your way through the crowd, and after waiting for some time are finally assisted by a scantily dressed young woman.

- **Home-made marc glass:** 1 zaifa.
- **Mead jar:** 1 zaifa.
- **Wine or beer jar:** 1 zaifa.
- **Roasted pork:** 2 zaifas.

- **Roasted fish:** 2 zaifas.
- **Bread:** 1 zaifa.

Once you have been served, you lean on the bar for a while, savouring the moment and enjoying a little peace after the many dangers you have had to face. Right then, a stranger approaches; a rough man with white hair who shouts at the waitress with a powerful voice.

"Beer, here! Bring me a huge tankard and another one for my friend!" he exclaims, pointing at you with his finger. When he sees the surprise on your face, as you are sure that this is the first time in your life that you have seen this man, he adds with a smile: "Come on, accept my invitation! I hate drinking alone! Only losers do that!"

As there's no reason to refuse, you nod shyly and the stranger laughs out loud.

"I can see that you are new here! It's a pleasure to find new faces in this den. My name's Dösser," he says, now firmly shaking your hand.

"Here are your beers," the waitress says, noisily placing the jars on the wooden bar. "Who's your new friend, Dösser? I've never seen him around here before."

"In fact, I don't know his name yet... What's your name?"

After answering his question and telling him about a few of the adventures that have brought you here, you seem to have earned some admiration from him. From the noticeable purple colour of his nose, he appears to have already drunk a number of tankards.

"I've been fighting in the war, way up north, near Fënz... fighting against those damned dreknars. Have you ever seen them? You feel like fleeing when you see them running into battle. They are wild men, real beasts eager for blood. I was lucky to escape with my life, but many comrades died on the battlefield. Many friends of mine lost their life there... Bring me another beer, woman!" he shouts before downing the jar in his hands in one huge gulp. "I tell you, I wish that you'll never have to fight those dreknars..."

Dösser now shuffles unsteadily on his feet (no doubt because of the alcohol he has consumed) and clumsily takes a couple of backwards steps, falling against a fierce-looking man who subsequently spills his glass of wine over his clothes.

"You bastard!" the angered man exclaims, pushing Dösser off of him. "Look at what you've done! You filthy moron!"

"It wasn't my..." your new friend starts to say, but he never finishes his words as the stranger forcefully punches Dösser in the stomach, sending him to the ground.

Somewhat stunned, Dösser tries to get up, but the stranger kicks him hard in the face. He falls again, and blood begins to spill from a cut lip.

Dizzy and short of air, Dösser reaches out, desperate for help, but nobody is willing to help him. Actually, the nearby patrons have taken a few steps back, not wanting to become involved, watching and waiting...

→ If you help Dösser: 79
→ If you don't want to involve yourself, and would rather get out of harm's way: 48

109

Interested in the two skillful hirelings, you come near to them to engage in a little conversation.

"I've never been to Lógadar, nor have I had the chance to meet many people born there..."

"Believe me, you wouldn't enjoy the experience," Tarúk, the tallest and stoutest of the brothers, suddenly interrupts you. "Spirits of Zedún, the priestly caste that rules over the lands of Lógadar, control everything... and if you face them, you will hardly be able to bear the horrible consequences! See this?" he says, indicating his left forearm, which is marked with many ugly scars. "I did these myself with my knife! One of those mentalists just spoke a single word and I lost control of my actions...! I was entirely at his mercy... I remember my right hand moving, cutting my own arm as if I were a damned butcher..."

"Stop that! Stop torturing yourself," his brother Jurköm says as he places his hand on Tarúk's shoulder. "As my brother has said," he adds addressing you, "you wouldn't like Lógadar... It's just a vipers' nest..."

"A vipers' nest that albeit offers a lot to learn. You'll have time to discover it one day," says Hormäz, now moving to your side. "Although, I'm afraid that will have to be at some other time. "We must get moving," he adds, now also talking to the rest of the group.

Keep on Reading. → Go to 123.

110

This second combat has been very noisy, drawing the attention of another sentinel who, without warning, pounces on you. Remember that after each combat, you recover all of your base life points.

◻ **Third guard of the Cult of the Golden Light:** Two-handed sword (SK). Damage: 1d6+2 / SK 2 / LP: 20 / Armor: Leather breastplate (C). Action area: trunk (values 2, 3 and 4). Protection: 2 LP. Helmet (H). Action area: head. Protection: 3 LP.

↓ If defeated, you lose 1 piece of armor of your choice, and, if you wish, you can fight him again.

If you don't feel ready, you can head back to the city of Verinfes (45) to find better equipment or to complete other missions to make yourself more powerful before attempting this quest again.

→ If you defeat your enemy: 120

111

It doesn't take long to pack up your improvised camp, so you soon resume your journey following Hormäz's instructions.

"We must step it up today," the merchant says. "I intend to reach 'The Caged Skeleton' before the estrio ends as I don't feel like spending another night in the open when an inn is within sight."

So, repeating the previous estrio's formation, you make your way through an area more wooded than the one you have left behind. The man-made path you're following can barely be seen within the dense vegetation here, as trees and bushes seem to have reclaimed much of this part of the forest. Thick, twisted trunks, fully covered in moss, grow all around you, creating a sinister atmosphere. This feeling is even more apparent because of the cloaking mist that hangs in the air here.

Although the estrio seemed to be clear after yesterday's rains, the surrounding mist rapidly grows thicker, up to the point that you can barely discern anything around you.

"This is very strange... too strange I would dare to say," the merchant says apprehensively. "Stop here, I don't like this at all! It's not been that long since I last passed through here, and I certainly don't remember all of these twisted trees. It's impossible that they would have grown this much since then."

"This mist isn't natural either," says the amazon. "Maybe we should turn back and look for an alternative route."

"It's too late!" says Süod-Helbórian, the dwarf sorcerer, who closes his eyes and reaches out before him as he begins concentrating his energy. "There's something in this forest... something mighty that doesn't want us to pass. I feel a powerful energy... Wait!" he exclaims, now concentrating even harder. "Quickly, come near, there's no time! Form a circle by placing yourselves around the carriages. We must fight back!"

So, following the dwarf's instructions you position yourself in the circle, waiting in a defensive stance with your weapon ready, looking for the thing that Süod-Helbórian fears so much. Your mounts are also restless and afraid, nervously pawing the ground while they neigh in alarm. Right then, you look at the forest directly in front of you, where you can barely discern anything clearly. The mist has grown thicker around you, producing a coldness that quickly chills your bones. Then, as if you were in a strange dream, you see a knotted trunk, fully covered in lichen, seemingly moving towards you; many vines creep along the ground around it, ready to catch you with their strong, thorny branches. Startled and rather horrified, you look around to see that your companions are also facing similar enemies. Get ready to face this strange forest creature. Remember to follow the rules for mounted combat, as you are currently riding Nëmster.

◘ **Spirit of the Forest:** Blow with branches (STR). Damage: 1d6+3 / STR 3 / LP: 20 / Armor: Bark. Action area: all areas (values 1 to 6). Protection: 3 LP / Special ability: Vines. The Spirit of the Forest, in addition to its tree form, attacks with 2 independent vines. At the end of every combat round each vine will take 1 extra life point as they begin to entangle you. When you win an opposed attack roll, you can choose to try and hurt one of the vines instead of the Spirit of the Forest. If you defeat one of them, you won't lose any further life points from it thereafter. If you succeed in defeating both vines, you will be able to focus on destroying the Spirit of the Forest. Vines have 7 life points, no armor, and the damage location does not apply to them.

→ If you defeat your enemy: 133
→ If the Spirit of the Forest has defeated you: 143

112

You proceed slowly through the thicket, and with the noise of running water nearby, you suddenly hear something else moving in front of you. Unfortunately, it is already too late to react, as you discover, in horror, that a massive wild dog is coming directly for you. Suddenly struck by fear, you notice a frothing about its jaws, which are already wide open, keen to taste your blood. You've been taken by surprise, so you must deduct 3 points from your first opposed attack roll.

→ Go to 135.

113

The fight continues on around you after finishing off your fierce enemy, so when you turn your head, Hormäz nods at you, acknowledging what you've just achieved. By his side, the amazon, the brothers and the two dwarves are still fighting. One of the dwarves seems to be a sorcerer, as a green fire shoots from the palm of his hands, quickly consuming one of the bandits. You don't have time to look on any longer, as another desperate assailant pounces on you...

- If you are still mounted (if you aren't, you would have already read this), you don't have the space to charge. Get ready and grab your weapon firmly, as your new enemy, who shouts in rage and has bloodshot eyes, seems to be far fiercer and much stouter than the previous bandit:

◻ **Third painted-face bandit:** Saw blade sword (SK). Damage: 1d6+3 / SK 3 / LP: 25 / Armor: Leather breastplate (C). Action area: trunk (values 2, 3 and 4). Protection: 3 LP. Helmet (H). Action area: head. Protection: 2 LP. Armbands and leather greaves (A) (G). Action area: arms and legs. Protection: 1 LP / Special ability: Whip. In addition to his sword, the bandit is carrying an intimidating whip in his left hand. Every time that the bandit wounds you, in addition to the regular damage inflicted with his sword, he rolls another dice. If he rolls a 5 or higher, it means that, in addition to the damage delivered with the sword, the bandit has also struck with his whip: deduct 1 extra life point. Additionally, the whip has also wrapped itself around one of your limbs, so deduct 1 point from your next opposed attack roll.

→ If you defeat the savage bandit: 158
→ If your enemy has defeated you: 97

114

Worried about the health of the amazon, you immediately go to her to check on her condition.

"Are you alright?" you ask, removing the cloth gag and the rope that ties her hands.

"Dirty bastards, sons of a thousand fathers!" Mhändara shouts as soon as her tongue is free, taken by an unspeakable rage. "They took me by surprise in the dark and I couldn't do anything..." she adds, now watching the soldiers escorting the two offenders away.

"Everything is over now. Luckily, I wanted some fresh air, too."

"Thank you kindly for your help. I'll not forget what you've done for me. You can be sure of that."

"All the Gods! Mhändara... are you okay?" comes Hormäz's voice, now rushing into the barn.

"Yes, yes... Don't worry," the amazon replies. "Fortunately, I've only got this bruised eye and a sore back. Nothing too serious that can be easily mended with a bit of time and a wine jar. Although I must admit that I owe it all to our friend here," she says, pointing at you. "I might be dead right now if not for his unexpected help. I'm sure that those bastards would have cut my throat after finishing with me. In a place like this, with a shut door and a building full of armed soldiers... they wouldn't have wanted to leave a witness behind."

"I can assure you that they have made a huge mistake," says an old man with white hair and beard, who now stands by the merchant. "My word is law here, and there is no doubt that those bastards are guilty. I'll deliver my judgement this very night!"

After saying these words, the stranger turns away and quickly leaves. That is when you look closer at his clothes: expensive and lavish.

"Who is he?" the amazon asks Hormäz.

"He is rarely seen in public. His name is Ágraszar, and he is the uncle of Xon Ágraster, King of Verinfes. As you have seen, 'The Caged Skeleton' is a very uncommon inn, and that is because Ágraszar moved here long ago. As he has said, his word is law here, as the rules of Verinfes are not followed here, even with it being part of the kingdom. I wouldn't want to be in the skin of those two derelicts, as if what's said is true, they'll suffer a slow death. He'll have no mercy on those bastards!"

"What do you mean?" Mhändara asks again as she is helped to her feet, interested in the old man's story.

"I heard that Ágraszar shut himself away in this place after finding his daughter brutally killed. It would appear that she had been struck violently and raped... Those responsible were never found, and Ágraszar sunk into the deepest sorrow..."

You slowly leave the barn, returning to the common room where great beer jars wait upon your table; their cost covered by Hormäz. You try to recover from what has happened, and as you do so you see that several guards now prepare a table at one end of the room.

"Our Lord Ágraszar will judge the two prisoners soon! Everybody get ready for the trial," one of them declares.

Shortly after that many guards enter the room, placing themselves at both sides of the table where the trial will be conducted. The audience, accustomed to these incredible trials, quickly falls silent while everyone finds a seat. A loud voice then announces the arrival of Ágraszar, who enters the room solemnly, almost majestically, covered by an elegant black cloak. He immediately takes his seat in front of the audience.

"Bring in the prisoners, and let the offended woman come forward," Ágraszar states with authority.

His orders are followed expeditiously, so Mhändara is soon standing by Ágraszar's table, watching the soldiers drag in her two offenders, their hands and feet chained.

"Well, the evidence seems to be clear, as these two travellers, these two unknown who don't deserve to be called by their names, have been surprised in the act of brutally assaulting the woman standing here. How do you plead?"

"Innocent!" the scoundrel who fought you exclaims.

"Guilty!" says his companion, completely downcast.

"Very well, one of them has already confessed... Now, the other one," says Ágraszar. "Woman! Did they try to rape you?"

"Yes."

"Both of them?"

"Yes, sir. Both of them!"

"What do you have to say to that?" Ágraszar asks, frowning, to the prisoner who pleaded his innocence.

"She was asking for it!"

"If that was the case, why did you have to hit her, tie her...? That is nonsense! No more questions! My decision is made. Both prisoners are declared guilty of attempted rape... and that, in 'The Caged Skeleton' can only be punished with death. The sentence will be carried out at dawn! They will burn on the stake together with the witch we hold in one of the cages; that alleged girl is just a creature from the Underworld. Get the stake ready immediately! Everything must be ready for Estrion's rise! So it is law here... everything will be fulfilled according to my saying!"

After saying these words, Ágraszar rises from his chair and, without looking back, immediately exits the room, leaving his men, who are already preparing to expeditiously follow their master's orders. Meanwhile, an intense murmuring has now replaced the previous silence within the room, as everybody discusses the harsh sentence passed by the uncle of King Xon Ágraster.

"That witch will finally burn!" you hear from a farmer sitting at a nearby table with two others.

"It is said that she comes from Nërkador, that little village more than an estrio's walk east of here," notes one of the other farmers.

"She's cursed!" says the third. "I was here when she was captured... She was talking with a voice that wasn't hers, and her face changed shape before my eyes. She killed two soldiers with her bare hands before she could be subdued. She bit one of the soldiers in the neck, tearing such a piece of flesh from him that he likely bleeds to death..."

→ If you want to talk to the amazon: 139

→ If you'd rather look into the alleged witch – the girl you saw shut in one of the cages: 151

115

Well done! That enemy was easy for you, but get ready for a new assault as you are surrounded by enemies. On this occasion, two enemies will attack you at the same time. You'll have to defeat them both, and the attacks come so frequently that you won't be able to recover any life point between the first combat and the next.

◘ **First soldier of Verinfes:** Two-handed sword (SK). Damage: 1d6+2 / SK 1 / LP: 20 / Armor: Leather breastplate (C). Action area: trunk (values 2, 3 and 4). Protection: 2 LP.

◘ **Second soldier of Verinfes:** Two-handed sword (SK). Damage: 1d6+2 / SK 2 / LP: 22 / Armor: Leather breastplate (C). Action area: trunk (values 2, 3 and 4). Protection: 2 LP. Helmet (H). Action area: head. Protection: 2 LP.

→ If the soldiers defeat you: 105
→ If you overcome both of them: 126

116

You have fought well, and fiercely, so the soldier now lies on the ground before you, completely at your mercy. You now realise that the second soldier gave the warning while you were fighting his partner, as you are quickly surrounded by twenty furious men of arms of Verinfes. Well equipped and armed to the teeth, they immediately pounce on top of you with the common goal of subduing you by force. Unable to defend yourself, you receive many forceful kicks and punches to all parts of your body, and soon collapse, falling flat on your face. Dizzy and stunned by their endless rain of blows, you surrender without complaint, are quickly tied with a rope and then dragged along the streets of the city.

↓ In the brawl, you have lost 1 item (of your choice) from your leather bag.

→ Keep on reading. Go to 87.

117

You have chosen to take the coins that the poor woman and her daughter offered. Because of this despicable decision, write down 30 zaifas on your character file, but be sure to deduct 1 experience point, as you have now left Landanar and Naira with nothing at all (Author's note: I hope you put the coins to good use). → Go back to the market square of Verinfes and continue your adventures: 45

118

With a final savage blow, Nödrik-Nígodar falls to the ground before the amazed members of the group. Immediately, Süod-Helbórian runs to his friend's help, who now writhes in pain on the ground.

"Mentor sigtar kànteos pür!" the dwarf sorcerer exclaims, gathering his energy. After saying these arcane words, a halo of yellow light shines between his short, thick fingers, twisting and stretching in an odd dance, matching the rhythm of the crackling fire. Little by little, the glow grows ever brighter; soon the surrounding forest is brightly illuminated, while a luminous sphere now wraps itself around the body of the fallen dwarf. After some minutes Nödrik-Nígodar raises his head a bit, looks at you and smiles weakly...

"Well... done...!" the dwarf says despite his troubled breathing.

"Shut up and don't speak right now, you moron!" says the sorcerer. "Can't you see that I'm trying to save your life? I should let you bleed to death, as that's what you deserve for all the stupid things that you do every estrio!"

Exhausted because of the hard fight, you now sit by the fire, trying to get your breath back. Keep on reading.

→ Go to 155.

Deciding to meet the needs of Rashtan, you approach the table at which The Golden One is seated. Without thinking about it twice, so that you now don't decide to retreat, you say:

"Is it really you, the bastard known to mistreat girls? I've been told that you need to be taught a lesson. Would a coward like you be able to fight somebody his own size?"

"His size, says this bighead!" exclaims one of The Golden One's two companions, a broad smile in his face. "Lad, you'd be best to flee now if you don't want to see your bones crushed!"

"I already knew he was a coward!" you add, looking at your objective.

"Are you crazy?" the other companion asks you, but he is suddenly interrupted by the powerful voice of The Golden One.

"Fine, leave him to me!" your opponent says at that moment, now rising to stand and removing his cloak. Looking closely at his fine physical appearance, a lump quickly forms in your throat, as you realise that Rashtan's description falls well short. Only the four golden teeth, his long black hair and his thick beard are accurate, otherwise, he is a real beast, far taller than you, with arms as thick as your own legs.

Intimidated by his unexpected power, The Golden One talks slowly in a resounding voice; he has a horrible cross-eyed look, and his loud breathing rises faster and faster:

"Flee now, little worm!" he shouts, causing the room to suddenly go silent.

"You are a coward and a miserable man who mistreats women!" you answer, mustering all of your courage so that you don't do exactly what he's just told you to do.

You now stand in the middle of a circle formed by an eager audience, and as soon as you finish speaking he grabs his weapon and, with a mighty, thrusting leap, pounces upon you. Get ready for the impending fight...

- At heart, The Golden One is just a coward. That's why, when he has 7 life points remaining, he will flee without looking back.

◘ **The Golden One:** Club (STR). Damage: 1d6 / STR 1 / LP: 21 / Armor: Leather breastplate (C). Action area: trunk (values 2, 3 and 4). Protection: 2 LP. Armbands (A). Action area: arms. Protection: 1 LP / Special ability: Extremely resilient. This enemy has outstanding resilience. When he rolls a 6 at any time, being an opposed attack roll or a damage roll, he instantly regains 1 life point (maximum of 21 life points).

→ If you defeat your enemy: 130

→ If he has been too tough and has defeated you: 88

120

With a final devastating blow, you break your opponent's sword in two; it falls to the ground together with your lifeless opponent.

↑ For reaching this point, you win 1 experience point (EP). Write this down on your character file.

You quickly hide in the shadows, unmoving and silent while you get your breath back. But then you hear a known voice whispering your name, and you see Jhaddïyä coming towards you.

"Quick, let's go!" she says without wasting time. "We've broken through their sentry circle. Nothing stands between us and the menhir. Let's go and kill those bastards!"

So, together with Jhaddïyä again, you make your way through the thick, dark forest, proceeding at a rapid pace towards your target. Another member of the Thornless Rose joins you momentarily but, after a brief chat with Jhaddïyä, returns to the thicket. You continue on for a while until you discern the strong smell of burnt wood, and in the distance you see the glow of a big bonfire.

"There they are! Let's move a little closer," Jhaddïyä quietly instructs, clearly nervous.

So you crawl slowly through the thicket until reaching the edge of the clearing where your enemies stand in clear sight. Shocked, you look on in horror at the stone altar in front of a menhir; on it lies the bleeding corpse of a boy no more than seven or eight liznars of age. You can see blood all around his body, and over it leans the merchant from whom Jhaddïyä stole the purse. By his side are other members of the Cult; all of their hands are red with dripping blood. Away from the altar stands a group of armed men, undoubtedly bodyguards of these members of the Cult of the Golden Light.

"Look over there!" Jhaddïyä suddenly whispers as she points away to her left. "That's Dëvian! She must not escape alive. She'll be our main target."

You focus in the direction of your companion's pointed finger, where you see a young, sexy warrior with remarkably loose blonde hair. She wears a pair of fur trousers and riding boots, a white linen blouse, a cloak and a fine leather breastplate. But there is something else that attracts your attention, as she is holding something small wrapped within a blanket –

possibly a little baby only estrios old that must have been stolen from her mother's arms.

"The turning point has now arrived!" Jhaddïyä states, immediately breaking your troubled thoughts. "Remember that other members of the group will try to kidnap the merchant, but our main objective is to kill Dëvian – don't forget! Now, get ready, because I'm going to give the signal for everybody to attack at the same time... But before that, drink this potion. You'll need it!"

She hands you a small wineskin and it is then that you witness Jhaddïyä's face changing its appearance before your astounded eyes. Her teeth grow bigger and her nose and mouth stretch out, like a snout. She then looks at the sky and howls powerfully like a wolf. A dozen arrows come from the thicket immediately, aiming for the followers of the Cult, who are completely taken by surprise. Thereupon, multiple shouts fill the silence of the night, as all the members of the Thornless Rose run towards your enemies, as you had agreed. You run past Jhaddïyä, and you glance at her furtively for a second, surprised to see that she has recovered her usual face again; that of a delicate, innocent girl. But there's no time to linger, as a bodyguard of the Cult now stands in your way. Get ready for the impending fight. → Go to 101.

121

"I don't think I've made myself clear," Brádoc tells you, grim faced. "I'm trying to be kind, and I can be a very reasonable guy... But your only chance is to accept my mission, otherwise, you won't ever leave this fortress. I'll lock you up in the deepest dungeon until the loneliness and isolation make you crazy. Do you want your estrios to end up like that? You wouldn't be the first... don't think that it will keep me from sleeping. You decide how we are going to solve this issue... by hook or by crook."

Between a rock and a hard place, you have no other option but to accept Brádoc's proposal, as you know he is perfectly capable of carrying out his threats.

"I'm glad to see that you're clever," Brádoc adds. "But before getting into details, keep one thing in mind. Remember, I have eyes and ears everywhere, so if you try to cheat me, or 'forget' your mission just as soon as you leave the city, you will face unpleasant consequences. Now, having corrected this small misunderstanding, we can resume our important conversation..." Keep on reading. → Go to 140.

122

With a deadly and very powerful blow, you finally defeat your enemy, who falls heavily to the ground, motionless. ↑ You win 1 experience point and can now resume your search for Korindor, the objective that has brought you here. → Go to 141.

123

Base camp
(write this number down on your character file)

So you resume your journey, moving along a narrow path surrounded by the vibrant green of many bushes and leafy trees; unhelpfully, these plants prevent you from being able to clearly see much of what's in the immediate distance. You maintain the same formation since the beginning of the estrio, so you continue to be the last in line, guarding the rear of this small caravan.

Not having any news, nor anything interesting to report, you ride placidly, deep in thought, watching the beautiful but monotonous landscape around you. Then late in the afternoon, Mhändara suddenly breaks the silence that had subdued each member of the caravan.

"Stop, something's wrong!" the amazon says, obviously nervous.

All of a sudden a tree trunk falls in the middle of the path, stopping the carriages, while echoing wild shouts now surround you. There is no doubt that this a well planned ambush; road blockers desiring Hormäz's merchandise. Hired for this exact purpose, you hadn't expected to earn your wage so soon, as you've not long left the city of Verinfes.

While a huge group of bandits emerge from the thicket, you turn your horse and see two men with black-painted faces run at you along the path you have left behind. Get ready for battle...

- You have the choice to charge with your warhorse against one of the bandits. Remember that Nëmster's charging rules are explained in section 140.

* If your enemy is still alive after Nëmster's charge, you can keep on fighting him from the saddle. Add 1 point (+1) to all of your opposed attack rolls because of the advantage of riding upon a horse. Also, you can't wound your opponent's legs as they are far too low for your reach. So, if you roll a 1 (legs) in any damage location roll, you will have to roll again. These rules are applicable whenever you fight from the saddle against an

unmounted enemy. The same will be true, with your enemy taking advantage of the situation, whenever you stand against a mounted enemy. Write down on your character file that the rules for mounted battle are in section 123, so that you can come back here whenever you need to.

◘ **First painted-face bandit:** Two-handed sword (SK). Damage: 1d6+2 / SK 3 / LP: 20 / Armor: Leather breastplate (C). Action area: trunk (values 2, 3 and 4). Protection: 2 LP.

> → If you defeat your enemy: 91
> → If you have been defeated: 102

124

Your cowardice in facing the dwarf, who accuses you of things that you cannot be blamed for, causes you to lose 1 experience point that you don't deserve because of this timid behaviour. Erase it from your file.

You ignore Nödrik-Nígodar's words and look the other way. After insulting and provoking you several times the dwarf seems to forget about the issue, soon falling into a deep sleep due to the lack of activity and the silence that has taken over the small camp. Sick and tired of this hard estrio, you use the limited time available to rest and recover, as it won't be long before your turn begins. Your watch blessedly passes placidly, so after a night of rest, a new estrio starts in Urowen. Keep on reading. → Go to 111.

125

Earning the admiration of the animated audience, you finally defeat your enemy with much enthusiastic applause and cheers from the crowd. Then, without delay, you help Dösser to his feet. He grabs your arm tightly.

"Thanks dude, I'll never forget what you've done for me! Let me pay for another beer," he adds, grinning shyly.

↑ You win 1 experience point (EP). Write this down on your character file.

> → Go back to 60.

126

With a final devastating blow, you defeat the second of your two opponents. ↑ You win 1 experience point because of all the strange events that you have endured up until to this moment. Now, grab your axe tightly as a new enemy, far more powerful than those previous, dares to face you.

◻ **Captain of Verinfes:** Two-handed sword (SK). Damage: 1d6+2 / SK 3 / LP: 25 / Armor: Leather breastplate (C). Trunk (values 2, 3 and 4). Protection: 2 LP. Leather armbands and leather greaves (A) (G). Action area: arms and legs. Protection 1 LP. Helmet (H). Action area: head. Protection: 2 LP / Special ability: War veteran. The captain of Verinfes is a skilled fighter, a master of swordplay. That is why he never rolls a 1. Re-roll any of the captain's dice with a value of 1.

→ If you defeat your enemy: 65
→ If the captain of Verinfes defeats you: 105

127

Full of rage after having recovered from all that has happened, you prepare to face a new enemy, but when you look around, the last of the bandits flee into the thicket. No longer in danger, you instead focus your attention on locating your horse, which you fortunately find several steps away by the thick trunk of an oak. You then make your way to the side of a carriage, where most of your companions have now gathered. When you get there, you see that one of the dwarves, apparently Nödrik-Nígodar, is lying on the ground with an arrow through his left leg.

"He's to blame!" the dwarf exclaims in rage when he sees you, pointing with an accusing finger. "He was bringing up the rear and I've been shot from that direction! Aaaahhh! Careful!" he shouts at the other dwarf, Süod-Helbórian, who would be the sorcerer according to what you witnessed during the fight.

"Don't grumble so much, you stupid dwarf!" Helbórian tells him, drawing everybody's attention. "I've seen you in worse situations than this, with far more serious injuries, so shut your damned mouth!" His companion looks him at him with fire in his eyes, causing Helbórian to take a deep, calming breath. "As far as I can see, the injury isn't too serious and I'll be able to easily heal it. The worst part will be removing the arrow, but I'll firstly numb you with my magic. Now, everyone else, move away!"

The two brothers now approach the group after having chased the bandits through the trees for a while.

"We are out of the woods for the time being," says Tarúk, now by your side. "All of the bandits have fled. They don't seem willing to come back for more."

"And fortunately they had to flee empty-handed," says Hormäz, visibly satisfied while looking at the corpses around you. "You have done a good job... All of you! But now we'd best leave this place as soon as possible. Finish tending to that injury," he orders Süod-Helbórian, who seems to be concentrating in casting a spell, "so that we can resume our journey."

After you have seen how the dwarf uses his amazing magic to heal his companion, you resume your journey, with Hormäz keen to make up for the time lost during your battle against the bandits.

So, always heading in the same direction, the estrio passes slowly, until the night begins to fall upon Urowen. You are in a forested and deserted terrain, surrounded by a green sea of vegetation that extends to where your sight reaches.

"Tarúk! Jurköm!" Hormäz exclaims suddenly. "Look for a sheltered location where we can spend the night!"

"At once!" both brothers answer in unison, just before spurring their horses to a gallop and advancing along the path.

They soon return, as according to what they now tell Hormäz, there is a small clearing nearby where you can spend the night. Keep on reading.

→ Go to 142.

128

"I'd rather be on my way, if you don't mind," you respond.

"We have orders from Brádoc," one of the soldiers responds with formal vigour. "We must take you to him immediately!"

"I have more pressing and important matters to attend to. Nothing binds me to this kingdom, nor do I owe loyalty to Brádoc!"

"But you are within the walls of Verinfes, and here Brádoc's word is the law. Come with us now or you'll regret it!"

"And what will you do if I refuse?"

"We won't hesitate to use all means necessary. It is to your benefit that you agree to come with us. I won't repeat our request again," he answers, subtly shifting a hand to his weapon's grip.

→ If you now accompany them: 95
→ If you are committed to your refusal: 144

129

Attracted by all that you have heard, you approach the place where the unusual fight will take place. There, the man who holds the wooden boxes containing the two combatants, explains the rules of the game:

- You can only bet an even number of zaifas, up to a limit of 20. No bet is allowed above that amount.

- Whether you bet on the tarantula or the scorpion, you'll get one zaifa for each zaifa that you have bet, if you back the winner. Therefore, if you bet 10 zaifas and you win, you'll get your 10 zaifas back plus an additional 10 zaifas: 20 zaifas in all. If you lose, deduct the 10 zaifas that you have bet.

After handing over your coins, you place yourself in the best spot available to enjoy the fight, which will take place on a wide table in the middle of the spacious room. The excited audience shouts and whistles loudly as the animals are readied, no doubt spurred on by the huge amount of alcohol that is being consumed. It doesn't take long for everything to be ready, so when the promoter makes a sign, the two men open the boxes and both contestants are set free on the table. The animals are immediately provoked into action, prodded by two small torches so that they attack each other. The fight has just begun...

- This fight is to be fought to the death, so the winner will be the animal that remains alive.

- In order to decide the result of the fight, you must roll dice for both the scorpion and the tarantula, as in a normal fight, according to the statistics below.

◘ **Scorpion:** Pincers and stinger (SK). Damage: 1d6-2 / SK 1 / LP: 12

◘ **Tarantula:** Fangs (SK). Damage: 1d6-2 / SK 1 / LP: 12

When one of the two animals finally wins, the shouts of those who have doubled their zaifas ring out loudly, as the winners now make fun of those who have lost their bet. If you've been lucky this time, you go straight ahead to collect your winnings. If the animal you chose has been defeated, you have now lost the zaifas you bet, so you return to your table, feeling sorry for your bad luck.

→ Go back to 106.

130

Although your enemy is a real beast, you have overcome this titan and defeated him. With a satisfied smile on your face you now witness The Golden One running from 'The Scarlet Goddess', humiliated and seriously wounded. Before the astonished eyes of his companions, who make way to let you pass, you quickly follow him outside; the crowd shouts with glee due to your bravery in the wonderful fight they have just witnessed. When you rush out to the street, you find Rashtan standing before you, delightedly waving a bag full of coins before your eyes.

"Let that dog flee! He's already had enough punishment for today! After what you've done to him, I think it will be a long time before we hear of him again... Oh, but here you are, 50 zaifas as promised. You have earned them well!"

Satisfied, you take the bag of coins and, after saying goodbye to Rashtan, head back into 'The Scarlet Goddess'. ↑ You win 1 experience point.

→ Go to 60.

131

With a savage attack you finally knock out your enemy, who now collapses to the ground. Just at that very moment, as you approach the rapist's accomplice, several guards run into the stables having heard your shouts for help. They immediately understand what has happened here and advance upon the remaining man without hesitation. Then, knowing that he is at the mercy of the guards, the accomplice decides to free the amazon and surrender.

↑ You win 1 experience point.

→ Keep on reading. Go to 114.

132

Totally exhausted, almost to the point of collapse, you finally defeat Dëvian with a thunderous, lethal blow. Only then do you take the time to glance around, now looking over a scene of horrendous carnage. Fortunately, luck is on your side, as many members of the Cult desperately fled into the thicket seeking escape. You now realise that Jhaddïyä is standing several steps away with a satisfied smile on her face, holding the young boy that Dëvian had left when she prepared to defend herself once the fighting had commenced.

She looks at you now, but just as she is about to tell you something, Vikord interrupts, urgently speaking these words:

"We have that wretched merchant, and I also see that Dëvian is defeated. Jhaddïyä, we must leave immediately!"

"You're right! We don't have a moment to lose!"

So you leave without delay, heading to the Izquion River, where members of the Thornless Rose have prepared an encampment. Safely hidden, you'll wait here for dawn to come, when the gates of the city will be open again and you'll be able to go back to Verinfes.

↑ You win 2 experience points

Write them down on your character file.

The next estrio, as evening falls, after having rested in the basement of a small building (another hiding place of the Thornless Rose), Jhaddïyä speaks to all of the reunited members of the group.

"Everything has gone better than expected. Dëvian is dead, and we have just been paid a lavish ransom for our merchant friend. It's time to celebrate, as we have dealt a devastating blow to the followers of the Cult of the Golden Light. A significant misfortune from which it will take a long time to recover!"

A great joy spreads through the room then, and someone even opens a small wine barrel, resulting in endless toasts that reflect their pride and enthusiasm. Jhaddïyä then comes near and asks you to follow her, as she wants to talk to you one-to-one. Once you are in a different room, she speaks:

"We couldn't have done it without you, as you were fundamental to our success in defeating Dëvian. As promised, here is your payment." After turning aside to a table, she lifts a heavy purse that she immediately hands to you. "There you are – 200 zaifas!" (Write them down on your character file). "It's a large amount, and I sincerely hope that you don't waste them on vices! Use them wisely and they might lead you to a more important treasure. If you want, I can take you to a place near the city walls where you'll find objects rarely for sale in the market of Verinfes. Very few know of this place, but as a final gesture of appreciation, I could show it to you."

→ If you want Jhaddïyä to show you the black market: 84

→ If you'd rather go back to the main square of Verinfes to start a new adventure: 73

133

Base camp
(write this number down on your character file)

With a powerfully destructive blow you split your enemy's trunk in half, causing the Spirit of the Forest to step back, retracting the countless vines that surround you. Temporarily paralysed by what you see, you watch on as your enemy gradually fades into the mist. Almost immediately, a beam of bright light tears through the cloud cover above you, illuminating the area where your small group stands. The other members now close ranks around the carriages, grasping their weapons tightly, worried about what may happen next. But nothing weird happens again, and a peaceful calm returns to the forest.

"What was that?" a surprised Jurköm asks, just as intimidated as the rest of the members of the caravan. "I've never faced such a strange enemy before."

"There are great powers hiding in this forest. We must have done something to upset them..." says Süod-Helbórian, closing his eyes to concentrate. "We must move away from this place as soon as possible. As long as we stay here, we will be in danger."

"You've heard Helbórian," says the merchant. "Quickly, take up your positions! We'll promptly be on our way. I don't want to meet that... thing... again. Hurry up!"

Fortunately, the estrio passes without further incident and, in mid-afternoon, after having covered a considerable distance, Hormäz's voice awakens you from your thoughts.

"We're getting there! Over there, you see – 'The Caged Skeleton'!"

Surprised by the news, you tightly grip the reins of your horse and look up with interest, attempting to see beyond the carriages. On elevated ground off to your left you discern a huge mansion, no doubt the inn that the merchant speaks of. It is an isolated small stronghold, perfectly walled, with defensive towers and a detachment of armed men – mercenaries all of them – on its walls. When you reach the massive steel gates of the mansion, you notice several cages hanging from high wooden poles; some of them have a host within. As you can see, two of these small hanging dungeons accommodate a decomposing human corpse, while another cage accommodates what undoubtedly is the skeleton of a dwarf. All of these bright white bones lost their flesh long ago, and are now cradled by the cold breeze. A bit farther on, in another cage, you are horrorified to see that the person locked within is just a girl, not yet of adolescenct age.

"Who approaches?" one of the men on top of the wall suddenly shouts down to the group.

"My name is Hormäz," replies the merchant. "We come from Verinfes and are strictly a commercial caravan. It's not my first time here. Your lord knows me."

"Wait a second!" the mercenary answers before disappearing behind the battlements.

Shortly thereafter you hear the sounds of dragging chains and wooden planks being trodden on behind the gates, and one of them then slowly opens.

"You may enter," another man tells you, after coming out to meet the group. "You'll find the stables to your right. You can leave the carriages before them, in the yard, and Riggard will take charge of your horses," he adds, pointing at a boy who runs forward to take the reins of the amazon's horse.

After leaving your horses behind, you enter the complex's main building; it is a strange configuration, something midway between a mansion, a military barracks and a small castle. As you enter, you are welcomed by the warmth of a massive chimney, where a roaring fire now burns. The stone walls are beautifully decorated with both tapestries in striking colours and mounted animal heads such as boars and deers. At the back a great bar extends the full width of the room, and behind it you can see numerous wine barrels, stacked high from the floor to the ceiling. Several maids tend to the customers, carrying roast meat and big jars full of beverage.

Several tables are to be found within this spacious common room, and following Hormäz's instructions, you make your way through to an empty table, which you take a seat at immediately.

"I'll be back right away," the merchant says. "I'm going to say hello to the innkeeper, an old friend of mine. Of course, I'll order something for everyone to eat and drink – you've certainly earned it today. 'Fill your stomachs while you can' is what my father used to say! How right he was, the poor bastard..."

Now shaking his head as memories from the past come back to him, Hormäz moves away and then disappears through a door by the bar. Shortly after that, a maid brings you a great jug of wine and a tankard of beer, as well as smaller mugs for each of you. Roast pork ribs arrive at your table shortly after, and you immediately eat your fill after such a hard estrio.

→ If you try to talk to the amazon: 145

→ If you'd rather talk to Nödrik-Nígodar during the meal: 156

134

With a final savage blow, the dwarf's fighting prowess causes you to collapse to the ground, before the onlooking members of the group. Immediately, Süod-Helbórian runs to you while you writhe in pain on the ground.

"Mentor sigtar kànteos pür!" the dwarf sorcerer shouts, gathering his power. After saying these arcane words, a halo of yellow light shines between his short, thick fingers, twisting and stretching in an odd dance, matching the rhythm of the crackling fire. Little by little, the glow grows ever brighter; soon the surrounding forest is brightly illuminated, while a luminous sphere now circles your body. After several minutes, in which dizziness begins to affect you, Nödrik-Nígodar walks towards you, a little smile upon his face...

"Well... done...!" says Nödrik-Nígodar, now finding it hard to breathe normally after the tough fight.

"Tha... thank you!" you answer faintly.

"Shut up and don't speak right now, you dumb bastard!" says the sorcerer. "Can't you see that I'm trying to save your life? I should let you bleed to death! That's what you deserve for such stupidity."

→ Keep on reading. Go to 155.

135

◘ **Wild dog:** Fangs (SK). Damage: 1d6 / SK 1 / LP: 14 / Special ability: Powerful bite. If the wild dog rolls a 6 in a damage roll, it has achieved a perfect bite with its powerful jaws, biting with all of its might: add 2 to its damage. Thus, as its damage is 1d6, if it rolls a 6, 2 points will be added, resulting in 8 damage points.

→ If you defeat it: 122

→ If you succumb to its attack: 63

136

When you are again with your companions, Hormäz orders that everything is arranged as you have previously agreed. Thus, after tying your horse to the second carriage, Nígodar ties your hands with a strong rope and you take your seat by the rough dwarf. Once everything is ready, you take to the road when the sky is beginning to clear, shortly before the first rays of Estrion caress the face of Urowen. At that very moment, when you are about to leave, you see several soldiers taking the men sentenced to death from one of the buildings to the massive pyre. It will be soon the witch's turn, as there are already four guards by her cage, ready to remove her from her prison. As you slowly walk by she points at you and then bursts out laughing; that is the last image you have of the witch, as the carriage now leaves her behind.

Fortunately, the estrio dawns clear, with a warm breeze caressing your body. This will help to lift your spirits after the tough experiences endured in 'The Caged Skeleton'.

In the late morning, Tarúk and Jurköm suddenly grab your attention with much excited shouting, pointing towards a hill to your left, not far from your location.

"Look, a wild boar! Tarúk and I could try to hunt it," says Jurköm with a smile on his face. "We could eat its meat for lunch and dinner, and even store supplies for estrios to come."

"I think that's a good idea!" answers Hormäz, aware of the tough estrios of travelling that you still have to endure. "Grab your lances and go for it, but don't be too bold. It could be dangerous!"

Without hesitation, both brothers approach the carriage of the merchant, lifting and then opening a massive bundle covered by thick fabric. They immediately grasp two magnificent long lances and, thereupon, spur on their horses and gallop after their prey...

→ If you're feeling restless, wanting to take part in the hunt, and decide to ask Hormäz for permission to run after the siblings: 153

→ If you'd rather stay where you are, leaving the dirty work for your companions: 164

137

◘ **Second bandit of the painted face:** Scythe (STR). Damage: 1d6+2 / STR 3 / LP: 24 / Armor: Leather breastplate (C). Action area: trunk (values 2, 3 and 4). Protection: 3 LP. Helmet (H). Action area: head. Protection: 3 LP.

→ If you defeat this tough enemy: 113
→ If you were unable to defeat him: 149

138

Despite your efforts, while the crowd shouts and whistles incessantly, you are unfortunately defeated. When you regain consciousness, you find yourself lying in the street, near the door of 'The Scarlet Goddess'. You can hardly get to your feet again, and when you do, you discover that you've been robbed. Delete 1 item, of your choice, from your character file. It can be an item from your leather bag, a piece of armor, a weapon, a magical item... → Go back to 60.

139

"How are you feeling?" you ask the amazon when she returns to your side.

"Fine, I'm fine. Somewhat surprised by what I've just seen, but fine. I didn't expect that they would burn those bastards alive, and even less in the company of a witch. Everything in this place is strange to me... I've never seen anything of the sort. I hope that Hormäz doesn't want to stay here any longer than necessary, as I'm willing to leave this place immediately."

"And what do you think of this girl, the alleged witch, that they are going to burn alive?"

"Who knows? Anything could be true. One thing I've learnt during my life is that you can never go by appearances. From what I've heard, there is strong evidence to sentence her, but you never know."

"Maybe we should do something to help her..."

"Don't count on me. I won't pointlessly risk my life. Even if she is an innocent girl, there's little that we could do to save her. She's already been sentenced to death... We would have to fight a full regiment to try and set her free... It's all too complicated. I'm sorry for her, but her destiny has already been written."

The words of the amazon leave you somewhat restless. You know that you won't be able to sleep tonight, so you decide to conduct some research to see if you can learn anything else about the witch. You soon leave the room, hoping to uncover something new that would change everyone's opinion about the unfortunate girl.

→ Go to section 151.

140

"Now I'll tell you all I know about Marok-häi. As I've already mentioned, she's one of the most influential amazons in the city, a great warrior in command of Zarkända's army. This is why she lives in the military headquarters in Bälkaar: that might be a good place to try to take her by surprise, sneaking in under the cover of darkness. As far as I know, that may be the best and only chance to kill her, as the rest of the time she is always guarded by several of her best warriors. But, of course, these are just my suggestions, as in the end you will be the one to deal with her, so if you discern a better opportunity or method to attack her, don't hesitate to take it. As for her physical appearance, you should be easily able to recognize her, as she has long red hair, usually braided. In particular, her eyes are bright blue and she lacks a little finger on her left hand... She lost that appendage in battle, severed by a sword. Aside from that, it should be easy for you to locate her, as it is impossible for her to go unnoticed, such is the respect and admiration that the rest of the amazons feel for her. Kill her mercilessly, as she is a terrible enemy who deserves nothing but death! Trust my words... You'll do Urowen a great favour upon her death!"

Trying to understand all that you have heard, you pay special attention to Brádoc's words, as he seems to be talking about Marok-häi with strong feelings. But then his face seems to relax all of a sudden and, after a short pause, he addresses you again.

"Time for serious talking is over... Let us go and collect the rich reward you've earned."

Brádoc steps away and gestures a clear invitation for you to follow him. So, you leave the room and walk with him down several corridors and stairs until you reach a distant room with two guards at its door. They quickly stand to attention when they recognize the approaching Brádoc, and then let you pass according to his instructions. When you enter this new room, you see a wide area, crowded with weapons.

"Welcome to the armory of the fortress of Verinfes! I've promised you armor and I think that we'll be able to find something suitable here."

- You can choose one of the following objects. Even if you are a thief, you can only choose one of them:

- **Dwarf leather breastplate (C).** Action area: trunk (values 2, 3 and 4). Protection: 4 LP.

- **Molfräch magical cape.** Action area: trunk (values 2, 3 and 4). It adds 1 protection point to any piece of worn armor (meaning a breastplate or doublet protecting areas 2, 3 and 4).

Note that the cape, if you are wearing it combined with another piece of armor, will not fill a slot in your leather bag. Regarding the dwarf leather breastplate, if you wear it instead of any other protection, the old item will fill a slot in your bag, but you can always dispose of it.

"You've made the right choice," Brádoc says when you finally choose your reward. "Now, let's go and get your horse! I was thinking of Nëmster, for you are both brash and bold... I'm sure that you'll get on rather well."

You now leave the armory and head for the weapons courtyard, where the stables are located. Overwhelmed by what you see here, you steer your way through a crowd of soldiers until you reach the massive building of the stables, home of the best horses in Verinfes. You keep on walking until Brádoc stops before an impressive horse.

"This is Nëmster. As promised, this magnificent animal is all yours. I hope that both of you can successfully serve our cause! I'll get him saddled and ready so that you can take him straight away."

Excited, you look proudly at your new mount, an imposing warhorse, totally black and very beautiful with a shiny coat and a majestic appearance. Write Nëmster down on your character file:

- **Nëmster, warhorse:** Charge (STR). Damage: 4d6+3 / STR 6 / LP: 35 / In order to inflict damage, charge is only effective against standing enemies, against whom you can spur your horse to a gallop (that is to say, there has to be a great distance between your horse and your enemy). If you charge, roll a dice to determine if your horse overwhelms your enemy. If you roll a 3 or higher, your attack is successful. However, your enemy will have a chance to dodge this charge by rolling a dice. If a 6 is rolled, they completely dodge your horse's onslaught. In case of a charge, there is no damage location: your enemy takes the full impact of 4d6+3 without considering any armor, which is useless before the overwhelming strength of your horse. Write Nëmster down on your file, together with this section number (140) so that you can return here to check the rules for a charge.

"Well, I'm a man of my word, so if you come with me again, I'll give you the zaifas that I promised," Brádoc says. You now follow him to a different building in the fortress, where he gives you a bag with 100 zaifas. "And that would be all of your reward, as agreed. Now, I must take my leave, as I have some pressing matters to attend to. I hope to see you soon, back here in Verinfes, as that would mean that you were successful in your mission. Remember that, if you achieve your goal, there will be a substantial reward waiting for you here. This war we are involved in is intensifying with every passing estrio. Zorbrak continues to gain power and we'll soon be surrounded. Dreknars are harassing us from the north, the mercenaries of Krénator advance from the Abyssal Sea, the amazons are getting ready in Bälkaar, and the Spirits of Zedún are plotting against us in Lógadar... We will soon be confined within a mousetrap from which we will find escape to be exceedingly difficult. May Sàgrast guide your steps, as your help will likely be critical in determining the outcome of this war. See you soon!"

After speaking these final words, Brádoc turns and leaves and, immediately, one of his men comes towards you, informing you that Nëmster is already waiting. → Go to 89.

141

After cutting through a dense field of sugarcane you finally reach the Izquion River, with its waters bathed in bright Estrion sunlight. According to Landanar's instructions, Korindor's refuge can't be too far from here, so you continue walking cautiously until you finally spot a humble hut standing beside the river in the near distance. You now close in on your destination, setting a fast pace, as you are eager to deliver justice for Landanar. You are somewhat unsure of exactly how to do so, however, as although Landanar told you that only by killing Korindor will the effects of his spell disappear, you think that it is too barbaric to simply attack and kill him in cold blood, regardless of the known justification. You decide to firstly talk with him, trusting that you can settle this matter without unnecessary bloodshed.

"Korindor?" you shout, now approach the hut. "Is this the dwelling of Korindor?"

"Who's looking for me?" a voice answers. "What do you want?"

"All you need to know is that I'm here on behalf of Landanar!"

"Landanar? Did you say Landanar? Who are you, her damned servant?"

Right then, you hear powerful and sinister laughter from inside the hut.

"Come out and talk so I can see you! What do you know of her?"

"That she should already be dead!" Korindor replies. "How long is she going to resist, the dirty bitch?"

His words make your blood boil, so you ask him directly if he is the one responsible for her suffering.

"Of course I am, and you should leave right now if you don't want to suffer the same fate."

The hut's rickety door now opens and a frowning middle-aged figure steps out towards you. Korindor is a tall, impressive man, with long hair featuring a few streaks of grey. He wears simple clothes, much like farmer's clothing, and he leans on a thick wooden stick.

"Well, didn't you hear me?" he suddenly shouts, growing angry. "I told you to leave!"

"I won't go anywhere until you free Landanar from your spell."

"And how do you plan to achieve such a request?"

"By killing you if it comes to that! I've already seen enough to know that's the fate you deserve."

"Come on then, come forward if you dare!" he exclaims, now waving a hand, inviting you to move closer.

Willing to advance regardless of peril, you take a step forward, but as you do so the sorcerer raises his wooden stick and pointing with it he shouts: "Nëkuondar, crissáldantar!"

Right then, a shining beam bursts from the base of the stick, aimed directly at you...

→ If you try to retreat to avoid the spell and flee without completing your mission: 74

→ If you courageously decide to stand firm: 82

142

Late at night, after having lit a fire and set guard duty, you eat a scanty dinner by the fire, mostly bread and salted meat, washed down by sweet wine from Verinfes. That is how you finally find some moments of peace, after your battle against the bandits and having ridden without a break for the whole estrio. You plan to make the most of your rest, as you have to take the third guard shift in the dead of the night, and that moment will arrive sooner than you would like. But not everything is quiet around you, as Nödrik-Nígodar, the dwarf injured by an arrow during battle, is continuously casting dark looks at you. He has been bothering you for the whole estrio, blaming you for what happened to him.

"You, rookie, next time execute your duty correctly!" he says rudely, breaking the silence. He looks at you intently from the other side of the fire, spitting several pieces of meat from his mouth as he talks.

"Leave him alone, Nígodar! He's done his best," says Hormäz, trying to calm the dwarf down. "I didn't even see an archer among the bandits... He must have been hidden in the thicket."

"How am I to leave him alone?" says the dwarf growing further annoyed with the situation. "Excuses! Excuses! I don't need excuses... That damned arrow could have killed me, or any of us, and it's all the fault of this bastard who doesn't know how to protect the flank. I give thanks for having Süod-Helbórian with us, as he has healed my injury with his powers. Otherwise, I would be bleeding like a pig... You deserve... you deserve a good beating!" he exclaims, angrily raising a fist. "That's the only way you'll learn to do your damned work!"

→ If you are sick of the dwarf and wish to respond appropriately to his insults: 104

→ If you prefer to remain quiet and to bow your head: 124

143

Despite all of your efforts, this enemy has been far too strong for you. With a final blow from one of its thickest branches, this strange forest creature easily unmounts you. Exhausted and aching from the fall, you try to catch your breath while rising to your feet to face your enemy again. If you had killed off a vine during the fight, the Spirit of the Forest will now have replaced it with another. Additionally, remember that you are now on your feet, no longer mounted on Nëmster. → Go back to 111 and fight this enemy again.

144

"I never would have thought that you'd be such a fool!" the first soldier says furiously. "But if it has to be... you asked for it! Get ready for battle!"

Now that battle is upon you, a second look at this experienced man-at-arms suggests that it may not have been a good idea to provoke him. Unfortunately, you must now face the consequences of your decision...

- This fight is not mortal. The first combatant to reach 5 life points will will surrender and suffer defeat.

◘ **Veteran soldier of Verinfes:** Two-handed sword (SK). Damage: 1d6+3 / SK 3 / LP: 25 / Armor: Leather breastplate (C). Action area: trunk (values 2, 3 and 4). Protection: 3 LP. Leather armbands and leather greaves (A) (G). Action area: arms and legs. Protection: 2 LP. Helmet (H). Action area: head. Protection: 3 LP.

→ If you win the fight: 116
→ If you are defeated: 152

145

"I think that we should hear from the only woman in the group," you say, trying to obtain some information from the enigmatic amazon. "As we don't know a lot about her, we would really like to hear her story."

Mhändara simply stops eating when she hears these words, and now stares at you in silence. You can't determine if her face shows hate or surprise, but just when you think that she's going to unleash her rage, your proposal is suddenly seconded by Süod-Helbórian, who is likewise curious about the strange woman.

"Yes, amazon, tell us something about yourself," the dwarf suddenly requests, raising a brow. "I don't think that anyone here was expecting you to join the group. How long have you known Hormäz?"

Under the pressure of your inquisitive looks, Mhändara is forced to provide an answer to avoid raising suspicion among the members of the caravan.

"I had only seen Hormäz once before, in Bälkaar. My grandmother, the matriarch of my family, is the one who does business with him and, as far as I know, they've known each other for a long time. She's sent me to travel with you and to guide you to our city. I can't tell you much more about the rest, as I don't even know the terms of the agreement between Hormäz and my family. I'm just a guide and a messenger, as I've told the merchant, following the words my grandmother told me before I left my city. There's nothing else. That's my whole story... Now, if you don't mind, I need some fresh air. The atmosphere in here is rather tense."

The amazon stands and then leaves through the door that leads to the courtyard where you left the carriages. → Keep on reading. Go to 106.

146

After your great victory over the sorcerer, you return to the city and immediately make your way back to Landanar's home. When you arrive, she is already waiting for you, standing by the door with a warm smile on her face, hugging little Naira.

"You've done it!" she exclaims as soon as she sees you. "I thank Sàgrast for having sent you to help me...! As you can see, I'm already much better. The effects of Korindor's spell will soon be gone for good. Here, have this! I know it's a poor payment for your help, but it's all that I have in the world. Take these 30 zaifas as a small token of my gratitude! That's all that Naira's been able to gather while I've been sick..."

→ If you accept the zaifas: 117
→ If you decide to refuse the offered coins: 103

147

After looking carefully at the ground and taking a deep breath, you decide to make your way through some tall bushes, as you are convinced that the wild boar has recently passed that way. You keep on running through this forested area until you come to a sudden halt; you have reached a small stream where your prey's trail is no longer clear.

■ Roll a dice for Perception (PER) again with a difficulty of 7 in order to determine which direction you will follow.

→ If the result is 7 or higher: 168
→ If the result is 6 or lower: 159

148

After a really tough battle amid much growling and gnashing of terrible teeth, you finally kill your prey, who succumbs to your superior skills. Then, exhaustion finally takes over and you sit upon a rock for some time, attempting to regain a little strength. You have definitely earned a few minutes of peace.

↑ You win 1 experience point.
→ Keep on reading. Go to 198.

149

After this humiliating defeat, if you were riding your horse, you fall to the ground, momentarily losing Nëmster. Deduct 1 experience point, as you are not able to protect the caravan's carriages and complete the duty for which the merchant hired you. Rising to your feet, your injuries aching, you have another chance to give this enemy his due.

→ Go back to 137 and defeat him.

150

Willing to know more about this barren, spooky village, you discreetly decamp to explore the surrounding area alone. You are soon walking along what had been a broad street until not too long ago, with humble wooden houses situated on both sides. One of these small buildings instantly draws your attention, because even though its roof is almost completely destroyed by fire, most of the walls still stand. Attracted by what this interesting place may offer, you approach the open entranceway; the door lies on the ground, brutally removed from its fixtures. You enter a room that, apparently, holds nothing of value, as it is a very simple, humble home. Nevertheless, it is quite roomy and due to the fading light, you can't see the rear too well, now hidden by the section of roof that remains in place. Intrigued, you walk further into the room...

Right then a strange, threatening sound reaches your ears. A strong hiss makes you shiver instantly, and very near, hidden in the darkness lurks an unusual creature. Awed, you see that this huge being towers menacingly over you, its heavy, coiled body as thick as a well-bred ram. You have in front of you a massive ardronte, a two-headed snake capable of spitting a blinding, paralysing venom.

The creature, with both heads raised and both mouths opened, makes a horrible, threatening sound that instantly freezes you. There's no doubt that it will attack at the drop of a hat. Do your best to save your life...

◘ **Ardronte:** Fangs (SK). Damage: 1d6+3 / SK 4 / LP: 28 / Armor: Silvery scales. Action areas: it covers all locations (from 1 to 6). Protection: 3 LP / Special ability: Two heads. The ardronte is capable of attacking with both heads simultaneously. At the end of each combat round, the head that you couldn't fight, the free head, will take 1 life point from you. Once you have reduced the ardronte to 18 life points or less, you have killed one of its two heads and will no longer lose the extra point at the end of a round. /

Venom. If the ardronte rolls a 6 for damage location (the attack aims at your head), it will spit paralysing venom into your eyes, causing additional damage. Therefore, from that moment on, deduct 1 point from all of your opposed attack rolls, in addition to the regular damage of that attack.

→ If you defeat the ardronte: 161
→ If the massive snake has been too tough for you: 171

151

Intrigued by all that you have seen and heard, you head to the wall where the entrance doors are located, thinking about the innocent girl now locked within one of the hanging cages. The night is silent and the clear sky allows for good visibility, so you head up a flight of narrow stairs to the top of the wall, just by the battlements, where a couple of guards warm themselves by a small fire.

"What are you doing here?" one of the guards asks.

"I just came to see the girl; the alleged witch. She is going to be burnt alive tomorrow, so I came out of curiosity. When I arrived and saw her, she didn't look like a witch, let alone dangerous, yet I've heard that she has killed two men."

"Just two men? If nothing else... It is known that she's been killing men for a long time, and not only men... boys, animals... There is no doubt that she is a witch who deserves to be burned. I'll enjoy the show!"

"Can I move closer to her?"

"Go ahead, if that's what you want."

After your short conversation with the guard, you keep on walking along the top of the wall until you finally reach the cage where the girl is locked, hanging outside the wall. You look now at the thick bars that form these tiny dungeons; horrendously narrow cells where prisoners are forced to stand, unable to crouch or sit. Just then, the girl slowly turns her head until she stares at you.

"Help me..." she whispers, shifting an arm between two bars to raise it towards you, her hand upturned. "Help me... please..."

Surprised by these words, you turn your head towards the soldiers, who apparently haven't heard anything. You then look back again at the girl, who shakes her arm insistently in despair. You know that you don't have any real reason to help her, as according to what you've heard, it would be clear that the little girl is a witch. You also understand that any attempt to help her would result in a lone fight against a full battalion, something you're not willing to do under present circumstances, as you have other missions and quests still to accomplish. For all of these reasons, you suddenly think that you shouldn't be here, as raising the suspicion of the guards could quite easily result in you being sentenced to death within the walls of 'The Caged Skeleton'. So you turn to leave, but a strange whistling calls your attention. You can't avoid it and now look back at the girl's cage; what you see there chills your blood. The face of the girl, not so long ago beautiful and sweet, is now the face of a terrifying, decrepit and withered old woman, who looks at you with indescribable hate, waving both arms unnaturally.

"You'll be damned now!" the old woman shouts. "You'll wish that you'd helped me. Your life will be miserable, with plenty of misfortune, as you will turn into an underworld creature little by little! Réskoidar, nimtos oÿc sedetín kar ástaloth!"

Suddenly feeling terribly dizzy, you stagger upon the wall. You look around, but you can't discern your surroundings clearly, as if a thick, blurry mist now covers everything. Right then, you realise that you have fallen to the ground. One of the soldiers leans over you, shouting inaudibly... Your eyelids become heavier and heavier, until you finally fade away... → Keep on reading. Go to 165.

152

Your enemy has fought fiercely, and you now lie on the ground at his mercy. The second soldier has raised the alarm while you were fighting his companion, so you are now surrounded by about twenty enraged men of arms of Verinfes. Well equipped and armed to the teeth, they immediately pounce on top of you with the common goal of subduing you by force. Seriously injured, you surrender almost without a fight, are quickly tied with a rope and then dragged along the streets of the city.

↓ During the fight you have lost 1 item, of your choice, from your leather bag. You also lose 1 experience point due to the defeat, and because you fought the soldiers of Verinfes.

→ Keep on reading. Go to 87.

153

After seeing the two siblings gallop away from your position, you are suddenly in a great hurry to take part in the hunt. You feel useless sitting here tied up, so you decide to stand and speak to the merchant.

"I want to hunt the boar, too. Set me free so that I can go!"

"I don't think that's a good idea after what has happened," Hormäz replies from the seat of his carriage. "Tarúk and Jurköm are more than capable of hunting that animal. We will continue our trip. I'm sure that they'll catch up with us shortly."

Unable to contradict his orders, you sit again by the dwarf, even though you feel terribly disappointed.

"Stay calm," Nödrik-Nígodar says to you, leaning a hand on your shoulder. "No doubt you'll have other chances to prove yourself during this journey."

But far from calming you, the dwarf's kind words seem to spur your pride, as if something unknown wakes inside you...

→ Go to 180.

154

You carefully crouch over the body and begin searching his clothes, looking for any clues as to what has happened here. You can't resist fumbling in his pockets, as you have noticed that there is something held within one of them. You remove a small scroll, which you unroll immediately to discover the instructions for a powerful spell:

* **Life suction.** Power points (PP) needed to perform it: 2. Effects: after casting the proper spell, you breathe in deeply and absorb your opponent's energy. Instructions: in order to use this spell properly, you have to win an opposed attack roll, using your character's MAG and the necessary PP. Damage: 2d6. Your enemy will lose those life points regardless of any armor, as they are useless against this spell – not even magic armor. These points are then added to your own life points, however, you can't exceed your base life points.

→ Keep on reading. Go to 202.

155

During the night, Tarúk and Jurköm, the two siblings, come to see how you are feeling after the difficult fight against the dwarf.

"You did well!" Jurköm says approvingly after sitting by your side and placing a hand on your shoulder. "That damned Nödrik-Nígodar deserved someone shutting his big mouth – and you have! Believe me, regardless of the result, the fact that you had the courage to fight him will have earned his respect. That's a genuine achievement."

"We don't like him much either," Tarúk adds. "Nígodar is just a loudmouth who spends the entire estrio in a bad mood, kicking up a fuss about anything. We have fought by his side more than once, and he is a powerful ally to back you up. You have earned his trust tonight... Congratulations!"

Satisfied by what has happened, although significantly bruised by the fight, you rest during the night as well as you can until the light of Estrion finally shows on the horizon. Right then Hormäz tells you to get ready to resume your trip as soon as possible.

Then, to your surprise, you feel somebody touch your back. You turn around immediately and see Nödrik-Nígodar holding something in his hands.

"I wanted to compliment you on last night's fight," the dwarf says. "You showed great courage, and a mastery of weapons... It is difficult to find somebody willing to initiate a fight like the one we fought. It was epic, unforgettable! I shouldn't have blamed you for the arrowshot I took from those bastards, and you've made me swallow my ill-considered words. Here, please accept this small present in appreciation of the fun you gave me last night. They are a spare pair of dwarf leather greaves that I was carrying in my bag."

Pleased by Nígodar's kind words, you immediately accept his gift. He then shakes your hand with incredible strength.

- **Dwarf leather greaves (G).** Action area: legs. Protection: 2 LP.

→ Go to section 111.

156

"Have you fought in many battles?" you ask the rough dwarf, keen to engage him in conversation.

Encouraged by the idea of talking about old fights and war injuries, Nödrik-Nígodar looks up from the tankard he is drinking, quickly draining it before responding.

"Oh, certainly. Hear this Helbórian! Our new friend here asks if we have fought in many battles... You wouldn't believe all that these two dwarfs have seen in their lives!"

"Do you remember that time in the Zend Marshes?" the sorcerer asks Nígodar, coming closer to better hear the conversation.

"I'll never forget it! Have you ever been in that horrible place?" the dwarf asks you directly, frowning.

"No..." you answer shyly.

"Good for you! Don't set foot there if you can avoid it." Right then, Nígodar turns his head and spits on the floor. "Oh! As I remember the smell of that place I can't help but taste rust. Returning to our topic, what my good friend Süod-Helbórian intends to remember is a terrible encounter we had in those stinking marshes. We had a mission and we were to accomplish it without hesitation... covered in dirt and mud up to our necks, but we never took a single step backwards. I remember that we'd been hired to find a strange orchid that grows only in the innermost and most unattainable areas of that huge, murky swampland. We had been hired by a sorcerer who needed the orchid for God's knows what concoction... Am I right, Helbórian?"

"Yes, he wanted it for an elixir, following the principles of alchemy... but who cares now? Tell your story, you are a far better teller than I."

"All right! All right! As I was saying, we went into the Zend Marshes where it was raining heavily that morning. Our company was Süod-Helbórian and myself, together with another dwarf that you don't know, a crazy and fearless dwarf, who claims to be the greatest thief throughout all of Urowen. Ax-Dimäk was his name... I wonder if he's still alive – we haven't heard of him for a long time. Well, we walked through the marshes for the whole estrio and, at dusk, we had an unfortunate encounter, as we ran into a disgusting silt slug. Have you ever seen one? They're huge, as big as two horses put together, and extremely poisonous. If we had seen it in advance we would have avoided it, but it was well hidden in the mud, sunk almost completely within it. Unknowingly, we walked by and it grabbed Ax-Dimäk's leg with one of its filthy limbs. His flesh began to rot immediately. I remember him lying on the ground, shouting in pain and rage as he saw the massive slug emerging from those black waters. Had he been alone, he would have met his end, but he was very fortunate to have us by his side. We immediately took up our weapons and faced it. My axe was quickly arcing through the air, and when I struck that filthy beast with my savage cuts, a nauseating, viscous liquid came out. Unfortunately, one of its tentacles touched me on the side... I still have a great scar there. But, in the end, we killed that monster... Yes, my friend, be very careful if you ever find yourself in those marshes, as it is likely that you won't easily escape." Now that his friend has refilled his tankard, Nödrik-Nígodar picks it up again and takes a long sip to soothe his dry throat.

"Excuse me," Mhändara says suddenly, surprising you as she rises from her seat. "I need to breathe some fresh air. The atmosphere in here is quite heavy!"

The amazon leaves the table and exits via the door of the common room, which leads to the yard where you left the carriages. Keep on reading. → Go to 106.

157

Tired of the hard estrio of travel, you look for a good place to lie near the fire that Süod-Helbórian has created with his magical powers. You fall deeply asleep after a scanty meal, enjoying a full night's rest as none of your companions trusts you enough to leave you alone and on guard duty. So, Hormäz himself wakes you up at dawn, and you all collect your equipment to resume your trip as soon as possible. You have moved closer the amazon's city, and after all that has happened you are very keen to reach it. You are soon riding Nëmster again, leading the group.

Several estrios of travel pass slowly without anything noteworthy occuring; you set a good pace and are now near to your destination, the city of Bälkaar. You've been travelling along a scenic path that follows the coast, and have left the Abyssal Sea now off to your right, having enjoyed the beautiful setting that this part of the route has provided.

"If we keep up this pace, tomorrow, at mid estrio, we'll reach Bälkaar," the amazon notes.

"That's wonderful news. Excellent!" says the merchant, holding the reins of his carriage. "Let's go a bit faster. I'm eager to get there."

So, following his instructions, you spur your horses to a quicker pace, continuing on along the idyllic path. However, the ground soon changes, and you discern the first farms and farming lands, clear signs that you are moving closer to the great city of Bälkaar. Then, when you are moving along a path that runs through an extensive planting of wheat, a column of black smoke rising from behind a hill catches your attention.

"That's not normal in this area," says Mhändara, clearly surprised. "No doubt some of my people are in danger. We must help them!"

The amazon immediately turns to the merchant, waiting for him to grant permission to help.

"Oh, fine," Hormäz responds, aware that he won't make the amazon change her mind. "But the carriages can't move through that wheat. Go with your horses and take a look," he says, pointing at you, Mhändara and the two brothers. "And be very careful! I'll wait for you here with the dwarfs... Come on, don't waste another second!"

Following the merchant's instructions, you now gallop towards the source of the smoke. You ride through the wheat planting and then up the slope of the hill to discover that a massive barn burns fiercely in the distance. Two men lie on the ground, surrounded by eight strangers...

"Raedënys!" shouts Mhändara without hesitation. "Quickly, we must help those on the ground – they'll be killed! These bandits hate the amazons. There's no time for explanations, let's go!"

With a loud cry, Mhändara gallops towards the bandits, and all of you follow her immediately, grasping your weapons tightly. As they see this powerful cavalry charging down the hill, the strangers flee without a second's hesitation, knowing they are at a disadvantage. Also, they have previously seen this amazon leading a charge, and they are fully aware of the intense hatred she feels for their kind.

You quickly shorten the distance from your enemies, who have spread out to mislead you; all running in different ways. You focus your gaze on one of the bandits and steer Nëmster towards him, galloping at full speed. Get ready to charge towards your enemy. Remember that the rules of the cavalry charge are in section 140 and those for horseback combat in section 123.

◘ **First raedënys:** Two-handed axe (STR). Damage: 1d6+2 / STR 3 / LP: 25 / Armor: Leather breastplate (C). Action area: trunk (values 2, 3 and 4). Protection: 3 LP. Helmet (H). Action area: head. Protection: 2 LP.

→ If you defeat him: 173
→ If you are defeated: 184

158

With a terrible blow, you kill your enemy, who collapses to the ground in a pool of blood. But as you are smiling out of satisfaction at your deed, you are powerfully struck on the back of your head. You are now stunned and at the mercy of an unseen enemy. Unable to stand, you fall to the ground (if you were riding your horse you fall from it). You now look up in horror to see that a new bandit stands above you, raising his axe to deliver a final blow. Right then, believing that these are the dying moments of your life, your enemy suddenly staggers with an arrow through his neck, making him collapse to the ground, drowning in his own blood. Incredulous at what you have just witnessed, you turn your head to see the imposing amazon in her saddle, holding the bow that has delivered the life-saving shot..

↑ You gain 1 experience point due to the good fight you fought.

→ Keep on reading. Go to 127.

159

You keep on moving for a lengthy distance, but you now start to think that you have lost track of the boar. You stop and look around the surrounding area, checking every small detail, hoping to discover the correct direction once again.

■ Roll for Perception (PER) with a difficulty of 8 as you try to reorientate yourself.

→ If the result is 8 or higher: 206
→ If the result is 7 or lower: 216

160

After having enjoyed plentiful good wine and some desired peace after the long estrio, you decide to take a break from the hustle and bustle of the common room to breathe a little fresh air outside. You are also wondering where the amazon is, as she has not come back inside after leaving the room. Outside in the great yard, you can see several men on the top of the walls; guards attempting to warm themselves from the heat of small fires. Off to one side of the yard are the two carriages that you have escorted all the way from Verinfes, so you decide to step over to them to check that everything is in order. Now by their side, you examine the stocky locks of the rear doors, wondering what type of merchandise you guard on your trip to Bälkaar. Right then, when you are only accompanied by silence, you hear what sounds like a whimper coming from the stables. Alerted by the unexpected sound, you decide to investigate, as you thought that the voice was vaguely familiar.

You walk cautiously but without delay until you reach the stable door. You open it very slowly, carefully attempting to remain unnoticed. Inside you see that several of your horses, Nëmster included, are very anxious. Deciding to approach your horse to calm it, you are surprised to see that two men lie on the straw that covers the ground, trying to subdue another person. You are shocked to discover that it is the amazon who struggles beneath the body of one of these strangers, her eye terribly swollen. This stranger has muzzled her with a rough cloth and tied her hands behind her back. Her clothes have been severely torn, but you seem to have arrived just in time to prevent the harsh rape that she was about to endure.

"Guards! Guards!" you shout immediately. But before anyone can help you, one of your enemies quickly pounces while the other still holds the amazon. Get ready to defend for your life...

◘ **Rapist:** Mace (STR). Damage: 1d6+2 / STR 4 / LP: 21 / Armor: Leather breastplate (C). Action area: trunk (values 2, 3 and 4). Protection: 3 LP. Leather armbands and greaves (A) (G). Action area: arms and legs. Protection: 1 LP / Special ability: Frenzied enemy. This enemy is out of his mind, driven by lust and now by rage for being interrupted. Therefore, he cannot roll a 1 in his opposed attack rolls. Re-roll any dice that result in a 1.

→ If you defeat this vile enemy: 131
→ If you are defeated: 177

161

After a hard, bloody combat, you finally overcome your opponent, who collapses to the ground, twisting its thick coils with one last drop of energy. You calmly watch the body of the defeated monster, now realising with a lump in your throat, that your end was near – very near. But you have fortunately overcome the hard test that destiny has placed before you.

↑ You win 1 experience point. Write this down on you character file.

→ Keep on reading. Go to 209.

162

You are surprised by the defensive skills of this elusive animal, and feel deeply disappointed by the fruitless result of your hunt.

↓ You lose 1 experience point because of this disappointment.

→ Keep on reading. Go to 198.

163

You have undoubtedly fought with extreme fierceness, helped by the improvement of your skills granted by the curse of the witch. Exhausted, Mhändara falls to the ground nearly breathless, weary and beaten, almost unable to stand.

"Leave him to me!" Nödrik-Nígodar cries out with his powerful voice, running towards you grasping his axe. "I'll reason with him!"

- Just before engaging in combat, you see that the dwarf gulps down the contents of a small bottle before throwing it to the ground. The dwarf has just drunk a powerful potion that will add 2 points to his strength (STR) throughout the fight.

◘ **Nödrik-Nígodar:** Battle axe (STR). Damage: 1d6+3 / STR: 4+2 = 6 / LP: 30 / Armor: Dwarf leather breastplate (C). Action area: trunk (values 2, 3 and 4). Protection: 4 LP. Helmet (H). Action area: head. Protection: 3 LP. Dwarf leather armbands and greaves (A) (G). Action area: arms and legs. Protection: 2 LP / Special ability: Dwarf rage. If Nödrik-Nígodar's life points fall below 10, his dwarf rage will awaken; a savage warrior rage that will make his strength grow stronger, now reaching a value of 7.

→ If you defeat the dwarf: 195
→ If Nödrik-Nígodar defeats you: 211

164

After the two brothers move away from the caravan, you settle in your seat, happy to enjoy these peaceful moments.

"Tarúk and Jurköm are more than capable of a successful hunt," Hormäz says from the seat of his carriage. "We'll keep on moving. I'm sure that they'll catch up with us sooner or later."

"Well," Nödrik-Nígodar says, leaning a hand on your shoulder. "I hope that those two do their job properly and that we will then enjoy a good boar roast. I really love the taste of its meat!" he adds, grinning widely.

You try to relax, but far from cooling off, a strange feeling starts to wake inside you...

→ Go to 180.

165

When you wake, the first thing that you see is Mhändara sitting by your side; beside her stand Süod-Helbórian and Nödrik-Nígodar. The latter looks at you, frowning with a serious face. Still dizzy, you look around and see that you are in a small room, lying on a straw-bed.

"How are you? Can you hear me?" you hear the amazon ask.

"I... it's..." Words hardly come out of your mouth, which feels rather swollen and sore. "What's... happened... to me?"

"We're not certain, but... in fact, no one's sure, really..."

"That damned witch has cursed you!" Nígodar interrupts her, bluntly answering your question. "She has cursed you and now you are doomed!"

"Is that... true?" you ask, scared to death.

"Unfortunately, all evidence points to that conclusion," says Helbórian, the sorcerer of the group. "As my companions have told you, I'm not actually sure of anything, but according to what I've seen, I believe that you've been possessed by some sort of animal spirit... Do you remember anything of what happened?"

"Just that witch shouting some words and then I felt dizzy... I think I fainted then, as I've woken up here... I can't remember anything else."

"Well... I'll tell you what happened then, as you deserve to know," Helbórian says. "As you say, you fainted and then fell to the ground, but you were unconscious for just a second, as you immediately opened your eyes. However, the eyes that opened didn't belong to you... they were an intense yellow, with a vertical almond-shaped pupil. Two large, sharp fangs emerged from your mouth, and your skin, which seemed to be scaly, had turned a greenish colour. You immediately sprang up, possessed by unnatural rage, and without a word of warning, attacked the guardians of the wall. You were lucky in that some of the guards had heard the witch's shouted words, so they immediately knew that you were under her curse, and they tried to restrain you without hurt. Up to six tough, armed men were needed to tie your hands and legs, then your body finally relaxed and you fainted again. That is when we brought you here, where we have been watching you ever since. Nobody wanted to set you free from the ropes that bound you, as Hormäz and the rest of the group are responsible for your actions... I hope that none of us regrets that... And that's all that has happened until just now, when you opened your eyes once again."

"But that can't be true! How...? How has that witch... done that?" Your words die on your lips, as you now feel that you are not able to finish them after what the sorcerer has told you. "Can you help me?" you ask the dwarf, who looks at you sadly.

"I'm afraid that my powers are not great enough for such a task... I'm not really sure of what's happening to you, for a start."

"I can't help you either," Mhändara adds. "But I might know somebody who could. She's a powerful amazon who lives in Bälkaar. She's very old, and all the matriarchs of my people revere her because of her vast arcane knowledge. She'll know what to do... Bringing you into her presence is the least I can offer for saving me. The bad news is that we must get to my town, and that may be terribly difficult, considering your present condition. Let's wait and see what Hormäz has to say about it, as he will be the one who decides if you stay with us or not, as you could be highly dangerous when we are travelling the remote roads we have to follow."

"How is he?" Hormäz asks as he enters the room. "Do we know anything new about what he's suffering?"

"He's awake and seems to be fine," Süod-Helbórian answers, "but we don't know anything new about what that witch has done. According to my experience, I think that this sort of curse is going to remain latent inside him. We won't know when or why it may show again, but I'm sure that it will do so sooner or later."

"Then what do you think about him travelling with us?"

"It will be a risk and a danger for us all, there's no doubt about it. However, if we don't leave him alone under any circumstances, and if he travels in a carriage with his hands tied, I think that we should have him well under control."

"Good!" says the merchant, apparently satisfied by these words. "I'm not willing to leave a man behind on the way to Bälkaar. Let's do as you say." Hormäz now looks directly at you. "Do you agree?"

Unable to think clearly, you accept the conditions imposed by the merchant, as your main goal now is to get to Bälkaar as soon as possible to meet the sorceress that the amazon has spoken of.

"In that case," says Hormäz, "we'll do as follows. You'll tie your horse to the carriage driven by Nígodar and you'll travel by his side with your hands tied. But don't worry, at the first sign of danger, Nígodar will set you free so that you can defend yourself and help us... I don't like the idea that much, but I think it's the safest thing to do, as I don't want to leave you behind... Now you should get ready to leave. It will be dawn soon, and we have a long way yet to go. Moreover, they'll soon light the damned bonfire they've been building the whole night, and I don't want to be here to hear the screams of those two bastards, or the witch, when they're burning alive."

→ Keep on reading at section 175.

166

You follow Tarúk and Jurköm without hesitation, soon joining them in their scouting mission – what you then discover is truly alarming. The flames have consumed a great part of the buildings, and in several places you see dark stains that seem to be blood. On the ground all around you are many objects of every day life, each completely shattered: pots, farming tools, bowls and more. Surprisingly, there is no trace of any person or animal. At least, that is what you think until you walk around a destroyed building and find a huge pyre where a number of corpses have been partially burnt. This shocking image is rather troubling and deeply upsetting. Overcoming this shared feeling, Tarúk moves closer to the bodies, where he crouches to inspect the remains of a hand that has not been touched by the fire.

"Look over there! What's that?" Jurköm suddenly shouts, pointing at a strange, moving bulk in the distance.

You look in that direction and notice a familiar profile. You quickly realise what it is that moves before your eyes.

"Crows! They're crows eating a corpse," you say coldly, walking towards the strange bulk. You only have to briefly wave your arms and stamp on the ground to scatter the hungry birds. Only then do you have a clear idea of the true horror before your eyes, as the body has a terribly mutilated shapeless face; a bloody pulp with empty eyes. Despite this dreadful image, you now look down at the lavish clothes that the corpse wears, and decide to search the remains of this unfortunate man.

→ If you are a sorcerer, a Sàgrast Knight Monk or an alchemist: 154.

→ If you are a hunter, a warrior, a minstrel or a thief: 187.

167

Intrigued by all that has happened while you have been unconscious, and now curious about the place you are in, you know that you will be unable to sleep again, no matter how tired you feel. So you decide to get up to try and find out more about your surroundings. So you swing your legs to the edge of the bed, dragging the thick chain that ties your ankles, and set your feet on the ground to stand. When you rise you instantly feel all of the estrios that have passed while you were in bed; you're very weak and unsteady. You slowly shift one of your feet and take just a short step, making the chain clink on the ground.

Right then the amazons guarding outside the doorway recognize the sound of your movement, and both quickly make an appearance at the threshold of the door.

"Where are you going?" one of them asks.

"I... I just wanted to stretch my legs," you answer quickly, startled. "I think it would do me good after the estrios that I've been in bed."

"Do as you like, but do not leave this room."

"Am I your prisoner then?"

"Prisoner wouldn't be the right word... Let's just say that you're here because Mhändara has asked us so. You'll be fed and you'll have a place to rest. In addition, you'll be safe here, but that's all. You've not been told anything that would give you the right to wander around our house, the home of a family of amazons, with all of its implications. And after what Mhändara has told us about the curse upon you, we have good reason to confine you here. If you don't like our rules or if you have any problem with them, I'll be pleased to show you the way to the door, and you'll be allowed to leave. It's up to you. You decide!

"Fine! I understand and accept your rules," you answer, intimidated by the threatening woman. But you also understand her words, as you are in Bälkaar, the glorious city of the amazons. "I won't leave this room."

"I'm glad to hear that."

So, you walk round your room several times to pump blood out of your legs, as you feel that all of your muscles are cramped. Thereupon, you go to the window and glance through it. You find that you are on the first floor, and under your feet you can see what seems to be a small square, with a fountain and a large washing area where several amazons are tending to their horses. You also see a wide street with buildings at both sides beyond the square. You stay by the window for a while, letting time pass by watching what little you can see of Bälkaar, absent minded, pondering all that has happened...

→ Keep on reading. Go to section 221.

168

After discovering several footprints on the other side of the stream, you are now certain about where you must continue the search; you run again in pursuit of your prey, feeling that you are drawing nearer. You run without pause and after rushing down a steep slope your sharp eyesight discerns the shape of the wild boar within a distant thicket ahead.

You immediately run towards this area, but when you arrive you are frustrated to discover the footprints of many different animals, and you are now in doubt about the direction that you must take.

■ In order to identify the correct direction, roll again for Perception (PER) with a difficulty of 8.

→ If the result is 8 or higher: 189
→ If the result is 7 or less: 206

169

"Here we are, we're finally here!" Mhändara says after having walked along several streets and now stopped before the door of a large building. "Now, listen to me carefully! The amazon that we're going to meet is highly respected here. Don't say or do anything that could offend her, and only talk to her when she asks you something. Do you understand?"

Surprised by the halo of respect that you can see in the strict society of amazons, you nod without hesitation, as you know that your fate rests in the hands of this sorceress.

"Well..." Mhändara says. "Now, follow me, always walking behind."

The amazon knocks on the door three times, using a great knocker hanging in the centre of the door. A middle-aged man soon opens the door and, after recognising your companion, lets you both in. As she had told you, Mhändara has already visited the sorceress to talk to her about your problem, and now you are expected.

"Wait here," the man says, pointing to a wooden bench located in the entrance. "I'll go and see if Sendhöra is ready to receive you."

Luckily, you don't have to wait long, as the man soon returns and waves for you to follow him; you now ascend a wide staircase that leads to the upper floor.

"You may come in, Sendhöra is waiting for you," he says after stopping before a door that attracts your attention due to its pitch-black wood – as black as the darkest night. Thereupon, the man moves away and leaves you alone before the entrance of the chamber of the sorceress.

Mhändara knocks on the door without delay, and it opens very slowly, seemingly pushed by an invisible hand.

"Come in, don't stay back there!" speaks a voice that seems to come from the back of the room.

Welcomed by these words, you enter this new room, the amazon leading the way with you one step behind. As soon as you set foot in this room, your eyes are distracted by different types of strange objects that fill this spacious chamber. Huge shelves stretch completely across the walls, from the ceiling to the floor, filled with books and bottles of many shapes and sizes, stuffed animals, different bones that you can't easily identify, skulls of several species, jars filled with strange products and so on. You also see several wooden tables in front of you, upon which are many flasks of brightly coloured products, parchments full of drawings and manuscripts...

A huge snowy-white cat jumps at your feet from one of the tables, unsettling you even further, as the strange atmosphere within this room, full of stale air, is highly intimidating. A whitish smoke with a sweet smell rises from a nearby flask, making you feel slightly dizzy, and in addition, the gloominess of the light is also concerning, as all the windows are tightly shut with only flickering light coming from a dozen thick candles placed here and there throughout the room.

"Is this the person you spoke of, the one who's cursed?" asks the voice who invited you inside.

"That's correct, madam," Mhändara answers at once.

You immediately turn your head, searching for the person who has spoken. Only then do you see an old woman who seems to be sitting at one of the big tables, with a black cat lying in her lap which she strokes continuously. Her long white hair is the first thing that grabs your attention, plus she has a very old face, heavily marked by many wrinkles. Otherwise, she seems to be a rather unaffected woman, dressed in a simple blue robe with a strange medallion resting upon her chest.

"It's all right... Come here. Come here by my side," the sorceress says. "I was waiting for you. Hold on just a moment."

Right then, the woman places the black cat on the floor, stands and walks over to a burning fireplace several steps away; you would have sworn that it wasn't there before. Then, she dips a wooden ladle into a bubbling cauldron placed above the fire, and pours it into a glass which she offers without hesitation.

"Drink this," Sendhöra instructs, peering deeply into your eyes.

Following Mhändara's earlier instructions, you do exactly as the sorceress asks.

So you take the glass and, after waiting a little for the dark concoction to cool, you drain it in one continuous draught.

"Now give me your hand. Close your eyes and relax."

Once again, you do as you are told, and suddenly feel very tired, too tired to stand, but you are no longer the master of your own actions. Right then you feel that your body collapses and falls heavily to the ground, where you stay now completely relaxed, detached from all that is happening around you. Your mind goes completely blank, plunged into a state of well-being that you would never voluntarily abandon...

After a long time, when you are once again aware of where you are, you see that you are sitting in Sendhöra's chair. The sorceress is right in front of you, staring at you, and several steps behind her stands the amazon.

"Well, now I know what's wrong with you!" Sendhöra exclaims, wiping her hands with a pristine white cloth. "As Mhändara told me, it is a curse, and a powerful one. It was a girl who cursed you, wasn't it? A girl who could transform herself, if I am not mistaken."

"That's correct," you answer confidently.

"A follower of Ancient Usshïres Rites, no doubt. Considering that, I can say that you are under an animal curse, a powerful evil that will progressively take hold of your body until it possesses you entirely and ends your own essence. It has to be removed at once, or you'll die. As for how I can help you, I've got good and bad news. The good news is that I know how to brew a concoction that will end your nightmare... The bad news... I won't beat about the bush! The bad news is that to make this concoction I need a strange root that grows in only a few places in Urowen. One of them, the nearest one, is an old mine abandoned by the duÿmors, the grumpy black-skinned dwarfs who live in the depths of the Úreher Mountains. As I say, that mine was abandoned long ago, and therefore it could be rather risky. Strange, dangerous creatures live in its depths, stalking any prey that they can cram into their mouth. Don't doubt that what I've just told you is very bad news, but you'll need to search this mine as soon as possible if you want to outlive the curse... But firstly we should talk about the payment for my services before we continue... What can you offer?"

"What do you desire? Zaifas?" you ask, nervous because of all that you've just heard.

"Zaifas!" the sorceress answers derisively before roaring with a sinister laugh. "Zaifas! Do you believe that this is a simple market stall? The payment for my services goes well beyond a mere purchase, but now that I know what's wrong with you, I think you're going to be lucky. Right before you arrived I had been thinking about how you could pay me, but as you're going into the abandoned mines of the duÿmors, I have an easy choice. I want the teeth from a zodonte, and it will be easy for you to find one down in those darkened galleries!"

When you hear that name, a cold sweat suddenly covers your forehead, and your nervous state is instantly reflected on your terrified face.

"Ah, you know what a zodonte is, do you?" Sendhöra adds when she sees that you are clearly troubled.

"Yes... and it is too dangerous. I won't be able to...!"

"That's my price, take it or leave it! But you should know that I will help you to succeed. I will tell you exactly how you will be able to kill one of those creatures, and I'll provide you with a very useful potion."

158

* Author's note: zodontes are creatures of the deep who live in a few underground locations across Urowen. Their oversized bodies are snowy-white, with slippery skin lacking fur or scales, and their tiny blackish eyes reveal its blindness, as sight is useless in the tunnels where they live. Because of that, they have developed a great number of tentacles to orientate themselves and explore their surroundings, and by doing so, can detect and catch their prey. Two small legs, located directly under their head, end in oversized claws which they use to make their way in the depths of the mountains. But what's really odd about these creatures is their mouth, ending in a sort of short tube that opens at the end and contains a myriad of curved fangs. Moreover, their skin features many small strands which are used to scan every inch of the ground, just as they use their tentacles.

Although you have never met a zodonte, you know about them because of the many stories and legends that are told across Urowen about these terrible creatures; disturbing stories of blood, death and missing people that now make you nervous and afraid.

"So, what have you decided? Are you willing to make your way through the old mines of the duÿmors to rid yourself of the curse?" the sorceress asks again.

Aware that you don't have any other option available to save your life, you nod slowly, accepting thus the new challenge that Sendhöra has posed.

"Excellent! Those teeth are very precious to me!" the old amazon adds, a wide smile on her wrinkled face. "I've been waiting for this moment for a long time, as I need them to brew a powerful elixir of many qualities... But back to our issue, as I've told you, I'll help you achieve your goal. Firstly, I must explain which type of roots I need for the concoction. They are really special plants that don't need light to live; they grow in the depths, in quite humid areas. Here, take this parchment. You can see a drawing of an alédoras, the plant that you must find."

Sendhöra immediately hands you the document (write it down on your character file, but it does not fill a slot in your leather bag). "Look here, you can see the shape of their long leaves, and their bulbous roots. These roots are what I need for the concoction. I'll require at least three of the biggest roots you can find... Regarding the zodonte, here you are," the amazon adds, now handing you a tiny flask. (Write it down on your character file. This tiny flask does not fill a slot in your leather bag either).

"What I've just given you is a concentrated potion with a strong aroma. That smell will bring forth any zodonte in the surrounding area. Choose a good place to use it, and then pour the content of the flask on the ground. Its effects will be noticed quite rapidly – I can guarantee you that.

But once you've done so, your problems will have just begun, as you'll be calling danger directly to your location. That's why I'm giving you this second concoction, an elixir you'll have to throw at the creature when you have it in front of you." (Write it down on your character file, but unlike the previous one, this potion does fill a slot in your leather bag). "This concoction will hurt its skin, and will prevent it from detecting you and moving normally. Don't forget any of what I've told you, as your life may depend on this information!"

Terribly nervous by the unfolding chain of events, and by all of the information you've been given, you try to clear your mind, but you don't have time to reconsider things, as the amazon continues on with even further instructions.

"Hmm... I nearly forgot... Once you've killed the zodonte and taken its teeth, the time will have come for you to look for the roots that you must find. Try to do this search last, as the fresher they are, the more powerful the resulting potion will be... But there's something else you must know if you're going to be brave enough to enter those dangerous mines. I'll give you one thing that might be very useful, as it is said that a duÿmors alchemist left great treasures hidden in those mines. Who knows? You might get lucky and emerge carrying a powerful object, or find yourself richer that you'd ever have dared to hope! Now look carefully, as what I'm going to reveal is a great secret..."

Sendhöra shows you another carefully rolled parchment that, with the naked eye, seems to be very old and has been damaged over the liznars. "What you're looking at is an original document of a duÿmors alchemist, a manuscript containing the Code of Vorduarán, the key they used to encrypt some of their documents. I'll make a copy so that you can take it with you (this does not fill a slot in your leather bag), as if you use this information wisely, you may be lucky and reward yourself with incredible treasures."

Now highly interested, you look carefully at what is written on the parchment. Write this code on a sheet of paper, or write down the number of this section (169) so that you can view the Code of Vorduarán at any time, the key of the duÿmors alchemists.

Code of Vorduarán

A - 3	B - 8	C - 1
D - 0	E - 5	F - 9
G - 7	H - 4	I - 2
J - 6	K - 8	L - 0
M - 2	N - 9	O - 1
P - 4	Q - 3	R - 6
S - 7	T - 5	U - 0
V - 3	W - 1	X - 6
	Y - 4	Z - 5

"Unfortunately," the sorceress goes on after a few moments of dead silence, "I'm afraid that I can't tell you anything more about this key, as you'll have to learn how to use it by yourself, if you have the chance to do so... Lastly, here is a map of the area that will allow you to find your way to the tunnels, a couple of estrios walk from here. (This last object does not fill a slot in your leather bag either). I can't do anything else for you until you have emerged victorious from your difficult task with the roots and zodonte teeth. I can only wish you luck and ask that you begin as soon as possible, as the curse that witch cast upon you will soon take hold. As a last piece of advice, I suggest that you visit the town's market, where you'll be able to find equipment better suited to such a difficult trip. Buy as many potions as you can, and I would suggest that you improve your armor, as you can never have too much protection in those dark galleries. That also reminds me that you must buy a lamp if you want to see anything down there... See you soon, traveller! I'll be waiting impatiently!"

→ Keep on reading. Go to section 230.

170

Intrigued by what this stranger may have to offer, you approach the table located in a corner of the room. The alchemist is an old man with a long white beard who reads a thick book while drinking wine, wholly detached from his surroundings.

"Excuse me, sir. I've been told that you're an alchemist and that you sell potions. Is this so?"

"Oh, please, have a seat. Yes, yes, that's correct. It will be my pleasure to help you. My name is Llerónimus, and all the potions I sell I've prepared myself. I have many liznars of experience in this profession, so I can guarantee the quality and effectiveness of all my products. I can tell by your appearance that you will need my potions. You're a man of action if I'm not mistaken, and with zaifas in his pockets, I guess."

"Of course I have coins to pay for your services. Provided that I'm interested in what you have to offer."

"I'm sure of that, my friend! Let me explain the different products that I've got right here, ready to be purchased."

Llerónimus turns and reaches down to locate a small bag that had been hidden under his seat. He opens the bag and then begins to place different types of bottles and flasks on the table.

"This is what I have for sale! Let me explain their qualities."

- Remember that, as long as you have zaifas, you may buy as many potions as you want. You can even buy several of the same potion, until you've filled your leather bag.

- **Healing potion.** How to use it: during combat, after winning an opposed attack roll, you can choose to drink this potion instead of hurting your opponent. There is potion enough for 1 dose. When you drink it, you'll recover 1d6+4 life points. Write it down in your leather bag, as this potion fills one of its slots. Price: 15 zaifas.

- **Exploding potion.** How to use it: during combat, after winning an opposed attack roll, instead of hurting your opponent with your usual weapon, you can choose to throw this potion at him. There is potion enough for 1 throw, as it is a tiny glass bottle that will burst when it strikes your opponent. When it explodes, a flammable and highly corrosive liquid will spread over their body (you do not roll for damage location), ignoring any armor, except for magical protection. The damage of this potion is 1d6+6 life points. Write it down in your leather bag, as this potion fills one of its slots. Price: 16 zaifas.

- **Elven elixir of bear fur.** How to use it: drink it right before combat. There is elixir enough for 1 dose. After drinking it, your muscles will immediately grow in size, as will your height, and you will become really strong and stout, with the rage of a bear. During that combat, you will add 1 additional point to all of your opposed attack and damage rolls. Write it down in your leather bag, as this potion fills one of its slots. Price: 18 zaifas.

- If you are a thief, you take advantage of a small lapse in Llerónimus' concentration and cleverly obtain a free potion of your choice.

→ When you've finished with the alchemist, you head back to your table. Go to section 106.

171

With a terrible strike of its tail, the ardronte throws you against a wall, which you hit with a sickening thud. Right then you can't breathe, and feel stunned and dizzy... You'll have to give your very best to survive this combat against such a lethal opponent. Nervous and knowing that you are at the mercy of this massive two-headed snake, you stand up immediately, ready to face it again. Focus on the fight, as your future in this adventure may depend on it...

↓ You lose 1 item, of your choice, from your character file. It can be 1 EP, 1 PP, an object, a piece of armor... For your next combat against the ardronte, keep in mind that, each time that you come back to this point you will lose a new element, as you must kill this enemy to go on in your quest.

→ Go back to section 150 and show that filthy snake what you're made of...

→ If you are defeated three times by this enemy, go to section 208.

172

You are surprised by the great strength of your opponent, who throws you violently to the ground. Now seriously injured, you are horrified to see the bear rising on his hind legs, growling menacingly with its foam-covered jaws wide open. And then, when you think that these are surely your final moments, Tarúk suddenly arrives upon his horse and charges the terrible bear with his spear. Injured and surprised by this new enemy, the bear instantly flees; Tarúk lets him go, and then dismounts to help you.

↓ During the fight you lose 1 item, of your choice, from your character file.

→ Keep on reading. Go to section 198.

173

You fight magnificently and your opponent soon bites the dust. However, you don't have time to enjoy your victory, as you see in the distance another enemy who, after stopping his horse, reaches behind him, grabs a bow and immediately aims it at you. After seeing that, you immediately head towards this new opponent.

- If you are still riding Nëmster (if this is not the case, the text would have told you so), you'll be able to charge against this opponent, using the rules for horseback combat. If you now attack on foot, you'll simply run towards him and won't be able to charge.

- Right before you reach him, your enemy shoots an arrow at you. The difficulty of the shot is 7. That implies that your enemy has to roll a 7 to hit your body. To do so, roll a dice and add 2 points to the result, as that is the value of the raedënys SK attribute. If he rolls successfully, he will have shot you, and you'll then roll for damage location and damage inflicted. After this one shot, you reach him. Damage of the bow: 1d6+1.

◻ **Second raedënys:** Club with spikes (STR). Damage: 1d6+3 / STR 3 / LP: 24 / Armor: Hardened leather breastplate (C). Action area: trunk (values 2, 3 and 4). Protection: 3 LP. Helmet (H). Action area: head. Protection: 2 LP. Leather armbands and greaves (A) (G). Action area: arms and legs. Protection: 1 LP.

> → If you defeat him: 191
> → If the raedënys defeats you: 200

174

Great! Extraordinary! You suddenly feel invincible and energetic, as knocking out Süod-Helbórian is a great exploit that very few people can boast about in Urowen. But now, what just a moment ago was a marvellous sensation suddenly turns into deep sorrow, as you feel terribly exhausted, so tired that you can't even stand; feeling dizzy you collapse to the ground, your eyes beginning to close. Everything that you are experiencing suggests that once again the effects of the curse are fading away (you now continue with your usual attributes). Thus, while trying not to lose consciousness, you see how your companions quickly tie you up with strong rope. You simply can't stay awake, and enter the world of dreams...

→ Go to section 237.

175

Once outside again, with all of your equipment ready for departure, you see that there is much activity in the parade ground, even though it is still night. Here a big pyre has been set, where those sentenced will be burned alive when the rays of Estrion appear and light the Lands of Urowen. There are many soldiers here busily seeing to different duties, as everything must be ready for the fast approaching execution. Surprised and terribly worried, you see that some of these men look at you with deep mistrust, no doubt due to what happened during the night.

You head towards the carriages, but when you get there you only find Tarúk at the entrance of the stables, saddling his horse. The rest of the group must be about to arrive, as Hormäz ordered everyone to prepare themselves quickly to leave. Right then, you realise that the gates have been opened, and that there are people entering the premises. You form an idea then, knowing that the witch must still be in her cage, alive and within reach. Who knows, she may take pity on you in the last moments of her life, or she might tell you something that would help rid you of the curse. On the contrary, talking to her might make things even worse...

→ If you decide to talk to the witch: 185

→ If you'd rather stay where you are to resume your journey as soon as possible: 136

176

"Leave the helpless dog alone!" you shout at the stranger, taking several steps towards him.

"And who the hell are you? Mind your own business if you don't want to receive your share. This bastard's my business!" he adds, just before kicking the dog in the snout.

"Mind your words or you'll get more than you can handle. And don't kick the dog again or else...!"

"What?" he screams, abruptly turning and now directly facing you. "Or else, what? Let's see! What will you do?"

The man now turns back towards the animal and, without speaking another word, kicks its head once again. The blow is so terrible that the dog collapses to the ground, bleeding from a recent injury that has now reopened because of that savage blow.

"You bastard. You'll regret that!" you shout, your words carrying all of the hate that you can convey.

Get ready to fight this opponent, who is already reaching under his cloak to grab his weapon...

◻ **Stranger from Bälkaar:** Rapier (SK). Damage: 1d6+3 / SK 4 / LP: 25 / Armor: Hardened leather chest (C). Action area: trunk (values 2, 3 and 4). Protection 3 LP. Hardened leather armbands and greaves (A) (G). Action area: arms and legs. Protection: 2 LP / Special ability: Skilled swordsman. Your opponent is a fencing master, a combat veteran who is very hard to overcome. Given his skills, he cannot roll a 1 at any point. Re-roll any of his dice that show this result.

→ If you defeat your enemy: 196
→ If your opponent beats you: 186

177

With a final terrible strike, your opponent causes you to collapse to the ground. Fortunately, as you're about to receive the death blow, several guards enter the stables having heard your shouts for help. They immediately understand what has happened here and advance upon the two men without hesitation. Then, knowing that they are at the mercy of their opponents, and with fear in their hearts, the rapist and his accomplice decide to free the amazon and surrender to the guards.

↓ Your opponent's mace has left you mortally ill, so your body will need time to recover from the fight. Therefore, deduct 1 point from all of your opposed attack rolls in your next fight. Write this down on your character file so that you don't forget this important consequence.

→ Keep on reading. Go to section 114.

178

As you did on the previous estrios, you prepare the camp to get some rest before the next estrio, when you should finally reach your destination; the glorious city of the amazons, Bälkaar. Thus, when night has fallen upon Urowen, you enjoy a nice dinner by the bonfire, sheltered by a small stand of trees. Exhausted by the hard estrios' journey, the discussion with the group after dinner is very short, as all of you are lacking sleep. Fortunately, you'll be able to rest all night, as you've not been asked to join the night watch again, as none of your companions know what you'll do if left awake and alone. Ruminating on that thought, you lean against one of the tree trunks and soon fall into a deep, restorative sleep...

"Wake up! Hurry!" Süod-Helbórian shouts nervously, waking you. Strangely, in your head, his voice sounds extremely distant, although the dwarf stands barely a dozen steps from you. "Wake up! It's the curse again!"

Süod-Helbórian looks on in horror, while the rest of your companions now rise from their slumber, alarmed by his shouting. You try to ask him what's going on, but the words won't come out of your mouth. Then, you try to stand up, but your legs won't respond either. At that very moment, you realise that you are no longer the master of your own actions. What's more, you're not even lying on the ground as you thought you were, but you are instead perched high in the trees, far above your companions. You have long fangs once again, and you now see that a long forked tongue comes in and out of your mouth at regular intervals.

"We have to get him down!" Nödrik-Nígodar shouts.

"We could try to catch him with a rope!" Jurköm adds.

"We must act fast, but we must also avoid hurting him," Mhändara says, clearly worried by what might happen to you. "Don't forget that he's our companion."

When you see the ongoing confusion at your feet, you suddenly feel threatened. Your heart races then, and you quickly become frightfully worried. Your troubled mind repeats a single idea: escape alive, kill all enemies who try to capture you. Enemies... Death... Escape... Your mind is taken over by a force that you can't defeat. You can't stop yourself from leaping onto your enemies, hungry to kill them all...

- Get ready to fight your companions. You can only think of killing or dying and, of course, you are not willing to die.

- You are now on the second stage of the transformation of the curse of the witch. As a consequence, you change somewhat. Don't forget to write down these changes. You should write them down on a sheet of paper and not on your character file, as the following changes are just temporary. The text will tell you when you are under the effects of the curse, as you are now. Add the following values to the value of your attributes on your character file:

- STR: +3 / SK: +3 / MAG: +3 / PER: +4 / LP: +8 / PP: +3

- As you are under the effects of the curse, you can exceed the limit of 6 points in these attributes.

"Depart, all of you!" the amazon suddenly exclaims as you jump on the group. "I'll subdue him!"

◻ **Mhändara:** Bälkaar curved blade (SK). Damage: 1d6+3 / SK 5 / LP: 27 / Armor: Hardened leather breastplate (C). Action area: trunk (values 2, 3 and 4). Protection: 3 LP. Hardened leather armbands and greaves (A) (G). Action area: arms and legs. Protection: 2 LP / Special ability: Deep cut. When Mhändara wounds you, if she rolls a 6 for her damage roll (damage: 1d6+3), not only has she inflicted 9 damage points, but she has also seriously injured you. Therefore, you will now lose 2 life points at the beginning of each round due to blood loss. You lose these life points just before rolling each opposed attack roll / Extremely skillful: the amazon can't roll a 1 in any roll. Re-roll any dice that has obtained this value.

→ If you defeat the amazon: 163
→ If Mhändara subdues you: 188

179

Exhausted by all that has happened, and with confused thoughts after processing the information you have heard, you leave the tray on a small table by your bed, and then lean back and close your eyes to calmly contemplate your situation. But your rest is soon interrupted by a sweet voice that immediately attracts your attention.

"What's your name?" you hear somebody ask. You see that the same girl that had watched you sleep, now stands by your bed. "What's your name?" she asks again, stubbornly.

After answering her, you see how the little girl sits by your side and looks at you with genuine curiosity. Right then, you look over her shoulder and see how one of the two amazons guarding the door looks at you, frowning with disapproval. It's clear that they don't trust you, especially with this girl. Surprisingly, they don't force her to leave the room.

"Mhändara has told me that you're sick," says the girl, "but she's going to heal you."

"And what else did she say to you?"

"She's told me that you've come from far away, and that it has been a very dangerous journey."

"Yes, little one. It really has. Tell me, what's your name?"

"Yao-shiäm."

"And is Mhändara your sister?"

"She's my aunt, and I want to be like her when I grow up. I practice with my bow every estrio to shoot as well as she does. She helps whenever she can, although she is usually busy with family issues."

"Yao-shiäm! Yao-shiäm! Where are you?" a distant voice calls, coming from somewhere down the corridor.

"She's here," one of the amazons at the door answers. "Come on, Yao-shiäm, your mother's looking for you. Go with her."

"See you later!" the girl says, smiling sweetly. "I'll come to see you later, when I can, to see if you're better."

The girl immediately turns and runs out of the room, calling her mother's name. Once again, you are alone, rather surprised by all that continues to happen around you. Keep on reading. → Go to section 221.

180

Your stomach begins to burn and your entire body feels overly stressed. You then feel the presence of the wild boar in the distance, and all of your senses are immediately set off. You can clearly taste the boar in your mouth, and the urge for a hunt quickly takes hold of you. Your perception of the world around you changes rapidly; your senses sharpening second by second. You feel even the slightest touch, see incredibly well over a vast distance, and your muscles gain superhuman strength as your blood boils...

You try to relax, but your breath quickens further and your heart races in your chest.

"Are you all right? Is anything wrong?" asks Nödrik-Nígodar, looking at you with concern. "Hormäz. Hormäz!"

You suddenly stand and violently pull apart the rope that tied your hands. You now only think about the wild boar, driven by an unrestrained desire to give free rein to your primary instincts; an unceasing urge to track your prey. You move your tongue and feel your canines transforming into fangs, and looking down at your hands, you see that your skin is now covered by greenish scales. Unable to restrain yourself any longer, you jump an incredible distance from the carriage as your companions look on in total disbelief. They are immediately left far behind...

- You are at the first stage of the transformation of the curse of the witch. As a consequence, your attributes change. Write these changes down on a separate sheet of paper – not on your character file – as these effects will be temporary. The text will tell you when this happens, as it is happening right now. Add the following values to the attributes of your character file:

- STR: +2 / SK: +2 / MAG: +2 / PER: +3 / LP: +5 / PP: +2

- You are able to exceed the limit of 6 points for your attributes when you are under the influence of the curse.

As you run through the forest at superhuman speed, all of your keen senses are focused on locating the trail of the wild boar. You soon smell your prey, but are not sure of the direction you must follow.

■ Roll for Perception (PER) with a difficulty of 7 to determine the direction you must follow. Remember, roll a dice and add the value of your PER attribute, plus the 3 extra points from being at the first stage of the transformation from the witch's curse.

→ If the result is 7 or higher: 147
→ If the result is 6 or less: 159

181

Wanting to get better equipped and to discover all that the great market has to offer, you enter the labyrinth of streets that give shape to the great bazaar of Bälkaar. You are soon offered endless goods and products, from sophisticated, richly coloured carpets to amphoras full of oils and essences. Grilled insects on skewers then attract your attention, as you have never seen crickets, grasshoppers, scorpions and spiders for sale as genuine delicacies. Surprised by all that you see, you keep on walking along these narrow, winding streets, trying hard to notice everything that may be useful for your arduous tasks. Here is a list of the main items that you can afford and that could prove useful in your quests.

Bälkaar Market

Armor:

- **Reinforced metal helmet:** 70 zaifas. Action area: head. Protection: 3 LP.

- **Bälkaar's hardened leather breast:** 90 zaifas. Action area: trunk (values 2, 3 and 4). Protection: 4 LP.

- **Reinforced leather armbands:** 40 zaifas. Area: arms. Protection: 2 LP.

- **Reinforced leather greaves:** 40 zaifas. Area: legs. Protection: 2 LP.

Weapons:

- **Amazon's bow (only for hunters):** 10 zaifas (SK). Damage: 1d6+2. Difficulty: 8.

- **Arrows:** 5 arrows cost 1 zaifa (they do not fill a slot in your leather bag).

- **Trident:** 110 zaifas (two-handed weapon, SK). Damage: 1d6+3. Special attribute: Triple hole. When you wound an opponent in a fight, if you roll a 6 in your damage roll you'll have delivered 9 damage points, and also seriously injured your enemy. Therefore, at the beginning of each subsequent round, your enemy will lose 2 life points due to their serious wound. They lose these life points right before rolling for an opposed attack.

- **Heavy mace:** 110 zaifas (two-handed weapon, STR). Damage: 1d6+3. Special attribute: Bonebreaker. When you wound an opponent in a fight, if you roll a 6 in your damage roll you'll have delivered 9 damage points, and also broken one of their bones. Therefore, from that moment on, your enemy will lose 1 point in all of their opposed attack rolls. If you break a second bone, they will deduct 2 points, and so on.

- **Úreher gemstone:** 110 zaifas (precious stone that casts energy against your opponent, MAG). Damage: 1d6+3. Special attribute: Lock on target. When you wound an opponent whilst carrying this gemstone, if you roll a 6 in your damage location roll, not only is your damage aimed at their head, but you have locked on it. From that moment on, all of your attacks will automatically aim at their head, adding the three extra damage points without the need to roll for damage location.

Miscellanea:

* If you are a thief, your clever hands will allow you to obtain 1 item, of your choice, for free from this miscellanea section.

- **Simple lamp:** 4 zaifas. You'll need this if you're going into the mines. It fills a slot in your leather bag. You'll be able to use a two-handed weapon even if you're holding the lamp, as right before a fight you quickly set the lamp on the ground.

- **Food rations for three estrios (days):** 4 zaifas. Remember that food never fills a slot in your leather bag.

- **Healing potion:** 20 zaifas. Instructions: during a fight, after winning an opposed attack roll, you can choose to drink this potion instead of wounding your opponent. There's enough potion for 1 dose. When you drink it, you recover 1d6+3 life points. Write it down in your leather bag, as this potion fills one of its slots. Once used, delete it from your character file.

- **Bälkian elixir:** 30 zaifas. Instructions: drink immediately before battle. There's enough elixir for 1 dose. After drinking it, your speed and reflexes will improve significantly, making you really tough to beat. During the fight, add 2 extra points to all of your opposed attack rolls. Write it down in your leather bag, as this potion fills one of its slots. Once used, delete it from your character file.

- **Mystic shield potion:** 30 zaifas. Instructions: drink immediately before battle. There's enough potion for 1 dose. After drinking it, a bluish halo will protect you from enemy strikes. Action area: full body (all values from 1 to 6 in damage location rolls). Protection: 2 extra life points, to be added to the usual points that your armor grants you. Write it down in your leather bag on your character file, as this potion fills one of its slots. Once used, delete it from your character file.

- **Chemical products (only for alchemists):** 6 zaifas. With these components the alchemist will be able to brew 1 healing potion that will restore 1d6+1 LP (to be added to his extra points granted by the special ability of the alchemist, that's to say, 2d6+1). It is used like the rest of the potions: during a fight, after winning an opposed attack roll, instead of wounding your opponent, you can chose to drink this potion. Each potion of this kind fills a slot in your leather bag. Once used, delete it from your character file.

→ Once you have finished shopping, you go back to the square: 230.

182

Base camp
(write this number down on your character file)

After having travelled for a large part of the estrio through uninhabited land without anything remarkable having occured, you now become aware that the amazon advances beyond the caravan, surely desiring to reach you.

"Hormäz requests that we speed up," she tells you. "Apparently we are quite near to a small village where he has some business to attend to, and he wants to arrive before dusk to spend the night there."

"All right, I'll hurry up and take the lead. By the way..." you add when Mhändara is already turning to return to the group, "thanks for helping me. If it wasn't for you..."

"I do my duty!" the amazon answers sharply. "I told you that I would help you, and I'll do so. That is all!"

She instantly spurs her horse and quickly moves away, leaving you alone once again. So you keep on riding, now a little faster, your focus on the surrounding area, but nothing strange happens or catches your eye. Finally, when night is about to fall, you discern a small column of smoke in the distant evening sky. It is probably the village that the amazon spoke of, the place Hormäz wants to reach before tonight, so you decide to advance to explore the area ahead. After a lengthy ride, you discover that the small settlement has been swept away. Almost every building has been burnt, and their blackened remains, some still smoking, are silent witnesses of the cruel barbarity that has occurred here. You see numerous signs of horrific violence and merciless fighting.

"What's happened here?" Hormäz's voice eventually asks from behind. You turn around and slowly approach the group.

"Whatever happened, it happened some time ago. I've had a look around and weirdly am yet to find a single corpse; everything has been swept away, however, there are clear signs of a terrible fight."

"There's no trace of magic here," Süod-Helbórian says. "It must have been a bandit attack... Maybe the survivors came back for the corpses of their loved ones before leaving this village for good."

"You may be right," Jurköm responds. He has unmounted his horse and now crouches by the charred remains of what until recently might have been a barn. "Two estrios may have passed since the raid; plenty of time to come back and recover the corpses."

"What will we do now? We were supposed to rest here," Nödrik-Nígodar asks, his face solemn.

"Night is upon us," the merchant says. "It's better to camp here, but we will do so on the outskirts of the village. Let's find a safe place. We should explore the village, as we might find something of interest in the smouldering remains."

According to Hormäz's instructions, you soon set up a simple camp in the shelter of a group of trees that have grown closely together. Once finished, the light of Estrion hasn't completely left the sky of Urowen as yet. Making use of the remaining light, Tarúk and Jurköm decide to explore the remains of the village, and you watch them move away from the camp.

→ If you use the remaining daylight to explore by yourself: 150
→ If you prefer to search with the siblings: 166
→ If you choose to stay and talk to Süod-Helbórian: 193
→ If none of these options are of interest, and you prefer to get ready for the night: 157

183

When you realise how dangerous this situation has turned out to be, you decide to leave the premises, as everything indicates that it will end badly for you.

↓ Because of your cowardice, you lose 1 experience point.

Once outside you breathe a sigh of relief. Right then, you hear a familiar voice calling your name.

"How are you? I'm glad to see that you're feeling much better! You made it really difficult for us the night before getting into town. Tell me, what about the curse?"

You turn to see a smiling Süod-Helbórian coming towards you. Ignoring his questions, you immediately warn him of the danger that the other dwarf is in.

"Come on, we have to help him if he's having the worst part!"

Without a second's delay, you re-enter the tavern, but now with the sorcerer who, as he assesses the situation, uses his powers to call on a terrible windstorm, that makes everyone freeze in shock. In the middle of the great common room, just above Nígodar, a thick black cloud suddenly forms and immediately shoots lightning at the dwarf's opponents as a strong wind throws numerous objects through the air.

"Quickly, take him from here!" Süod-Helbórian yells, momentarily looking from the storm that he has summoned.

Following his instructions, you run to the dwarf and hurriedly pull him outside, while many others also jostle their way to the door. Taking advantage of the chaos, you finally get out of the tavern, and once you are in the streets of Bälkaar, you head to the outskirts, attempting to do so unnoticed. Keep on reading. → Go to section 201.

184

In spite of the superiority of fighting on horseback, this enemy has been too tough. With a final devastating strike, he dismounts you. Quickly, and now gritting your teeth because of the pain you feel all through your body, you stand up and try again to win this terrible fight. → Go back to 157 and fight your opponent once more. Remember that you are now fighting on foot, so you won't be able to charge against your enemy, nor will you'll have the other advantages of fighting on horseback.

185

Desperate to find a solution to the terrible curse, you take courage and walk outside, where you see the cage that holds the witch. You approach with faltering steps until the strange girl acknowledges your presence and fixes her eyes on you with a sweet but penetrating gaze, now revealing a wicked smile.

"Oh, but here you are, my new pet!" she says sweetly, a voice completely different to the one she used to curse you. "Have you come to say goodbye? Or maybe to help me escape? Tell me, will you help me? I don't have much time."

"I've come to ask for mercy. What have you done to me? Release me from this curse. I beg you!"

A terrible guffaw comes out of her throat and she spits a lumpy glob of green sputum, which directly hits you in the face. You look away and hurriedly wipe your face with your sleeve, and when you look back at the girl, she has changed again into the horrific old woman you've seen before.

"You'll spit like me, my pet...! I'll never show mercy! My body may be dead soon, but the effects of my spells will keep on wreaking havoc – I'll laugh at that from hell! I'll laugh at you as I'm laughing at you now, you stupid, big-headed fool! You've come begging for mercy, but you won't find any of that here."

"I haven't done you any wrong..."

"I know, but I don't give a damn! However, as you've made me feel much better, I'll tell you exactly what's happening to you. I'll do so because I know that you'll suffer more from the knowledge, as you'll be aware of what's coming next. Do you really want to know?"

"Yes," you answer without hesitation.

"Fine... you asked for it!" says the witch. "I've cast a powerful curse upon you. Some witches know it as the Curse of Ardronte..."

* Author's note: ardrontes are massive snakes that live all around Urowen, especially in forest areas rich in flora and fauna. It is well known that these dangerous animals attack their prey by spiting a blinding, paralysing venom in their face. Their heavy but nimble bodies are massive and very impressive, as they are huge two-headed snakes with two tiny, twisted horns at the top of their heads. As thick as lambs, their bodies are covered with hard, bone-white scales, making their appearance even more menacing and dangerous.

"Your body is now possessed by the very essence of the ardrontes," says the witch after a pause. "Little by little, their animal strength will take hold of you and... oh! you didn't think that I was going to ruin the surprise, did you? You'll soon find out for yourself! Unless you remedy the situation, of course... but that's quite difficult, and time's quickly running out."

A wicked laughter comes out of her throat again, but right then you hear a voice calling your name.

"What are you doing there?" Nödrik-Nígodar asks you from the gates. "Let's go! Hormäz is looking for you. We're all ready to leave!"

Knowing that the rest of the group is waiting for you to start the journey, you leave the witch behind and follow the dwarf into 'The Caged Skeleton', where you meet your companions. Keep on reading.

→ Go to section 136.

186

In spite of your admirable courage and your numerous blows, you haven't been able to deal with this difficult opponent. Finally, your opponent brings you to the ground, where he steals an item from your leather bag while you are still dizzy. He then runs away along the alleyway, taking the bleeding dog with him.

↓ Delete 1 item from your leather bag. You can choose any item that you are carrying, other than the lamp (if you have already bought it) or the elixir you need to attack the zodonte, as the stranger doesn't show any interest in these.

After a long while, when you have caught your breath and recovered a little from the many blows and cuts that now mark your body, you stand and slowly return to the square, your pride hurt by the experience. → Go back to section 230.

187

You carefully crouch over the body and begin searching his clothes, looking for any clues as to what has happened here. You now dig into his large pockets as you have noticed that there's something held within them. You remove a well-folded parchment, which you unfold immediately, revealing a beautiful ring with an eye-catching green stone:

- **Ronwën ring:** you'll gain 1 extra protection point on your arms while you're wearing this ring. For the purpose of the game, it will protect you for 1 life point (to be added to the protection granted by any armbands) in location 5 (arms). It will only have effect when your opponent rolls a 5 for damage location. (Magical item; it does not fill a slot in your leather bag).

> → If you are a thief, go to section 213.
> → If you are not, go to section 202.

188

Although you have fought fiercely, helped by the enhancement of your attributes granted by the curse, the amazon has turned out to be too tough as an opponent, and she has knocked you down. Exhausted, breathless and terribly weary, you remain on the ground, unable to stand up. Keep on reading. → Go to section 226.

189

Convinced by what your senses now tell you, you rush on, aware that your prey is near – really near. Your ears sense vibrations that you've never previously experienced, and your tongue, now extremely sensitive, detects the presence of the wild boar thanks to a series of intense sensations that you can't understand. So you keep on running, at a speed which you have never reached before in your life. Your legs are so powerful that you are barely tired from all of this exertion, so correspondingly your breath is slow and steady. You make your way through the thick forest, until you finally spot your prey among a group of rocks, easily within your reach. You have tracked a majestic male boar with large fangs; you pounce on it without hesitation. Get ready to face it...

◘ **Wild boar:** Fangs (SK). Damage: 1d6+3 / SK 3 / LP: 28 / Armor: Fur and thick skin. Action area: the whole body (values 1 to 6). Protection: 1 LP / Special ability: Fangs hook. If the boar rolls a 6 in a damage roll, this means that it has sunk its teeth into your skin and then violently shaken its head, causing a terrible cut. Therefore, at the beginning of each subsequent round, you will lose 2 life points due to the great loss of blood. You lose these life points right before making an opposed attack roll.

→ If you defeat the wild boar: 148

↓ If you are unable to defeat it, you lose 1 object from your leather bag, and then immediately fight it again.

190

With the first rays of Estrion light Mhändara knocks on your door. You have hardly slept at all during the night, so you are already wide awake and ready to leave.

"Well," the amazon says, "as we are going to leave, I'll remove the chains from your hands. I hope I don't have reason to regret it."

Then, with a small key, Mhändara releases you from your chains so that you can finally move freely again; you immediately stretch your stiff arms and legs. The amazon is keen to keep her word by paying a visit to the alleged sorceress, so you linger only long enough to collect all of your equipment and weapons before leaving.

You now realise the real size of the huge mansion once you've left your guarded room. A wide staircase leads you to the ground floor where several corridors spread in different directions grant access to other rooms, as you can tell by the many doors in sight. But you don't have time to see much more, as Mhändara leads you to some kind of inner courtyard, where a couple of lackeys open the huge gates that lead out to the street.

Once outside, you note that the estrio is grey and cold, in spite of a couple of rays of light that pass through the thick clouds.

"Let's go!" the amazon says. "It's not far, so we'll travel by foot. Your horse will be kept at my family's stable until you decide to take it. The animal is well cared for – don't worry about it," she adds, noticing the upset expression on your face.

You walk along a spacious, perfectly cobbled street, and are pleased by that fact that it is not usual to find this kind of road in Bälkaar. Surprised, you look with fascination at the numerous details that make the city of the amazons different from the rest of places you know. You are powerfully drawn to the beautiful architecture, as this big city seems to be full of high towers finished with decorated pinnacles that hide a myriad of bells. Beautiful arches cross the streets at a great height above your head, forming bridges that link one building to another. You have never seen anything so wonderful, so strong but so light at the same time.

After turning a corner you come across a group of amazons riding muscular horses. Each grasps a long spear, and their heads are crowned by striking helmets decorated with feathers.

"Look down at the ground! Quickly!" Mhändara orders, clearly nervous. "Don't dare to look directly at these amazons if you value your life! Let's stop and wait here until they pass."

You immediately do as your companion instructs, intimidated by this situation. You are surprised to see that she does exactly the same, looking down at the ground silently until the danger passes.

"Who were those women?" you ask Mhändara once their horses have left you behind.

"They were the honor guard of Queen Zarkända – some of her closest amazons. Everybody else owes them allegiance and respect. They are the best among our warriors, perfectly trained and naturally gifted for fighting."

→ If you want to seize this moment to ask Mhändara about Marok-häi, the amazon you must kill: 215

→ If you decide that it is too risky to do so, and leave it for a later time: 169

191

In spite of your enemy's excellent combat skills, you get the better of him due to greater determination and a stronger sense of survival. After regaining your breath, you look around to see your companions in the distance; the amazon now approaches having killed another raedënys.

↑ You gain 1 experience point for these difficult combats.

When your group finally reunites after the mounted charge, you are pleased to discover that all are well after their battles against the raedënys. Then, Mhändara spurs her horse towards the two men that are still lying on the ground before the burning barn.

"Are you all right?" the amazon asks after coming to their side.

"You have saved our lives!" one of the peasants answers joyfully. "We would be dead now if you had arrived only a little later!"

"What did those bastards want?"

"The same as usual – to steal all they can and take vengeance on the amazons!"

"Which family do you belong to?" Mhändara then asks.

"We belong to Ästharaz guild. Darviana is our matriarch," one of the men answers.

"I know her," the amazon replies, now thoughtful. "Fine, we have saved your life and you are my responsibility until I hand you to Darviana – she must know all about it. You'll join my group until we reach Bälkaar. Come, let's get moving! We've lost too much time already, and Hormäz will be impatient!"

So, while you head back through the wheat field with the two peasants trailing your horses, you approach the amazon, curious to know more about the enemy.

"Who were those raedënys?" you ask her.

"Exiled, banished...! All of them bastards! They're men who dared to rebel against their matriarchs, against the ruling power of Bälkaar – ruled by women, as you know. The only punishment for such action is death... Raedënys are those who have escaped from the wrath of their families, of their matriarchs. They are outcasts now, and they're attempting to take control of our lands. Amazons and raedënys hate each other intensely. As soon as we reach the town, we must inform Darviana of this raid against the Ästharaz guild. She will undoubtedly fly into a rage and then send a group of her best warriors to scout this area..."

"What's happened?" Hormäz asks from afar as soon as you are within hearing distance.

Mhändara immediately rides across to him and explains exactly what has occured. You're soon riding again, with both peasants travelling on the second carriage with Nödrik-Nígodar. You set a rapid pace as you're now anxious to reach the town, yet in spite of your efforts, night falls while you are still on the road.

According to the peasants, you are now half an estrio from Bälkaar, and the merchant decides to stop for the night and set a new camp, the last one before reaching your destination. As on previous nights, you get everything ready for dinner, and then prepare to spend another night in the open air.

→ If you want to take advantage of these quiet moments to talk with the peasants: 204

→ If you want to ask more questions of the amazon: 219

192

Hungry as a lion, and with a growling stomach, you are driven by the enticing aroma to the tavern, which appears to be more than acceptable from the outside. But to your own grief and sorrow you have to forget all about food as soon as you set foot inside, as you immediately encounter a terrible fight. However, your surprise grows even greater as, when you look at the angry contenders, you realise that several men face just a lone opponent, a sturdy dwarf – Nödrik-Nígodar – who is completely drunk and in a foul, argumentative mood.

"Bastards!" he shouts in rage at the men who surround him. "You do not deserve to be alive! Come! Come and get me if you're brave enough! I'll make you all swallow your tongues!"

"What's happened here?" you ask a boy who's trying to escape from danger.

"That dwarf's crazy! I'm not quite sure what happened, but he was suddenly in a great rage. He says that he's been insulted... I don't know! It's likely to be the result of the thirteen tankards he's drunk. You can believe me, I've counted each of them!"

"I believe you boy, I believe you... Fine! I'll go and see if I can stop this madness!"

You take several steps towards the fight and speak loudly. "Damn it, Nígodar! What's happening here?"

"Oh, my good friend! Do you want to join me?"

You take a breath to answer, but right then the fight intensifies and two men pounce on the dwarf who, in spite of his fierceness, is bleeding heavily because of a deep cut across an eyebrow. Surprised by this new attack, you have to quickly duck as a huge tankard now flies directly at your head...

■ Roll a dice to try and dodge the tankard, which has a difficulty of 5 in a PER roll. If the result is 5 or higher, you have dodged the tankard, otherwise it will hit you in the face. The damage of the tankard is 1d6 and you'll have to add 3, as the strike is aimed at your head. When you have finished, keep on reading.

Stunned by what is happening here, you stand up again and look at the dwarf, who is being beaten mercilessly. Completely drunk, Nödrik-Nígodar can barely stand, so it is impossible for him to face the four opponents who surround him.

→ If you choose to leave the tavern, thinking that you will only receive a good kicking: 183
→ If you simply can't leave a friend in a tight spot: 210

193

"What do you think is wrong with me?" you ask the sorcerer once you've approached him. "Have you ever seen anything similar to what that witch has thrown at me?"

"Just once, a long time ago..."

"What happened?" you ask, instantly interested.

"I remember that I used to live north of the Srimost Mountains back then. I was still very young and I was with my parents in what you could call a border barracks. My father was the dwarf in command of that fortified place, a stronghold that protected one of the main entrances to the Kingdom of Ternostan, one of the many galleries that made their way through the Srimost to our glorious city. That place, that... community... had many inhabitants and was partly underground, in the shelter of a massive mountain. But, on the outside, there were tall stone walls with battlements, with a myriad of defensive towers, a real obstacle for anyone wanting to enter our lands without permission. It is still in place as I remember it, in spite of the long time that has elapsed since then. But thinking about it again, I remember that there were several abandoned galleries not far from there. These were tunnels that my people started digging, but had forgotten, and there was a strange dwarf that everybody else thought that had suddenly gone crazy. I remember that my father wouldn't let me go to that area, as he said that it could be dangerous. There were cracks on the ground, holes that would make you trip over, and besides there was that dwarf supposedly disturbed...

Then, a short time after that, a strange creature appeared and started killing people indiscriminately... At the beginning only a few people claimed that they had seen it, but as time went by, the creature grew bolder and more dangerous. I saw it just once, as it fled after having committed one of its hideous crimes. I remember that it was very elusive, with grey fur and sharp claws that helped it to climb the walls and ceilings of our galleries. It always killed the same way, slicing its victims with its claws to later eat a part of the corpse. It took scores of lives... and we were all terrified by its enigmatic presence, as it disappeared as if by magic.

To kill such a terrible creature, my father prepared a trap, an ambush using several dwarfs as bait. That was how they led that sinister creature to a dead-end tunnel. Once it was surrounded by more than twenty warriors, the beast defended itself bravely until it was finally killed by several spears. It was right then, while it lost its life, that the strange creature started to transform to our great surprise. It lost its fur, its terrible claws shortened, and it progressively became the form of that exiled dwarf, the one that everybody thought had gone crazy. A curse...! The victim of a terrible curse! That was the conclusion we came to after analysing all that had happened. Nobody knew how the sentence that forced the poor guy to isolate himself had started, even though his sacrifice wasn't enough...

I sense that you're going through something similar. That witch cursed you and, from what I've seen, I think that you're becoming another... creature. If my concerns turn out to be true, things will get much worse as times goes by. Your soul will fade little by little and it will be replaced by the grim spirit of that creature, until you are completely transformed. You have to get rid of that evil! If you want my advice, and you want to save your life, stick to that amazon as if you were her shadow, and don't leave her until she leads you to the sorceress she says she knows. I'm afraid that you don't have much time, so this might be your only choice of survival."

"Come, let's get dinner ready and set the shifts for the night guard," Hormäz says, interrupting your conversation.

After having chatted with the dwarf, you have two choices:

→ If you want to explore the village, go back to 182.
→ If you'd rather get ready for the night: 157.

194

Your combat ability is highly impressive, as it is not easy to kill such a strong and powerful creature. Fortunately, luck was on your side this time and now the massive body of the zodonte lies dead at your feet, bleeding thick black blood.

You have achieved your goal, but rather than resting for a period, you take only a few moments to regain your breath, wishing to be far away from this place as soon as possible. The smell of the first potion still floats in the air, which may draw another zodonte here, and if so, it would find you still exhausted from your previous battle. That is why you don't delay and now approach the head of the beast, whose mouth, finished in a sort of short tube that opens at one end, shows a myriad of curved teeth. You begin pulling teeth without hesitation, and only stop when you have collected about thirty of these small, sharp fangs. You quickly store them inside your leather bag. (Write them down on your character file; they do not fill a slot in your leather bag).

↑ In addition to the teeth, you win 1 experience point because of the terrible fight you have just won.

Suddenly feeling another vibration, you immediately look around to see if something else is going on, yet everything is calm and quiet. You pick up your lamp, which you had previously placed on the ground before the fight, and move off through one of the tunnels, looking for the mysterious roots of alédoras, your next objective in these mines.

You make your way along another artificial tunnel. You are quite sure that it has been dug by duÿmors because of the many marks on the walls and ground, which could only have been made by tools. As there aren't any branches or forks along the length of this passage, you safely gain ground before entering another large, square room; a perfect cube carved in stone, with four ways out – the tunnel that you have just come through, plus three others. Curiously, the room is also notably cold and wet, with muddy ground that your boots sink into when you walk.

■ Before going on, you must roll for PER with a difficulty of 4. Remember, roll the dice and then add the value of your PER attribute.

→ If the result is 4 or higher: 243
→ If the result is 3 or less: 257

195

With a superhuman strike, you finally knock the dwarf out, and he falls heavily to the ground. It has been a titanic, epic fight and you begin to feel very weary, but you can't rest yet, as a new opponent is running towards you.

↑ You gain 1 experience point for knocking out the dwarf.

"Nígodar, No!" Süod-Helbórian yells, immediately running to help his companion, ready to end the threat that you pose for the group. "Get away from here!" he shouts at the others. "I'm going to deploy all of my powers!"

■ **Süod-Helbórian:** Electric ray (MAG). Damage: 1d6+4 / MAG 6 / PP: 4 / LP: 30 / Armor: Dwarf leather chest (C). Action area: trunk (values 2, 3 and 4). Protection: 4 LP. Helmet (H). Action area: head. Protection: 3 LP. Dwarf leather armbands and greaves (A) (G). Action area: arms and legs. Protection: 2 LP / Special ability: Invisibility charm. Power points (PP) needed to cast it: 4. Effects: after saying this charm, the dwarf becomes totally invisible. Instructions: when Süod-Helbórian's life points drop below 8, he will cast this charm as soon as he wins an opposed attack roll. His body will then fade from view for two combat rounds. Therefore, the dwarf will roll two damage rolls against you, with no opposed attack roll, as Süod-Helbórian automatically wins them as you can't decide which direction you must choose for your attack, nor what to do to protect yourself. The only thing that you can try is to dodge his rays at random. To do that you will roll a dice for each of these two attacks: if you roll a 6, you have luckily dodged that ray. Once both of the dwarf's damage rolls have been completed, he reappears and the fight continues as usual.

→ If you defeat this terrible opponent: 174
→ If Süod-Helbórian makes you bite the dust: 226

196

In spite of your opponent being highly credentialed, you defeat him in an extremely skillful way, leaving him on the ground with wounded pride and a body covered with cuts and bruises. Satisfied with the lesson that you have now taught this bastard, you decide to keep his stylish wide-brimmed hat as a trophy; the spoils of a well-earned victory. (If you are wearing a helmet, you can keep the hat for a special occasion. Write this down on your character file – it will not fill a slot in your leather bag).

You carefully approach the poor dog and immediately cut the rope that holds it, setting him free. Eager to move on, and satisfied that you have done enough to help the animal, you return to the square, but are surprised to see that the dog now follows you. You try to scare it off by shouting, waving and kicking at the ground but, far from being afraid, the abused animal comes even closer, its attitude submissive and somewhat endearing. Although your first thought is that you simply don't need an animal companion, you see something within this dog that makes you decide to let it travel with you on your adventures. You give it the name Rödjod, and it happily wags its tail in agreement. Nobody could tell for sure, but your new friend might just save your life... Add your new companion to your character file.

* Rödjod, attack dog: Fangs (SK). Damage: 1d6+2 / SK 2 / LP: 17 / Armor: none / Special ability: Defense. During combat, whenever your life points fall below 6 (that is to say, when you have 5 life points or less, but are still alive), Rödjod will attack your enemy to defend you. For the purposes of the game, as your enemy will be busy trying to defend themselves from your attacks, the dog will directly make a damage roll against your opponent. This roll represents the extra attack of the dog, and will occur at the moment your life points fall below 6, immediately before your next opposed attack. Remember that you must roll for damage location first, then roll damage for Rödjod (1d6+2). Your new companion can only attack once in each combat. / Powerful bite. If Rödjod rolls a 6 in a damage roll, it has achieved a perfect bite, clenching its jaws with all of its might. This will add 2 points to its damage. Therefore, as its base damage is 1d6+2, if it rolls a 6, 2 points would be added due to powerful bite, and it would cause 10 damage points altogether / Write down the number of this section (196) next to Rödjod so that you can easily return to these rules.

That is how, with your new companion at your heels, you finally leave the alleyway and return to the square of Bälkaar, looking for new challenges to face. → Go back to section 230.

197

After lighting the lamp you have brought all the way from Bälkaar, you immediately head down the first tunnel. Your eagerness to move without delay is very strong, as you want to rid yourself of the curse as soon as possible, but a strange unsettling sensation causes your steps to falter. 'Fear? No! Who said fear?' you repeat in your mind to lift your spirits, even if this place is rather intimidating. Trying to keep your mind busy with other things, you look at the walls and the ground of this gallery, surfaces undoubtedly chiseled by the picks and hammers of duÿmors.

You keep on walking, following a passage that suddenly becomes narrower and narrower until a sharp turn forces you to change direction. This way leads to a wide gallery where you think that you can discern a doorway on one of the distant walls. The darkness here doesn't allow you see it clearly, but as you move closer you discover that it is indeed a rather well-preserved wooden door.

→ If you try to open it to see what is hidden behind the door: 212
→ If you'd rather pass it by and keep on moving through the tunnel: 259

198

When you finally return to the road with Tarúk and Jurköm, you are surprised to see the deer that the siblings have killed. There is no doubt that the hunt has gone well, and you will all enjoy some good roast meat.

By then, the effects of the curse of the witch have completely disappeared from your body. (Regarding the rules of the game, forget all the modifiers, your attributes are back to the values written down on your character file). Your senses now work normally, as do your hands, which show no trace of scales. But your mind is restless, as you are now fully aware of the horrible effects of this curse and its capability to overwhelmingly possess you. Suddenly, a nearby voice questions you:

"Why did you do that?" Hormäz asks, clearly angry. "And how could you tear apart your bonds so easily? There's no doubt that you're cursed!"

"It's not his fault," Süod-Helbórian interjects, trying to help you. "He's just a victim. Although that doesn't mean that he isn't dangerous... Who knows what could happen in the future. It's best that we reach Bälkaar as soon as possible so that he can find someone to help him."

"And what will you do with me now? Will you tie me up again?" you ask, aware of the danger you pose for your companions.

"There's no point in tying you up!" Hormäz replies strongly. "You would easily break free again. I think it is best to... I don't like this idea, but I believe it's best that you leave the group. You have done your duty well, but we must now part ways."

"You can't just abandon him to his fate!" the amazon exclaims, surprising all the members of the caravan. "He must reach Bälkaar as soon as possible, where he will find help. And the best way he can achieve that is by travelling with us!"

"I'm afraid that it's simply too risky, particularly after all we have just witnessed," the merchant replies. "As I've said, I don't like the idea, but I can't find a better solution. He's best to go his own way."

"His way leads him to Bälkaar and that's our destination," answers Mhändara. "Besides, I promised him that I would help, and that's what I intend to do. I won't rest until I can take him to the powerful sorceress who lives in Bälkaar. I owe him at least that after what he did for me. He saved my life!"

"But..." Hormäz tries to speak up again, but the amazon doesn't allow him to finish.

"It's now beyond dispute!" the amazon exclaims. "Hormäz, you know that my word of honor is more sacred to me than any oath, so don't try to stop me from keeping it! If you refuse to let him travel with us, our agreement ends right now. I will no longer be your guide and you won't be able to enter my town..."

"Are you crazy? You can't break the commercial agreement I signed with your matriarch," the merchant shouts back in rage.

"How dare you to talk to me like this!" Mhändara immediately responds, determinedly approaching Hormäz. "I see that you are completely unaware of the code of honor of the amazons – don't dare to put me to the test! Our friend will come with us or you can turn and go all the way back!"

"Why...? Oh, fine," the merchant says, dispirited. "If that's your will, so it will be done... but only because I couldn't otherwise get into Bälkaar and would lose plenty of zaifas. I know that I won't change your mind, so we'll stick together, but it will be done as I say."

"That's fair," Mhändara agrees.

"From now on we change our formation," Hormäz says, wiping sweat from his forehead. "Our friend will now ride his horse again, but he will go first, far in front of us. That way we will be able to see if something's happening, and we will have time to react."

The issue seems to be resolved with these words, so you resume your journey in an uneasy atmosphere, now travelling upon Nëmster again. You soon cover a decent stretch of the winding path, leading the way by yourself... Keep on reading. → Go to section 182.

199

"Going back to our previous subject," you say, continuing the interrupted discussion. "Do you think that your master could be interested in hiring me?"

"I don't know. As I've told you, we've just come back from a long journey. If it had been before our departure, I'm sure he would have, but now..."

"Where have you been?"

"I shouldn't really talk about that," Toljröm answers, clearly intimidated. Yet the booze is apparently taking effect and his tongue is suitably loosened, adding "as we were following orders from Krénator himself"

Toljröm receives your full attention when you hear these words.

"It was the wizard himself who ordered this mission of my master, Bors of Raidyón, and that made us travel to the Desert of Stone, specifically to the oasis of Alda..."

"Toljröm, you damned idiot! You would talk to this foreigner about our business?" You jump at the sound of the powerful voice saying these words, as you hadn't realised that their owner was so near. When you see terror on Toljröm's face, you immediately turn and see that one of the men accompanying Bors of Raidyón is standing right behind you. He is a fierce opponent exhibiting angry, threatening behaviour, as he has clearly overheard your discussion.

"I'm sorry but this stupid Toljröm has sentenced you to death!" the stranger adds, grabbing his weapon. "You've heard too much, and I can't let it pass!"

You hardly have time to react, as your enemy raises his broadsword and directly aims at your head. You are lucky enough to dodge it and the sword resoundingly hits the table, chipping the wood... Chaos then takes hold of the room, as the call girls shout and run in all directions, afraid of danger. Those who try to protect the girls demonstrate bravado, while those who desire to take money from the gaming tables insult and punch each other without restraint. In the blink of an eye the tavern becomes a battlefield where there is only one rule: everyman for himself.

Get ready for the impending fight, as after quickly standing, your enemy with the broadsword is already preparing to strike again... Keep on reading. → Go to section 301.

200

This opponent has been too tough for you. You will have to give your best if you want to move on with your quest, as your companions have spread out, chasing enemies in different directions, leaving you to fight alone. Grab your weapon firmly, focus on the task ahead and fight him again. As a penalty for having lost the previous fight, you now face the raedënys on foot (if you were riding your horse, you have now fallen from it), and you must also deduct 2 base life points due to the consequences of the previous combat. If you defeat him, you'll get your usual life base points back for the next combat. As an only advantage, your opponent is no longer shooting at you with his bow. → Go back to 173 and fight with all your heart to kill this enemy.

201

"Nígodar, are you all right?" Süod-Helbórian asks his companion once you reach a small, isolated square with a fountain and a water pipe. "You're bleeding!"

"Why did you pull me out of there? I was giving them a good kicking!" the dwarf answers, clearly upset and moody.

"Oh, come on, for God's sake, don't be so cocky!" Helbórian says, a bit angry with his friend. "Well, fine... come on, come over here and let me see to that injury on your forehead... and drink some water, that will do you some good."

While the sorcerer tries to heal his permanently complaining companion's injuries and bruises, Helbórian asks how things have turned out since you parted ways.

"I went to see the sorceress that Mhändara told me about," you answer the dwarf, "and she told me that she knows a remedy to remove my curse. The bad news is that she needs strange roots to make this concoction, and now I have to locate them in some abandoned mines near here."

"You're not going to the old duÿmors mines, are you?"

"I'm afraid so..."

A shade of sadness is cast over Süod-Helbórian's face, who stares at you before speaking again.

"I wouldn't like to be in your skin, my friend. That's a damned, dangerous place. Nobody really knows what you may find in those tunnels. Some people say that the duÿmors abandoned that place because they drained all of its minerals, but others suggest that they were forced to leave the place because of something they found there, which they wished they had never seen... Anyway, if you have to go there, I wish you the best of luck, as you're going to need it."

"And what about you? Maybe you could come with me," you say with a half smile on your face, intimidated by the dwarf's words of warning and hoping for two unexpected companions.

"Oh, shit! I won't deny that, in the bottom of my heart I'd love to go with you, as it is also said that duÿmors alchemists left extraordinary treasures hidden in those mines, but I'm afraid it's going to be impossible. We're leaving town tomorrow, escorting Hormäz again. That old fox has already finished his business with the amazons and has filled his carriages again with new merchandise that we'll have to transport to God knows where... So I'm afraid that we'll have to postpone the fun. It's a pity... but as we won't be able to go with you, I'd like to give you something that will prove useful in those galleries. Here, put this on and don't ever take it off. It might save your life.

- **Enhanced life necklace:** while you're wearing it, your base life points (LP) will increase by 3 points. (Magical item; it does not fill a slot in your leather bag). Remember that you can only wear one necklace at a time.

After sharing some time in the company of the dwarfs, you finally say goodbye, as all of you hear the call of duty and it is here that your paths must split.

"I hope to see you soon, my friend!" Nödrik-Nígodar says, looking respectfully at you.

"And in better circumstances!" Süod-Helbórian adds immediately after shaking hands. "May Sàgrast want us to meet again!"

With these words, you finally depart and again walk to the square of Bälkaar, alone this time. → Go to section 230.

202

After your encounter with the corpse, you again locate Tarúk and Jurköm, who have found another body, almost hidden among the remains of a small wooden building that collapsed due to the flames.

"This place could be very dangerous," Tarúk notes. "According to what we've seen, all the evidence suggests that bandits razed the village – and they've done a thorough job. They've left almost nothing standing, nothing that we can benefit from... Best that we leave now. This place is beginning to give me the chills."

Agreeing with Tarúk's summation, you had back to the simple camp, where your companions are resting. → Go to section 182 and choose another option.

203

"Come! Come closer – don't be afraid," the stranger says when he sees you approach. "My name is Tórkuod, and I'm a servant of the great amazon Rámada. Have you heard about her?"

"No, I don't know of her," you answer, sure of your words.

"Oh, then you should meet her, as she can teach you great things! I assume that you're not from here... and you look like a warrior, a battle-tested warrior. It would be very interesting for you to visit Rámada. I can bring you to her."

"And what am I supposed to see her for?"

"Well, you'll see, my lady is one of the best masters in Bälkaar. She has trained hundreds of amazons and she could teach you combat techniques you've never heard of. Anyone can tell you about her wonders – you only have to ask around if you don't believe me. Rámada masters the arcane arts and the power of magic, as well as the steel of the sword or the heaviest of axes. She can teach you great things, if you have the time and the zaifas to pay for her services."

"How much money are we talking about?"

"She won't teach you anything for less than 80 zaifas, although I can assure you that it will be worth more than that... If you decide to hire her, you'll spend five estrios at her home, by her side, training without rest until you master the technique you've chosen to learn."

Although you find Tórkuod's proposal interesting, 80 zaifas is far too much to pay, and you don't have enough time available to train with her, as you must leave at once for the abandoned mines.

"Although I'm tempted by the idea, I've got some pressing matters to attend to, so I can't learn her method," you finally say to Tórkuod. "I'm going to be several estrios out of town, but when I get back I might be interested in hiring the services of Rámada. Where would I find you then?"

"Good... good... I'm glad to hear this. When you want to learn from my master, you must go to the north of the town and ask for directions to Rámada's home. Everybody in Bälkaar knows her and anyone will be able to guide you to her door. I hope that I'll see you there soon – you won't regret the investment!"

After saying goodbye to Tórkuod, and thinking about visiting Rámada in the near future, you return to the square of Bälkaar.

→ Go to section 230.

204

"How are you?" you ask the two peasants after approaching them.

"We are fine, thanks to you," one of the peasants answers. "Unfortunately, the raedënys grow in number every estrio and we who work in the fields feel more and more unprotected every day."

"Sooner or later," the other man says, "this escalating issue will end badly if the amazons aren't able to root it out."

"Are you in favour of the amazons?" you ask out of curiosity.

"But, of course! They're part of our culture, our way of life. It's them who have been born to fight and protect us! We just serve them... That's how it is and that's how it should remain. Those raedënys bastards fight against everything we believe in, and they have already killed many. I won't feel safe again until I am behind the walls of Bälkaar. May they burn in hell!"

After your short conversation with the two men, you approach the dwarfs, who seem to be lighting a fire. You now focus on the task of setting up camp for night. Keep on reading. → Go to section 178.

205

This has been a rather unequal fight, as you have been brutally overwhelmed by the combined strikes from two of these ferocious beasts. They have brought you to the ground, where you try to defend yourself the best you can, aching in pain and with your body now covered in cuts and bruises. Given the poor combat you've just fought, you lose 1 experience point to help you learn this lesson.

→ Delete the experience point from your character file and go to section 235.

206

Highly focused, you make your way through the thicket. Although it now seems that you have lost track of the wild boar, there is another prey nearby. You walk cautiously without making a noise until you finally discover a pheasant right at your fingertips. You feel somewhat disappointed for having let the wild boar flee, but you now focus on this new prey that will satisfy your thirst for blood. It is a magnificent specimen, a fat cock with striking feathers. Get ready to kill it...

◘ **Pheasant:** Peck (SK). Damage: 1d6-4 / SK 3 / LP: 15 / Special ability: Escape. If the pheasant rolls a 4, 5 or 6 in a damage roll, this means that it flies away to perch, out of reach, in the branches of a tree.

→ If you kill it: 198
→ If the pheasant escapes: 162

207

You have determinedly fought a superb fight, savagely striking to the left and right at these dangerous creatures. You immediately decide to quickly leave this place, not knowing if more of them will suddenly emerge from the numerous holes. You hurriedly move off at a rapid pace, leaving behind the corpses of the dreaded sistöliums.

↑ You win 1 experience point (EP). Write this down on your character file.

→ Go to section 282.

208

Unable to kill your opponent, you collapse again before the dreaded ardronte, entirely at its mercy... But when you reopen your eyes, you find yourself at the improvised camp on the outskirts of the village. Alerted by the sounds of the fight, all of your companions ran to help you, reaching the battle just before the two-headed snake swallowed you alive. After killing the ardronte, they carried you back to the camp, where you have just woken from restless, nightmarish dreams.

↓ As a consequence of the multiple defeats, you lose all that you had in your leather bag, plus 1 piece of armor.

→ Go to section 182, as you are again at the camp.

209

Drawn by the noise of the fight, Mhändara and Nödrik-Nígodar emerge through the door of the building, as they had also gone scouting and heard your struggle in the distance.

"I can't believe it. It's an ardronte!" the dwarf exclaims, approaching the oversized corpse of the two-headed snake. "And one of the largest I've ever seen! No doubt that it's a great specimen to have killed on your own."

"Are you all right?" the amazon asks you then, interested in your health.

"Yes... yes... I'll bounce back," you answer, breathing with some difficultly due to the tough fight.

"I think that this ardronte had a hidden surprise," Nödrik-Nígodar says suddenly, calling you while he crouches by one of the coils of the oversized creature.

"What's happened?" Mhändara asks.

"Can you see that? It's last meal!" the dwarf answers, pointing at a huge bulk located in the snake's body. "And I'd bet that it's one of the villagers, looking at its size and shape."

"Tiny gods, you're right!" Mhändara says. "We can't leave them in there... We should remove the body and bury it." The amazon approaches the ardronte and warily inspects it.

"That won't be very nice," says Nígodar. "He must be in the middle of the digestive process... but I think you're right... Stand aside, I'll cut the monster open!"

Without delay, the fierce dwarf grabs a hunting knife that he uses for meals and, after looking for a moment at the body of the snake, raises his weapon with both hands and then thrusts downward with all of his might into the flesh of the beast. Immediately, and making a great effort, he starts to tear at its scales, slicing the body lengthways. A nauseating smell emanating from the guts of the beast fills the room, turning the air into an almost unbreathable gas. Stunned, you stagger slightly while seeing how the dwarf determinedly continues on with his task, overcoming the terrible stench flowing from the huge open wound.

When Nígodar finally ends his difficult task, you see a terrifying scene, as inside the snake is the shrunken corpse of an adult woman with a terrified expression on her face. Much of her flesh has now slid off her bones as a result of the ardronte's digestive acids. And that smell... that filthy smell gets into the deepest part of your lungs, making it hard to breath easily.

"Let's finish this as soon as possible!" the amazon exclaims. "Come on, help me!"

You respectfully remove the crushed corpse from inside the snake, and then dig a grave using tools found on the ground nearby. When you finally finish all of this exhausting work, the night has already fallen upon Urowen, so you head back to the camp to rest with the group. → Go to section 182 and choose another option.

210

If you were struck by the tankard that was just thrown, you will start the following combat without the life points that were lost in that strike.

Determined to help your companion, you approach Nödrik-Nígodar to set him free from his opponents, who hound him mercilessly. You quickly grab a nearby chair and, without saying a word, slam it down on the back of a real hulk that has just punched the dwarf in the stomach. Surprised by your attack, this opponent is knocked to the ground, but another enemy immediately stands in your way, raising his fists...

- As is usual in tavern brawls, weapons are not used, as only the honor of the contenders is at stake, not life. You are not allowed to use weapons or any magic charm or potion during this fight. You'll both be punching each other, and the damage that both of you inflict is 1d6. In your case, you can roll on STR, SK or MAG, at your choice.

◻ **Tavern opponent:** Fists (SK). Damage: 1d6 / SK 3 / LP: 26 / Armor: Leather breastplate (C). Area: trunk (values 2, 3 and 4). Protection: 3 LP.

- **Special ability for both opponents:** in this combat both combatants can try to grab objects from the bar or nearby tables to strike their opponent with – jars, bottles, a chair... These objects will add extra damage to your blow. You'll know if you or your opponent have managed to grab one of these objects when one of you roll for damage. If a 6 is rolled, an object has been used, so in that turn (and only in that turn), the damage is automatically 1d6+3. That's to say, the damage is 9, as you can only pick up an object when you roll a 6.

→ If you defeat your opponent: 223
→ If you are unfortunately defeated: 233

211

Although you have fought courageously, the dwarf has been too tough for you. Exhausted, you are surprised by the many powerful strikes that Nödrik-Nígodar launches at you, until you are finally knocked out and now lie at his feet. Keep on reading. → Go to section 226.

212

Out of curiosity, you push the door with one of your feet and it begins to open slowly, issuing a loud creak that echoes around the gallery. Alarmed by this unexpected sound, you stand still and hold your breath, hoping that the noise hasn't alerted any dangerous creatures... Thankfully, their seems to be no nearby reaction, so you carefully push the door wide open. Holding your light aloft, you poke your head beyond the doorway to see what is hiding in there. It appears to be a small room dug from the stone, a guardroom or something of the sort. In the middle stand several upturned chairs and a wooden table on its side; scattered jars and two bowls also lie on the floor. Your attention is drawn to a shelf at the back of the room, so you decide to check if there is anything useful to be found there. Right then, as you step into the room and walk by the table, your breathing quickens and your heart races as you discover unexpected skeletal remains on the ground.

Now recovered from the shock of this find, you look more closely and deduce that they are the remains of a dwarf, no doubt a duÿmor who, according to the positioning, must have died a violent death. Your suspicion is confirmed when you round the table to take a better look and discover that his skull is crushed on one side. You decide to search his rotting clothes, but find nothing of value, so you again focus on the shelf that is now at your back. However, after moving a number of dusty bowls and glasses you still don't discover anything of interest and immediately decide that you're just wasting your time. Disappointed not to have found something, you leave the room and move on.

→ Go to section 259.

213

Your soul of a thief makes your clever hands tirelessly continue the search of the corpse, eager for further reward. You soon find a small sachet in another pocket containing 20 shining zaifas. You immediately store them safely (add these to your character file).

→ Go to section 202.

214

Although you fought courageously, your enemy finally defeats you with a terrible strike, knocking you to the ground, unconscious. When you come to your senses, you are completely disoriented in time and place, as you don't know what estrio it is nor the way you've been carried to be where you now are. Anxiety immediately takes hold of you when you realise that you are chained by hand and foot; you are a prisoner in a small cage that is being dragged by a carriage pulled by horses. You can't see your weapons or armor, and you're not dressed the way you were either, as you're only wearing a stinky, shabby robe that's not yours. Additionally, your feet are bare.

Dispirited, you try to discover where you are, but you can't see far as it is late at night and is very dark. With some difficulty you discern that you are moving forward along a cobbled and lonely path, just one part of a caravan composed of several carriages like yours, pulled by horses, full of cages overcrowded with prisoners and driven by a large group of seasoned... duÿmors!

Feeling a lump in your throat, you look around and see that, by your side, within this cage of thick bars, is a young, burly man, also chained, who looks at you silently.

"Where are we? What has happened?" you ask in a whisper.

"Don't you know? I'd seen that you were unconscious, but I didn't know that you weren't aware of your destination," he answers, also whispering. "I'm afraid it is not good news. We now belong to the duÿmors. We are their slaves, and the best we can hope for is to die soon. Right now we're been carried to the Úreher Mountains. These dwarfs live in its depths, and I would bet that we are supposed to work in their mines until our death, as it is said that everyone who enters those mines never see the light of Estrion again. I'm sorry to be the bearer of this unpleasant news, but it is better to know what you can hope for in the future."

"Quiet in there, you dogs!" interrupts one of the many duÿmors walking by the carriages. He strikes the bars of your cage with a long spear. "You'll have all the time you want to chat in the mines! And you won't whisper! You'll shout to the rhythm of the whips of our foremen!" There are fates much worse than death, and it would seem that this time luck has turned its back on you.

You have come far, much farther than many would have dared to expect, but a cruel trick of destiny has seen you meet a miserable end... Such is life and death in the relentless Lands of Urowen, a highly dangerous place, where you never know what each new estrio may bring.

→ Go to section 400.

215

Intrigued by what Mhändara may know about your next objective, you ask about Marok-häi in a concealed manner so that she doesn't become suspicious.

"Some time ago, in an inn near Verinfes, I heard some hirelings talking about an amazon... Marúk... Marúk-häi, as I recall."

"You mean Marok-häi?"

"It's... it's possible... They said that she was the best of your warriors, and that she was in command of the armies of your queen."

"So it is! No amazon can eclipse her in hand-to-hand combat and, as you say, she is in command of our armies and the guard of honor of the queen. The women that you have just seen riding their horses are not only in charge of protecting Zarkända, they're also the personal bodyguards of Marok-häi, her most trusted amazons. Every one of them would give her life defending any one of those two amazons."

"Where do they live, in a castle?" you ask, encouraged by the answers provided by Mhändara.

"More a stronghold than a castle, I would say. In the middle of town there is the great palace of the queen, a walled citadel that has reserved barracks for Marok-häi and her amazons, the guards of honor of Zarkända. I'm sure that you'll get to see it if you stay some estrios in town... Oh, let's go, it's this way. We're near now."

And with these words, Mhändara puts an end to this conversation and turns into a narrow alleyway that leads you to a real labyrinth of streets.

→ Go to 169.

216

Despite all your efforts, and the effectiveness of your enhanced senses, you have lost track of the wild boar. However, your efforts haven't been completely in vain, as you now hear a loud noise nearby. Surprised, you turn immediately to the source of the sound and see an enraged bear running towards you. It's an impressive specimen, a big male with thick, bright, black fur. Get ready to defend yourself...

◘ **Black bear:** Claws and fangs (STR). Damage: 1d6+4 / STR 5 / LP: 33 / Armor: Thick fur and skin. Action area: whole body (values 1 to 6). Protection: 2 LP / Special ability: Lethal swipe. If the bear rolls a 6 in a damage roll, this means that its claws have struck with terrible consequences, seriously wounding you. Therefore, at the beginning of each subsequent combat round, you will lose 2 life points due to the extreme loss of blood. You lose these two life points right before making an opposed attack roll.

→ If you kill the bear: 148
→ If the bear defeats you: 172

217

After looking closely at the thick bars, the wall, the ground and the ceiling, you finally give up as you can't find anything that helps you to figure out how to move the impassable obstacle in front of you. Frustrated by this situation, you eventually decide to return to the entrance to try your luck with another tunnel. So you leave this claustrophobic dead end tunnel, and now have the three wooden buildings before you again, with their corresponding tunnels.

The moment has come to choose a new option. Think carefully, as your future may depend on your decision...

→ If you choose the first tunnel, the one with the door lying on the ground: 197
→ If you choose to go down the second tunnel: 224
→ In the third tunnel you have found the grill blocking the way: 238

218

Attracted by the strange sounds, you enter the alleyway to find a very odd predicament: a man incessantly hitting a dog with a stick. This large, intimidating animal howls in pain from the many strikes that the man inflicts, unable to defend itself as it is tied to a grill by strong rope.

After recovering from the sight of this unusual situation, the angry man, who wears a wide-brimmed hat and a dark coat, begins shouting at the poor animal.

"May you be cursed! You've made me lose a bucket full of zaifas! I will teach you to become a fighter! I'm going to kick you so badly that you'd rather die in the next fight you're in rather than deal with me! Damned bastard...! Come on, attack!"

→ If you move closer to try to end this abuse: 176
→ If you decide that it is none of your business and return to the square: 230

219

"What's wrong with you? You seem a little strange," you ask Mhändara as you approach her.

"There's nothing wrong with me. I'm fine," she answers categorically, but the brightness of a single tear in one of her eyes doesn't escape your scrutiny, so you don't give up your questioning.

"Well, something's happening. Of that I have no doubt! I've never seen you like this. Does it have anything to do with the raedёnys?"

"No! Well... yes..." the amazon adds with a straight but sad face. "But don't expect me to tell you anything about it. It's something I've buried deep in my heart, something that I'm not proud of. I shouldn't even be saying these words! Forget that we had this conversation."

Mhändara turns back and hastily moves away from the group. Worried by what has happened, you move to follow her, but Hormäz stops you by placing his hand upon your chest.

"Leave her alone, my friend... Leave her to her pain."

"Do you know what happened?"

"From what I've heard," the merchant replies, "a brother of Mhändara's, one who she was strongly attached to, is now one of the raedënys. He was, and still is, a source of great shame for her family, and especially for her, as she tried to help him escape the rage of the amazons. Her brother finally escaped and he's now doing his own things, attacking his own people. That is why it's better to leave her alone. Don't ask her anything else about this issue."

After your brief conversation with Hormäz, you approach the dwarfs, who seem to be lighting a fire. You focus again on the task of setting up camp for the night. → Go to section 178.

220

Finally, after the long, hard travel from Verinfes, and after the many sufferings you have endured to get here, you can focus your efforts on doing the job Brádoc entrusted you with: killing the powerful amazon Marok-häi. To do so, before taking any other action, you go to an isolated place and sit quietly, mentally collecting all of the information you have gathered so far. As far as you know, Marok-häi is the most skillful warrior of all the amazons of Bälkaar, and she is in command of the armies of the Queen Zarkända, and of the guard of honor. These guards also protect Marok-häi with their lives. You have fortunately discovered in the last estrios that she spends most of her time in the so-called Tower of the Drum, where she is waiting for important news that a carrier pigeon is supposed to bring. You are thinking about these things when an unexpected voice draws your attention...

"Excuse me, sir, but I've been asked to give you this."

You look up to discover a boy talking to you, under eight liznars old. He holds two items in his hands, which he offers to you: a carefully rolled parchment tied with a blue ribbon, and a small leather bag.

"Who has given you these things?" you ask without hesitation, startling the boy, who immediately turns around to look across the street.

"That woman over there..." the boy answers pointing at a dark alleyway, but when you look over there, nobody can be seen. "She was there just a moment ago!"

"Who was she?"

"I couldn't see her well, as she was hiding under a cloak, but she was young."

"It's all right, don't worry," you answer, convinced that by now it would be impossible to track and follow the stranger, so you'd rather concentrate on what the boy brings to you. "Come and give me what you've got there."

You immediately take the parchment and the bag (and, if you feel generous, you can give the boy a coin for the inconvenience).

"Thank you very much for your services, you may leave now."

As soon as the boy turns the corner and you lose sight of him, you look around to check that you are alone. As there seems to be nobody in the vicinity, you open the bag quickly and discover 100 zaifas (write them down on your character file). Surprised by this unexpected gift, you unwind the parchment's blue ribbon, and read the following text:

So far so good, but you have the most difficult part of your task ahead; the reason why you are here, and why we are going to help you. For the moment I will only say what you need to know for time is running out, but for your peace of mind you may want to know that B... sends us. We have followed you from the moment you left his town. We have been tempted to intervene on some occasions, as you have been in grave danger, yet you have managed to continue on your own. However, you have the most difficult part of your quest still ahead. Marok-häi is your main objective, and ours, so tomorrow, at dusk, will be the best moment to attack. I think that you already know that Marok-häi passes part of the night in the Tower of the Drum. We will attack her there. I know I'm asking too much by asking you to trust me this way, but you don't have another choice if you want to leave this damned place alive.

If you want to succeed, follow my instructions to the letter. Tomorrow, when Estrion sets, you must be near the door of the Tower of the Drum. We will take care of tearing it down. That will be the signal to take action. You'll have free passage up to Marok-häi, who will surely be found in the upper part of the tower. There will be many amazons guarding the building, but you won't enter alone. We will launch a coordinated attack, and we will get rid of the guard of honor. Then, it will depend on you, as B... himself entrusted you with this mission. If you succeed and kill her, we will then join you and flee through the sewers of Bälkaar, which can be accessed in the Tower of the Drum. We have planned it all thoroughly. Now, memorise this message and destroy it at once, as if you are discovered carrying it, you can consider yourself a dead man. Remember that we will be watching you and, if you are willing to fight that amazon, put the zaifas we gave you to good use and improve your equipment.

Once again, trust me and don't let us down.
In return, I swear by my honor that we won't let you down.

D...

Surprised by what you have just read, you try to understand the contents of the message. It seems rather believable to you, as it doesn't make any sense that an enemy would have written it. If your intention had been discovered, you would have been put under arrest at once, or you would have been killed in the alleyway you're now in. Also, the information about Marok-häi matches what you have discovered so far, and the help offered is very difficult to reject. For all of these reasons, you decide to follow the given instructions after carefully thinking it through, remaining alert to any setback or betrayal that may arise. If there really is someone willing to open the doors of the Tower of the Drum and to give you backup for such a dangerous mission, then you must seize such an opportunity. Keep on reading. → Go to section 284.

221

You pass the estrio alone, slowly recovering and thinking about the curse of the witch. You become rather bored, as you have nothing else to do but lie on the bed and look up at the ceiling. Luckily, a new visitor cheers you up somewhat; at night, Mhändara comes back to your room.

"How are you? I hope you're better."

"Yes, I'm much better."

"I'm glad to hear that, because there is some business that will take me out of town. I won't be able to stay in Bälkaar much longer, so if you agree, and you feel strong enough, we will go and see the sorceress tomorrow. What do you think?"

"That you've made my estrio. I'm desperate to get rid of this curse. Damned witch! And damned be the moment that I came near her!"

"Fine! I'll get you something for dinner. Eat well and try to sleep so that you bounce back for good. Tomorrow, at dawn, I'll come for you and we'll leave together. Rest now."

With these words, Mhändara departs, leaving you alone. But a spark has shone inside you, a spark that makes your blood run hot, as you're about to face a new challenge. So far, you have fulfilled the first mission that brought you to Bälkaar. You've successfully escorted Hormäz and his caravan to the city, but you still have two main quests to accomplish. The first one, extremely urgent, is to rid yourself of the curse of the witch. The second, the important and risky mission that Brádoc entrusted you with in Verinfes, is to kill Marok-häi, one of the most influential amazons in Bälkaar, the most skilled of their warriors, the leader of the armies of the Queen Zarkända. Thinking of this challenge makes you realise that you are not safe, as you are within an enemy city. According to all the spies of Verinfes, the amazons have allied with the followers of Zorbrak, the

Dragon God, and everything suggests that a big war is about to start, a war that will set the disciples of that god against all the free people of Urowen.

"Excuse me, I've brought your dinner," a servant says, quickly returning your thoughts to where you are. You quietly enjoy the meal, wishing that the new estrio would arrive forthwith so that you can discover more of what the wonderful city of Bälkaar, home of the legendary amazons, has to offer. → Go to section 190.

222

You have fought an extraordinary fight, as killing these two ferocious animals is a mighty deed worthy of song. ↑ Unfortunately, there isn't a minstrel to immortalize your exploit, so you gain 2 experience points for your bravery and skill in hand-to-hand combat. → Go to 235.

223

With a final devastating punch, you knock your enemy to the ground. A faint smile forms on your face, but you don't have time to enjoy your victory, as a new opponent faces you and, if you now trust your eyes, he seems to be even fiercer and more dangerous than the first. Take a deep breath and get ready for a new fight...

You'll fight with bare hands once again, so you won't be allowed to use weapons or any kind of charm or potion. Your damage is 1d6, and you'll be allowed to roll on STR, SK or MAG, at your choice.

◘ **Second tavern opponent:** Fists (SK). Damage: 1d6 / SK 4 / LP: 29 / Armor: Hardened leather breastplate (C). Action area: trunk (values 2, 3 and 4). Protection: 3 LP. Hardened leather armbands and greaves (A) (G). Action area: arms and legs. Protection: 2 LP.

- **Special ability for both opponents:** in this combat both combatants can try to grab objects from the bar or nearby tables to strike their opponent with – jars, bottles, a chair... These objects will add extra damage to your blow. You'll know if you or your opponent have managed to grab one of these objects when one of you roll for damage. If a 6 is rolled, an object has been used, so in that turn (and only in that turn), the damage is automatically 1d6+3. That's to say, the damage is 9, as you can only pick up an object when you roll a 6.

→ If you defeat this second opponent: 245
→ If you are defeated: 233

224

After lighting the lamp that you bought in the town of the amazons, you start heading down the second tunnel. You're anxious to move forward, as you want to rid yourself of the curse as soon as possible, but a strange unsettling sensation causes your steps to falter. 'I can't be afraid!' you repeat in your mind to inspire courage, even if it is true that this darkened space is rather unnerving. Trying to think of something else, you remember the tune of an old song, although you don't dare to hum it here, fearing that you may draw undesired attention.

So you keep going down into the depths of the mines, already wishing to be outside again, even though you've barely begun your underground journey. Somewhat overwhelmed by the situation, you continue on step by step, until you reach a wider section, where you find a sort of abandoned carriage, whose wood is completely rotten because of the passing of time and the general humidity. Right then your attention is drawn to a number of holes in the walls. They are about the size of a ripe melon, and there are about thirty to be found within this area. Out of curiosity, you approach one with the lamp to try and determine what they are, but a sudden noise coming from the back of the hole makes you take a couple steps back, as it does not bode well. Surprised and intimidated by this unexpected situation, you watch in horror as the head of some kind of oversized insect emerges. It has a frightening appearance with a horrible pincer-like mouth. It hisses strongly, and in response, four more of these creatures immediately come out of other holes. They have elongated bodies full of legs, and they expertly move across the floor and walls at an incredible speed. After seeing what it is now happening, you are sure that these creatures are surrounding you, and their threatening behaviour makes you prepare to defend your life. You will have to do your best if you want to succeed in your fight against these five sistöliums, the name given by some to these nightmare creatures.

◘ **Sistöliums:** Pincers (SK). Damage: 1d6+3 / SK 4 / LP: 7 / Armor: Exoskeleton plates. Action area: whole body (values 1 to 6). Protection: 2 LP / Special ability: Group attack. The great danger of these lethal, carnivorous 'insects' is their ability to organize and initiate a group attack on their victims, who are usually overwhelmed by numerical superiority. Therefore, at the beginning of each round you will lose 1 extra life point (regardless of the armor you have equipped) for every two sistöliums that are still alive, besides the one you are fighting against right then. (If there are three of them, you'll lose 1 point). You lose these life points immediately before making an opposed attack roll. For example, in this first combat round you are facing 5 sistöliums. As you are fighting one of them, there are 4 others free, so you will lose 2 LP at the beginning of each combat round. When you kill the first one and there are only 4 alive, there will now be 3 of them free, so you will only lose 1 LP in each round. And so it will be until there are only 2 of them alive, when you will no longer lose any extra life points.

→ If you defeat these horrible creatures: 207
→ If you can't defeat the sistöliums: 247

225

Successfully fighting against the underwater beast is a hard test that very few can pass. Exhausted, you allow yourself a few moments to regain your breath while you look at the beast's body, now floating belly-up, showing its yellowish scaly skin. But while resting you notice a long trail in the water, moving quickly towards you. Everything suggests that this is another of these sinister creatures, so you immediately swim to the shore, guiding yourself by the glow of your lamp on the sand. As soon as you get there you immediately pull up several roots (they do not fill a slot in your leather bag), and swiftly rush for the tunnel without looking back.

↑ You win 1 experience point (EP). Write this down on your character file.

→ Keep on reading. Go to section 325.

226

Up until this moment you have felt invincible, energetic. But now, what just a moment ago was a marvellous sensation suddenly turns into a deep sorrow, as you feel terribly exhausted, so tired that you can't even stand; feeling dizzy you collapse to the ground, your eyes beginning to close. Everything that you are experiencing suggests that once again the effects of the curse are fading away (you now continue with your usual attributes). Thus, while trying not to lose consciousness, you see how your companions quickly tie you up with strong rope. You simply can't stay awake, and enter the world of dreams... → Go to section 237.

Because of your mastery in the completed fight, you win 2 experience points, which may be crucial in improving your character file for the impending combat. Bors of Raidyón now advances after having watched your previous fight from a distance. You have humiliated his men, killing them before his eyes – such an offense can't pass unpunished. He grabs his weapon and runs at you, continuously staring you in the eye. Do your best or you may not survive to tell the story...

* Author's note: to win against this toughest of enemies, throw everything you have at him, such as the items in your leather bag, because, in case you are defeated, there are fates much worse than death.

◘ **Bors of Raidyón:** Charmed combat axe (STR). Damage: 1d6+5 / STR 6 / LP: 36 / Armor: Reinforced helmet (H). Action area: head. Protection: 4 LP. Coat of mail (C). Action area: trunk (values 2, 3 and 4). Protection: 5 LP. Armbands and greaves (A) (G). Action area: arms and legs. Protection: 2 LP / Special ability: Shield of fire. When you roll a 6 for damage, your enemy will automatically cast this charm (without rolling any dice), concentrating his vital energy to create a shield of fire before him that protects his body from your strike. Thanks to this charm, your enemy doesn't suffer any damage from that blow / Bonebreaker. When Bors of Raidyón hits you during combat, if he rolls a 6 for damage (Damage: 1d6+5), not only has he inflicted 11 damage points, but he has also broken some of your bones. Therefore, from that moment on you'll deduct 1 point from all of your opposed attack rolls (only during this combat). If he breaks a second bone, you'll deduct two points, and so on.

→ If you get rid of this powerful enemy: 239
→ If Bors of Raidyón defeats you: 252

228

Surprised by the lethal attacks of this regal creature, you have been unable to face the mountain lion that, with a thunderous roar, brings you to the ground with a viscious swipe, leaving you at its mercy. You will have to give it your absolute best effort if you want to defeat this true wonder of nature.

↓ During the fight, a piece of armor has been so seriously damaged that it will now grant 1 point less of protection. You can choose the piece of armor: H, C, A or G. The one you choose will lose 1 point of protection. Update your character file with this new value, as this deduction lasts for the rest of the game, until you can purchase replacement armor.

↓ If you come back to this section (for a second, a third time, and so on) you will keep on losing 1 protection point from a piece of armor.

→ Go back to 241 and make that fierce mountain lion bite the dust.

229

Unfortunately, luck has turned its back on you this time, as the many projectiles that have struck you now bring you to the ground, seriously ill. You drag yourself away from the danger area and then tend to your injuries, nervous and fearful due to the experience of being so close to death.

↓ You lose 1 experience point, and must be more vigilant in the future. This time you have activated a trap of the duÿmors – the next time it may be something far worse...

→ Go back to 257 and choose another tunnel.

230
Base camp
(write this number down on your character file)

After leaving the house of the sorceress, Mhändara now leads you to the large square where the great market is located. Here merchants loudly proclaim the many benefits and advantages of their products, keen to make a sale and add extra zaifas to their pockets.

"Well, as promised, I have helped you as much as I've been able, but now we must part ways," the amazon says. "I have to leave town today, as I can't delay my departure any longer. I wish you all the best of luck with ridding yourself of the curse and, who knows, we may meet again."

"Thank you very much, Mhändara. I appreciate all that you've done for me. I don't know what I would be doing right now if it wasn't for you. At least I have a chance to save my life, even if that sorceress hasn't make things easy. I wish you luck in your journey, too, and I hope to see you again real soon."

"What are you planning to do?" Mhändara asks out of curiosity.

"I think it would be best if I locate some better equipment, and I'll then tour the town for a bit, in case I find something of interest before leaving for the mines."

"Head back to my family's home when you want your horse back. Remember, you must ask for the location of the Nhemïta guild. Everybody in town knows us and they'll lead you there easily... Well, I'm afraid the time has come to say goodbye. Best of luck. Náskälez!"

You watch the amazon depart, now leaving you alone in a strange town – an enemy city almost entirely unknown to you. You have two important missions to complete: visiting the abandoned mines of the duÿmors, and killing Marok-häi to keep your word with Brádoc. But for the moment you can only think of visiting the town to find better equipment and get ready for the tough journeys ahead. Once again, the dice have turned...

→ If you want to visit the Bälkaar market: 181

→ You can smell delicious grilled meat from a nearby tavern: 192

→ A strange man beckons you to talk with him: 203

→ You hear loud noises coming from a dark alleyway, as if someone was kicking an animal. If you go to see what's happening: 218

→ If you feel totally ready to leave for the mines: 241. Before playing this last section, remember that you are in a base camp, so you'll be able to play one or several of the other sections and then leave for the mines. This option will take you far from town, and therefore unable to choose the remaining options offered here.

231

Even though you have fought courageously, the zodonte has proven itself as a very tough enemy to overcome. That is why you will have to do your absolute best to defeat it, as without its precious teeth the curse of the witch will completely take hold of you, shortly ending your life. You must face it again to continue on with your adventures, but the following consequences have been added because of your defeat.

↓ Due to the brutality of the combat, and to the many tentacles strikes, a piece of armor has been so seriously damaged that it will now grant 1 point less of protection. You can choose the piece of armor: H, C, A or G. The one you choose will lose 1 point of protection. Update your character file with this new value, as this deduction lasts for the rest of the game, until you can purchase replacement armor.

↓ If you come back to this section (for a second, a third time, and so on) you will keep on losing 1 protection point from a piece of armor.

↑ You still have the second potion that the sorceress gave you in your bag, so you will be able to throw it at the zodonte again to try to harm it and to reduce its SK.

→ Go back to section 282 and kill this monstrosity of the depths.

232

Totally frightened, you watch on in horror as a deformed creature emerges from the thicket, aggressively attacking without delay. From the little that you have seen of it before entering combat, it is a real beast, a mixture of a human with some kind of giant scorpion. It has many pitch-black legs, two oversized pincers where you would expect to see arms, and a long tail ending in a pointed, intimidating stinger. You can't see nor do much more right now: get ready to sell your life dearly...

◘ **Arachnid monstrosity:** Pincers (SK). Damage: 1d6+3 / SK 4 / LP: 25 / Armor: Strong plates. Action area: whole body (values 1 to 6). Protection: 4 LP / Special ability: Stinger strike. If this beast rolls a 6 in a damage roll, not only has it inflicted 9 damage points, but it has also struck with its stinger, not the pincers. Therefore, at the beginning of each subsequent combat round you lose 1 life point due to the lethal effects of its venom. You lose this life point right before making the opposed attack roll. In addition, deduct 1 point from all of your opposed attack rolls due to the paralysing effects of the venom.

→ If you defeat this horrifying creature: 286
→ If your enemy crushes you like an insect, go to section 258, but don't lose this page or forget that you are in section 232.

233

Although you have fought fiercely, your opponent has unfortunately exhibited greater skills. A powerful punch knocks you to the ground, where one of his companions takes advantage of the situation to kick you hard in the stomach; this kick is so terrible that vomit immediately rises into your throat. Exhausted and humiliated, you try to stand, but you receive another blow that makes you collapse once again. Your opponents vastly outnumber you, and as you are clearly at a disadvantage, you start to think that it has not been a good idea to take part in this nonsense. But then, when you see that another enemy is pouncing on you, something totally unexpected happens. Keep on reading.

→ Go to section 260.

234

Although you fight fiercely and very bravely against a much superior opponent, you can't do anything to avoid the fatal outcome, as after collapsing on the boat completely beaten, you see helplessly how the huge mouth of the sea snake closes around your body, just before violently taking you high up in your small boat. The pain you are feeling is unbearable, as some of your bones now break due to the terrible strength of your opponent's powerful jaws. You scream in pain for help, but it's useless, as your fate has already been decided. Luckily, your torment is short, because after crushing you even harder within its jaws, you literally burst your guts, and the giant snake swiftly gulps you down. While your life's last heartbeats fade away, you briefly see that everything around you darkens as you move deeper into the stomach of the beast, where gastric juices will soon start to digest you...

You have come very far, much farther that many would have expected, but a cruel trick of destiny has led you to an unhappy ending... Such is life and death in the implacable Lands of Urowen, a highly dangerous place, where you never know what each new estrio may bring.

→ Go to section 400.

235

When you see that the remaining lions still surround you, now roaring aggressively, you fear for your life, realising that it will be extremely difficult to escape from this grave situation. Increasingly growing anxious, a rapidly spreading fire begins to burn inside you, in your chest, in your stomach... Right then, you look down at your hands to see that they are once again covered by scales. You feel your teeth turning into fangs and your senses sharpen; it takes only a few more moments to be possessed by a blind fury that makes you suddenly jump to a more advantageous location to fight your opponents. You are no longer the master of your own actions; you can hardly control the body that now moves without your will. With only a shred of lucidity remaining, you realise that the curse is taking more and more hold of your body; you're now becoming something more than powerful enough to face the beasts that stalk you. You are turning into a real monster, and that frightens you much more than the possibility of dying here, a victim of the mountain lions.

- Get ready to battle two other lions, as in the previous fight, but now things have changed dramatically...

- You are in the third stage of the transformation of the curse of the witch, which has the following consequences. Write them down on a separate sheet of paper without modifying your character file, as everything that is explained hereafter is only temporary. The text will tell you when you are under these effects, as you are now. Add the following values to the attributes on your character file:

- STR: +4 / SK: +4 / MAG: +4 / PER: +5 / LP: +10 / PP: +4

- As you are under the effects of the curse, you can exceed the limit of 6 points in each attribute.

- Once again, you are facing two enemies at the same time. Play each turn the usual way but, at the end of each turn (whether you have won the opposed attack roll or not), you receive an additional injury to represent the attack of the second lion, because, as you are facing the other lion at that moment, you can't defend yourself from the second. Therefore, make the usual attack rolls for the second animal. Firstly, roll for damage location and then, roll for damage with 1d6+2. If you defeat the first lion, the second one will back away and you will be the winner of the fight.

◻ **Third mountain lion, leader of the pride:** Fangs and claws (SK). Damage: 1d6+4 / SK 5 / LP: 31 / Armor: Thick fur and skin. Action area: whole body (values 1 to 6). Protection: 2 LP / Special ability: Lethal swipe. If the lion rolls a 6 in a damage roll, it has strongly sunk its claws into your flesh, inflicting serious damage. Therefore, at the beginning of each subsequent combat round, you lose 2 life points due to blood loss. You lose these life points immediately before making the opposed attack roll.

→ If you are the winner of the fight: 250
→ If you have been unfortunately defeated: 264

236

Despite many powerful strikes, this horrible monstrosity has been too tough for you. Every legend about Krénator seems to be true, as after what you have seen, it is clear that the sorcerer is using his powers to crossbreed men and beasts. ↓ As a penalty for having lost this combat, you lose 1 base life point because of the terrible consequences of the injuries that the jailer has inflicted. Delete it from your character file, remembering that you have permanently lost this point. If you come back to this section, you will lose another base life point, and so on. Now, take courage and face this sinister creature again. → Return to section 371 and kill that beast.

237

Base camp
(write this number down on your character file)

When you regain consciousness, you feel terribly achy, as if your whole body had been stretched and beaten. Regardless, you try very hard to focus your mind, as your memory is strangely confused and your vision is somewhat blurry. You recover little by little, and then realise that you are constrained by a new situation: your hands and feet are now securely shackled with thick chains. In spite of this, you are not held in any type of prison, but are lying upon a soft, comfortable bed covered with a thick, and very warm, blanket. Surprised, you look around to see a ceiling with many wooden beams and a large window. Right then, you notice a girl sitting on the bed, staring at you.

"¡Cotloc! ¡Cotloc mulpüri!" the girl says in what seems to be an archaic language, now running out of the room.

Before you can talk to the girl, she has already disappeared and a different voice answers in the distance:

"Néitar árnoszen. Nin kai cotloc, símuren dälmen."

The girl returns shortly after in the company of a woman who, at first glance, you take for Mhändara, as her features arc much alike.

"How are you? I bet you have woken up hungry!" the stranger says in your own language.

"Where...? Where am I?" you ask, bewildered.

"You are at the home of the Nhemïta guild, Mhändara's family. She brought you here. We've been looking after you since then, even watching over your sleep."

"How long...? How long have I been here?"

"Three estrios, the same estrios that have passed since your caravan reached Bälkaar."

"My goodness!" you exclaim, stunned by this information. "And Mhändara, is she home?"

"She had to go out, but she'll be back soon. Don't worry, as I've told you, she'll come back really soon and, from what I've heard, you have an outstanding issue. Rest and recover in the meantime, you must be exhausted. I'll order something for you to eat."

Without another word, the woman turns and quickly leaves the room, leaving you to your thoughts. But you are not alone for long, as two slim, beautiful amazons armed to the teeth now enter, and they wait at your door, as if they were guarding it. Surely, everybody in the house knows about your threat, and that is why you are chained and why guards stand at your door. However, in spite of your curse, they have treated you well, and they will keep on doing so, as you soon appreciate when a man carrying a tray full of food enters into your room. A bowl of steaming soup, roasted meat, bread, cheese and a big glass of wine makes your mouth water and your stomach loudly rumble. You devour the food without delay, having not eaten for three long estrios.

"I'd been told that you were already awake! How are you?" Mhändara asks, catching you in the middle of the feast.

"Fine... or I think so, at least. What happened?"

"Can you remember any of it?"

"Vaguely..."

"The effects of the curse of the witch took hold of you again, and you attacked us all, without mercy. We were lucky to be able to subdue you, but you gave us all a really tough time. Thanks to heaven, Süod-Helbórian was with us and he helped to heal our wounds. After that, there's not much to tell. You fainted. I think that happened because of the curse, too, and then we reached Bälkaar the following estrio. I brought you here, as I'm still in your debt and... that reminds me that we have an outstanding visit. I've gone to see the sorceress I told you about and she has agreed to meet you. As soon as you have recovered a little more, we'll go and see her. You have to get rid of that curse as soon as possible... By the way, your horse is in our stable, and by your equipment you'll see a bag of coins Hormäz gave me to give to you. He told me that there are 250 zaifas in the bag. That was the amount promised to you for escorting the caravan to our city (write down these coins on your character file). Everything else is in that chest," the amazon adds, pointing to a large trunk at the foot of your bed. "But, for the time being, eat and rest. I've got business to deal with, so I'll come back later to see how you're feeling."

→ If, after the meal, you decide to lie on the bed again to regain strength: 179

→ If, on the contrary, you choose to get up despite your chains: 167

238

Equipped with the lamp that you have brought from Bälkaar, you enter the tunnel hoping to leave these mines as soon as possible, once your mission is fulfilled. It is rather intimidating to be alone in such a threatening place, isolated from the rest of the world and unable to ask for help. You clench your teeth and move along the narrow, winding tunnel, feeling that the temperature drops as you walk on, and detecting the strong smell of humidity. After taking a closer look at the walls, you realise they are wet; you are now walking over a real quagmire, with many insects hurriedly moving through the arc of light projecting from your lamp.

After turning into a new section of tunnel you find something ahead that you would never have expected. A large grill completely blocks the way forward. Surprised by this unexpected obstacle, you look at it closely to try and discover a way of crossing to the other side.

At first glance you would say that this is some kind of gate that slides upwards, as you can see an elongated, narrow slot in the ceiling above it, where it should rise into. You attempt to raise it, but it is far too heavy for you to move it on your own, despite your best efforts. Now exhausted and gasping, you lean on the wall and try to regain your breath.

Frustrated, you realise that if there is any way of moving the grill, it will be thanks to the brain, not the muscles. Consequently, you decide to look closely around the surrounding area, hoping to find any clue that shows you how to open the grill...

■ Make a roll for PER with a difficulty of 5. Remember that you must roll a dice, and then add the value of your PER.

→ If the result is 5 or higher: 251
→ If you obtained 4 or less: 217

239

You have been truly remarkable, magnificent, and have showed great mastery, once again, in hand-to-hand combat. (↑ You win 1 experience point). But you don't have time to enjoy the victory, as danger still surrounds you. Even if you have killed Bors of Raidyón, he seems to have many more followers in the room claiming vengeance. That is why you immediately flee to the exit, as your life is in danger as long as you remain inside the tavern. → Go to section 398.

240

Your good luck and rapid reflexes have helped you to escape from this ancient trap of the duÿmors. You have been really lucky, maybe too lucky, as the complex mechanism is a lethal deathtrap. But you have crossed to the other side alive, so you win 1 experience point; write this down on your character file. You continue along the tunnel, attracted by strange runes carved into the walls that seem to form a sort of poem, but it is impossible for you to decode its content. Keen to not waste time, you keep on walking and soon follow a tight curve that leads you down a new tunnel.

→ Go to section 288.

241

Base camp
(write this number down on your character file)

After the long estrio you have passed in the city, searching for new equipment to take on your trip to the mines, you decide to spend the night in a humble inn where you enjoy an agreeable dinner. (If you have any zaifas, delete 5 coins from your character file to pay for this. On the contrary, you'll have to sneak into and then sleep in a stable, with an empty stomach of course, unless you have bought some food). You intend to leave at the beginning of the new estrio, fresh and fully rested to face your new adventure in the best physical condition.

You wake up to the first rays of Estrion, to what seems likely to become a hot estrio, with a clear sky. You wake up quickly and are soon under way, walking to Mhändara's home to collect Nëmster. Once there, you take your horse and ride to the gates of the glorious city of Bälkaar.

Once you have left the walls of the city you find yourself in the middle of a road full with merchants and peasants. As they continue to come in and out of the populous city, you stop to take a close look at the map that Sendhöra provided, showing the route to the mines. From what you see on the map, you'll have to ride two estrios south-east, towards the Úreher Mountains. If you follow the instructions correctly, you shouldn't have any trouble in finding, at the foot of a steep and lonely cliff, a huge excavation. Here you will find the entrance to the mines and access to a tunnel that will lead you to the very inside of Urowen.

In good spirits for this new adventure, even if somewhat intimidated by what you may find, you spur on your horse and begin a quest that will decide your destiny. For the time being, progress is easy, as you ride along a path beside extensive farmlands, which provide plentiful produce to the city of the amazons. But at mid estrio this situation changes dramatically, as the path now ends. To directly reach the mines you must head into a thick forest of high pines, whose leafy branches don't allow the light of Estrion to pass. Shadows surround you instantly, and a light breeze makes the atmosphere significantly colder, as it brings with it the cold of the mountains. What had been, up to that moment, a pleasant ride on Nëmster rapidly becomes a sinister march through a dark, bleak landscape, lowering your spirits as you are again aware of the danger ahead, and of the reasons that have brought you here.

However, you maintain a good pace, making your way through this old forest. You follow the paths indicated on the map without deviating from your course, until the night begins to fall. You look for a safe place to camp because, as you already know, you will have to sleep out in the open air for at least this one night. Luckily, the next estrio, you should find the entrance to the mines. Following your instincts, you explore the area until you find a place that seems adequate; a small depression under a large rock protruding out of the ground. This arrangement will keep you protected from cold air currents, and you will even be able to light a fire that will be hidden from view, just as Tarúk and Jurköm taught you during your long travel from Verinfes to the city of the amazons.

You finally settle down in your improvised camp, by the small fire you have lit in a hole dug into the cold ground. Total darkness is all around you by then, as night has finally fallen upon the Lands of Urowen. Tired from the hard trip of the estrio, you decide to lean on the trunk of a tree to sleep for a while, and your eyes close immediately, out of pure tiredness...

Unfortunately, your sleep is soon interrupted by a frightening roar that makes you wake and stand at once. You look around nervously, and now in a stressful state, you see an oversized mountain lion with bright dark brown fur with black spots, just several steps from you. The intimidating beast pounces immediately. Get ready to defend for your life...

◘ **Mountain lion:** Fangs and claws (SK). Damage: 1d6+2 / SK 3 / LP: 26 / Armor: Thick fur and skin. Action area: whole body (values 1 to 6). Protection: 1 LP / Special ability: Lethal swipe. If the lion rolls a 6 in a damage roll, it has strongly sunk its claws into your flesh, inflicting serious damage. Therefore, at the beginning of each subsequent combat round, you lose 1 life point due to blood loss. You lose this life point immediately before making the opposed attack roll.

→ If you defeat the lion: 255
→ If you have been defeated: 228

242

After having made up your mind you resume walking, now on firm and dry ground, moving through a tunnel built from big stone blocks that are perfectly aligned and dovetailed. As you don't really know what to expect ahead in this silent tunnel, you walk forward cautiously, noticing many insects crawling about on its cold walls. You soon turn a corner and are immediately shocked to find a guard stationed here. He is a fearsome enemy, with a frightening tattooed face and a massive axe that he now grabs with both hands.

"Stop there and tell me the watchword!" he barks with a powerful voice.

Unable to answer such an unexpected request, you hesitate for a moment, time enough for your enemy to clearly understand that you are an intruder. He doesn't wait any longer, instantly raising his weapon to attack. Give it your best shot if you want to escape alive...

◻ **Hireling leader under Krénator's command:** Battle axe (STR). Damage: 1d6+5 / STR 5 / LP: 29 / Armor: Reinforced helmet (H). Action area: head. Protection: 3 LP. Coat of mail (C). Action area: trunk (values 2, 3 and 4). Protection: 4 LP. Reinforced armbands and greaves (A) (G). Action area: arms and legs. Protection: 2 LP / Special ability: Superior lethal mirror. When you roll a 6 in a damage roll, the hireling leader will automatically cast this charm, channelling part of his vital energy against you. Therefore, although the hireling will continue to receive your strike and damage as usual, part of that damage bounces back: you lose 3 damage points at that very moment, regardless of the armor you are wearing.

→ If you succeed in such a titanic battle: 377
→ If you are crushed by your enemy, go to section 277, but don't lose this page or forget that you are in section 242.

243

As you move across the room under the dim light of your lamp, you think that you see something of interest in a corner, on one of the walls. You approach out of curiosity, and begin to rub the wall with your hand to remove a layer of wet dirt, discovering a strange symbol carved in the stone. You look at it closely and discern a thin, square recess, possibly some kind of door or trapdoor. After pressing in one corner, you finally disengage it, making this panel slide to your left, opening slowly with a subtle scraping sound. But what lies hidden inside is even more surprising, as you discover some kind of puzzle. At least, that's what you think when you look at the strange vertical pad carved in stone and composed of eighteen small cells. Some of these cells are empty, while others contain placed pieces where you see different letters. Also, three of these small cells are turned as a diamond, as if you have to insert the missing tiles this way. At the bottom of the pad is a drawer full of square tiles, with the various letters of the alphabet carved upon their faces. You don't have any doubt that these tiles are supposed to be inserted into the empty cells, as from their size and shape they will fit perfectly. But you don't have a clue as to the order in which they must be inserted to achieve its unknown purpose...

→ Next page...

- If you want to try and solve this puzzle, remember that you have a drawer full of many tiles featuring the letters of the alphabet. From what you can deduce, these tiles must be inserted into the empty cells, and three of them must be inserted on end, like a diamond...

- If you think that you have deciphered this puzzle, you only have to follow the instructions given... You'll know that you have been successful if you read the following: 'Terrible is the life of the one who wants to unveil the mysteries of Urowen.' Do not continue reading if this is not the first sentence of the section you turn to; you must now restart this section, as the pad is still a true mystery to you.

* Special note: if you are a thief and you want it so, your unique skills automatically allow you to solve the puzzle. You won't need to decipher anything; just go to section 332 and keep on reading. In case you don't want to take this advantage, you can try to solve the puzzle like the rest of the characters.

→ If you can't solve the puzzle, or you don't want to waste your time solving this so-called enigma, simply be on your way and forget about the mysterious pad: 257

244

◻ **Black tiger:** Fangs and claws (SK). Damage: 1d6+4 / SK 5 / LP: 29 / Armor: Thick fur and skin. Action area: whole body (values 1 to 6). Protection: 3 LP / Special ability: Fangs attack. If this beast rolls a 6 in a damage roll, it has pierced your flesh with its long fangs and then violently shaken its head, inflicting serious damage. Therefore, at the beginning of each subsequent combat round, you lose 2 life points due to blood loss. You lose these life points right before making each opposed attack roll.

→ If you kill your enemy: 384
→ If the black tiger defeats you: 396

245

The fight has gone well, very well, as your opponent was really difficult to beat. ↑ Because of your success, you gain 1 experience point (write this down on your character file), and great satisfaction for having beaten two opponents without a moment's respite. However, your troubles are far from over, for when you look over at the dwarf you see that he fights three opponents at the same time. You immediately try to help him again, but one of these strangers blocks your way. Right then you see another opponent pouncing on you, but then something totally unexpected happens. Keep on reading.

→ Go to section 260.

When you finally recover your breath and your heart beats normally again, you look around to see that you are within an area of thick vegetation placed between two hills. Right then, a dim glow attracts your attention, so you walk towards this light. You walk along the small valley and hide among the feathery branches of a tall bush, trying to remain unnoticed, as you see something from your position that is very interesting.

In the distance before you stands a large building with huge open doors, although its portcullis is down, blocking the entrance. Beyond these bars is a fire, and sitting beside it is a guard. This fortress is protected by very tall walls, but you notice that there is a large wooden shed nearby, not far from the outside wall. You creep towards the shed, but suddenly come upon a new fence forming a pen. What is being held inside this pen really surprises you, as you find an oversized aurochs with massive horns; a powerful animal belonging to the largest and most feared of the bovine races on Urowen. Fortunately, the animal is completely relaxed, almost asleep you would dare to say, and your presence seems to be of little interest to the unperturbed beast.

You memorise all that your eyes see to then share this valuable information to the elves, as what you have discovered so far proves that Dhaliara's suspicions were correct. You are in a kind of large laboratory, a place where Krénator carries out his experiments, crossbreeding dangerous animals with humans, elves and dwarfs. You now approach the large wooden building and see that the door is closed, but it is only secured by a thick bar blocking the entrance. Thanks to that, you immediately move it out of the way and cautiously step inside. Your surprise is even greater now, as you are astonished to find many animals from different species here, locked inside large cages set side by side. You see a mountain lion, a saber-tooth tiger and a pitch-black feline. You can also see a type of reptile that reminds you of a dragon, although its size is rather smaller and its body is flat to the ground. Two small bear cubs curl up in another cage, while in a cage of huge dimensions there is an animal you have never seen before: a majestic specimen featuring long fangs, oversized ears and an elongated snout that almost touches the ground.

After having inspected this exotic stable a little longer, you decide to move on, not wanting to alarm the animals and subsequently draw undesired attention towards you. You leave the building with the satisfaction of having fulfilled your mission, as it would seem that the suspicions of the elves about the practices of Krénator are utterly correct. However, you decide to investigate a bit more, and you head back to the entrance where the guard was sitting. But something totally unexpected happens on your way there, as while you move forward among the bushes, you see an enormous beast on top of one of the nearby hills, a creature that seems to have come out of nowhere. Right then, the clouds part and you get an immediate lump in your throat as the light reveals a mighty, muscular beast. This monstrosity looks at you directly and points an enormous battle axe in your direction; it has detected you, and just a moment later the beast is running towards you.

It is a real hulk, oversized and terrifying as it seems to be both human and animal. Both essences have combined to give birth to a monstrosity half-man, half-aurochs; a beast that sends shivers down your spine. The body of the aurochs remains almost intact, although its size and physical strength has grown. Its four powerful legs now finish in deadly hooves that can strike with devastating power. In the place where you would find the neck and the head of an aurochs, there is now a grotesque human trunk, horrible and deformed, with longer than normal arms, and its chest and shoulders are covered with a thick black fur that makes its powerful mass of muscles even more intimidating. In addition, the face has also changed, as its features are now a combination of both victims. The nose has widened and the jaw protrudes much more, and the eyes now sink into the skull. Two oversized horns, strong and curved, crown the top of its horrible head. Standing, this monstrosity is taller than you by far, and its disproportionate size is even more frightening.

Intimidated and fearing for your life, you get ready for the impeding battle. It is going to be something quite savage...

* **Author's note:** to defeat this toughest of enemies, don't hesitate to use everything at your disposal, such us every item you have in your leather bag, because if you are defeated, mind that there are much worse fates than death.

◘ **Krénator deputy:** Double-edged battle axe (STR). Damage: 1d6+6 / STR 6 / LP: 40 / Armor: Thick fur and skin. Action area: whole body except the head (values 1 to 5). Protection: 4 LP / Special ability: Extreme fierceness. If this beast's life points drop below 7, an uncontrollable rage will take hold of it. As a consequence, it won't roll a 1 or a 2 from that point on. Re-roll any dice showing one of these values / Thundering roar. If the beast rolls a 6 in an opposed attack roll and wins that roll, not only does it have a chance to wound you, but it also roars powerfully while it does so. This thundering roar will make the earth move under your feet, temporarily stunning you. Therefore, deduct 1 point from your next opposed attack.

→ If you survive this battle of titans: 293
→ If this monstrosity defeats you: 387

247

Brutally overwhelmed by the lethal sistöliums, which have seriously injured you and caused major blood loss, you flee desperately to try and save your life. You hurriedly return back to the surface, as the only thing that you wish to see right then is the light of Estrion. Fortunately, sistöliums seem to be satisfied with the blood that you have spilled, as they seemingly haven't chased you from the scene of the attack.

↓ Unfortunately, during your crazy retreat, you have lost not only your dignity, but also 1 experience point due to your behaviour. Erase this from your character file.

You stand again before the three wooden constructions with their corresponding entrances to the mines. You finally have some time to rest and recover, but you know the future that's awaiting you. → Go back to section 270 and choose the same tunnel if you want to take your revenge on the sistöliums, or try another, hoping for better luck...

248

Despite all your effort, all of the combats fought and won against your enemies, and all of the missions that you have fulfilled, simple greed has been your downfall, undermining your honor and the good reputation you had built up so far. But who gives a damn about honor and reputation when you have vast riches to live on? (↑ You win 1 experience point for having reached this point). The answer to that question is clear in your mind, so you decide to escape alone, to flee towards a comfortable life, far from the dangers of war. Therefore, you move away from the city to find a safe place where you cannot easily be found. You're not sure of the best direction to take, but you decide to follow a path that follows the coast, seemingly heading to the east. You know you will have to take great risks to protect your booty along the long trip you have to make to reach a safe place, but you are willing to take that risk. You decide to go from village to village without drawing too much attention to yourself, moving away from Krénator's domain and, by extension, from war. You might even hire the services of a mercenary to guard you... Be that as it may, you decide that the best thing you can do is to go as unnoticed as long as possible until you reach a safe place... but, as it is usually said, that's another story.

Long after, now an old man sitting by a big fireplace in your cozy home, on top of a hill in the fertile lands of Berwald, you remember your exciting moments in the city of Wastmur, where you discovered a wondrous surprise that changed your life forever...

Although you betrayed those who trusted you, there is no doubt that you have come far, much farther than anyone would have expected when you started your adventures. Luck smiled on you after all, making your future something far better than you would ever have dared to dream of. Because of your dishonorable decision, you are far from becoming a real 'Hero of Urowen', as you once hoped... Who gives a damn about honor when you possess so many treasures? That is why nobody can deny that you've had a much better ending than that of most so-called 'Heroes'. Such is life in the relentless Lands of Urowen, a highly dangerous place, where you never know what each new estrio may bring. Keep on reading.

→ Go to section 400.

249

Intrigued by what Rámada may have to teach you, you walk to the north of the city, as Tórkuod told you and, after asking several people, you finally find your destination; a big, beautiful mansion with magnificent entrance doors. Without a moment's hesitation, you knock several times using a knocker shaped as the head of a dragon, and the door is soon opened for you. To your surprise, it is Tórkuod himself who comes to welcome you and, by the expression on his face, he seems to recognize you immediately.

"Oh, it is you traveller... I see that you finally decided to pay us a visit! Well, well... I'm really glad to see you here! But don't just stand there, come in, come in if you are looking for the great Rámada!"

"It's a pleasure to see you again. As you say, I'm rather curious about what your lady may have to teach me, and I'm bringing plenty of zaifas to pay for it."

"I told you 80 zaifas, didn't I?"

"That's correct, and I'm willing to start my training."

"Well, you have come at a good time! Usually the house is full of apprentices, but at the moment we only have a girl aged ten liznars, a young and promising amazon who wants to know the secret ways of fire... But, come in... Let's go to the kitchen and have a drink. Rámada will meet us there soon."

You follow Tórkuod along several of the mansion's corridors to a spacious kitchen where a servant is cooking a tasty stew. Your host hands you a wine jar before serving a generous measure for himself. But you don't have the time to talk much more, as Rámada herself soon enters the room.

You are rather surprised by her appearance, as she is a muscled yet beautiful amazon aged around thirty five liznars, with a shaved head, which contrasts powerfully in comparison to the beautiful long hair that women usually have in Bälkaar. A striking spiral tattoo highlights the back of her head, and her penetrating gaze seems to carefully evaluate you.

"So tell me, Tórkuod, who is this?" she asks suddenly with an intimidating voice.

"My lady, this is a traveller I met in the streets of the city, and who is interested in hiring your services."

"Have you been told my price?" Rámada asks you.

"80 zaifas."

"And do you have that much? I want to see the money before starting your training, although you will pay me in five estrios, when you are fully satisfied with what you have learnt, as you must know that you won't be allowed to leave my house during that time. I will teach only one technique of my choice, the one that I think most suitable once I've evaluated your abilities. That technique will be related to magic or steel, you'll be allowed to choose that. Do you agree with my conditions?"

"I do."

"Excellent. I see that Tórkuod does his job correctly. And now tell me stranger, what will you choose, magic or steel...?"

→ If you are a sorcerer, a Sàgrast Knight Monk or an alchemist, you should choose magic. Go to section 280.

→ If you are a hunter, a warrior, a minstrel or a thief, your best option is steel. Go to section 294.

250

You have done exceedingly well in your battle against the two lions. Your strikes have been so lethal that a bestial rage now takes hold of your body and you pounce on those that remain. Terrified, they run to escape when they see how agitated you are, but now that you are not the master of your own actions, you begin a relentless pursuit through the forest, unprepared to leave any of them alive. Many sounds and wild actions mingle within your troubled mind, and you seem to be living all of this at breakneck speed. You lose contact with reality and think that you've lost consciousness. To your sorrow, that's not what happens, but you simply don't remember anything of this period of time...

When you reopen your eyes you are back in your own self, master of your body and actions. (Once again, the effects of the transformation have disappeared, so you are playing again with the attributes on your character file, not applying the modifiers of the curse). With blurred vision and relaxed muscles, you seem to have had a good nights rest, as it is now dawn and you don't remember anything from your first battle against the lions. Suddenly, as you think of them, you instantly become alert again, as you don't know if danger is close by or not. But when you look around, everything is much worse than you would have expected. Although you seem to be safe, the scene before your eyes is truly shocking. Several dismembered mountain lion corpses are spread before you, broken mercilessly into a strange mass of blood and guts. There are traces of skin and bone fragments everywhere, and you see two lion heads completely cut off, with empty eye sockets that form two dark pits in their bloodied skulls. The stench is really nauseating, an offensive mixture of guts and dead meat now beginning to rot under the continuous buzzing of the hundreds of flies that have attended this feast.

Now, really sick in your stomach, you desperately need to leave this awful place as you are about to puke. You try to resist this feeling by breathing slowly, but when you turn to move you become horrified by what you can do, as you are certain that what you are seeing is all your own work...

Right then, in a vivid flashback, you remember scenes from the previous night. You see yourself fighting, killing and eating the bodies of the fierce lions and what's worse, killing Nëmster, your own horse, to feed with his meat still warm...

You can't avoid it any longer. Vomit pours out of your open mouth; a cascade of blood and raw meat that you had previously eaten enthusiastically. At the same time, you can't help but look at the remains of your horse, atrociously mutilated, cut open and partly eaten, bearing the marks of your own teeth. The curse of the witch, that until this moment was something that you could live with, now becomes a genuine nightmare, a burden you have to rid yourself of as soon as possible. You feel a great urgency to be on your way, to locate the mines and find the elements you must gather to then return to Bälkaar. You recover a little and start gathering your equipment, desperately keeping your unsettled mind numb to save yourself from the reality of your grim sentence. You soon begin walking to your destination, moving rapidly away from this place full of death.

↓ After the unexpected death of Nëmster, delete your mount from your character file, as you have lost your precious horse. From now on, you'll have to travel by foot.

→ Go to section 270.

251

After spending a long time inspecting every detail of the grill, the walls, the floor and even the ceiling, you finally discover a small ring hidden on the wall, almost completely covered over with mud. You release it from the enveloping mud and pull it firmly. What happens next surprises you, as a small trapdoor opens nearby, revealing a kind of swivel wheel with several grips, surely the necessary leverage to trigger the mechanism that will open the gate. You should have thought that something of the sort would exist, although now that you think about it, you are surprised that this wheel is only found on the outside, on this side of the grill. That can only mean one thing, you decide after thinking it through... the barrier was built to stop people from leaving...

You place your lamp on the ground and grab the wheel with both hands, and then pull on it strongly to make it turn. Initially, nothing happens, as the old mechanism seems to be stuck, but after trying several times you finally move it a little and the grill begins to rise. With great effort you encourage the gears and chains to move further and finally lift the heavy grill to waist height. Satisfied with the result, you grab your lamp and swiftly cross to the other side. Now breathing calmly, you proceed deeper underground.

Moving along the tunnel, which abruptly slopes further downward, you see great cobwebs hanging above you, and spot their weavers moving upon the walls. Not wishing to be distracted, you focus on your goal, and when you check where you next set your feet, a small reflection on the ground ahead draws your attention. You immediately approach this spot to see what it is and discover something metallic partially hidden under the mud. You free it from its muddy resting place and are surprised to find that you now hold a small bracelet.

Intrigued by this unexpected find, you clean the mud from its surface and now scrutinize the runes that cover every surface. These are very strange symbols that you have never seen before in your life, incredible characters that seem to imbue it with powers, as while you hold the bracelet you feel a great energy coming from it; it even warms with the contact of your skin. Thinking that it can only be a magical object, you slip it on immediately, neglecting the possible danger from doing so. Fortunately, you weren't wrong, as from the moment you wear it round your wrist, your senses sharpen so that you seem to see more clearly in the darkness. ↑ Write down the bracelet on your character file. As you are wearing it round one of your wrists, it does not fill a slot of your leather bag.

- Duÿmor mystic bracelet. It adds 1 PER point as long as you are wearing it.

→ Go to section 282.

252

Your terrible opponent has brought you to the ground, crushing and humiliating you. But to escape alive you will have to defeat him, and that won't be an easy task because, as a consequence for having been defeated, from now on one piece of armor will grant you 1 point less of protection, as it has been seriously damaged during the fight. In addition, you also permanently lose 1 base life point. Update your character file accordingly, stand up and return to section 227 to try and kill Bors of Raidyón... Before leaving this section, don't forget to read the next paragraph:

* **Special ability of this section: Escape.** If you have come back here for the second time (enduring the consequences of having been defeated again), and think that you won't be able to defeat your enemy, you'll be able to attempt to escape, as the ongoing chaos in the tavern makes it possible. If you try to flee by taking advantage of the fact that several fighting hirelings stand between yourself and your enemy, giving you time enough to escape, go to section 312.

253

You stand still, in complete silence, and would swear that you hear a creak some distance away. You immediately look in that direction but see nothing unusual ahead, however, your gaze lingers there for a minute and eventually you notice movement. Between two tree trunks, you briefly see what you would say is long hair, even if you can't be assured that your eyes hadn't simply played a trick on you.

Alert and now ready for a confrontation, you run to the spot where the hair would be, but you don't find anything unusual. You look carefully at the ground to try and discover any footsteps, but there is nothing, absolutely nothing that indicates that something, or someone, was ever there. You relax and resume your journey, remaining alert, just in case.

→ Go to section 291.

254

"I'd love to face that bastard, but I'm afraid that I'm just not prepared to drink that much," you say to your companion. "I would surely make a fool of myself. That guy seems to be able to stomach anything."

"You can be sure of that. As I've already told you, he's unbeatable at drinking..."

"Well, back to our business, do you think that your master would want to hire me?" you ask, driving the conversation towards your issue of interest. "Let's go and talk at a table with a jar between us. Waitress, please, another round for us!" you say to the girl waiting at the bar, before draining your drink in one continuous draught. Your companion does the same, keen for the possibility of getting drunk for free.

"Thank you, my friend. I think that's a wonderful idea!"

So, once you hold new drinks in your hands, you head over to an isolated table where you'll be able to resume your conversation.

→ Go to section 199.

255

Despite your initial surprise, you overcome the fierce creature. When the mountain lion finally falls motionless to the ground, your blood begins to boil in your veins, and you feel strangely euphoric, anxious to keep on fighting. And you're going to need these potent feelings, as when you look around you can see that a whole pride of mountain lions, with not less than six members, is now desiring to taste your blood. Right then, two of these great animals pounce on you at the same time with the clear intention of killing you. A new battle begins...

- This time, you fight two enemies at the same time. Play each turn the usual way but, at the end of each turn (whether you have won the opposed attack roll or not), you receive an additional injury to represent the attack of the second lion, because, as you are facing the other lion at that moment, you can't defend yourself from the second. Therefore, make the usual attack rolls for the second animal. Firstly, roll for damage location and then roll for damage with 1d6+2. If you defeat the first lion, the second one will back away and you will be the winner of the fight.

◻ **Second mountain lion:** Fangs and claws (SK). Damage: 1d6+2 / SK 3 / LP: 26 / Armor: Thick fur and skin. Action area: whole body (values 1 to 6). Protection: 1 LP / Special ability: Lethal swipe. If the lion rolls a 6 in a damage roll, it has strongly sunk its claws into your flesh, inflicting serious damage. Therefore, at the beginning of each subsequent combat round, you lose 1 life point due to blood loss. You lose this life point immediately before making the opposed attack roll.

→ If you defeat the lions: 222
→ If you are defeated by these lethal animals: 205

256

After deciding which tunnel to follow, you start moving slowly to the light of the she-elf's ring. Not sure of what you may find ahead, you are completely alert and constantly checking where you set your feet, knowing that danger is all around. You walk for a long stretch along a tunnel that descends constantly, going down into the depths of the land. In addition, the dampness of the atmosphere becomes more noticeable, and there are areas where the walls and the ground are rather wet. Fortunately, you only slip on the wet ground once, luckily steadying yourself at the last moment.

With a hand following the wet wall to maintain balance more easily, you keep on walking, thinking that you may be wasting your time in this expansive labyrinth of underground passageways. But you haven't come this far to turn back now, so you move forward, knowing that nobody would take the trouble to fake the presence of a dragon if there wasn't a good reason for it. You are thinking about these circumstances when a strange noise draws your attention. It is a kind of fluttering sound that makes you stop and stand still, listening attentively. A new flutter now calms your nerves, as you think that you have recognized this sound, even if you think your explanation rather unlikely. That is why you keep on walking and soon reach a room lit with a torch that's set in a bracket on the wall. What you find here is a good few farm animals, locked in small wooden pens: hens, goats and even a couple of pigs. There's nothing here to delay you so you keep on walking along another tunnel.

→ Go to section 329.

257

Keen to leave this cold room as soon as possible, you approach the three exits to see if you can discover anything that will help you to choose the way forward. But these three passages each seem to be exactly the same, offering nothing to help you make an informed decision. Once again, you will have to rely on your intuition to successfully negotiate your way through these dangerous mines.

You now look at them according to the tunnel by which you entered the square room...

→ If you choose the tunnel to your left: 268
→ If you follow the passageway in front of you: 278
→ If you'd rather try the one to your right: 288

258

The monstrous beast has crushed you. It has humiliated you and there's no other way to move forward until you kill it. As a penalty for having been defeated, you must choose one of the following options before fighting your enemy again: lose 1 experience point, delete 1 item from your character file or decide that one piece of armor now protects you 1 point less, as it has been seriously damaged during battle. Choose one of these options, update your character file, and then go back to the noted section from where you came.

* Special ability of this section: Escape. If you have already returned to section 258 several times, and now believe that you won't be able to defeat your enemy, you can try to escape into the dark night. You won't have to roll dice to escape, but you will have to endure the following consequences:

↓ You lose 1 experience point.
↓ You lose 1 object from your leather bag.
↓ You lose 1 piece of armor, of your choice (H, C, A or G).

→ If you choose to escape, update your character file, and then go to section 246.

259

You keep on moving slowly forward, your eyes searching the shadows before you, as the last thing that you want is to turn these tunnels into your tomb. You walk along a straight stretch until a sound draws your attention. Instantly alarmed, you stop and listen... Nothing of concern happens as you silently wait, although the sound, weak and continuous, comes from somewhere not far ahead. Moving forward cautiously, your fears subside after only a few steps, as it is now clear that what you've heard is some kind of underground stream. With renewed strength, you keep on moving forward until you discover a landslide partially blocking your way. Although part of the ceiling has collapsed into a ragged opening, you are fortunately able to pass without difficulty. From below, within the hole, you hear a small subterranean stream that seems to run parallel to the tunnel in which you stand.

Attracted by this discovery, you attempt to use your light to illuminate this space below, however, you can't see much in the total darkness and so quickly forget about this landslide as your mind resumes its focus on your mission.

→ Go to section 282.

260

Right then, a strong, rushing sound draws your attention and you look at the ceiling, as something is happening there that makes everyone freeze in shock. In the middle of the great common room, just above Nígodar, a thick black cloud suddenly forms and immediately shoots lightning at the dwarf's opponents as a strong wind throws numerous objects through the air. You then look around, intimidated by the situation, and see Süod-Helbórian standing several steps away with a look of deep concentration on his face; he is undoubtedly the creator of this terrible windstorm.

"Quickly, take him from here!" Süod-Helbórian yells, momentarily looking from the storm that he has summoned.

Following his instructions, you run to the dwarf and hurriedly pull him outside, while many others also jostle their way to the door. Taking advantage of the chaos, you finally get out of the tavern, and once you are in the streets of Bälkaar, you head to the outskirts, attempting to do so unnoticed.

→ Go to section 201.

261

After paying attention to your surroundings for some time, you neither hear nor see anything unusual, so you decide to move forward. But then something happens that terrifies you, as the ghostly shape of a black tiger emerges from the thicket and instantly attacks. Unfortunately, this unnoticed lethal enemy has surprised you, so before beginning the fight as usual make a damage roll for the tiger (first damage location roll, then damage roll itself). This represents the first attack of your enemy, to which you were unable to defend. The fight will then start as normal with an opposed attack roll. → Go to section 244.

262

"Who wants to fight Cäshdor?"

Attracted by these words, you approach to see what is happening and discover a man bleeding profusely from his nose, lying on the ground before Cäshdor, who smiles at the many curious spectators that have assembled. He raises both arms to the sky in a sign of victory. By his side, a rather old man is encouraging people to participate.

"Come on! Isn't there anyone here brave enough to match their strength against Cäshdor? Double your zaifas if you defeat him!"

Interested by the possibility of multiplying your coins, you look closely the opponent that you must defeat. Cäshdor a real hulk, a giant whose shoulders are far wider than yours, with bulky arms and strong legs as thick as tree trunks. He has also a fierce, horrible face, with an ugly scar disfiguring his left cheek.

"Eh, my friend, you look like a worthy candidate!" the old man says to you. "Do you want to try your luck?"

"How would be the fight proceed... rules?

- As in previous occasions, you won't be allowed to use weapons, nor magic charms or potions; it will be a straight fist fight. Your damage is 1d6 and you'll be allowed to roll on STR, SK or MAG, at your choice.

- As for placing bets, contrary to what has previously occured, there is no limit this time. You can bet any amount you desire, and you will double it if you win the fight. If, for example, you bet 100 zaifas and you win the fight, you will receive both the coins you bet, plus 100 zaifas more. If you lose the fight, forget about the money you've bet.

- If you decide to fight Cäshdor, here are his attributes:

◻ **Cäshdor:** fists (STR). Damage: 1d6 / STR 4 / LP: 26 / Armor: Hardened leather breastplate (C). Action area: trunk (values 2, 3 and 4). Protection: 3 LP / Special ability: Accurate punch. Due to his great experience in fist fighting, and the many street fights he has fought, Cäshdor has +1 in all of his damage location rolls, so it is more likely for him to hit you in the arms or the head, and he will never aim a punch to your legs.

- Once you have finished the combat, or if you preferred not to fight this opponent, go back to the streets of Bälkaar to be on your way.

→ Go to section 335.

263

It is said that the life of every hero gives birth to a legend. Undoubtedly, if it continues this way, yours will be written in golden letters. You have become a skilled spy and warrior, so your skills will be very valuable and may even be decisive in the horrendous war that is about to begin in the Lands of Urowen...

After all that you have lived through during the night, with your mission now fulfilled you flee to safety with the elves as soon as possible, as there is no doubt that alarms are about to sound all over the city because of your actions and for the actions of the other elves. That is why you go directly to the port of Wastmur, as you are eager to reach the ship where you will meet Dhaliara again. Your group travels very quickly, hidden in the shadows of the night, so you are somewhat surprised to discover that you are the last to arrive, as by then all of the elves, skilled warriors each and every one, have succeeded in their missions and safely returned to the ship.

A smiling Dhaliara welcomes you when she sees that you have rescued Eddmont. As soon as you come aboard you hear someone shout 'ropes away', and the vessel moves slowly away from the city where, before too long, the streets will be crowded with people in revolt due to all of the mischief your group has caused.

"Set our course for Verinfes!" Dhaliara orders the elves. "We must get there as soon as possible to inform Brádoc and the king about all we have discovered tonight, as this information may be crucial for the development of the war. Let's hope that the winds are favorable and we therefore reach our destination soon."

So you begin the journey that will take you from the enemy city of Wastmur to Verinfes, where you will finally find refuge in a safe place. Fortunately, luck seems to be on your side for such an important journey, as the favourable winds grant you great speed, helping you to reach your distant destination sooner than expected.

As soon as he knows of your arrival, Brádoc, the Major Soldier of the city, wishes to see you personally, and you are therefore driven to the stronghold of Verinfes. Dhaliara speaks on behalf of your group and presents Brádoc with the reports that had been written during your long journey across the sea, using all of the information unearthed during your dangerous missions in Wastmur. The Major Soldier then asks to be left alone with the she-elf and they talk together while the rest of you wait in another room, where you are regaled with plenty of food and well watered by the best wine in town.

Dhaliara now approaches. "Brádoc desires to talk with you – alone," she says. "Report yourself to him. He's waiting for you."

You immediately follow Dhaliara's instructions and leave all the elves of the snow behind to meet the Major Soldier of Verinfes.

"Come in and have a seat," Brádoc says as he sees you. "I'm glad that you are back, safe and sound. I sent you on a really risky mission, and you not only succeeded when you killed that amazon, but you helped Dhaliara in Wastmur, rescuing the king's cousin. When you left I promised that if you succeeded in your mission, you would have another great reward waiting for you here. So it will be, if you stay with us. Dhaliara and her elves of the snow will soon leave for Krindaslon, and I don't want you to follow them. That is why I ask you to stay here in Verinfes, as we will need people like you in this war that is about to begin. If you do so, the king himself, Xon Ágraster, has asked me to tell you that he is extremely grateful for Eddmont's release. Because of that, he offers you not only a place on the honor guard of Verinfes, commanding a garrison, but he also promises high pay, concordant to your new position, and the title of Guardian of the Kingdom, the highest distinction in our army. This distinction also places you in command of another army unit and provides a respectable amount of lands nearby. You'll be by my side, and you'll be able to build up a good future for yourself in this kingdom. It is a more than generous offer, as I've very rarely seen the king be so generous, but you have won his trust by safely returning Eddmont. So, what do you think? Do you accept my offer?"

→ If you decide to accept Brádoc's generous offer: 326
→ If you decide to tactfully decline it: 337

264

Against the odds, given your superiority in hand-to-hand combat due to your transformation, you have been defeated by the mountain lions, They now lick their lips in satisfaction, your blood staining their jaws.

↓ Due to the many bites and swipes you have suffered during the fight, a piece of armor has been so seriously damaged that it will now grant 1 point less of protection. You can choose the piece of armor: H, C, A or G. The one you choose will lose 1 point of protection. Update your character file with this new value, as this deduction lasts for the rest of the game, until you can purchase replacement armor.

↓ If you come back to this section (for a second, a third time, and so on) you will keep on losing 1 protection point from a piece of armor.

→ Stand again, go back to 235 and kill these two mountain lions to continue on with your adventures.

265

To wild cheers and applause, you stagger half drunk to your feet. Görlok's fat body is now slumped on the ground in front of you, unconscious. When he passed out his head hit the table with such force that it violently shook out the contents of the jars still to be consumed. As the winner, you rightly claim the zaifas you have won (add these to your character file).

When you look around you see that Toljröm approaches your fallen opponent. He stops before the prone body and spits a thick green phlegm on him, no doubt a retaliation concocted for such an august occasion. He immediately moves towards you and offers his shoulder to lean on, as the alcohol makes you stagger and it is somewhat difficult to stand erect (deduct 1 point from all of your opposed attack rolls in your next combat due to the effects of the booze).

"Come on, let me help you to a table. We've got to celebrate this victory!" your companion says, smiling broadly.

So you walk towards two free chairs and immediately have a seat. Toljröm momentarily disappears into the crowd and then quickly returns with two tankards of beer crowned with foam. He sets one of them before you with great pleasure, hitting the jar on the table as he does so.

"Here you are. You earned it when you beat that swine!"

"Thanks," you answer unenthusiastically, as the last thing on earth that you want right now is to keep on drinking.

However, you try your best to bounce back from the drunkenness, as this is the right moment to gain some information.

"Back to our previous business," you continue, beginning to feel a little more sober. "Do you think that your master would want to hire me?"

"I don't know. As I've told you, we've just come back from a long journey. If it had been before our departure, I'm sure he would have, but now..."

"Where have you been?"

"I shouldn't really talk about that, but damn it, you're now one of us," Toljröm answers, his spirits raised by the booze and the emotion of the moment after your great victory. "We were following the orders of Krénator himself."

Toljröm receives your full attention when you hear these words.

"Yes, it was the wizard himself who hired my master, Bors of Raidyón. The mission led us to the Desert of Stone, specifically to the oases of Alda-Xakheç, where we met Assharid Almansshura, a chief of chiefs who leads the clans of the desert. He rules over all the nomad tribes. He is a very intimidating man, dressed completely in black, with a tagelmust that covers all of his head and face, except for the eyes. I can tell you that I was often frightened in that place, as the nomads of the desert are highly dangerous. Besides, escorting Assharid were the so-called Asshitas Riders, who were riding their famous dromedaries, legendary all over Urowen, as only the bravest among their people earn the honor to ride those desert animals. They were all really strange, and they have those savage customs that give me the chills..."

"And what was your exact mission in those lands?" you ask impatiently when you realise that Toljröm pauses for a long time, absent-minded.

"Oh, we were representing Krénator himself and we were supposed to convince Assharid Almansshura to join our side in the upcoming war."

"And did you succeed?"

"Absolutely. The wizard can count on the hordes of the nomad tribes of the desert, who are being assembled right now by Almansshura himself."

When you hear this valuable information, your mind begins to race, as it would seem that the intelligence from the elves was mistaken. This man isn't a spy from Verinfes, as suspected, but some kind of emissary in charge of the recruitment of troops for Krénator. You now know that the tribes of the desert have joined the ranks of your enemies, and you're anxious to report this fact to Dhaliara...

"Toljröm, you damned idiot! You would talk to this foreigner about our business?" You jump at the sound of the powerful voice saying these words, as you hadn't realised that their owner was so near. When you see terror on Toljröm's face, you immediately turn and see that one of the men accompanying Bors of Raidyón is standing right behind you. He is a fierce opponent exhibitng angry, threatening behaviour, as he has clearly overheard your discussion.

"I'm sorry but this stupid Toljröm has sentenced you to death!" the stranger adds, grabbing his weapon. "You've heard too much, and I can't let it pass!"

You hardly have time to react, as your enemy raises his broadsword and directly aims at your head. You are lucky enough to dodge it and the sword resoundingly hits the table, chipping the wood... Chaos then takes hold of the room, as the call girls shout and run in all directions, afraid of danger. Those who try to protect the girls demonstrate bravado, while those who desire to take money from the gaming tables insult and punch each other without restraint. In the blink of an eye the tavern becomes a battlefield where there is only one rule: everyman for himself.

↑ You win 1 experience point for defeating Görlok and having learned Toljröm's valuable information.

- Get ready for the impending fight, as after quickly standing, your enemy with the broadsword is already preparing to strike again...

→ Go to section 301.

266

You stand still and silent trying to sense anything unusual, but you hear only the sound of the breeze moving leaves and branches, and your eyes are also unable to detect anything unusual. After standing still for a long while, you decide that you should just relax and continue your journey to reach to your destination as soon as possible. However, you think it is better to stay alert, just in case.

→ Go to section 291.

Once total darkness has fallen over the city, you head to your objective to attack it openly, head-on, almost as a suicide mission. Thanks to Dhaliara's instructions, you soon locate the great building where the cousin of the King of Verinfes is being held prisoner. You then take up positions some distance from the gates of the mansion, with Kúdinar leading the way. He starts gathering his energies. A short nod of his head tells the rest of you that he is ready, so you must stay alert, prepared for action, as you have a very simple plan. Once the elf has destroyed the door, the group will sprint into the great mansion, looking for a way down to the dungeons, killing anyone that comes across your path. You can't foresee too much in such a direct mission with a lack of reliable information, so you place your trust in the power of your weapons.

"Nekoy sudläs, sífales dáuramar!" After saying those words, a huge, deep green fireball flies out of Kúdinar's hands and instantly smashes into the building's gates, blowing them to pieces. The moment of truth is here, so you run into the sinister mansion. Get ready for battle, as your welcome is much more hostile than you had expected...

- Firstly, remember the characteristics of your new weapon, the Scepter of Sàgrast, and don't ever forget them, as they could save your life.

- Secondly, remember that you now have 100 life points, but unlike what usually occurs, you won't regain lost life points between battles, unless the text specifically tells you so. From now on you must only follow the book's instructions to know the LP you recover as you progress in your mission. For instance, in the following fights, if you defeat the fourth guard, you won't have your full 100 LP back, as you only recover the life points that the text indicates.

- In addition, potions that usually reveal their effects during a single combat will now do so during a full sequence of combats. For instance, the four combats that you are about to fight in a row against four guards will feature this circumstance.

- Now, give it your best shot to defend your life while your companions do the same around you against other enemies, as this building is heavily defended...

◘ **First guard:** Two-handed sword (SK). Damage: 1d6+4 / SK 5 / LP: 25 / Armor: Leather breastplate (C). Action area: trunk (values 2, 3 and 4). Protection: 3 LP. Helmet (H). Action area: head. Protection: 3 LP.

◘ **Second guard:** Two-handed axe (STR). Damage: 1d6+5 / STR 5 / LP: 30 / Armor: Leather breastplate (C). Action area: trunk (values 2, 3 and 4). Protection: 3 LP. Helmet (H). Action area: head. Protection: 2 LP. Leather armbands and greaves (A) (G). Action area: arms and legs. Protection: 1 LP.

◘ **Third guard:** Heavy mace (STR). Damage: 1d6+6 / STR 6 / LP: 33 / Armor: Leather breastplate (C). Action area: trunk (values 2, 3 and 4). Protection: 4 LP. Helmet (H). Action area: head. Protection: 3 LP. Leather armbands and greaves (A) (G). Action area: arms and legs. Protection: 2 LP / Special ability: Dodge. This opponent is very agile. Every time you try to hit him (that is to say, every time you make a damage roll), he will try to dodge. Roll a dice: if you roll a 6, your enemy has successfully dodged your blow and won't take any damage.

◘ **Fourth guard:** Heavy morningstar (STR). Damage: 1d6+7 / STR 6 / LP: 38 / Armor: Leather breastplate (C). Action area: trunk (values 2, 3 and 4). Protection: 4 LP. Helmet (H). Action area: head. Protection: 3 LP. Leather armbands and greaves (A) (G). Action area: arms and legs. Protection: 3 LP / Special ability: Dodge. This opponent is very agile. Every time you try to hit him (that is to say, every time you make a damage roll), he will try to dodge. Roll a dice: if you roll a 6, your enemy has successfully dodged your blow and won't take any damage. / Critical damage. When your enemy hits you, if he rolls a 6 in his damage roll (Damage: 1d6+7), not only has he inflicted 13 damage points, but he has also seriously injured you. Therefore, at the beginning of each subsequent combat round, you lose 2 life points due to bleeding. You lose these life points right before making the opposed damage roll.

→ If you defeat all of your enemies: 394
→ If you are defeated: 327

268

After walking for a long while along this cold and narrow tunnel, you suddenly feel very tired, so you stop for a few moments to regain your breath. Right then, you begin to feel worried, as despite all of the time now spent in the mines and the many tunnels you have travelled, you're yet to see any trace of the special plant you must find for the amazon's concoction. However, you know that no matter how deeply you may worry, you won't find anything without a thorough search, so you soon resume walking these tunnels once again.

But then a sudden gut feeling tells you that something is wrong...

■ You immediately stop and listen carefully, eager to discover what is now happening... Before you continue walking, roll a dice for PER with a difficulty of 5 to check if you can sense anything unusual. Remember, roll a dice and add the value of your PER attribute.

→ If the result is 5 or higher: 285
→ If the result is 4 or less: 300

269

Intimidated by the dark, descending tunnel, you begin to get nervous, knowing that you are wasting precious time. You quickly decide to head to the stone building with a small window that would allow you to peep inside. You cautiously make your way out and, after closing the door, go back to the carriage again. Keep on reading.

→ Go to section 371.

270

Base camp
(write this number down on your character file)

After walking at a steady pace under a dull grey sky you believe that you are near to your destination at mid estrio, as what you now lies before you is very close to what is drawn on the map. You see a wide plain covered with green knee-high grass, and in the distance beyond the plain rises a steep mountain, at whose foot, the great excavation that you are looking for must surely be waiting for you.

Now in good spirits, you establish a faster pace, encouraged by a cold breeze that promises rain. The last thing in the world that you need now is to enter the mines soaked with water. Walking in a straight line towards the mountain, you stumble upon some kind of abandoned old path. It's a badly maintained cobbled road that may have been built by the duÿmors, who could have used it to carry the minerals taken from the mines to their real home, down in the depths of the nearby Úreher Mountains. No matter what its original purpose was, you now find it useful, as in this isolated and uninhabited region of Urowen, you think that it is very likely to lead you directly to the abandoned mines. With that in mind, you keep on walking at a good pace until you find what you were looking for in the afternoon. You now stand before a huge excavation; a gigantic quarry full of ramps that are carved into the hard stone, leading on to the depths of the mines.

Overwhelmed by the impressive scale of this open space, you stop and look around, searching for a possible entrance. But, after long minutes of close observation, you see nothing suggesting an opening, so you decide to walk down one of the ramps, being careful of where you place your feet as everything is rather old and you fear a landslide that would drag you to a certain death. However, you descend quickly and, after walking some distance, discover some sort of man-made corridor that turns left beyond a massive rock that protrudes from the ground. You follow this new route which then leads on to a spacious area, also carved in stone, where you see three wooden buildings set against the wall. At a glance, they are all in bad condition, with one of their doors lying on the ground.

As you move closer, you realise that these are rather strange buildings, as they don't appear to have any depth; you begin to think that they are just wooden facades leaning against the stone wall. These suspicions are confirmed when you take a closer look. You peer inside the building without its door and find a small, completely empty room. At the back of that room, a wide tunnel begins, going down into the depths of the earth. There is no doubt that you have found the entrance to the mines, what you were looking for so intently. You think that the other two buildings may hide tunnels similar to the one you have already seen, meaning that you would have found three entrances, not one, and you will have to reluctantly choose one of them.

Unfortunately, your thoughts are confirmed when you open their doors; as feared, you will have to decide which of the three tunnels will lead you into the depths of the mines, at least, theoretically...

→ If you choose the first tunnel, the one with the door on the ground: 197
→ If you choose to go down the second tunnel: 224
→ If you want to try your luck with the third tunnel: 238

271

You make your decision and then walk along a winding tunnel that progressively descends, reaching further into the depths of the earth. Thankfully, everything seems to be empty and calm. That is why your surprise is rather enormous when you suddenly come across a silent stranger heading the other way. He pushes a wheelbarrow containing half of a recently slaughtered pig, his way lit by a lamp bound to this small cart. Everything suggests that he is the person taking care of the beast, and that he was about to feed it. But you don't have time to think about much more, as he releases his grip on the wheelbarrow and grabs his weapon to attack the intruder that has entered his domain...

◻ **Cavern keeper:** Cutlass (SK). Damage: 1d6+3 / SK 5 / LP: 27 / Armor: Leather breastplate (C). Action area: trunk (values 2, 3 and 4). Protection: 3 LP. Helmet (H). Action area: head. Protection: 3 LP. Leather armbands and greaves (A) (G). Action area: arms and legs. Protection: 1 LP / Special ability: Whip. In addition to his cutlass, this enemy holds an intimidating whip in his left hand. Each time he hits you, in addition to the regular damage of the cutlass, roll another dice. If the result is a 5 or 6, he has also whipped you. Therefore, you lose 1 life point, and the whip immobilizes one of your limbs: deduct 1 point in your following opposed attack roll.

→ If you defeat your enemy: 351
→ If your enemy kills you: 283

272

With a devastating, powerful blow, you make the amazon fall flat on the ground, where she dies after convulsing several times, with her body now lying in a great pool of blood. You immediately turn your head to look for the she-elf, who has also defeated her enemy, although she hasn't emerged unscathed, as you can clearly see that she is bleeding profusely from her left leg.

"Quickly, they have backup on the way!" your companion shouts after peeking back down the stairs. "Go ahead on your own and find Marok-häi! Get to the next floor and fulfil your mission! I'll watch your back."

You are surprised to see that the she-elf sheathes the daggers she has fought with and instead grabs two curved swords that have been hidden under her long cape. "Hurry up, don't waste any more time!" she cries right before going down the stairs, where you clearly hear the running footsteps of new enemies. No doubt your companion wants to take advantage of that narrow stairway, as she would be able to fight one enemy at a time without worrying about attacks from behind. You understand that there is much at stake and that you must maximise every moment, so you run up the stairs in front of you, leading to the upper floor of the tower. You are now aware that you have entered a mousetrap full of deadly enemies, but you can only try to succeed in your mission and fight as well as you can to try and save your life.

Now focused on every detail around you, you keep on moving. To your dismay, once you get to the upper floor you see another staircase going up even further still. No enemies hide in the room you are in, so you run towards the staircase that will take you higher up the tower. But your run comes to a sudden halt when a dust devil forms on the ground before you and you are forced to take several steps backward due to the force of the violent, swirling wind. Before your surprised eyes, the air starts to drag a huge pile of sand in circles, forming a strange creature that blocks your way. Distressed by what this monstrosity may be, you try to approach to the stairs, but there's no way to reach them. You don't have to wait long for the wind to subside, but you now look in disbelief at the strange creature that has arisen before your eyes. It is an oversized hulk, so tall than its hideous head almost touches the ceiling. Its body, also deformed and terrible, is truly frightening, and this monstrosity repeatedly beats its chest with two impressive arms. But the worst thing about it is its rough skin, as this unusual beast seems to be made only of solid stone. Now that the wind has abated, the stone monstrosity steps forward and is quickly upon you with a thunderous roar...

◻ **Earth elemental:** Fists of stone (STR). Damage: 1d6+3 / STR 5 / LP: 30 / Armor: Layer of stone. Action area: whole body (values 1 to 6). Protection: 4 LP / Special ability: Grip. If the earth elemental rolls a 6 in a damage roll, it has caught you in its arms and attempts to break your bones. Due to such a brutal attack, your breastplate will be damaged (regardless of the result of the damage location roll that will determine the LP you lose). Your breastplate is now permanently damaged, granting 1 point less of protection (update your character file). If the elemental crushes you in its grip again, you'll have to repeat this process; once your breastplate is reduced to 0 points, it will be useless and must be deleted from your character file.

→ If the elemental defeats you: 378
→ If you defeat this enemy: 321

273

You don't know exactly in which direction you must head, and are rather nervous because of all fuss you caused at the tavern when you were supposed to go unnoticed. You look around and are surprised to discover Toljröm running to the end of the street before you. You run after him without thinking, sure that you can gather some more information as Dhaliara asked. He attempts to lose you once realising that you are following, and now runs faster, although you seem to be a little faster than him, and will catch up soon...

That is your greatest wish right now, to catch your prey and extract all that he knows. However, fortune seems to turn her back on you, as when you turn a corner, there is no trace of Toljröm and you find two possible directions leading out of a small square. You have to decide which to follow to resume your quest...

→ If you choose to go along a narrow alleyway to your left: 304
→ If you'd rather continue by the wider street to your right: 322

274

Mentally exhausted after the many struggles of your journey so far, you decide to relax and to just enjoy the moment. That is why you choose to look for a propitious tavern to give full rein to your instincts. You begin by asking some merchants that soon cross your path, seeking the most qualified people to help you find a suitable place. Thanks to them, you go to the outskirts of the town, to some kind of tavern named 'The spider in its web'.

Once inside, you can see that it is overcrowded, especially with foreigners – merchants for the most part – as the amazons from Bälkaar, being extremely well-behaved, don't usually frequent this kind of establishment where the wine and beer flows freely. Cheered by what you see, you go directly to the bar, where a youngster asks you:

"What will you have?"

- **Spiced wine jar:** 1 zaifa.
- **Black beer tankard:** 1 zaifa.
- **Mead jar:** 1 zaifa.
- **Firewater glass:** 1 zaifa.

The bartender speedily serves your drink (taking your money at the same time), and right then, you are surprised to hear a voice talking to you:

"Hi, handsome! Your drink looks good. I'd love to be invited to share a drink with someone like you."

You turn to discover that the person who spoke is someone of the opposite sex (or the same, according to your personal preference). They are a rather attractive person, immediately drawing your attention. In addition, you realise that they have already consumed several mead jars, and you can see that their cheeks have blushed.

"And... what do you say? Are you going to invite me to a drink?" this person adds, seeing your hesitation.

→ If you decide to talk to them and buy them a drink: 297
→ If you'd rather forget this person, who is obviously drunk: 309

275

With a final powerful blow, your enemy collapses to the floor of the cavern, lifeless. You have fought fiercely, showing great courage, and have defeated an enemy that was vastly superior to you. With your heart now beating at its normal pace, you look down with satisfaction at the corpse by your feet, a mountain of flesh and blood that had been about to kill you. But you don't have any further time to waste in contemplation, as something now draws your attention. When you look towards the sea you see the glowing lamps of a great ship in the distance, and three smaller lights that seem to be approaching from it. Everything suggests that they are boats coming to the cave, pirates who must have been on their ship and who are now heading here to land.

You quickly check the nearby table, but all you find there is food and wine. Now frantic because of the oncoming danger, you keep on searching desperately trying to locate anything to take with you, but all of your efforts are in vain until you open one of the barrels. What you see inside causes you to shudder, as the barrel is full of priceless objects, mostly gems, although there are also rings, necklaces and bracelets made of gold. Knowing that you don't have time to waste and that you won't be able to carry this heavy barrel, you empty your leather bag (get rid of all your items), and quickly fill it with treasures instead; more than enough riches to live a comfortable life, oblivious to war.

The lights of the approaching boats draw ever closer, so as soon as you have filled your leather bag, you run towards the tunnel that led you here, desperate to escape the pirate cave. Fortunately, you have time to flee before being detected, and luck is on your side as nothing inconveniences you as you make your way back along the tunnels. You are soon in the open air again, in the area of the forest burned to suggest the presence of a dragon.

Nobody can deny that you have fulfilled the she-elf's mission beyond expectations. Not only have you discovered the trick of the pirates, but you have also taken a valuable quantity of treasures at the same time. You start to consider a new thought then, as you have two possible options. Let's see what you are willing to do...

→ If you decide to return to the harbour as promised to meet the elves, go to section 293. You will be able to keep the gems hidden in your leather bag, but that will be a secret you will have to keep, as if Dhaliara knows about them, she will require those riches to pay for the incoming war against your enemies, the followers of Zorbrak, the Dragon God. However, you have the right to keep them, and to join her army.

→ On the contrary, if your honor isn't worth as much as you have taken in the pirates cavern, and you now choose to leave the city alone, carrying all these riches to live a good life, oblivious to war; go to section 248.

276

Following your instincts, you quickly resume your march in the shadows. You walk stealthily in your chosen direction, trying to find a place where you can climb the fence. You walk cautiously for a long stretch, attentive to everything around you, yet you don't find a place to sneak in until something odd about the fence draws your attention. One of the boards seems to have been splintered outwards, as if something had crashed into it from the other side, almost breaking it in two. Interested by this circumstance, you push the upper side of the board and see that it moves, almost coming loose. You push and pull several times until the upper side of the board gives away and falls to the ground, leaving a narrow space halfway up where you think you could set your feet and then jump to the other side. You do as planned and soon find yourself on the ground, inside the ranch, and so far you've done so unnoticed by any sentinel.

→ Go to section 317.

277

This ruthless enemy has crushed you. Unless you can overcome this painful humiliation, you won't be able to proceed any further in your adventures. As a consequence for having been defeated, you must choose one of the following options before fighting again: lose 1 experience point, delete 1 object from your character file or lose 1 protection point from one piece of armor, as it has suffered serious damage during the fight. Choose one of these options, update your character file, and then return to the section that sent you here to fight your enemy again.

278

Looking forward to achieving your objective as soon as possible, you walk at a good pace along a tunnel that gradually becomes much narrower and lower; so low that you soon have to crouch to progress. You think about turning back to try another route, but decide to keep on moving forward, slowly making your way through the impenetrable darkness of these old duÿmor mines.

A sudden claustrophobic sensation takes hold of you, as you now feel the weight of the whole mountain over your head. Fortunately, this strange sensation quickly vanishes as you enter another room with a high ceiling. A rickety wooden door stands on the opposite side; curious, you open the door which simply leads to another room. You can see that it is a kind of miners' bedroom, as there are many sleeping compartments carved into the walls, forming practical bunk beds. The remnants of straw mattresses are also found here, as are deteriorating blankets.

You approach a wooden table where someone long ago abandoned the leftovers of their dinner: a pile of thin, whitish bones and a small opened jar. You move your lamp to better illuminate the sleeping compartments, and in one find a pair of old boots. When you move them you discover that they hide something inside: 20 rusted zaifas, but zaifas all the same. Satisfied with your unexpected find, you take the coins without hesitation, a half-smile on your face.

You leave via a small, shadowed tunnel beyond the table, and keep on exploring, keen to locate the roots that the sorceress requires.

→ Go to section 288.

279

Although you continued for as long as possible, your resistance to alcohol hasn't matched that of your opponent. You collapse to the ground hearing the joyous shouts of the audience, while the fat Görlok smiles in satisfaction, taking the zaifas he has won.

Only after a long while do you try to focus your eyes again, and you are surprised to see Toljröm standing by your side, watching you silently.

"You did well," he says. "But I warned you that Görlok had never lost. Come on, you'd better stand up!"

You follow his instructions, raising your head and trying to keep your nausea and dizziness under control. (↓ due to the effects of the booze, you must deduct 1 point from the value of all your opposed attack rolls in your next fight, and you will start that fight with 2 life points less). When you do finally stand, you remember the mission that brought you here, and up until this moment you are failing disastrously at it. So you determinedly focus your mind to control the situation and take in all of the information that you can learn from Toljröm.

→ Go to section 199.

280

As you start your training Rámada performs many tests to understand your magical and physical abilities. That is only the beginning of several hard estrios in which you will barely sleep, as you won't have the time to do all of what the amazon requires. You undergo numerous exercises of concentration to enhance your arcane powers, and you follow a rigid training schedule that will harden your muscles. The amazon also teaches you how to calm your spirit and free your mind.

Under this tough and rigid training, time passes slowly until the five estrios eventually pass. You are barely aware of exactly how you have done it, but after finishing such hard training, you have learnt this special ability. Write it down on your character file and delete the 80 zaifas that are Rámada's payment.

* **Lethal mirror:** as this technique exhausts part of your energy, it can only be used once during each combat. When an enemy rolls a 6 in a damage roll, you will have the chance of automatically making this charm (no need to roll dice or use a power point), which concentrates part of your vital energy and channels it to your enemy. Because of that, even if you take damage in the usual way (that doesn't change), part of that damage bounces back to your enemy. Therefore, your enemy takes 3 damage points that they lose straight away, regardless of any armor worn.

After saying goodbye to the amazon and leaving her residence, you return to the streets of Bälkaar to continue your adventures.

→ Go back to section 335 and choose another option.

◘ **First charmed and trained guard dog:** Fangs (SK). Damage: 1d6+5 / SK 5 / LP: 24 / Armor: Energy field that protects its whole body (values 1 to 6). Protection: 3 / Special ability. Bite power. If the dog rolls a 6 in a damage roll, it has achieved a perfect bite, puncturing your skin with its jaws: add 3 points to its damage.

◘ **Second charmed and trained guard dog:** Fangs (SK). Damage: 1d6+6 / SK 6 / LP: 27 / Armor: Energy field that protects its whole body (values 1 to 6). Protection: 4 / Special ability: Bite power. If the dog rolls a 6 in a damage roll, it has achieved a perfect bite, puncturing your skin with its jaws: add 3 points to its damage.

◘ **Third charmed and trained guard dog:** Fangs (SK). Damage: 1d6+7 / SK 7 / LP: 35 / Armor: Energy field that protects its whole body (values 1 to 6). Protection: 5 / Special ability: Bite power. If the dog rolls a 6 in a damage roll, it has achieved a perfect bite, puncturing your skin with its jaws: add 4 points to its damage.

◘ **Charmed and trained white wolf:** Fangs (SK). Damage: 1d6+8 / SK 7 / LP: 40 / Armor: Energy field that protects its whole body (values 1 to 6). Protection: 5 / Special ability: Bite power. If the wolf rolls a 6 in a damage roll, it has achieved a perfect bite, puncturing your skin with its jaws: add 4 points to its damage. / Venom: when this magical monstrosity hits you, if it rolls a 1 in its damage roll (damage: 1d6+8), not only has it inflicted 9 damage points, but it has also inoculated the venom in its fangs. Therefore, you lose 2 life points in each subsequent combat round due to the lethal effects of the venom. You lose these life points right before making each opposed attack roll.

→ If you defeat these real beasts: 386
→ If your enemies beat you: 327

282

You keep on moving forward trying to fulfill your mission as soon as possible, always attentive to your surroundings in case you come across the required plant, although your first priority is to kill a zodonte and take its teeth.

Slowly but surely you walk along the winding tunnel that suddenly opens out into a great natural cavern featuring impressive stalagmites and stalactites. There seems to be several ways out of here, as you count up to five different openings within it, aside from the one that led you here.

Impressed by what you see, you explore the area, discovering a couple of abandoned wheelbarrows and some tools (several spades and a couple of rusty picks) that lean against one of the walls. With a new idea in your mind, you turn around and scan the area: this seems to be a good place to ambush the zodonte. Having now made up your mind, you follow the instructions of the sorceress by pouring the contents of the small flask onto the ground. This strong-smelling concentrated potion should soon attract any zodonte in the surrounding area.

Thereupon, you locate an isolated place and hide behind a huge stalagmite that rises overhead; now you only have to wait for one of these beasts to make an appearance. You prepare yourself by removing the second potion from your leather bag, the one that you have to throw at the body of the zodonte to gain an advantage against this fearsome enemy.

You wait impatiently in complete silence, almost holding your breath, for the moment when your enemy appears. In the meanwhile, the atmosphere fills with a strong sweet smell. It reminds you of the scent of flowers, but it is extremely intense, even somewhat excessive. It must be an attractive scent for the zodonte, but it doesn't seem to be having any noticeable effect so far. Worried by this lack of activity, you poke your head out from behind the stalagmite to try and see something, but everything before you is pitch-black beyond the limited light of your lamp. You scrutinize the shadows, impatient to discover your enemy, but you only see a pit of silent darkness. After a long while you begin to despair, unable to keep your nerves under control, but right then, in your darkest moment of discouragement, you feel a slight vibration underfoot. In the beginning it is only very slight, so slight that you believe you may have imagined it, but after a short time you hear a clear noise, like the sound of many hands scratching at the ground. You then look out at the area before you, and are absolutely shocked by what you now see...

Little by little, the ground breaks open in clods of earth that crumble down a small mound which grows ever larger. A tentacle appears from within this hole: it is snowy white and glows under the light of your lamp. Covering the skin of the tentacle are a myriad of small strands that move to explore every inch of the ground around it... Suddenly, it seems to detect something, as right then this appendix moves directly towards you. It is only one step from your feet and you nervously consider the idea of escaping the cavern, although you know that your life depends on this fight.

The massive body of the zodonte emerges out of the hole that it has dug with its claws. Like the tentacle, it is snowy white, with slippery skin lacking hair or scales. Its tiny eyes remind you that it is blind, as sight is useless in the dark tunnels where zodontes spend their lives. That is why they have developed a great number of tentacles to scan the ground, and to detect and catch their prey...

Suddenly, three of these tentacles reach out for you...

- After detecting your presence, the zodonte prepares to attack. Immediately, before starting hand-to-hand combat, you open the second flask and throw this concoction at the beast. According to the sorceress, this will harm its skin and will prevent it from moving easily.

- As the zodonte is so near and so large, you should find it very easy to hit it with the elixir. Only nerves, a cruel trick or destiny could make you miss this shot. Roll a dice and cross your fingers, as if you roll a 1, the flask will crash to the ground and shatter without having touched the body of the zodonte. Thereupon, get ready to fight this monstrosity which desires to taste your blood...

◘ **Zodonte:** Strike and grip with tentacles and claws (SK). Damage: 1d6+3 / SK 6 (if you have succeeded in striking the zodonte with the potion, this value will be reduced to 5) / LP: 23 / Armor: Very thick layer of fat and skin. Action area: whole body (values 1 to 6). Protection: 2 LP / Special ability: Multiple attacks with its tentacles. The zodonte also attacks with three tentacles that act independently. At the end of every combat round, each tentacle will take 1 extra life point from you, as they trap you while you attack the body. When you win an opposed attack roll, you can choose to attack one of these tentacles to try and chop it off, instead of attacking the body of the zodonte directly. If you chop a tentacle off, you won't continue to lose the extra life point that it was taking. If you chop off all three tentacles, you won't lose any more of these extra life points, and can focus on killing the zodonte. Each tentacle has 7 life points, no armor nor damage location.

→ If you kill the zodonte: 194
→ If this monstrosity defeats you: 231

283

Although you have fought bravely, all of your efforts have been useless against such a skilled and experienced enemy. ↓ You lose 1 experience point because of this defeat, although you now quickly rise to face your enemy again. → Go back to section 271 and kill that bastard.

284

Base camp
(write this number down on your character file)

You decide that it would be best to head to the tower, as you must locate it, study its overall situation and get familiar with the surrounding area. You'll also have to look for a good place to rest and spend the night, and you realise that a visit to the market could be a good idea to improve or complement your equipment for the upcoming battles.

→ If you choose to locate the tower and study its situation... (For the purposes of the game, you shouldn't skip this option until you have comprehensively explored the objectives of your mission. Remember that you have reached a base camp and therefore will be able to return to this section): 316

→ If you want to visit the market of Bälkaar to spend some zaifas: 330

→ If you'd rather look for a nice place to spend the night and then rest until the time to fight Marok-häi has come... (Once you choose this option you won't be able to return to the base camp): 359

285

After moving your lamp about to light the enclosing darkness, you kneel by one of the walls, thinking that you spotted something low to the ground there. When you look closer, you clearly see a perfectly round small hole that immediately gives you bad feelings... But your surprise grows even greater when you discover another hole exactly like the first, although positioned a little higher. You also have the impression that there is, at least, another hole beyond that.

Uncertain about what this is all about, you think that something strange may take place here.

→ If you decide to continue on regardless: 313
→ If you walk back to the last room and choose another tunnel: 257

286

Simply extraordinary. You are undoubtedly becoming a real master in hand-to-hand combat. That is why, and because of your fight with such a sinister creature, you win 3 experience points to improve your character. Update your character file. Continue on like this and you will soon become a full 'Hero of Urowen'. → Go to section 246.

287

After paying close attention to your surroundings for a moment, you notice slight movement in the nearby thicket. Then, while terror instantly takes hold of you, the head of a black tiger appears very close to your position; it turns and looks at you intently, and then springs forward to claim its dinner. But you've fortunately seen it in time and face it with some preparation.

→ Go to section 244.

288

Although you are rather exhausted, you decide to keep on moving forward, as you don't wish to spend a second more than is necessary in these horrible mines. It must now be dark outside, although down in these depths there is nothing to tell the passing of the estrios. You long to again breathe the pure air of the surface, so you quicken your steps as you move along the dark tunnel before you. You walk on until you hear a distant murmur. Attentive should a new danger arise, you move a little futher forward and then breathe a sigh of relief, as you would swear that what you now hear is just a gentle stream of water. Happy with that outcome, you continue until the end of the tunnel, which opens to an enormous cavern where you can see a wide, calm river.

You approach this somewhat surprising underground waterway and notice in the near distance to your right, close to the bank, several plants with elongated leaves that seem to match the drawings that Sendhöra gave to you. Now moving closer, you have no doubt that they are the rare alédoras whose roots you need so badly. Satisfied to be about to fulfill your mission, you go towards them and kneel on the warm sand by the river. You place your lamp down and pull one of the plants from the ground; it comes out easily, showing a thick, bulbous root similar to an onion. After looking at it for several moments, you are about to store it in your leather bag before taking a second, when something completely unexpected happens. In the blink of an eye, a terrible beast emerges from the calm river, instantly snatching you in its jaws and dragging you under the water. There is nothing to do but let it happen...

- You'll have to fight fiercely to try and escape alive, as you are fighting in water (this will severely limit your movements), and a great part of your efforts will be to keep your head above water to allow you to breathe. Therefore, deduct 1 point from the value obtained in all of your opposed attack rolls. Fortunately, you have all of your equipment at your disposal, so think carefully about how you can best use what you carry.

◻ **Unknown aquatic creature:** Fangs (SK). Damage: 1d6+4 / SK 3 / LP: 23 / Armor: Scaly skin. Action area: whole body (values 1 to 6). Protection: 2 LP / Special ability: Choking. If this creature rolls a 6 in any damage roll, it has caught and sunk you in the water, preventing you from breathing for this turn. Therefore, you will lose 10 points from its attack (1d6+4) before considering the modifications from the damage location roll and your armor. You will then lose 2 extra life points to represent the moments spent choking underwater. Those two points are only lost in that round, as you finally escape and resume breathing for the next round.

> → If you defeat this creature: 225
> → If you are defeated in spite of all your efforts: 305

289

◻ **High fire elemental:** Fists of fire (STR). Damage: 1d6+8 / STR 7 / LP: 90 / Armor: Coat of incandescent lava. Action area: whole body (values 1 to 6). Protection: 5 LP / Special ability: Grip. If the elemental rolls a 6 in a damage roll, it has caught you in its arms, and now attempts to break your bones in a mortal hug. Because of this brutal attack, your breastplate will be damaged (regardless of the result of the damage location roll). Aside from the regular damage, this piece of armor will now permanently protect you for 1 life point less (update your character file accordingly). If the elemental catches you more than once, these points will accumulate until the object grants 0 LP protection. In that case, it will be useless and must be erased from your character file.

> → If you defeat this terrible enemy: 376
> → If the elemental defeats you: 327

290

After a long and epic fight, you finally defeat the frightening beast. Due to your exploit you win 1 experience point, as it isn't easy to face such a lethal and sinister creature. When you finally calm down a little and restore your breathing to normal, you look and listen for several moments, happy to see that you haven't drawn the attention of any other guard.

You resume your descent, keen to discover what these underground corridors may offer, and quickly reach a straight, narrow corridor with several doors on both sides. It is undoubtedly some kind of dungeon. You walk on to the first solid timber door, reinforced with thick ironworks. It is locked and, unlike in other dungeons, there isn't a small window allowing you to see inside the cell. You don't have time to waste, more so considering that you've just left a corpse behind, so you decide not to linger and keep on walking until you find another descending staircase. You go down it without hesitation and, once at the bottom, instead of finding another dry gallery, you now find yourself standing in a sewer full of filth, with black, foul-smelling water that rises up to your knees. Luckily, you have some light down here, even if you do find it odd, as there is a lit torch in a bracket on one of the walls. Its flame is weak and dim; this means that it was lit some time ago, although it also means it is likely that you are not alone in these underground tunnels. Regardless, you rule out that idea for the moment, and grab the burning torch to continue moving forward. You cover a good distance, until you reach a small room where several passageways converge.

→ Go to section 339.

291

You continue walking, coming nearer and nearer to the city of Bälkaar. You arrive again at the crop fields outside of the city, although night now falls upon you once again. You are lucky to find an old abandoned farm, where you can rest under the shelter of a roof, however, before Estrion rises you are on your way again and by mid-morning you see the high walls of the city of the amazons in the distance. This vision lifts your spirits and you walk the remaining distance with renewed energy, until you finally cross the gates of the great city. Anxious for a meeting with the sorceress, you go directly to her home, although you need to ask for directions from several people you find in the labyrinth of streets. Luckily for you, the powerful Sendhöra is well known and you are soon at her door.

You knock and the same middle-aged man greets you at the door once again; he recognizes you immediately and lets you in. He asks you to wait by taking a seat on the wooden bench in the entrance.

You don't have to wait too long, as shortly after that Sendhöra herself comes to meet you with a smile on her face.

"So you're back," the old lady says as she stares you in the eye. "And that can only mean one thing; you have succeeded. Am I wrong?"

"It has been tougher and much riskier than I initially thought, but as you say, I have succeeded..."

"Do you have the roots I need? And what about the zodonte teeth? Do you have them?"

"Everything is in my bag, as requested."

"Very well. Let me see. I want to check that you have brought what I asked."

You do as the sorceress asks and give her the zodonte teeth and the roots of alédoras. Sendhöra looks at these treasures enthusiastically.

"I must admit that you have surprised me," the old amazon finally says. "I didn't expect you to do such a good job, and in such a short time, too. There's no doubt that there is something inside that makes you stand out over the rest... But I'm digressing, as I guess that you are willing to get rid of the curse. As promises should always be kept, I'll immediately put myself to the task of brewing the potion that you require. It will take me a whole estrio to get it ready, so you will spend the night here. Those teeth you brought me are worth my hospitality. I'll get you installed in a room, and you will have dinner at my table. Now, if I may, I will go and start with the preparation of the potion. Hans will take care of you in the meanwhile," the sorceress says, indicating the man who after previously opening the door, has stood several steps from you and has heard all of the conversation.

"As you wish, my lady," the servant says and makes a small bow. "If you'll come with me," he now says to you. "I'll guide you to your room."

So your paths diverge, as Sendhöra goes upstairs to her workroom, while you walk along a corridor on the ground floor.

"If the lord requires so, I can get a bath ready for you."

These words are like a sweet song to your ears, as you can't even remember the last time that hot water touched your dirty skin. You accept his offer willingly and take an agreeable bath that makes you forget all of your recent hardships and misfortunes, finally enjoying a well-earned rest. This rest also comes with a clean robe and a pair of sandals offered by the servant who, when night has come, leads you to a spacious dining room where the amazon is waiting for you by a table full of glorious food. Freshly baked bread, grilled fish, wine in great abundance and many different types of fruit make you enjoy a wonderful night in the company of the sorceress who, against all odds, is very solicitous and warm with you. Because of that, you are now sure that the teeth you brought from the mines are extremely valuable to your hostess, as you doubt that she wouldn't treat you like this otherwise.

You get on so well that the after-dinner conversation lasts well into the night, so Sendhöra, after having enjoyed a couple of the wines that you are also tasting, is so tipsy that you think it may be a good opportunity to gain some information on Marok-häi, the leader of the amazons that Brádoc has asked you to kill. Hopefully, that will be during the next estrio, with Sendhöra's help.

"Before I came to this city for the first time, I had heard much about Marok-häi. Is all that is said about her true?" you ask, directing the conversation to your interest.

"Probably, although chatterboxes tend to exaggerate... But Marok-häi is the most skillful of our warriors. She has no equal with the bow, and you won't find a better rider in Urowen – she would die to protect our queen."

"From what I've heard, Marok-häi and the queen are well protected..."

"That's true! Both of them have a guard of honor. Let me tell you that long ago, I was one of those guards."

"I can't believe it!"

"Well, you should, as it is true! We protected Queen Zarkända's mother then, as she wasn't yet born. What memories! Those were glorious estrios, better times... Not like now. Honor was valued then... But now everything has changed..."

"How did you happen to be part of the queen's guard of honor?" you ask to cheer her up. Your question seems to work, as Sendhöra answers proudly, with a wide smile on her face.

"Of course I had to pass the three tests! They are always different, so it is impossible to know in advance what you will have to do in such a serious test. You may be asked to kill somebody or steal an object, or to show your skill with the bow, complete some exploit like survive in the desert, or run an incredible distance... And you have to do three of these things. But, as I've told you, those were other, different times... Now, even if the tests continue to exist, and all of those amazons... Bah, sometimes everything seems a charade, as it doesn't make any sense to me that Marok-häi passes most of her time in the Tower of the Drum. She isn't doing anything useful there, even if some people say that she is waiting for news – a dove that will carry a message that will decide the future of our people. But that's absurd! No message can be so important that Marok-häi wastes her estrios and most part of her nights on top of that tower."

"Why does it have to be her?" you ask, interested in the information you have just discovered, as it could be very useful for you mission.

"She is the only one who's trusted by the queen, so that's why Marok-häi keeps watch."

"What is the Tower of the Drum? Where is it?"

"You can see it from almost everywhere in the city. It's a tall stone watchtower that is used to watch the sea in case of a possible attack. It's an extremely high tower, and you can only reach its upper part by a long and narrow staircase. There are many drums there, taller than any amazon; when all of the drums sound at the same time, they can be heard all over the city, and that sound means danger... I kept guard myself on top of that tower many times! But let's cease talking of these issues, as they only bring me sad memories that I'd rather forget."

You bow to her wishes, and begin talking about other issues so that the sorceress doesn't suspect your intentions. You continue to share a good time with her until you leave to rest, enjoying a quiet and restful sleep, helped by her promise that the potion will be ready the following morning.

So after a peaceful night you finally awake to the light of a new estrio, and after having a light breakfast, you are led once again to the rooms of Sendhöra, where she is already waiting for you.

"Here it is!" the amazon exclaims as soon as she sees you. "This is the potion that will rid you of your curse. Drink it all, right now, and my services will have finished, as you will be free from the death sentence of that witch."

You approach Sendhöra and take from her the dark bottle she holds in her hands.

"I wouldn't smell that potion if I were you – it stinks," she says when you look at it doubtfully. "Drink it up. Come on... Trust me."

So you drink the thick, lumpy concoction which seems to stick to your throat. Far from surrendering to the revulsion that you begin to feel, you swallow more eagerly, eager to empty the bottle.

"Well done!" says the sorceress. "Now you'd better sit, as you may feel somewhat dizzy."

As the amazon had expected, you start feeling unpleasantly dizzy, and feel a terrible stinging pain in your stomach.

"Don't be worried, it's perfectly normal. The potion is acting as it should." You now hear the voice of the sorceress from far away, as if in a dream. "Relax... Can you hear me? Relax!"

But the words of Sendhöra are soon lost, as you are no longer aware of what is happening around you.

→ Go to section 335.

With a broad smile forming on her face once she knows that you are willing to stay, Dhaliara pats your back and immediately announces your decision to the rest of the elves, who seem proud to have you join their exclusive group of elite warriors. You are told that the plan is to arrive in the city of Wastmur at night, hidden by darkness, to reach a small warehouse of the elves; a sure refuge where they can organize themselves before their important missions.

* **Author's note:** in the estrios in which your adventure takes place, Wastmur, the colossal city on the shores of the Abyssal Sea, is now overcrowded, entirely due to the gold offered by Krénator (lieutenant of Zorbrak, the Dragon God) to those who wish to enlist in his mercenary army. That is why the streets and avenues have stretched beyond its walls, creating neighborhoods outside the walled city, now home to a myriad of hirelings, bounty hunters, pirates and whores. Wastmur and Wruldor are the heart of Krénator's empire, the center of the now called 'Kingdom of the Hundred Moons'. For this reason, many ships full of thieves and killers travel to enlist in Krénator's army, as the gold he offers to his followers is a substantial payment. Nobody in Urowen is sure about from where the sorcerer accumulates his vast riches, but the truth is that the gold truly exists and for now seems to have no end. All this, together with the promises of conquest and power that Krénator offers, has turned Wastmur and Wruldor into two dangerous places, full of criminals who waste their zaifas on entertainment and who never hesitate to draw their sword at the slightest provocation. Fights are common, and every estrio several people breathe their last breath because of these changed circumstances. Wastmur, the glorious city from which Zorbrak led his dragon hosts, has become a viper's nest in which life is valueless. That is the destination you will soon glimpse before your eyes.

You approach the city late at night and carefully dock the ship on the edge of the harbor to slip in unnoticed. You all cover yourselves with hooded capes to hide your face and hair, and once ashore move cautiously along the darkest streets you can find, making your way to the outskirts, to one of the many neighborhoods that have proliferated outside its walls. Luckily, everything is calm and quiet, so you reach your intended location without difficulty. There you are welcomed by another elf who has everything ready for your arrival, as after barring the entrance door, he leads you to a room where a great table full of food awaits. Nothing further happens that night, as after your hard journey and having had a late dinner, you sleep until the following estrio, which promises to arrive full of new dangers.

"I've brought you something for breakfast," Dhaliara's voice wakes you, with her immediately offering cheese and bread. "Estrion is already up in the sky and we must get ready to fulfill our missions as soon as possible. Staying in Wastmur is very dangerous for all of us, so we will have to be quick and cautious to escape from this city as soon as possible. We have to do the same thing that we did in Bälkaar, act and disappear. Today, we will distribute the different jobs, but first of all, you need to upgrade your equipment," she adds, smiling at your weapon and armor. "If you are going to help us, you will be equipped like us. I'll be waiting for you. Come and see me when you're ready."

The she-elf walks out of the room after saying these words, leaving you alone with your breakfast. You devour it quickly, as her words have left you intrigued, and are almost immediately before her; she smiles at you once again.

"Come on, follow me. I'll take you to our little warehouse, and you'll be allowed to take anything you want from it."

You follow the she-elf by candlelight down a narrow spiral staircase that leads you to some kind of basement, where she stops before a door secured by an impressive padlock. She opens it quickly with a key she had been keeping, and then speaks again:

"Wait here while I light some lamps."

Then, she steps into a new room, and you can see from the outside that she lights several oil lamps placed around the room.

"Ok, you may come in now."

You follow Dhaliara's instructions and what you see inside leaves you speechless, as the spacious room is crowded with weapons, armor and potions...

"You can take whatever you want," says the she-elf. "Come on, don't be shy. Get equipped the best you can, as I can guarantee that you'll put everything you select to good use."

- As Dhaliara has told you, you can take whatever you want and you don't have to pay for any of it. Get rid of your old armor, if you want; delete them from your character file and write down the new armor instead. Do the same with your weapons, if you want to change the one you're carrying with anything inside this room. And fill your leather bag with potions. Remember it only has capacity for six items, so delete what you don't want or won't need and take any of these potions, as you won't have to pay a single zaifa! Now, think through what you should take or leave, and enjoy this wonderful 'shopping'.

Equipment of the elves of the snow

Armor:

- **Elvish helmet of Krindaslon.** Action area: head. Protection: 4 LP.

- **Elvish coat of mail (very light).** Action area: trunk (values 2, 3 and 4). Protection: 5 LP.

- **Armbands of Krindaslon.** Action area: arms. Protection: 3 LP.

- **Greaves of Krindaslon.** Action area: legs. Protection: 3 LP.

Weapons:

- **Bow of the elves of the snow (only for hunters):** (SK). Damage 1d6+3. Difficulty: 9.

- **Arrows:** 15 (they do not fill a slot in your leather bag).

- **Vopkhësh:** a feared and famous two-handed sword forged in Krindaslon with a complex, curved design that has no equal in Urowen (two-handed weapon, SK). Damage: 1d6+4. Special characteristic: extremely easy to handle. Given the easy movement that the vopkhësh allows, while using it you can't roll a 1 in any roll. Re-roll all dice that result in a 1.

- **Warhammer:** a beautiful and stylish weapon forged by the blacksmiths of Krindaslon. It is a rare item among elves, but extremely effective in hand-to-hand combat (two-handed weapon, STR). Damage: 1d6+4. Special characteristic: extremely easy to handle. Given the easy movement that the elfish warhammer allows, while using it you can't roll a 1 in any roll. Re-roll all dice that result in a 1.

- **Ice crystal:** a magical gem that uses the cold of the snow against your opponent (MAG). Damage: 1d6+4. Special characteristic: it improves the channelling of energy. As it is extremely powerful, you won't roll a 1 in any roll. Re-roll all dice that result in a 1. If you are a sorcerer, given your special ability that changes the result of your damage rolls (turning your 1 into a 3), you will add another point to your special ability whenever you are carrying the ice crystal (now turning your 1 into a 4).

Other equipment:

- **IMPORTANT NOTE:** You can take as many potions as you want for free until you fill your leather bag. The only restriction you must take into account is that you cannot take more than two potions of the same kind.

- **Food rations for a week** (they don't fill your leather bag).

- **Kandrist healing potion.** How to use it: during combat, after winning an opposed attack roll, instead of hurting your enemy you can choose to drink this potion. There is potion enough for 1 dose. When you drink it, you recover 1d6+4 life points. Write it down in your leather bag, as this potion fills one of its slots. Once used, delete it from your character file.

- **Vital essence (potion).** How to use it: drink immediately before combat. There is potion enough for 1 dose. After drinking it, you will feel a strange energy throughout your body. It is the vital essence of the Kandrist Mountain Range, where the Ice City of Krindaslon, home of the elves of the snow, is located. The effects of this potion are immediate, so during that combat you will have an additional 8 life points. Write it down in your leather bag, as this potion fills one of its slots. Once used, delete it from your character file.

- **Elvish venom.** How to use it: spread over the blade of a weapon or chosen magic object immediately before combat. There is venom enough for 1 use. During that combat, when you hurt your enemy for the first time, you will not only inflict damage points, but you will also inoculate the venom of your weapon. Therefore, at the beginning of each subsequent combat round, your enemy will lose 2 life points due to the effects of the venom. These points are lost right before making each opposed attack roll. Write the flask of venom down on your character file in your leather bag, as it fills one of its slots. Once used, delete it from your character file. Note that these points are accumulative to the effects of a weapon that, for example, can inflict critical damage, such us the trident.

- **Major arcane potion.** How to use it: drink immediately before combat. There is potion enough for 1 dose. After drinking it, you will feel that the magical energies within you travel through your body with renewed strength. The effects of this potion are immediate, so you will have 3 extra power points during that combat. Write it down in your leather bag, as this potion fills one of its slots. Once used, delete it from your character file.

- **Bälkian elixir.** How to use it: drink immediately before combat. There is elixir enough for 1 dose. After drinking it, your speed and reflexes will improve considerably, and you will become very hard to beat. During that combat you will add 2 extra points to all of your opposed attack rolls. Write it down in your leather bag, as this potion fills one of its slots. Once used, delete it from your character file.

- **Mystic shield potion.** How to use it: drink immediately before combat. There is potion enough for 1 dose. After drinking it, a bluish halo will appear around your body, protecting you from your enemy's attacks. Action area: whole body (values 1 to 6) in a damage location roll. Protection: 2 extra LP, to be added to the regular points granted by your armor. Write it down on your character file, as this potion fills one of its slots. Once used, delete it from your character file.

→ Once you have finished selecting your new equipment, go to section 381. Think carefully about what you take because you won't be allowed to come back to this room again.

293

It is said that the life of every hero gives birth to a legend. Undoubtedly, if it continues this way, yours will be written in golden letters. You have become a skilled spy and warrior, so your skills will be very valuable and may even be decisive in the horrendous war that is about to begin in the Lands of Urowen... ↑ You win 2 experience points.

After all that you have lived through during the night, with your mission now fulfilled you flee to safety as soon as possible, as there is no doubt that alarms are about to sound all over the city because of your actions and for the actions of the other elves. That is why you go directly to the port of Wastmur, as you are eager to reach the ship where you will meet Dhaliara again. You travel very quickly, hidden in the shadows of the night, so you are somewhat surprised to discover that you are the last to arrive, as by then all of the elves, skilled warriors each and every one, have succeeded in their missions and safely returned to the ship.

As soon as you come aboard, you hear someone shout 'ropes away', and the vessel moves slowly away from the city where, before too long, the streets will be crowded with people in revolt due to all of the mischief your group has caused.

"Set our course for Verinfes!" Dhaliara orders the elves. "We must get there as soon as possible to inform Brádoc and the king about all we have discovered tonight, as this information may be crucial for the development of the war. Let's hope that the winds are favorable and we therefore reach our destination soon."

So you begin the journey that will take you from the enemy city of Wastmur to Verinfes, where you will finally find refuge in a safe place. Fortunately, luck seems to be on your side for such an important journey, as the favourable winds grant you great speed, helping you to reach your distant destination sooner than expected.

As soon as he knows of your arrival, Brádoc, the Major Soldier of the city, wishes to see you personally, and you are therefore driven to the stronghold of Verinfes. Dhaliara speaks on behalf of your group and presents Brádoc with the reports that had been written during your long journey across the sea, using all of the information unearthed during your dangerous missions in Wastmur. The Major Soldier then asks to be left alone with the she-elf and they talk together while the rest of you wait in another room, where you are regaled with plenty of food and well watered by the best wine in town.

Dhaliara now approaches. "Brádoc desires to talk with you – alone," she says. "Report yourself to him. He's waiting for you."

You immediately follow Dhaliara's instructions and leave all the elves of the snow behind to meet the Major Soldier of Verinfes.

"Come in and have a seat," Brádoc says as he sees you. "I'm glad that you are back, safe and sound. I sent you on a really risky mission, and you not only succeeded when you killed that amazon, but you helped Dhaliara in Wastmur. When you left I promised that if you succeeded in your mission, you would have another great reward waiting for you here. So it will be, if you stay with us. Dhaliara and her elves of the snow will soon leave for Krindaslon, and I don't want you to follow them. That is why I ask you to stay here in Verinfes, as we will need people like you in this war that is about to begin. If you do so, I offer you a place on the honor guard of Verinfes, commanding a garrison. You'll be by my side, and you'll be able to build up a good future for yourself in this kingdom. So, what do you think? Do you accept my offer?"

→ If you decide to accept Brádoc's generous offer: 326
→ If you decide to tactfully decline it: 337

294

As you start your training Rámada performs many tests to understand your use of weapons and physical abilities. That is only the beginning of several hard estrios in which you will barely sleep, as you won't have the time to do all of what the amazon requires. You are subjected to numerous exercises using different types of weapons, and follow a rigid training schedule that will harden your muscles. The amazon also teaches you how to calm your spirit and free your mind.

Under this tough and rigid training, time passes slowly until the five estrios eventually pass. You are barely aware of exactly how you have done it, but after finishing such hard training, you have learnt this special ability. Write it down on your character file and delete the 80 zaifas that are Rámada's payment.

* Edge of fire: as this technique consumes part of your energies, it can be used just once during each combat. When you roll a 6 in a damage roll, you have concentrated part of your vital energy, your essence, and then channelled it through your weapon. Its blade now bursts into flames when you attack, adding 3 extra damage points to your blow (and just that blow). As always, you'll have to consider your enemy's armor. If you are a warrior, don't forget that you must also add 2 extra points due to the special ability of your character, if you roll a 6 in a damage roll.

After saying goodbye to the amazon and leaving her residence, you return to the streets of Bälkaar to continue your adventures.

→ Go back to section 335 and choose another option.

295

Somewhat reluctantly, you head down the old wooden staircase, which appears to be half rotten. You move forward in total darkness as there isn't any lamp to light this cold, damp place. Step by step, little by little, you arrive at the foot of the stairs and again set your feet on the ground; or at least, that would have been your preference, as instead of finding a dry tunnel, you now stand in a sewer full of filth, with black, foul-smelling water that rises up to your knees. Luckily, you have some light down here, even if you do find it odd, as there is a lit torch in a bracket on one of the walls. Its flame is weak and dim; this means that it was lit some time ago, although it also means it is likely that you are not alone in these underground tunnels. Regardless, you rule out that idea for the moment, and grab the burning torch to continue moving forward. You cover a good distance, until you reach a small room where several passageways converge.

→ Go to section 339.

296

This terrible monster has crushed you. You are totally at its mercy and won't be able to continue your adventures until you successfully kill it. ↓ As a penalty for having been defeated you must choose one of the two following options: lose 1 experience point or delete 1 item from your character file. → Choose one of these options, update your character file, and then go back to section 374 to fight your enemy again.

297

Appealed by such unexpected company, you accept their offer without hesitation; you call the bartender again to ask for another jar of the same beverage. If you have zaifas enough, you will meet the cost of three more rounds, as you feel cheered by the drink and appealed by your partner who is being extremely responsive and charming. (Delete 7 coins from your character file to pay for these drinks).

"Do you want to come with me?" your partner asks you then, surprising you once again. "I've got a room upstairs. We could have a good time! You know what I mean..."

Without waiting for a response, you are guided through the crowded room, a stupid smile on your face, now willing to reach your destination as soon as possible to enjoy the pleasures of the flesh...

- Now you'll have to make a roll using 2d6. Add the results and compare that value with the 'Atmosphere table'. Follow then the instructions of the table, and if you are told to do so, make another roll with 2d6, whose result you'll have to compare with the 'Pleasure table':

Atmosphere table:

- **2:** How unlucky! Go to section 319.
- **3:** When you are about to take action, your partner suddenly feels remorseful and talks about a lover she doesn't want to betray by cheating with you. Completely frustrated, you leave the tavern, willing to forget what happened there and anxious to continue your adventures. Go back to section 335 and choose another option.
- **4:** Your partner takes out a bottle of a strange liquor, which you drink, ending up with a hangover: -1 in your next roll. Roll for pleasure.
- **5:** This so-called room is a stinky, dirty hayloft full of bedbugs and ticks. You now have numerous bites that will trouble you for many estrios. You'll

start your next combat with 3 life points less. Write it down on your character file and then roll for pleasure.

- **6:** A loud crack in your back will now cause it to hurt for several estrios. You'll start your next combat with 2 life points less. Write it down on your character file and then roll for pleasure.

- **7:** Your partner turns out to have poor grooming, but you realise it too late and, once you are in the middle of your performance, you decide to go ahead. Roll for pleasure.

- **8:** Your partner looks even better naked, and that arouses your passion even further: +1 in your pleasure roll.

- **9:** Your partner takes out a rope and suggests that they use it to tie you to the bed: +1 in your pleasure roll.

- **10:** Your partner is an expert, so you do things that you had never done before: +2 in your pleasure roll.

- **11:** Before starting, your partner gives you a massage with a strange, fragrant oil that favourably warms your blood: +3 in your pleasure roll.

- **12:** Your partner brings a bottle of what you are told is a strong potion. They take a good swallow before passing it to you. This potion will turn both of you into real beasts: +4 in your pleasure roll.

Pleasure table:

- **2:** You are so quick that everything is over before it has really started, making your partner very angry. You lose 1 experience point (EP).

- **3:** Lack of motivation makes it impossible for you to go ahead. You lose 1 experience point (EP).

- **4:** Attempting a strange position hurts one of your shoulders. You win 1 experience point (EP), but you will have 1 point less in all of your opposed attack rolls in your next combat.

- **5:** When your partner begins action, they turn out to be a major disappointment, so you end up frustrated and wanting for more. It's as if nothing really happened.

- **6:** The experience has turned out to be short but satisfactory. However, it could have been much better. You will try your best next time.

- **7:** After resting for a short period of time you resume action again, letting yourself go with unrestrained passion. Roll again for pleasure, but you'll have to deduct 1 point from the result this time. If your two dice total is 2, the final result will be 2.

- **8:** It has been extraordinary, so you feel elated, energised to continue your adventures. You'll add 1 point to all of your damage points in your next combat.

- **9:** You feel very proud, with an extremely high morale. That was just what you needed to go ahead and keep on facing new challenges. You'll add 1 point to all of your opposed attack rolls in your next combat.

- 10: It has been so wonderful that you feel that you can finally die in peace after this extraordinary exploit. You win 1 experience point (EP).

- 11: Simply sublime. Your fully satisfied smile won't fade off your face for the whole estrio. You win 1 experience point (EP).

- 12: Your exploit has been so incredible that the chronicles of Bälkaar should record what has happened, no doubt about that. You win 1 experience point (EP).

- After you have finished here, you go back down to the common room and decide to continue your adventures. → Go back to section 335 and choose another option.

298

Although it seemed that a real beast would emerge from the thicket, you have been very lucky, as what now blocks your way seems to be a rather weak creature, almost near death. Before you is a grotesque, sickly monstrosity with a single arm, the combination of a human and some other animal you are completely unable to identify. By its appearance you would say it looks more like a failed attempt of the sorcerer Krénator, than a menace to be sent to war. After seeing it, you no longer have any doubt that the sorcerer is playing god, experimenting monstrously with all of the creatures that live in the Lands of Urowen. However, the fierceness of this deformed creature seems to now rise, as it comes towards you with the clear aim of launching an attack. Kill this beast if you can, as you will set it free from the sentence imposed upon it by the wizard...

▫ **Deformed monstrosity:** Claws (SK). Damage: 1d6 / SK 2 / LP: 22 / Armor: Thick fur and skin. Action area: whole body (values 1 to 6). Protection: 1 LP.

→ If you defeat this creature: 286

→ If, against all odds, this monstrosity defeats you, go to section 258, but don't lose this page or forget that you are in section 298.

299

You rush on, continuously searching for your objective, looking in all of the cells. Then, a really horrible creature suddenly appears at your back, moving forward aggressively to kill you. You don't know for sure what it is, as its ghastly appearance is rather deformed and grotesque. But you don't have any more time to study it closely, as the combat is about to begin...

◘ **Monstrosity created by Krénator:** Strike with tentacles, claws (STR). Damage: 1d6+5 / STR 6 / LP: 50 / Armor: A type of bark. Action area: whole body (values 1 to 6). Protection: 4 LP / Special ability: Tentacles. In addition to this deformed monstrosity's powerful claws, it also attacks with three tentacles that act independently. At the end of every combat round, each tentacle will take 1 extra life point from you, as they trap you while you attack the body. When you win an opposed attack roll, you can choose to attack one of these tentacles to try and chop it off, instead of attacking the body directly. If you chop a tentacle off, you won't continue to lose the extra life point that it was taking. If you chop off all three tentacles, you won't lose any more of these extra life points, and can focus on killing this monstrosity. Each tentacle has 9 life points, no armor nor damage location.

→ If you defeat this horrible creature: 361
→ If you are crushed by this monstrosity: 327

300

You continue on your way but as soon as you've taken a couple of steps, you hear a faint click that instantly makes you fear the worst. To your great sorrow, your fears have come true, as numerous arrows shoot from the holes in the walls.

- Twelve arrows have been shot at you.

- Roll two dice to represent the amount of arrows. The sum of both dice will be the number of arrows that have hit you.

- Roll for damage for each arrow that has struck you, as if you had suffered a blow from an enemy. Take notes on a sheet of paper as you make a damage location roll for each arrow, and then roll for damage, deducting the protection granted by your armor. The damage of the arrows is 1d6+1.

→ If you are still alive after being struck by the arrows: 240

→ If you've been killed by the arrows: 229

301

❏ **Expert warrior working for Bors of Raidyón:** Battle broadsword (STR). Damage: 1d6+4 / STR 4 / LP: 32 / Armor: Reinforced helmet (H). Action area: head. Protection: 3 LP. Coat of mail (C). Action area: trunk (values 2, 3 and 4). Protection: 4 LP. Reinforced armbands and greaves (A) (G). Action area: arms and legs. Protection: 3 LP / Special ability: Upper edge of fire. Every time this expert warrior rolls a 6 in a damage roll, he has channelled part of his vital energy, his very essence, to his broadsword. The blade of the sword now bursts into flames, adding 3 extra points to that attack. Additionally, that blow will inflict critical damage, so from that moment on you lose 1 life point at the beginning of each new round, right before every opposed attack roll.

→ If you defeat your enemy: 331

→ If your enemy defeats you, go to section 380, but don't lose this page or forget that you are in section 301.

302

Although you have fought bravely, the balls of your enemy's flail have hit you quite brutally, finally making you bite the dust. However, you recover enough to fight her again. As a penalty for having been defeated you will have to delete 1 experience point from your character file or 1 item from your leather bag, at your choice. Stand up, return to the section that sent you here and give your best to keep on moving up the Tower of the Drum.

→ Go back to section 341 and fight the amazon again. This time, she won't shoot her bow.

303

Before your surprised eyes, the ground beneath your feet immediately begins to crumble – it isn't rock as you had thought. You stand above a trap now activated, opening a wooden gate that exposes a deep pit full of sharp upward-facing spears. Unfortunately, you have reacted too late, and can't stop yourself from falling into a mortal trap. Your life is now at stake, so pray to your gods to see the light of Estrion again...

■ As you have fallen into the trap, roll a dice to determine how many spears have hurt you. The result of your roll will be the number of wounds inflicted.

- The damage of each spear is 1d6+4. Determine the damage received by making a damage location and damage roll for each spear that has hurt you. You'll also have to consider the protection granted by your armor, as in a normal combat.

→ If you are still alive: 318
→ If you are dead: 366

304

You run tirelessly to find Toljröm, but either he has dissipated into the air or you have gone the wrong way, as there is no trace of him. Now desperate, you're thinking of going back to where you came from when a shout comes from an alleyway. Immediately, you make your way over there and are surprised to discover, in the distance, Toljröm kneeling on the ground, a stranger pulling his hair and pressing a knife against his throat.

"Stop! Don't do that!" you shout in the silence of the night, but your words are useless, as the stranger savagely thrusts his knife in Toljröm's neck and cuts his throat from side to side.

No doubt that poor bastard had other enemies aside from yourself, and his loose tongue had sentenced him to death. He has paid with his life for his reckless actions in such a complicated situation, with an impending war in which information is a valuable commodity. You won't be able to gain any more information from his lifeless corpse, and your mission has come to an unexpected end...

The dark, hooded killer now raises his hand and points his knife at you, moving back along the alleyway to attack.

The most important thing right now is to escape alive, return unnoticed to the ship to meet the elves, and then flee from this city. However, you still have a choice to make...

→ If you want to run away to try to escape from that enemy: 334
→ If you choose to run towards him to kill him: 347

305

The terrible strength of the beast, plus fighting underwater, has been too much for you. You finally surrender, totally exhausted and at the mercy of your enemy, which now prepares to eat you. But right before this strange creature is going to tear off your head, another beast similar to the first appears. This second beast is almost double the size of the first, and it now fights against it to steal its meal. Before your astonished eyes, a violent struggle begins between both creatures, so you use these moments to regain your breath and immediately swim to the shore, guiding yourself by the glow of your lamp on the sand. As soon as you get there you immediately pull up several roots (they do not fill a slot in your leather bag), and swiftly rush for the tunnel without looking back.

↓ You have saved your life for the time being, but you haven't come out of this incident without consequences. During the fight you have lost 1 object, of your choice, from your leather bag; delete this now, noting that you can't choose the lamp as you need it to escape from the mines. In addition, the beast tore off one piece of armor, and it has been lost in the depths of the river. Delete 1 armor item of your choice (C, H, A or G).

→ Go to section 325.

306

You rush on, continuously searching for your objective, looking in all of the cells. Then, a really horrible creature suddenly appears at your back, moving forward aggressively to kill you. You don't know for sure what it is, as its ghastly appearance is rather deformed and grotesque. You don't have any more time to study it closely, as the combat is about to begin...

◻ **Monstrosity created by Krénator:** Strike with tentacles, claws (STR). Damage: 1d6+7 / STR 7 / LP: 55 / Armor: A type of bark. Action area: whole body (values 1 to 6). Protection: 4 LP / Special ability: Tentacles. In addition to this deformed monstrosity's powerful claws, it also attacks with three tentacles that act independently. At the end of every combat round, each tentacle will take 1 extra life point from you, as they trap you while you attack the body. When you win an opposed attack roll, you can choose to attack one of these tentacles to try and chop it off, instead of attacking the body directly. If you chop a tentacle off, you won't continue to lose the extra life point that it was taking. If you chop off all three tentacles, you won't lose any more of these extra life points, and can focus on killing this monstrosity. Each tentacle has 10 life points, no armor nor damage location.

→ If you defeat this horrible creature: 361
→ If you are crushed by this monstrosity: 327

307

You have fought a titanic combat in which you have been able to defeat a vastly superior enemy. However, you now feel terribly exhausted, so you quickly grab the oars to try and reach the nearby shore as soon as possible. This way, you are soon onshore and throw yourself to the ground, enjoying the rays of Estrion, as you are happy to still be alive, having believed that the sea snake would easily consume you. Right then, you remember the foul creature and immediately stand, looking at the water to see its colossal corpse being slowly pushed by the waves to the shore. When it is finally beached upon the sand, you approach the corpse to inspect it better. It is really huge, massive, with an ugly, oversized head. But what immediately draws your attention are four tiny legs, which seem to have atrophied, standing out from the scales of its lower parts. You immediately think of some rumours you've heard about the return of dragons to Urowen. A question arises inside you then: what if this creature was some kind of dragon, a descendant of its lethal ancestors, which flew in the sky long ago?

This question consumes you while you look at the corpse of the beast, as according to old legends, when a dragon lost its life, its heart turned into a gem, a precious stone worth a genuine fortune. Encouraged by that idea, you decide that you have nothing to lose if you look for the heart of the snake, so you grab your weapon and begin cutting the beast's stomach, where you think its heart should be. Thanks to that, you soon find what you are looking for, as a strong glitter draws your attention when the warm rays of Estrion reflect on something unusual. In the guts of the snake you discover a gem the size of your fist, coloured a deep green, and extremely beautiful. Excited, you take it in your hands and raise it into the light to look at it better. With a broad smile, you see that the light is deviated from its trajectory when it crosses the twenty polished faces of the gem.

You have no doubt that this is the greatest treasure you could ever find in your adventures, as you know that in any market you would surely receive many thousands of zaifas for this wonderful gem. That is why, you soon stow it in your leather bag and immediately embark on the path to find the highest bidder.

You'll live many new adventures to locate your desired price, as the reward for the gem is great – a real booty that makes you immensely wealthy. But that's another story.

→ Go to section 400.

308

Choosing the safer path, you walk along the cliff through a forested area, at some distance from the precipice. According to the instructions from the she-elf, the cavern shouldn't be too far ahead, so you are hopeful that you will find it very soon, although it may be a bit more complicated than you had initially thought. You are contemplating the possibilities when you detect something odd around you, so you stop and stand in complete silence, attentive to your surroundings, as you would swear that you heard something nearby...

■ Roll for Perception (PER) with a difficulty of 5 to determine if you detect something. Remember, roll a dice and add the points you have in your PER attribute to the result obtained from the dice.

→ If the result is 5 or higher: 287
→ If the result is 4 or lower: 261

309

"I don't think you've found the right person. Go and bother another man and leave me alone," you say without hesitation.

"Stupid moron! Who on Urowen do you think you are? How...? How dare you talk to me like that!"

Indifferent to her words, you turn and move away to a quiet corner, leaving the stranger at the bar. Soon after you notice that one of those present approaches her and accepts the offer you have declined.

After drinking the remainder of your jar, you decide to leave the tavern, as you haven't found what you had in mind and are now eager to continue the mission you have to fulfill.

→ Go back to section 335.

310

Simply masterful, an extraordinary performance! You are becoming a real master in hand-to-hand combat. For that reason, and for your wonderful fight against such a dangerous creature, you win 3 experience points to help you improve your character file. Continue on in this way and you'll soon become a full 'Hero of Urowen'.

Once you've regained your breath after the bloody combat, you look at the corpse of the monster, thinking about what you've seen here. Somebody must have pretended that this reptile was a dragon, burning the cave surroundings to keep strangers away, spreading the idea throughout Wastmur that one of these dangerous creatures lurks here. Besides, the beast that you have killed couldn't have chained nor fed itself, and the cavern floor is crowded with old bones. Somebody is clearly responsible for all of this, and so much effort would only be made for a very good reason, such as hiding something precious within the cave. That is the first idea that comes into your mind, and after thinking it through for a while it makes even further sense. Somebody has faked the presence of a dragon, using this creature to guard the entrance to the cavern, in which case there must be something worth taking such disproportionate measures. You now begin exploring the area, using the light of the she-elf's ring. Unfortunately, it is not going to be quite as easy as you had expected, as it seems that the beast at the entrance was only the first of your problems. You reach a crossroads and now have four tunnels to choose from. All of them are alike, so there is nothing to help you with your decision. Once again, luck and intuition will decide your destiny...

→ If you choose the first of the tunnels, the one to your left: 271
→ If you choose one of the centre tunnels: 342
→ If you'd rather go into the third: 256
→ If you go into the tunnel to your right: 364

311

You have fought bravely against an enemy who was an expert warrior. But in spite of your victory, your nightmare is far from ending, as you hardly have time to regain your breath when a new amazon pounces on you, taking you by surprise. Right then she aims her weapon directly at your heart, ready to deliver a mortal stab that will surely end your estrios on Urowen. But when you think that everything is lost, a small dart accurately strikes the slender neck of the beautiful amazon. Your enemy instantly falls to the ground and starts to convulse, while a black foam starts to dribble out of her mouth. You turn your head and see another couple of hooded shapes, grabbing strange blowpipes with which they are shooting similar darts at all of the amazons that remain standing. You are soon the only ones left standing in the room, as all of your enemies have lost their life to the lethal effects of the venom in which the darts shot by your new companions are oiled.

"Quick, let's continue climbing," the she-elf now tells you, as she turns to climb another flight of stairs. "They'll watch our backs! Hurry up, let's go!"

You follow her without a moment's delay, while her companions fall behind. ↑ As you've won your first combat, you also win 1 experience point.

→ Go to section 341.

312

You fear for your life fighting against an enemy so superior, so you take advantage of the confusion to run towards the exit, hoping to reach it without being intercepted. All of your attention is focused on that objective, but luck will play an important role, as the goddess of fortune will determine if your way is blocked. Roll a dice and say your prayers, as your life may depend on it:

→ If you roll a 1 or 2: 324
→ If you roll a 3 or 4: 340
→ If the result is a 5 or 6: 369

313

Although you have discovered these mysterious holes, you decide to keep on walking, ignoring your gut feeling. There is no doubt that your adventures have made you a brave person, but being so bold in a situation like this can come with a heavy cost... Once again the die is cast, and there's no turning back.

→ Commit your soul to the gods and go to section 300.

Having chosen your mission, the she-elf gives you further details, more specific information on the objectives you have to fulfill. From what she tells you, the tavern you must go to is marked on a small map that she now hands to you. It is on the outskirts of the town, beyond the city's walls. Once there, your mission will be to find the alleged traitor Toljröm, to gain all of the information you can about his treason. If that crime is confirmed, he should pay for it with his life, and you will be in charge of carrying out the sentence. To do so, you'll have to gain his trust, and given that a good way to do so is with buying a few drinks, the she-elf gives you 30 zaifas so that you can pay for several rounds.

Aside from that, Dhaliara doesn't know much more about your mission, so everything depends on you now. The estrio passes calmly, as everyone studiously prepares in the best possible way to face the dangerous challenges waiting that night. It's already dusk when Dhaliara gathers you all again to address you.

"Good luck to all of you, my companions and friends, as we part ways again. You know what you must do! Fulfill your missions as best you can. I hope to see all of you on the ship in the harbor. Neuköulos kan, sínfulas dänder ànfer!"

After hearing her words, you leave the room in small groups, slipping out of the building through different doors and windows to go unnoticed. When it is your turn, you leave the hiding place of the elves by a rear door, and you move into the alleyways of Wastmur, which are already in shadow, as the night is close. You walk to the southern area of the city and wait for darkness to fall upon the Lands of Urowen. Only then do you decide to leave your position and head for 'The Sword in Flames', which you find easily, guided by the she-elf's map. It is a huge building, with a door ajar by which you can hear voices and smell the mouth-watering aroma of grilled meat.

You step inside without further delay and a broad smile immediately spreads across your face. Many prostitutes in scanty clothing swing their hips among many tables crowded with dangerous looking people. For this very reason, Wastmur is one of the most treacherous cities in Urowen, a hiding place for pirates and bounty hunters, killers, thieves and hirelings who like to enjoy the pleasures of life whenever they have a zaifa or two in their pockets. And it looks like you are in the right place for that, as tankards of beer and jars of wine come and go, while some people have fun with the girls and others try their luck in games of chance.

You are grateful that nobody seems to pay you the slightest attention, and now move towards the bar to try and find out some information about Toljröm.

"A tankard of beer!" you say to an attractive female servant. She collects one zaifa from you as she serves it. "I'm looking for Toljröm. Have you heard that name?"

"You hear many things here," the girl answers, "but I can't remember if I've heard that name. I'm sorry, but I can't help you."

She moves away at once, as there are other thirsty customers incessantly asking for drinks. You took a risk asking directly about your objective, but time's against you and at this moment you have few available options. However, luck seems to be on your side, as a toothless, stinky old man, who was standing several steps from you, stops by your side and tells you:

"Toljröm? Why are you looking for that bastard?" he says with a hideous smile.

"That's my business, although I would appreciate your help. Do you know him?"

"Oh, of course I know him, but my throat is too dry to talk," he says, looking at the tankard in your hands.

After asking the girl servant for another beer for your new companion (delete 1 zaifa from your character file), the old man seems far more prepared to talk.

"Toljröm is a regular of this den. He's been lost for a long time though... even I thought he must have died. But the truth is that he was travelling out of town. Fortunately for you, he's back and he's been coming here for several estrios now, every night. He'll be here soon, I bet."

"Can you tell me when he's here if you see him?"

"Of course, my friend, you can count on it. As soon as I see him, I'll come and tell you."

"Do you know where he travelled to?"

"I don't know that, but as I told you, he's been away for a long time."

"Why do you know him, if I may ask?"

"That mad dog and I have sometimes worked together for his master."

"His... master? I thought that Toljröm... What kind of person are we talking about?"

"That jerk is just a 'sewer cleaner', always stuck to his master's ass to pick up his shits."

According to your information, Toljröm should be some kind of soldier or hireling, someone bold and capable of betraying his people, nothing like what this old man says. It now seems likely that the reports from the elves are incorrect, and that your true objective will be Toljröm's master. Therefore you must be very careful and highly attentive to all details to try and fulfill your mission. These are your thoughts when the voice of your companion suddenly brings you back to reality.

"Look...! Speaking of him... There you are, Toljröm."

→ Go to section 367.

315

◘ **First elite soldier:** Curved sword (SK). Damage: 1d6+4 / SK 5 / LP: 29 / Armor: Hardened leather breastplate (C). Action area: trunk (values 2, 3 and 4). Protection: 4 LP. Reinforced leather armbands and greaves (A) (G). Action area: arms and legs. Protection: 2 LP. Reinforced metal helmet (H). Action area: head. Protection: 3 LP / Special ability: Deep cut. When your opponent hurts you, if he rolls a 6 in a damage roll (Damage 1d6+4), not only has he inflicted 10 damage points, but he has also seriously injured you. Therefore, at the beginning of each subsequent combat round, you lose 1 life point due to blood loss. You lose this life point right before making each opposed attack roll. / Extremely skillful: your enemy can't roll a 1. Re-roll any dice that show 1 as a result.

◘ **Second elite soldier:** Curved sword (SK). Damage: 1d6+5 / SK 6 / LP: 33 / Armor: Hardened leather breastplate (C). Action area: trunk (values 2, 3 and 4). Protection: 5 LP. Reinforced leather armbands and greaves (A) (G). Action area: arms and legs. Protection: 3 LP. Reinforced metal helmet (H). Action area: head. Protection: 3 LP / Special ability: Deep cut. When your opponent hurts you, if he rolls a 6 in a damage roll (Damage 1d6+5), not only has he inflicted 11 damage points, but he has also seriously injured you. Therefore, at the beginning of each subsequent combat round, you lose 1 life point due to blood loss. You lose this life point right before making each opposed attack roll. / Extremely skillful: your enemy can't roll a 1. Re-roll any dice that show 1 as a result.

◘ **Third elite soldier:** Curved sword (SK). Damage: 1d6+6 / SK 6 / LP: 35 / Armor: Hardened leather breastplate (C). Action area: trunk (values 2, 3 and 4). Protection: 5 LP. Reinforced leather armbands and greaves (A) (G). Action area: arms and legs. Protection: 3 LP. Reinforced metal helmet (H). Action area: head. Protection: 3 LP / Special ability: Deep cut. When your opponent hurts you, if he rolls a 6 in a damage roll (Damage 1d6+6), not only has he inflicted 12 damage points, but he has also seriously injured you. Therefore, at the beginning of each subsequent combat round, you lose 2 life points due to blood loss. You lose these life points right before making each opposed attack roll. / Extremely skillful: your enemy can't roll a 1 or 2. Re-roll any dice that show these results.

→ If you defeat all three enemies: 349

→ If you are defeated: 327

316

Willing to gather as much information as possible about the Tower of the Drum, you head to the north of the city. You keep on walking for some time, sure of your direction, as you have asked many passers-by about the watchtower's location. Thanks to that, you soon find it easily, as you can now discern the tall tower's distinctive shape in the distance; it rises well above all of the buildings that surround it.

When you reach it, you immediately note that it has been wisely built on top of a hill situated inside the walls of the city; this further helps to highlight its impressive height. From your discreet position, half-hidden in the shade of a wall, you can see that only small buildings are built nearby, the workshops of craftsman and merchant for the most part. There is no doubt that these low-rise buildings were designed to offer maximum visibility from the top of the tower, from where there must be a magnificent view of the whole city, and the nearby Abyssal Sea.

You see a single entranceway into the tower: two oversized gates reinforced with thick ironwork – no doubt extremely resistant going by their sturdy appearance. Two heavily armed amazons in uniform guard that entrance, one of them standing at each side of the door.

The tower is impressively tall, with its top well above your head. And it really isn't a tower, as it is more of a huge mass of stone, extremely wide if measured from side to side, with several windows at different heights; a fortress whose interior layout you are unable to imagine. As it isn't as slender as you had initially thought, such a massive building could contain a great number of staircases, rooms and corridors – you don't want to think about all of the amazons that you will likely find inside its walls. According to what you now see, you really do believe that you'll need the help offered by the strangers in their letter.

Finally, after watching the tower for a while longer without finding anything else that may be useful, you decide to move away so that you don't raise suspicion. At the very least, you already have some basic information about the Tower of the Drum, such as its exact location and where its gates are, so the following estrio you'll be able to go directly to your destination when the night comes to Urowen.

→ Go back to section 284.

317

From what the she-elf has told you, there must be many wild and dangerous animals held here, some of the fiercest in Urowen, foul monsters that the sorcerer Krénator uses to crossbreed with humans, dwarves and elves... Completely alert, you move forward through the tract of land before you, a succession of hills full of thick vegetation where danger could hide in every shadow. It is late at night by then, and the clouds have covered a great part of the sky, so you proceed in almost total darkness. Right then, you see how the tall bushes before you shake violently, indicating the near presence of some creature. Grab your weapon tightly and clench your teeth, as it seems that danger stalks you once again...

■ To determine if fortune smiles on you or not, roll a dice and pray to your gods to have mercy. Compare the result of the dice to the following table and keep on reading in the indicated section.

→ 1, go to section 393.
→ 2, go to section 360.
→ 3, go to section 345.
→ 4, go to section 333.
→ 5, go to section 298.
→ 6, go to section 232.

318

You had been about to lose your life in that absurd lethal trap, but luckily your reflexes have saved you in the nick of time. Although slightly wounded, you quickly recover and take a little time to calm yourself and rest. Only when you feel ready do you stand again and, using some grooves on the walls, climp out of the pit. Thanks to that, you can keep on searching the depths of the cavern, as after what you have just seen, you have little doubt that something really valuable is hidden down here...

→ Go to section 329.

319

When you are about to let yourself go with passion, a loud strike is heard upon the door. A stocky, out of control man armed with a huge, knotty club bursts into the room and immediately attacks you, shouting that your partner is his, and his only. His sudden charge completely surprises you, so all of your clothing and gear remains scattered across the floor. Although you have grabbed your weapon, you wear no armor in this fight. Additionally, the archer won't be able to shoot their bow, nor will you be able to use any potions, or any other item from your bag. Get ready to fight...

◻ **Jealous enemy:** Club (STR). Damage: 1d6+2 / STR 4 / LP: 25 / Armor: Leather breastplate (C). Action area: trunk (values 2, 3 and 4). Protection: 3 LP. Leather armbands and greaves (A) (G). Action area: arms and legs. Protection: 2 LP / Special ability: Frenzied enemy. This enemy is out of control, seething with jealousy and rage having discovered his partner in this situation. Because of his uncontrolled anger, he can't roll a 1. Re-roll any dice that result in a 1.

→ If you defeat him: 353
→ If you are beaten: 370

320

Luck has certainly turned her back on you this time, so fortune has definitely been against you. This warrior was as skillful and experienced as he looked, and there was nothing you could do against him – nothing. Unable to avoid it, you watch helplessly as your enemy's huge axe falls upon you at great speed; you can't block it nor dodge it. The pain you feel is indescribable, but it lasts for only a moment, as you feel your strength failing and then immediately faint, your mind falling into total darkness...

A bucket of iced water brings you back to reality. When you recover consciousness you do not know how much time has passed, and to your horror you discover that your hands and feet are tied and that you are lying on the deck of a great ship, now cold and soaked. Apparently, night has already passed, as Estrion is shinning in the sky of Urowen, burning your many wounds. You feel that your lips and face are badly burnt, and are suddenly aware of your terrible thirst.

"Look! The bastard is awake. Call the captain!"

You turn your head at these words and see a group of pirates nearby, looking at you with interest. You think that you recognize some of the men you saw previously leaving the cave, but you can't be sure.

"Well, if he's already awake, attract our friends and throw him overboard! I don't want to keep him on my ship any longer!"

The bearded man who said these words now disappears through a door that must lead to the cabins.

"You've heard the captain!" another of the sailors shouts, accompanied the laughter of his companions. "Use bait to attract the sharks!"

This last phrase almost paralyses you, but you immediately start to shout, begging for mercy. Only laughter and insults answer your demands, while the sailors collect a couple of buckets full of fish remains mixed with blood. They throw this bait overboard and the desired consequence is obtained soon, as you can tell from the excited shouts of the sailors, who point at the water while laughing crazily.

"Is he still here?" the captain, who has come back to the deck, asks then. "End this show and set course for the north. Hurry up! We're wasting too much time!"

The orders of the captain are carried out quickly so you are lifted over the gunwale in spite of your shouts and moans, and then ruthlessly thrown overboard. The terrible impact on the water is just the beginning of your nightmare, as you immediately see a fin coming out of the water and heading towards you. Another fin and a strong splash make you shudder while you try to stay afloat, although that will be the least of your worries when one of the sharks bites and almost tears off a leg. You stop hearing the shouts of the pirates when you are dragged to the depths, pulled by the strength of several sharks, frenzied by the taste of your blood. Fortunately, your torture ends soon, as another savage bite inflicts more pain and everything darkens as you drift away...

You have come far, much farther that many would have expected, but a cruel trick of destiny has led you to a terrible end, maybe the worst that you could have imagined... Such is life and death in the relentless Lands of Urowen, a highly dangerous place, where you never know what each new estrio may bring. → Go to section 400.

321

That combat was really savage, as you fought a hulking beast who, after suffering your last destructive strike, has collapsed before you as a windswept sandcastle.

↑ You win 1 experience point for having defeated such a powerful enemy.

Unfortunately, you don't have time to enjoy your victory, and can't even pause to rest, as the urgency of the situation forces you to keep on going up the stairs of the Tower of the Drum.

You hear battle noises coming from the lower floor, and that reminds you that you have to fulfill your mission as soon as possible, so that you can flee from the mortal trap in which the tower has turned into. That is why you don't lose another moment looking at the sandy remains of your last enemy, and you run to the stairs that will lead you to the upper floor. You bound up the stairs and quickly arrive at a room that seems to be at the very top of the tower, as you can't see a way to keep on ascending. You see large windows on the walls of this room, but above all you can't help but look at the huge drums kept here. A dozen drums are placed in a horizontal position, held within massive wooden structures, the drum heads oriented towards the center of the room. You are surprised by how big they are, as these impressive drums are massively oversized, as tall as even the tallest of the elves. You have little doubt that their sound is heard throughout the city, even well beyond its walls. But when you remember what has brought you here, you immediately forget all about the drums, as if you now stand on the top floor of the tower, Marok-häi must also be here, as all of your information assures. You instantly focus on your senses and walk very slowly, as your enemy may be hidden behind any of these colossal instruments. But a sudden voice makes you stop at once, as the amazon decides to reveal her presence.

"Well, well! Who do we have here then? You must surely be someone extremely powerful and brave if you have been bold enough to come up to the top of this tower alone." This voice comes from the back of the room, off to your right, so the person now talking hides behind one of the drums. "Come, come closer if your dare... I want to see you better... Oh, I see that I'll have to come and catch you," the voice adds when you remain stationery, "but let me do this first!"

Right then, a beautiful heavily-armed woman shows herself at the back of the room, with some kind of mallet held in her hands. She immediately raises the mallet over her head and strongly strikes the skin of the drum before her. Moving wholly out of instinct, you run to her as she continues to pound on the drum, but just as you reach her, she throws the mallet on the ground, takes a couple quick steps backward, and faces you – ready for battle.

"Are you Marok-häi?" you shout at her, full of rage.

"I am, and I guess that you've come to kill me! The alarm has sounded and soon the whole city will be alerted. Even if you achieve your objective... do you think that you'll be able to escape alive? But anyway, that doesn't matter, as you will have to walk over my dead body, and that won't ever happen! Let's find out who's been sent to kill me. Come on, come closer!"

Get ready for the toughest of the combats you have fought up until this moment, considering all of the enemies you had to defeat just to get here...

◘ **Marok-häi:** Curved sword of Bälkaar (SK). Damage: 1d6+3 / SK 5 / LP: 27 / Armor: Bälkaar hardened leather breastplate (C). Action area: trunk (values 2, 3 and 4). Protection: 4 LP. Reinforced leather armbands and greaves (A) (G). Action area: arms and legs. Protection: 2 LP. Reinforced metal helmet (H). Action area: head. Protection: 3 LP / Special ability: Deep cut. When Marok-häi hurts you, if she rolls a 6 in a damage roll (Damage 1d6+3), she inflicts 9 damage points, but has also seriously injured you. Therefore, at the beginning of each subsequent combat round, you will lose 2 life points due to the great loss of blood. You lose these life points right before making each opposed attack roll / Extremely skillful: the amazon can't roll a 1. Re-roll any the dice that show 1 as a result.

→ If you kill your enemy: 338
→ If Marok-häi makes you bite the dust: 356

322

You keep on running without a break, trying to find any trace about where on Urowen that damned Toljröm could have got to. There is nothing to indicate the direction that you must follow, until something draws your attention in the distance: a large pool of blood in a dark alleyway. You immediately slow fearing danger, and walk forward cautiously, attentive to everything around you. The narrow, gloomy alleyway is silent and empty, and also stinks of urine. What you see leaves you shocked, as before your eyes on the ground is the corpse of Toljröm, his throat cut from side to side. No doubt that poor bastard had other enemies aside from yourself, and his loose tongue had sentenced him to death. He has paid with his life for his reckless actions in such a complicated situation, with an impending war in which information is a valuable commodity.

You won't be able to gain any more information from his lifeless corpse, so your mission has come to an unexpected end... You must focus on escaping alive now, returning unnoticed to the ship to meet the elves and flee from this city, as there is no doubt that the one who killed Toljröm is nearby, and you could easily be their next victim. So you rush again along the streets of Wastmur, keen to reach the ship of the elves safe and sound.

→ Go to section 293.

323

Having chosen your mission, the she-elf gives you further details, more specific information on the objectives you have to fulfill. From what she tells you, the cavern you will have to enter is marked on a small map that she now hands to you. It is located on the outskirts of town, near the coast. Once there, your mission will be to find any evidence of the presence of the dragon in that cavern. If you find out that the dragon is indeed there, you'll have to gather all possible information about such a terrible enemy.

"Take this! You'll find it useful to get into the cave," the she-elf says, handing over a beautiful ring with an engraved blue gem. "When you wear it, you'll only have to wish it so and it will emit light in dark places." (↑ Write it down on your character file. This magical ring does not fill a slot in your leather bag).

Aside from her gift and the accurate location of the cavern, Dhaliara doesn't have much more information on your mission, so now everything depends on you. The estrio passes calmly, as everyone studiously prepares in the best possible way to face the dangerous challenges waiting that night. It's already dusk when Dhaliara gathers you all again to address you.

"Good luck to all of you, my companions and friends, as we part ways again. You know what you must do! Fulfill your missions as best you can. I hope to see all of you on the ship in the harbor. Neuköulos kan, sínfulas dänder ànfer!"

After hearing her words, you leave the room in small groups, slipping out of the building through different doors and windows to go unnoticed. When it is your turn, you leave the hiding place of the elves by a rear door, and you move into the alleyways of Wastmur, which are already in shadow, as the night is close. You walk toward the west and wait for darkness to fall upon the Lands of Urowen. Only then do you leave your concealed position to head for the cavern, where you will have to carry out your risky mission.

Leaving the last buildings of Wastmur behind, whose lights recede in the distance, you head to a tall cliff where you view the waves of the immense Abyssal Sea breaking over rocks well beneath your feet. You quickly continue your journey, following the instruction of the she-elf's map, although not every detail seems to be correct, as you soon reach a confusing crossroad that does not appear on it. Here a narrow path descends along the wall of the cliff before you, but you can also walk along the top of the cliff, and the correct way isn't clearly indicated. Once again, you'll have to trust your intuition to try and reach your destination...

→ If you choose to head down the pathway: 354
→ If you'd rather go along the top of the cliff: 308

324

You run towards the exit like a bat out of hell, but when you think that you'll be able to escape, just several steps from the exit, Bors of Raidyón himself blocks your way, ready to kill you. Luckily, something has now changed, as he seems to have been seriously injured in the brawl and is no longer as powerful as he was before. Take advantage of this situation to kill him...

◘ **Bors of Raidyón:** Enchanted battle axe (STR). Damage: 1d6+4 / STR 5 / LP: 29 / Armor: Coat of mail (C). Action area: trunk (values 2, 3 and 4). Protection: 4 LP. Armbands and greaves (A) (G). Action area: arms and legs. Protection: 2 LP / Special ability: Bonebreaker. When Bors of Raidyón hits you during combat, if he rolls a 6 in his damage roll (Damage 1d6+4), not only has he inflicted 10 damage points, but he has also broken one of your bones. Therefore, from that moment on, you'll deduct 1 point from all of your opposed attack rolls. If he breaks a second bone, you'll deduct two points, and so on.

→ If you finally defeat him: 398
→ If Bors of Raidyón defeats you again: 388

325

Base camp
(write this number down on your character file)

You've finally located the three roots that the sorceress needs to brew the potion, and you also have the zodonte teeth to pay for her services. However, you are totally exhausted, so when you reach a quiet spot, you decide to sit and rest. You know that you have to build up your strength as you have both a long way ahead to get out of the mines, and a hard journey back to Bälkaar, which is going to be particularly long without the use of your horse. That is why you use as much time now to rest; you are so exhausted that you can't help but close your eyes and have a deep, restful sleep.

When you finally wake, you feel deeply relaxed, as if you had been sleeping for estrios. You have lost track of time by then, although that is not something that particularly worries you. However, you want to get out of these overwhelming mines as soon as possible, so you're soon under way again. You walk a long way until reaching the cavern where you killed the zodonte, where to your sorrow, a new surprise is waiting. You hear an odd fluttering noise that immediately draws your attention. Alerted in case of danger ahead, you walk cautiously, trying to hide yourself behind the gigantic stalagmites that crowd this area. Then, you can hardly believe your eyes as you discover something truly frightening; several ghastly creatures ravenously devour the corpse of the zodonte, which is still lying where you left it. Their appearance reminds you of vultures, but their wings are membranous, without feathers, similar to those of bats. As for their heads, their most predominant attribute is their huge, powerful beak that can easily tear flesh...

One of those creatures now flies very near to your head and, due to the horrible croaking noise it makes, it seems to be alerting the rest of the flock to danger. It seems that luck has turned its back on you again, as the entire group of creatures quickly focus on the strange intruder who stalks them...

When you see the frightening image of these beasts flying to your position with evil intention, an extreme rage arises inside your chest. But then the effects of the curse of the witch appear again, heightened even further this time, as your senses sharpen and you feel overwhelmingly powerful. Luckily, there is no place here where you can see your reflection, as your physical transformation is rather dramatic... You drop the lamp to the ground and get ready to face your enemies. Fight fiercely or you will not leave this place alive...

- You are in the fourth stage of the transformation of the curse of the witch. As a consequence, it has the following effects on you, and therefore, on your character file. Note down these characteristics on a separate sheet of paper; do not alter your character file, as all of these effects are temporary. The text will tell you when you are under these effects, as you are now. Add the following values to your attributes on your character file:

- STR: +5 / SK: +5 / MAG: +5 / PER: +6 / LP: +40 / PP: +5

- As you are under the effects of the curse, you can exceed the limit of 6 points in your attributes.

* **Special ability: Venom.** You are in a highly advanced state of your transformation, about to surrender to its effect, so you can now spit venom. This attack aims at the eyes of your enemy, and its purpose is to blind it and cause a certain paralysis, what will make its movements extremely difficult.

Therefore, you will only be able to use this special ability when your attack aims at the head of your enemy. So, if you roll a 6 for damage location (head), you'll be able to choose whether to make your regular attack or spit venom. If you choose the venom option, you have to make a damage roll (1d6 is the damage of the venom itself, +3 as it's an attack aimed at the head), but in addition, it will have a blinding and paralysing effect on your enemy, who will then deduct 1 point from all of its opposed attack rolls as long as it still lives. You're only allowed to spit venom once at each enemy.

- Due to the many enemies that are attacking, the following is a special combat. As the many blows and strikes will be delivered at a frantic pace, you won't recover any life points between one combat and the next. Remember that, thanks to the fact that you are in the fourth stage of the transformation, you have added 40 LP, so your total life points will be around 60. Use all of these points wisely to escape from this cavern's mortal trap, where the echoing croaks of these foul monsters hammers insistently inside your head. Get ready for the incoming fight...

◘ **First winged beast of the caverns:** Claws and beak (SK). Damage: 1d6+2 / SK 6 / LP: 20 / Armor: Thick skin. Action area: whole body (values 1 to 6). Protection: 2 LP / Special ability: Stunning croak. If the beast rolls a 6 in an opposed attack, and it wins that roll, not only does it have the chance to strike you, but while it does so, it will shriek a powerful croak right by your ear, temporarily stunning you. Because of that, you'll deduct 1 point from your next opposed attack roll.

◘ **Second winged beast of the caverns:** Claws and beak (SK). Damage: 1d6+3 / SK 7 / LP: 22 / Armor: Thick skin. Action area: whole body (values 1 to 6). Protection: 2 LP / Special ability: Stunning croak. See first beast.

◘ **Third winged beast of the caverns:** Claws and beak (SK). Damage: 1d6+4 / SK 8 / LP: 25 / Armor: Thick skin. Action area: whole body (values 1 to 6). Protection: 3 LP / Special ability: Stunning croak. See first beast.

◘ **Fourth winged beast of the caverns:** Claws and beak (SK). Damage: 1d6+5 / SK 8 / LP: 26 / Armor: Thick skin. Action area: whole body (values 1 to 6). Protection: 3 LP / Special ability: Stunning croak. See first beast. / Lethal peck. If the creature rolls a 6 in a damage roll, it has pierced your armor and has inflicted serious damage. Therefore, you lose 2 life points due to blood loss. You lose these life points right before each opposed attack roll.

→ If you defeat your four enemies in a row, and you still have some life points remaining after the final combat: 346

→ If you are defeated before killing the fourth beast, try it again or go back to the previous base camp. Every time that you are defeated, you will have to choose one of these consequences:

a) You lose 1 EP.

b) You lose 1 item from your leather bag.

c) During the fight, a piece of armor has been so seriously damaged that it will now grant 1 point less of protection. You can choose the piece of armor: H, C, A or G. The one you choose will lose 1 point of protection. Update your character file with this new value, as this deduction lasts for the rest of the game, until you can purchase replacement armor.

326

Pleased with this new opportunity that destiny has offered, you accept the proposal of the Major Soldier of Verinfes without a moment's hesitation. From that moment on, you turn your life around, working towards a future where you do great things with your life. You have chosen a side in the great war that is about to begin; a war will send a tremor throughout the Lands of Urowen. You have succeeded so far in many combats, gaining reputation and experience, and a prominent position in the Kingdom of Verinfes. There's no doubt that is much more than you had expected when you started your adventures, and you have become a hero, a real 'Hero of Urowen'. However, in spite of your exploits, what you have lived so far means nothing when compared to what is undoubtedly to come... but, as minstrels say, that's another story.

You have come far, much farther that many would have expected, and fortune has smiled on you, bringing you an end worthy of a real hero...

→ Go to section 400.

327

Although you have fought bravely, this powerful enemy has crushed you, leaving you collapsed upon the ground, bleeding like a cut pig. You die in terrible pain while looking on at the ongoing battle that is still being fought around you; the elves are being defeated one by one, slaughtered, eviscerated... You couldn't do anything against such violent enemies, and your risky mission has turned out to be a massive failure, as you've not only failed to rescue Eddmont, but the entire group will perish in the attempt.

If, as you were advised, you have left your character file untouched, as it was before starting this mission, you can go back to section 368 and restart this dangerous mission if you wish.

Otherwise, this has been your unfortunate end. You have come far, much farther than many would have expected, but a cruel trick of destiny has led you to a bloody end... Such is life and death in the relentless Lands of Urowen, a highly dangerous place, where you never know what each new estrio will bring.

→ Go to section 400.

328

You have fought bravely but your nightmare is far from ending. Right then she aims her weapon directly at your heart, ready to deliver a mortal stab that will surely end your estrios on Urowen. But when you think that everything is lost, a small dart accurately strikes the slender neck of the beautiful amazon. Your enemy instantly falls to the ground and starts to convulse, while a black foam starts to dribble out of her mouth. You turn your head and see another couple of hooded shapes, grabbing strange blowpipes with which they are shooting similar darts again all of the amazons that remain standing. You are soon the only ones left standing in the room, as all of your enemies have lost their life to the lethal effects of the venom in which the darts shot by your new companions are oiled.

"Quick, let's continue climbing," the she-elf now tells you, as she turns to climb another flight of stairs. "They'll watch our backs! Hurry up, let's go!"

You follow her without a moment's delay, while her companions fall behind.

↓ As you were defeated, you lose 1 experience point.

→ Go to section 341.

329

You cautiously descend a long and winding tunnel that continues down into great depths until reaching a huge cavern. Here you hide behind a protruding rock, inspecting the area carefully for several moments, as it would seem that you have found what you were looking for. You are within a cavern that opens to the sea, now crouching out of sight on an elevated area, with a ramp that goes down to the water and into the cavern, creating a natural lagoon full of rocks. All of this area is well lit by many torches, and also by a bonfire where meat is being roasted. You also see a table covered with plenty of unidentifiable objects, and several stools and barrels. A dozen or so sailors, surely pirates going by their appearance and stance, currently push a boat towards the water, encouraging one another as they do so. When the water rises to their waists they leave the rocks behind, clamber onto the boat and row offshore, taking advantage of the fact that the water is calm. Only one of these men remains. He is some kind of sentinel who guards what appears to be their camp, but he is not a simple watchman, as you would swear that he is a full Servant of Neucen; a stout, hulking dreknar giant with a tattooed face. He is sitting by the fire, with his impressive battle axe within easy reach.

If the pirates have been celebrating, as you would swear they were, then they may have a considerable amount of booty hidden down there. Unfortunately, they haven't left it unprotected, as that guard is a real monster, a butcher whose appearance from afar is enough to intimidate anyone.

→ You have already fulfilled the mission that Dhaliara entrusted you with. You have investigated the presence of the dragon, which you now know is a fraud orchestrated by these pirates to conceal their hideout. That is why you can be satisfied and go back to Wastmur to meet the elves. If you choose this option, go to section 372.

→ If you'd rather get to the bottom of this issue and are keen to fight the Servant of Neucen and then search the cave to your heart's desire, go to section 357.

Market of Bälkaar

Armor:

- **Reinforced metal helmet:** 70 zaifas. Action area: head. Protection: 3 LP.

- **Bälkaar hardened leather breastplate:** 90 zaifas. Action area: trunk (values 2, 3 and 4). Protection: 4 LP.

- **Reinforced leather armbands:** 40 zaifas. Area: arms. Protection: 2 LP.

- **Reinforced leather greaves:** 40 zaifas. Area: legs. Protection: 2 LP.

Weapons:

- **Amazon's bow (only for hunters):** 10 zaifas (SK). Damage: 1d6+2. Difficulty: 8.

- **Arrows:** 5 arrows cost 1 zaifa (they do not fill a slot in your leather bag).

- **Trident:** 110 zaifas (two-handed weapon, SK). Damage: 1d6+3. Special ability: Triple hole. When you hit an enemy during combat, if you roll a 6 in a damage roll (Damage: 1d6+3), not only have you inflicted 9 damage points, but you have also plunged the trident deeply into your victim. Therefore, at the beginning of each subsequent combat round, your enemy will lose 2 life points because of these serious injuries. They lose these life points right before making each opposed attack roll.

- **Heavy club:** 110 zaifas (two-handed weapon, STR). Damage: 1d6+3. Special ability: Bonebreaker. When you strike your enemy during combat, if you roll a 6 in a damage roll (Damage: 1d6+3), not only have you inflicted 9 damage points, but you have also broken a bone. Therefore, your enemy will deduct 1 point from the value of all subsequent opposed attack rolls. If you break another bone, they will deduct an additional point, and so on.

- **Úreher gemstone:** 110 zaifas (precious stone that casts energy to your enemy, MAG). Damage: 1d6+3. Special ability: Lock on target. When you hit an enemy, if you roll a 6 in your damage location roll, not only will your strike aim at their head, but thanks to the power of the gem, it has locked on to its target and all of your subsequent strikes will automatically strike your enemy's head (taking advantage of the three extra damage points without the need to roll for damage location).

Other gear:

* If you are a thief, your clever hands allow you to obtain an item from this section for free.

- Food rations for three estrios (days): 5 zaifas.

- Healing potion: 20 zaifas. How to use it: during combat, after winning an opposed attack roll, instead of hitting your enemy you can choose to drink this potion. There is potion enough for 1 dose. When you drink it, you recover 1d6+3 life points. Write it down in your leather bag, as this potion fills one of its slots. Once used, delete it from your character file.

- Small healing potion: 10 zaifas. How to use it: during combat, after winning an opposed attack roll, instead of hitting your enemy you can choose to drink this potion. There is potion enough for 1 dose. When you drink it, you recover 1d6 life points. Write it down in your leather bag, as this potion fills one of its slots. Once used, delete it from your character file.

- Bälkian elixir. 30 zaifas. How to use it: drink immediately before combat. There is elixir enough for 1 dose. When you drink it, your speed and reflexes will improve considerably, so you'll become very hard to beat. During that combat, you will add 2 extra points to all of your opposed attack rolls. Write it down in your leather bag as this potion fills one of its slots. Once used, delete it from your character file.

- Small bälkian elixir. 5 zaifas. How to use it: drink immediately before an opposed attack roll. There is elixir enough for 1 dose. After you drink it, your speed and reflexes will improve momentarily. Add 2 extra points to your following opposed attack roll (only in that roll). Write it down in your leather bag, as this concoction fills one of its slots. Once used, delete it from your character file.

- Mystic shield potion. 30 zaifas. How to use it: drink immediately before combat. There is potion enough for 1 dose. After you drink it, your body will emit a bluish halo that will protect you from attacks. Action area: whole body (values 1 to 6). Protection: 2 extra LP, to be added to the protection granted by your armor. Write it down in your leather bag, as this potion fills one of its slots. Once used, delete it from your character file.

- Chemical products (only for alchemists): 6 zaifas. With these components the alchemist will be able to brew 1 healing potion that can heal 1d6+1 LP (to be added to the extra points due to the alchemist's special ability, i.e., 2d6+1). You use it in the usual way with potions: during combat, after winning an opposed attack roll, instead of hurting your enemy you can choose to drink this potion. Each potion of this kind fills a slot in your leather bag. Once used, delete it from your character file.

→ Once you have finished your shopping, go back to section 284.

331

↑ You win 1 experience point thanks to the terrific display of power you've just shown in hand-to-hand combat. Unfortunately, you don't have time to enjoy your victory, as while chairs and bottles fly around in the dangerous battlefield of the tavern, another henchman of Bors of Raidyón blocks your way, ready to kill you...

◻ **Man-at-arms at Bors of Raidyón's service:** Heavy club (STR). Damage: 1d6+5 / STR 5 / LP: 28 / Armor: Reinforced helmet (H). Action area: head. Protection: 3 LP. Coat of mail (C). Action area: trunk (values 2, 3 and 4). Protection: 4 LP. Reinforced armbands and greaves (A) (G). Action area: arms and legs. Protection: 2 LP / Special ability: Shield of fire. When you roll a 6 in a damage roll, your enemy will automatically cast this charm (without rolling any dice), channelling part of his vital energy, his very essence, to build a huge shield of fire before him that protects his whole body. Therefore, your enemy does not suffer a single damage point during that round.

→ If you get rid of this fierce enemy: 227
→ If your enemy defeats you, go to section 380, but don't lose this page or forget that you are in section 331.

332

As instructed in the previous section, if you are a thief and have chosen this option, you won't have to solve anything to know the solution to this complex puzzle. Therefore, instead of struggling to decipher it, you can simply go to section 365 and enjoy one of the advantages for being such a bold thief.

333

Frightened and alarmed, you look at the creature that now moves directly towards you. It is a magically created monstrosity that is a cruel combination of a human and what you think is a saber-toothed tiger, going by the sight of the oversized fangs that protrude from its jaws. The beast looks at you intently, pauses and then roars horribly before running on its four legs towards you at a frantic speed. Get ready to defend for your life...

◻ **Saber-toothed monstrosity:** Claws (SK). Damage: 1d6+5 / SK 5 / LP: 30 / Armor: Thick fur and skin. Action area: whole body (values 1 to 6). Protection: 2 LP / Special ability: Fangs attack. If this beast rolls a 6 in a damage roll, it has pierced your flesh with its fangs, and then violently shaken you, inflicting serious wounds. Therefore, at the beginning of each subsequent combat round you lose 3 life points due to blood loss. You lose these life points right before each opposed attack roll.

→ If you defeat this horrible creature: 286
→ If your enemy can bring you to the ground, go to section 258, but don't lose this page or forget that you are in section 333.

334

You run through the labyrinthine streets of Wastmur attempting to mislead your pursuer. Apparently, you have succeeded, as when you stop to regain your breath, there is no trace of him to be seen. Everything suggests that fortune has smiled on you this time, and your pursuer has lost your path or quit his chase. You finally decide to head directly to the elven ship to escape, as you don't want to spend another minute in this city's filthy streets. You set a quick pace for the harbor.

→ Go to section 293.

335
Base camp

When you regain consciousness, you see that you are lying on a bed in which you have spent the night. The sorceress is in front of you, showing you a small glass.

"I guess you feel better now, don't you?" she says. "Here. Drink this. It will help you to recover and it will make the stomach ache disappear for good... don't worry about its taste. You'll like it; it's sweet."

Grateful for the kindness of the amazon, you gulp the contents of the glass and immediately start feeling better. So much so that you are soon standing, rapidly regaining strength.

"Well, my friend," Sendhöra adds when she checks that you are all right, "the potion has fulfilled its role effectively, so I can guarantee that you have gotten rid of that curse for good. You can leave when you want, as nothing's keeping you here. Anyway, if you want to have some further rest, you can stay as long as you need to. I, for one, must say goodbye now, as there are important issues that need my attention. It's been my pleasure to know you. If you ever need my services again, don't hesitate to pay me a visit, even knowing my high price. See you soon. I hope that our paths will someday cross again."

After saying these words, the sorceress leaves the room and you are left to your thoughts. The idea of the mission that Brádoc entrusted to you becomes more and more important. That is why you leave the home of the amazon soon, ready to fulfill this new challenge. Once you are back on the street, you have several options to choose from...

→ This section is subject to the fact that you have played as instructed in section 203 in your previous visit to the city. You should refresh your memory and have a look at that section to check if you have the information given there and, therefore, if you can play this option and go to Rámada's place. If you have the information but you don't have enough zaifas, you can choose another option before playing this one. If you already have the information and the zaifas, and you are willing to spend them, go to section 249.

→ You hear a man shouting out these words: 'Who wants to fight Cäshdor? Double your zaifas if you defeat him!' If you want to try your luck with this easy way to win some coins: 262

→ If after the many pains that you've now lived through, you decide to waste some time enjoying the pleasures of life, you can choose to look for a tavern in which you may find some fun: 274

→ When you decide to focus on the mission that Brádoc entrusted you with and all your efforts are devoted to kill Marok-häi: 220. (Keep in mind that when you go to this section, an independent adventure will start, so you won't be allowed to come back to this base camp and, therefore, you won't be able to play the other options).

336

◘ **Ázer:** Magical attacks with his wand (MAG). Damage: 1d6+6 / MAG 6 / PP: 4 / LP: 70 / Armor: Energy field protecting his whole body (values 1 to 6). Protection: 4 / Special ability: Dodge. Ázer is extraordinarily nimble. Every time you try to hurt him (that is to say, every time you make a damage roll), he'll attempt to dodge your attack. Roll a dice: if you roll a 6, he has successfully dodged your attack and doesn't take any damage / Freeze: when Ázer hurts you, if he rolls a 6 in his damage location roll, the discharge will have a lethal effect on you. Therefore, you lose 1 life point at the beginning of each subsequent round due to the chill that now spreads throughout your body (in addition to the regular damage of this attack). You lose this life point right before making each opposed attack roll / Invisibility charm. Power Point (PP) needed to cast it: 4. Effects: after casting this charm, your enemy suddenly becomes invisible. How to use it: when Ázer's LP drop below 10, he will cast this charm as soon as he wins an opposed attack roll. Right then, his body will disappear from view for two combat rounds. This means that Ázer will be able to make two damage rolls (with their corresponding damage location roll) directly against you. There will not be an opposed attack roll in these rounds as your enemy wins them without needing to roll dice, as you don't know where you should attack nor what you should defend yourself from. You will only be allowed to randomly try to dodge his attacks. Roll a dice for each attack: if you roll a 6 you have luckily dodged that attack. Once Ázer's has made these two damage rolls, he is visible once again, and the combat continues in the usual way.

→ If you knock Ázer out: 263
→ If your enemy makes you bite the dust: 327

337

Intimidated by the new opportunity that destiny seems to offer, you decide to refuse it, pleading that you still have a lot to learn before becoming a real hero. And that is your goal, to become a real 'Hero of Urowen', and you think that it is better to keep on travelling throughout Urowen searching for new and greater challenges to face. From this moment on your life will reach a turning point towards a journey with no particular destination in mind, guided by the wind and reaching the destination where your tired feet drag you. But that's the destiny you have chosen for yourself, a path that Brádoc accepts and perfectly understands.

A bloody war is about to begin, a conflict that will send a tremor throughout the Lands of Urowen, and although you have no doubt that you will play some part in the conflict, you choose to do so in a different way, without being an active part of any army, just another regular soldier on the battlefield. You have succeeded in many battles so far, gaining fame and experience that will help you on your chosen path. However, despite all of your exploits, what you have lived so far is nothing compared to what is still to be lived... but that, as good minstrels usually say, is part of another story.

You have come far, much farther that many would have expected, and luck has smiled on you with an ending worthy of a real hero... Keep on reading. → Go to section 400.

338

Magnificent! ↑ You win 1 experience point because it is a real exploit to have progressed this far. You are standing with the lifeless corpse of the amazon at your feet... However, even with a fatal blow to her throat, you double check that she no longer lives, something you don't doubt any longer when you see that her head is separated from her still body. You then remember Brádoc's description of the amazon, so you check that it is really her. Her long red hair, deep blue eyes and the lack of her left little finger confirm without a doubt that you have killed Marok-häi...

Now that you have fulfilled your mission, nothing else is to be done here. Time runs against you if you value your life, as your priority must now be to escape this damned tower. But there is only one way out, and that goes down the same stairs that led you here. Turning to flee, you see the she-elf standing several steps from you, her clothes torn and almost completely covered in blood, which isn't, for the most part, hers. She gives you a small smile.

"Well done. You have fulfilled the mission that brought us here," the beautiful she-elf says solemnly. "Now you'd best follow me if you want to escape alive. Quickly, let's get out before it's too late!"

So you rush down the many stairs, your injuries aching, but you don't have the time to waste on complaints or healings. As you go down, you realise in amazement the bloody trail of bodies that you have left behind on the Tower of the Drum's different floors. Only when you reach the ground do you come to a halt, as you see that a large group of elves fiercely hold off numerous amazons at the smoldering gates, who are desperate to access the tower and abruptly end your life.

"Kúdinar, have you found the entrance to the sewers?" the she-elf asks one of her companions as he approaches.

"Aye, Dhaliara! It's where our map indicated."

"Well then, what are you waiting for? Proceed as planned!"

Without a moment's respite, Kúdinar takes a couple of steps towards you, closes his eyes and immediately begins to focus his energies.

"Watch there!" Dhaliara shouts then from the rear to the rest of the elves who are fighting at the gates. "Nemöi sidof, Kúdinar kai tan ämnem!"

From that moment on, everything seems to happen really quickly, as several things occur at the same time before your amazed eyes. A huge fireball comes out of Kúdinar's hands and flies at a frantic speed towards the upper part of the tower, which then bursts apart in a powerful explosion. Meanwhile, the elves on the ground quickly retreat while the amazons hungrily pounce on them, however, as they do so the ceiling and part of the outside wall crumbles away, burying these seasoned amazons under a mountain of stone. Although more amazons wait outside only two of the skilled warriors, who were at the forefront, avoid this horrible death. They stand on this side of the collapse, but to their sorrow they die soon under the swift blades of the elves.

Although you are momentarily safe having blocked the entrance to the tower, the explosion has been so powerful that all of you remain stunned; so much so that you only hear a horrible buzzing noise that mercilessly punishes your aching ears. That is why you don't hear the words of the she-elf Dhaliara and you can only guide yourself by her signs. She waves at you to move away from the entrance and to follow Kúdinar, who is leading the way along one of the tower's corridors.

You rush on again, now surrounded by elves who flee down the narrow staircases to what are, undoubtedly, the sewers of Bälkaar. You would have never otherwise wanted to go down here, as after passing through a heavy grate opened by the elves, you have to walk in filthy, chest-high waters that reek of disease and death.

"Everybody in silence now. Follow Kúdinar, as he has the map," Dhaliara orders as you follow your guide. He carrys some kind of bluish gem in one hand, with which he lights the way; the other hand holds a parchment, which he consults constantly.

Trying not to eject the contents of your stomach due to the terrible stink that fills this narrow duct, you move forward with a firm step, very attentive to everything around you. More than once you have to look away when you see roaches running across the wall less than a hand from your face, as you know that your only chance is to go with the elves.

You continue to move along an ongoing labyrinth of tunnels, making many twists and taking many deviations, until Kúdinar finally comes to a halt.

"Dhaliara, we've arrived. It's right there."

"Fine, take the grid off and let's hurry for the ship. This isn't a safe place. We must sail away from the coast as soon as possible," the she-elf responds.

Following her instructions, some of your new companions move forward along the tunnel until stopping at thick bars that now block your way. However, they have already been forced by the elves in the estrios before the assault of the tower, and the grate no longer blocks the tunnel, just appearing to still do so. With a push, the grid falls easily onto tall grass beyond it and you quickly head outside, leaving the sewers of Bälkaar behind. You immediately realise that you are outside the walls of the city, on a sheer cliff full of vegetation that stands above the waters of the Abyssal Sea. Dhaliara is now leading the way, and she heads down a narrow path made of slippery stones. Luckily, you reach the bottom quickly, to a narrow beach where the elves have hidden a couple of boats within the thick vegetation.

Led by your new companions, you are soon rowing one of their boats, fleeing from the city of the amazons. After a short while, you spot a dim light that seems to be signaling at you; shortly thereafter, in the darkness of the night, you are surprised to discern the dark shape of a ship, anchored near the coast, waiting for your arrival.

"Did it go well?" you hear someone ask from aboard the ship.

"Better than expected!" Dhaliara answers. "Quickly, let's get out of here immediately! Set course for Wastmur!"

→ Keep on reading. Go to section 390.

339

You are in a strange kind of sewer that doesn't really look like one, particularly because of the three different pathways now before your eyes. Two tunnels rise out of the water and then continue on at ground level, while the third seems to simply fall deeper and deeper into the ground ahead.

→ If you decide to take the tunnel on your left: 352

→ If you choose to follow the tunnel on your right: 242

→ If you'd rather go along the tunnel in the middle, the one that seems to sink into the water: 363

340

You rush outside like a bat out of hell, but right when you think that you might have escaped, just a few steps from the door, you stumble into a drunk hireling who feels instantly insulted. Without a word's warning, he unleashes a punch that you can hardly dodge and immediately grabs his weapon. Do your best to get rid of this bastard as soon as you can, as Bors of Raidyón is already running towards you...

◻ **Drunk enemy:** Sword (SK). Damage: 1d6+3 / SK 4 / LP: 23 / Armor: Leather breastplate (C). Action area: trunk (values 2, 3 and 4). Protection: 3 LP. Leather armbands and greaves (A) (G). Action area: arms and legs. Protection: 2 LP / Special ability: Frenzied enemy. This enemy is out of control, totally driven by rage and the excessive amount of alcohol he's consumed. Therefore, he cannot roll a 1 or a 2 in any opposed attack, damage location or damage roll. Re-roll any value of 1 or 2.

→ If you kill him: 398
→ If your enemy makes you bite the dust: 379

341

You rush up the narrow stairway to an upper floor, but just as you reach a spacious room, two hidden amazons shoot their bows at you. One of these arrows is flying directly at you; deal with it by following these instructions:

- The amazon who has shot at you, like every amazon in the guard of honor, is a real master of the bow. Because of that, to represent her mastery with the bow, roll a dice. The amazon will only miss her shot if she gets a 1 or 2 in that roll. If that's the case, the arrow will miss, hitting the wall at your back. Therefore, if you roll 3 to 6, the arrow will strike you. Roll for damage location and then for damage itself: 1d6+1. If the arrow has hit you, deal with it with in the same way as in regular combat.

As soon as the amazon has fired her first arrow, she raises her hand to take another arrow from her quiver. You immediately respond by rushing her position to prevent her from shooting again. You are lucky enough to run that distance before she can prepare her bow again, so the amazon leaves her bow and takes up her flail. A new combat is waiting for you while your companion, the she-elf, is trying to defeat the other amazon...

- If you've been hit by the arrow, you'll start this combat after having deducted the life points of that strike.

◘ **Second amazon:** Flail (SK). Damage: 1d6+3 / SK 4 / LP: 27 / Armor: Hardened leather breastplate (C). Action area: trunk (values 2, 3 and 4). Protection: 3 LP. Hardened leather armbands and greaves (A) (G). Action area: arms and legs. Protection: 2 LP / Special ability: Critical damage. When the amazon hurts you, if she rolls a 6 in a damage roll (Damage: 1d6+3), not only have you suffered 9 damage points, but she has also seriously hurt you. Therefore, at the beginning of each subsequent combat round, you will lose 1 life point due to blood loss. You lose this life point right before making each opposed attack roll.

> → If you can defeat your enemy: 272
> → If the amazon beats you: 302

342

You walk on for a long stretch, moving deeper into the depths of Urowen. From the outside you wouldn't have thought that this cavern would be so large, but the truth reveals that it is an extensive labyrinth of tunnels. Nothing of interest draws your attention until a wooden door suddenly blocks your way. Fearing what you may find on the other side of the door, you set your ear to it to try and hear something, but everything seems to be silent. It opens easily and what you find beyond the door leaves you in amazement: a spacious room full of supplies, such as wine casks, barrels full of apples, roasted meats, and different kinds of spices... Plenty more things fill that room, which also features another door that you now decide to open.

> → Go to section 329.

343

The she-elf provides you with further details, adding specific information related to the goals you must achieve. She tells you that the location you have to go to is marked on a small map that she hands over, right in the middle of the town; some kind of walled barracks in which she believes some of the gold is kept. In fact, she doesn't know much more about this place, so you'll have to find a way to sneak in unnoticed. However, the elves have discovered it is not a well-guarded place, possibly because it is believed that being in the middle of Wastmur, any attack would be absurd. Apparently, nobody thinks that a small-scale infiltration like the one you are about to try could be successful, and that is why Dhaliara gives you a long rope ending with a strong hook.

"Take this and put it to good use," the she-elf says.

(This object is considered special, as you are going to carry it in your hands, hidden under your cloak, and you will use it as soon as you start your mission, so it doesn't fill a slot in your leather bag).

Once there, your mission requires you to gain as much information as you can about the origin of the gold, and to steal as much of it as possible. Everything is in your hands now. The estrio passes calmly, as everyone studiously prepares in the best possible way to face the dangerous challenges waiting that night. It's already dusk when Dhaliara gathers you all again to address you.

"Good luck to all of you, my companions and friends, as we part ways again. You know what you must do! Fulfill your missions as best you can. I hope to see all of you on the ship in the harbor. Neuköulos kan, sínfulas dänder ànfer!"

After hearing her words, you leave the room in small groups, slipping out of the building through different doors and windows to go unnoticed. When it is your turn, you leave the hiding place of the elves by a rear door, and you move into the alleyways of Wastmur, which are already in shadow, as the night is close. You head downtown, as you have to be at the walls before the gates of the town are locked.

Nothing happens before you get to your new position, so you wait for the night to lord over the Lands of Urowen. Only then you decide to leave your hiding place in a dark alleyway, and begin walking, following the instruction of the she-elf's map. Luckily, you don't have to walk for long, as you soon locate a kind of stronghold. Without making any noise, you place yourself strategically to watch and evaluate the barracks. There is a large, closed gate barring access to the premises, which seem to be rather spacious. A guard walks on top the walls in one direction, and shortly thereafter you see another guard heading in the opposite direction. After waiting and watching for a long time, you discover that these two guards cross before you several times, therefore they follow a circuit that is retraced again and again.

You then formulate a plan. As there are only two men guarding the walls, when they cross, if you are on the opposite side, you'll have enough time to scale the wall before the first guard returns to your position.

So you move again in the darkness, looking for the most distant point of the walls, opposite to where the sentinels will cross their paths again according to your calculations. But before you get to your destination, you see a new entrance door, not the main door, and it looks significantly less difficult to deal with than the other. However, it is locked, and you can't get in that way. You stick to your plan then, hidden in the shadows, waiting for the exact moment when you have to throw your hook to climb the wall...

Hidden at the rear of the stronghold, you see that the guards, after crossing their paths in front of you, move along the upper side of the walls heading in opposite directions. This is your moment, and you immediately throw the hook praying that it doesn't make too much noise when it impacts the battlements. Everything seems to go better than expected as the hook is rapidly secured and the rope, when tightly stretched, seems to be sure enough to climb. Using your considerable strength and skill, you are soon on top the wall. A staircase descending several steps away from your position offers a new way out, so you take up your rope and run down the staircase, immediately hiding under a carriage by the wall, in what looks like a weapons courtyard.

After relaxing and regaining your breath a little, you decide that this is a good place to hide the rope and hook, so you leave it under the carriage, believing that it might be helpful to escape the same way you entered. You stop for a moment to closely scan the scene before you: a courtyard with several stone buildings, with nothing to inform you about what each of them may be used for.

→ If you choose to enter the nearest one, whose door is just ten steps from your position: 358

→ If you'd rather take the risk of moving to one of the remotest buildings to look inside through a window: 371

344

Luck wasn't on your side this time. Your opponent was as skillful and experienced as he looked, and you couldn't do anything to defeat him. Unable to avoid it, you were helpless under his massive axe, and you were unable to dodge or block the blow that sped towards your neck. You feel overwhelming pain and distress, yet it lasts for only a second, and you don't even utter a sound of anguish before everything turns dark and your head falls from your body, which then collapses to the ground, pouring out blood through the grisly open wound.

You have come far, much farther than many would have expected, but a cruel trick of destiny has led you to an unhappy ending... Such is life and death in the relentless Lands of Urowen, a highly dangerous place, where you never know what each new estrio may bring. Keep on reading. → Go to section 400.

345

You are really surprised by what you see, as now before you is a grotesque, deformed and truly horrible creature. By what your eyes tell you, it's some kind of mixture between a dwarf and a giant spider, so the result really can't be any more disturbing. The beast, walking on many articulated legs, makes a hissing sound and runs directly towards your position. Get ready for the impending combat...

◘ **Arachnid Monstrosity:** Sting (SK). Damage: 1d6+2 / SK 4 / LP: 25 / Armor: none / Special ability: Venom. When this beast hits you, if it rolls a 1 in its damage roll, not only has it inflicted 3 damage points, but it has also injected the powerful venom within its fangs. Therefore, at the beginning of each subsequent combat round, you lose 4 life points due to the venom's lethal effects. You lose these life points right before making each opposed attack roll.

→ If you defeat this deformed and disgusting creature: 286

→ If the creature defeats you, go to section 258, but don't lose this page or forget that you are in section 345.

346

Your battle was titanic, outstandingly epic and worthy of rememberance. For that reason, and for having survived that mortal trap, you win 2 EP that will help you to improve your character file.

You almost can't believe that you have won against so many lethal enemies, Suddenly, you find yourself running along one of the tunnels, the same one that led you to the cavern when you entered the mines, so you know that, if you don't get lost, this tunnel will take you outside. But your troubled mind, exhausted by the effort and possessed by the curse of the witch, is tired and confused, mixing the past and the present so much that you begin to lose touch with reality. This sensation only grows more and more powerful and you now feel dreadfully dizzy, as everything spins around you, fading away as you faint...

When you regain consciousness (forget about the modifiers of the curse, as you are again playing with the values of your character file), you surprisingly discover that you are already at the surface, in one of the small wooden buildings that protects the entrance. You remember only vaguely what has happened since you defeated those strange winged creatures... Terribly worried, you quickly check the contents of your leather bag, unsure as to what might have happened with the roots of the alédoras. Luckily, you still have them with you, as well as the zodonte teeth, both safely kept within your bag.

You stand and discover that you are fully rested and are again the master of your own actions, so you pick up your meagre possessions and set off for Bälkaar. Luckily the estrio is clear and the temperature is mild so you now travel with renewed strength and hope, keen to reach your destination without delay. On the second estrio you reach the forested area, but luckily, everything seems to be calm and you set a fast pace, rapidly shortening the distance to your destination. However, in the afternoon, a strange sensation takes hold of your heart as, although you can't describe what it is really happening, you feel that you're being observed, as if many looming eyes were fixed on you. Unsettled by the possibility of danger, you stop and look around...

■ Roll for Perception (PER) with a difficulty of 7.

→ If the result is 7 or higher: 253
→ If the result is 6 or less: 266

347

As soon as you face your opponent, you realise that maybe this wasn't the best of ideas, as your enemy seems to be just like a shadow, moving very quickly towards you. When he is several steps from your position, he moves his cape to the side and grabs two scimitars that make you feel a lump in your throat. But it is too late now to retreat or try to escape, so you can only grind your teeth and fight fiercely to outlive this confrontation...

◻ **Hooded stranger:** Two scimitars (SK). Damage: 1d6+4 / SK 5 / LP: 30 / Armor: Coat of mail (C). Action area: trunk (values 2, 3 and 4). Protection: 4 LP. Reinforced armbands and greaves (A) (G). Action area: arms and legs. Protection: 2 LP / Special ability: Multiple attacks. Every time your opponent hits you, he rolls two dice for his damage location rolls instead of just one, representing his attacks with both scimitars at the same time. You will only be hit with one scimitar, but it will be the one whose result is higher in the damage location roll. Thanks to this circumstance, your enemy will hit your arms and head more easily.

→ If you kill your enemy: 382
→ If you are defeated: 392

348

Keen to act as soon as possible, you decide that you can't wait any longer and begin climbing the helpful tree. Thanks to that, you are soon above the fence and can see the creature that stalks you – some kind of massive black dog, with two shining red eyes and dreadful jaws covered in white foam. One of its legs seems to be somewhat atrophied and that makes it clear to you that it is a dip: a crossbreed of dog and wolf known for its fierceness and lust for blood. Many atrocities are told about dips, as they don't hesitate to attack livestock or the shepherds that guard them.

You don't waste another second due to its loud growls, so you fall down from the tree to face the dip. Get ready for the fight...

◘ **Dip:** Fangs and claws (SK). Damage: 1d6+4 / SK 5 / LP: 27 / Armor: Thick fur and skin. Action area: whole body (values 1 to 6). Protection: 4 LP / Special ability: Lethal swipe. If the dip rolls a 6 in a damage roll, it has strongly attacked with its claws and then violently shaken you, inflicting serious damage. Therefore, at the beginning of each subsequent combat round, you lose 2 life points due to blood loss. You lose these life points right before making each opposed attack roll / Terror: the red eyes of the dip, shining intently in the dark, paralyse their victim in terror. Therefore, when the dip hits you, if it rolls a 6 in a damage location roll, it has looked you in the eye, making you tremble in fear. Deduct 1 point from all of your subsequent opposed attack rolls (in addition to the usual damage of that attack).

→ If you kill this sinister creature: 373
→ If it makes you bite the dust: 385

349

Once again you've fought gloriously, demonstrating skill and power worthy of a real 'Hero of Urowen'. Therefore, you win 1 more experience point, and regain 50 life points (with a maximum limit of 100). Besides, thanks to your overwhelming victory, your way is now clear, so you run upstairs with all of your might until you reach the floor where the exit waits. As you already know your way, you move quickly throughout the manor and are soon at the building's shattered door. Right then, when you think that you will be able to escape easily, an explosion bars your way; a blast of fire and a huge cloud of smoke from which the shape of a short human emerges. His face shows that he's suffered extensive torture; a wrinkled face despite his youth, as you believe that he can't be much older than yourself. He has a sharp, pointed nose and hollow eyes, which together make him look quite dreadful. In addition, his narrow mouth shows black, decaying teeth, and he wears a plain blue robe with a cincture about his extremely thin body.

"Stop right there!" this short human says, apparently in command. "You have come really far, but you'll never leave this place alive!"

"Who are you? Out of our way or we will kill you like the others!" you shout at this ugly bastard.

"You ask me who I am? Dumb idiot! I'm Ázer, if that name means anything to you. I'm Krénator's right-hand man... and I'll kill you at once!"

The fight is imminent. The elves will take care of the hirelings, but Ázer seems to have chosen you as his first victim. Good luck, brave warrior, as you will need it... → Keep on reading on section 336 and don't spare anything you have at your disposal to defeat this enemy.

350

Exhausted after so many adventures, you decline the she-elf's offer, deciding to make your own way back to a safe city, away from danger and from the threat of war. You aim to head east, probably to the Srimost Mountains, where you will be allowed to pursue your apprenticeship in a rather less risky way. And that is how, as Dhaliara had assured you, the elves of the snow set one of their boats ready for you, with food enough for several estrios. After a brief farewell, you are soon on board, rowing on still waters, while the ship of the elves is already far off on the horizon. You are quite near to the coast where you see a strip of white sand, so if you keep up your pace, you'll soon be on dry land. But when you are about to reach shallower waters, and thinking of the new route you'll take, something you would have never expected then occurs. Directly in front of you, now barring your way, is the massive head of a sea snake rising out of the water. Its appearance is terrifying, as it is covered with long spikes and thick black scales. Right then, you see its tail coming out of the water towards the rear of your boat, while its coils surround your small vessel, which is now completely at this monster's mercy. Luck seems to have turned its back on you this time, as you have unexpectedly encountered an enemy that greatly exceeds your might. Get ready to fight an unequal combat against a dangerous, powerful enemy...

◘ **Giant sea snake:** Fangs / Head and tail strikes (SK). Damage: 1d6+4 / SK 6 / LP: 34 / Armor: thick scales. Action area: it protects all locations (from 1 to 6). Protection: 4 LP / Special ability: Grip. If the snake rolls a 6 in a damage roll, it has caught you in its massive jaws, lifting you up over

311

the boat, unable to escape. If this happens (regardless of how many life points you have at that moment), keep on reading in section 375.

→ If you defeat your enemy: 307
→ If the sea snake defeats you: 234

351

With a final, mighty blow, you knock out your enemy, who now lies on the floor of the cave, completely at your mercy. You have fought fiercely, crushing a really powerful enemy. ↑ Because of this latest victory, you win 1 experience point and can keep on exploring the cave, positive that it hides a great secret.

You move on through a narrow tunnel that goes deeper and deeper, endlessly twisting its way downward. → Keep on reading at section 342.

352

After having made up your mind you resume walking, now on firm and dry ground, moving through a tunnel built from big stone blocks that are perfectly aligned and dovetailed. You walk cautiously, passing a fat rat, and after turning a corner you unexpectedly encounter a guard, stationed at this point. He is a very stout man, a genuine hulk, well equipped for hand-to-hand fighting.

"Watchword?" he asks, his resounding voice coming out of the slits of a beautiful helmet that hides everything but his dark eyes.

Unable to give him the correct answer, you hesitate just for a moment, but that's time enough for your opponent to realise that you are an intruder. The hulking guard grabs his massive broadsword and attacks. Make your best effort to escape with your life...

◻ **Skilled warrior, follower of Krénator:** War broadsword (STR). Damage: 1d6+4 / STR 5 / LP: 30 / Armor: Reinforced helmet (H), Action area: head. Protection: 3 LP. Coat of mail (C). Action area: trunk (values 2, 3 and 4). Protection: 4 LP. Reinforced armbands and greaves (A) (G). Action area: arms and legs. Protection: 3 LP / Special ability: Major fire edge. Every time this skilled warrior rolls a 6 in a damage roll, he has concentrated a part of his vital energy, his very essence, to channel it through his broadsword. His blade will burst into flames when he strikes, adding an extra 3 damage points. Additionally, this blow will inflict a critical injury and you will subsequently lose 1 life point at the beginning of each combat round from that moment on (this additional damage point does not stack, i.e., your opponent cannot inflict two critical injuries).

→ If you win this fight: 377

→ If you are defeated, go to section 277, but don't lose this page or forget that you are in section 352.

353

Despite your initial surprise and the compromising situation in which your enemy found you, you finally defeat him and knock him out. ↑ You win 1 experience point because of the incredible combat you have fought, being clearly at a disadvantage, half naked and barely equipped. However, you return to the main room somewhat frustrated, as you haven't been able to finish what you wanted so badly.

→ Go back to section 335 and choose another available option.

354

You walk with a hand on the wall of the cliff to feel a little safer, as the abyss below your feet is rather intimidating, with the roaring waves constantly hitting the rocks beneath. But you walk on steadily and soon reach a kind of ravine that takes you away from the sea. It is an area of lush vegetation, which subsequently makes progress more difficult, but you now move without the risk associated with walking by a cliff. You follow an even path that descends gently towards what seems to be the entrance of a cave. The cavern! You have undoubtedly been lucky to find this place without having suffered any form of mishap, however, this is just the beginning of your mission and danger may be waiting in any place, and if the legend of the dragon is true, it might already be stalking you.

→ Keep on reading on section 374.

355

TRAP: if you read this section at any time during your game, it means that you are cheating, as there isn't anywhere within the adventure that will direct you to this section. You must now read this paragraph fully, as you will be punished for having read what you shouldn't have. You have walked into a trap, and this will teach you to read only what you are told to read within your journey. As punishment, you lose 1 experience point and 1 item from your leather bag. You can now resume your game at the last section you had read, but be careful with devious traps such as this one from now on.

356

With a lethal blow of her curved sword, Marok-häi makes you collapse to the ground, bleeding profusely. You'll have to fight more fiercely next time to defeat such a skilled opponent. As a special gift, given because of the many tough enemies you've had to defeat to reach Marok-häi, you won't be punished this time. Thank the gods for their benevolence towards you! Stand up again and get ready to fight the terrible warrior who stands before you.

→ Go back to section 321 and kill this ferocious amazon.

357

Taking courage, you come out of your hiding place and directly face the Servant of Neucen. He quickly gets to his feet and menacingly grabs his axe as soon as he sees you. The dreknar sentinel doesn't waste words, running directly towards you. Get ready for the impending fight, as this will be a titanic combat...

* **Author's note:** in order to defeat this really tough enemy, don't spare anything at your disposal, such as all of the items in your leather bag, as you must bear in mind that, if you are defeated, there are much worse destinies than death.

◻ **Dreknar sentinel, Servant of Neucen:** Battle axe (STR). Damage: 1d6+6 / STR 7 / LP: 40 / Armor: none / Special ability: Extremely tough. This enemy has outstanding endurance. Whenever your opponent rolls a 6 in any roll, he instantly regains 2 life points (up to a maximum of 40 points) / Lethal attack. If your opponent rolls a 6 in a damage location roll and then rolls a 6 in a damage roll (damage 1d6+6), he has made a lethal attack. Therefore, his blow will aim directly at your neck, cutting it like butter, severing your head from the rest of your body.

→ If you can defeat this real beast: 275
→ If the Servant of Neucen finally defeats you: 320
→ If your enemy makes his lethal attack and cuts off your head: 344

358

After checking the exact location of the guards, you take the opportunity when they are next out of sight to run across to the door of the nearest building, which fortunately opens as soon as you push on it. Once again, luck seems to be smiling upon you as you find an empty hall with nobody inside. There is just a large wooden table standing on a floor full of straw.

You walk along a passage at the back of the hall and discover something very strange there, as from the outside you would have sworn that this was some kind of tower, and that the building consisted of several stories, yet your way is now barred by a stone wall. You look around but there certainly isn't a staircase leading upwards, just the hall with the table and that absurd passage leading nowhere. That is why you search everywhere, trying to find something that could have remained unnoticed...

■ Roll for PER with a difficulty of 5.

→ If the result is 5 or higher: 383
→ If the result is 4 or less: 395

359

Tired of a tough day, you decide to look for a place where you can rest and regain strength, waiting for the hard test of the next estrio. If you have zaifas and you are willing to spend some, you can choose to lodge in an inn. On the contrary, you can always choose to try to sneak into a barn as, although it isn't the most comfortable of places, it is much cheaper. Whatever you do, take into account what is stated next:

- If you decide to lodge in a rather luxurious inn and have a good meal, delete 15 zaifas from your character file. Due to the magnificent rest and the restful sleep that you've had, you will gain 3 additional life points in your next fight (and only in the next fight).

- If you decide to lodge in a humble inn, and sleep in their common room, delete 6 zaifas from your character file. You enjoy only moderate rest (the best you are allowed), and your life points won't be modified for your next fight.

- If you decide to sneak inside and spend the night in a barn, don't delete any zaifa from your character file. If you choose this option, you will hardly have any rest, as you won't be able to sleep and will be exhausted the next estrio. Deduct 2 life points in your next fight (and only in the next fight).

Impatient and nervous about all of the events that are about to happen, you spend the estrio as quietly as you can, until the evening falls. Then, you prepare for the assault on the tower, checking your equipment, weapons and armor thoroughly. Once you are ready you leave your resting place and walk decisively to the Tower of the Drum, arriving as Estrion is about to hide. You have done everything that you were told to do in the letter, and now have only to choose a good spot to wait for your alleged partners to open the entrance to the stronghold.

You approach the tower, always remaining within shadow so that you don't draw any undesired attention. You finally decide to wait by the door of one of the nearby buildings, whose wide sill forms a suitable dark space in which to hide. Everything is calm and quiet when the night has taken the streets of Bälkaar, with only two amazons visible by the entrance, who try to warm themselves by the great braziers placed on both sides of the gates. Everywhere else you see nothing but silent, empty streets, plunged into total darkness by a sky filled with thick, black clouds.

So you wait impatiently fearing discovery and, despite what you had expected, nothing happens. On the contrary, everything is completely still and the only thing that you can hear is the sound of a few dogs barking in the distance. Nothing happens and time passes slowly, testing your nerves. Many thoughts come into your mind then, as you don't know if everything is a lie or, even worse, a deadly trap. You become so desperate that you choose to leave your hiding place, as you think that you must have been cheated, but suddenly your eyes reveal otherwise...

Before your astonished eyes, a huge fireball rapidly crosses the space to the gates of the Tower of the Drum, which then bursts into a thousand pieces from the destructive impact. You clearly see that the fireball has been shot from the roof of one of the nearby buildings. It came from out of nowhere, without warning and without previously showing the glow of the fire, so you think that it must have been a magic ball. But you don't have time to think of anything else as, now that the gates have been destroyed by the fireball, the moment for action has come. Without delay you sprint towards the entrance of the tower, with a view to entering it and efficiently locating Marok-häi.

As you move nearer to your objective you see that one of the amazons guarding the gate now runs about in flames, shouting in terror; an arrow shot from the darkness quickly puts an end to her suffering. The second amazon, still somewhat shocked by the blast, runs into the tower, but a cloaked shape quickly emerges out of the shadows several steps ahead of you and runs immediately after her.

When you reach the entrance of the stronghold and pass through the remnants of the broken gates, you finally see the inside of the tower: narrow, steep staircases ending in total darkness. Without delay, you start running up stairs, looking for your objective. You hear people shouting ahead of you; no doubt the sounds of a fight. Nervous, you keep on going up this lengthy staircase that doesn't seem to end, but you soon reach the top where you discover the concealed shape that ran after the second amazon, whose corpse now lies at her feet.

"Quick, let's look for Marok-häi and kill her!" the concealed shape tells you with a voice that is undoubtedly female. "My companions will cover us!"

You don't have time to answer nor to think anything else, but when you come near to her you see clearly that she is an elf. You don't have time to see anything else, as when you turn to check where you are, you see several amazons running towards you. Get ready for the impending fight...

◘ **First amazon:** Rapier (SK). Damage: 1d6+3 / SK 4 / LP: 25 / Armor: Hardened leather breastplate (C). Action area: trunk (values 2, 3 and 4). Protection: 3 LP. Hardened leather armbands and greaves (A) (G). Action area: arms and legs. Protection: 2 LP / Special ability: Skilled fencer with rapier. Your opponent is a real master in fencing, as she has trained for all of her life, specialising in this weapon. Given her mastery of the rapier, she can't roll a 1. Re-roll the dice whenever she gets a 1 as a result.

→ If you defeat your opponent: 311
→ If you are defeated: 328

360

A massive horn emerges from the thick vegetation and, immediately following it, the impressive creature that owns such an enormous horn. You are positive that this is a vrölek, a strange breed of rhinoceros that lives in very few areas of Urowen. The huge beast thunders directly towards you: get ready for combat and pray that the vrölek misses its charge. Read the special ability of this creature and play it right before the fight...

◘ **Vrölek:** Horn (STR). Damage: 1d6+5 / STR 6 / LP: 42 / Armor: Extremely thick skin. Action area: whole body (values 1 to 6). Protection: 5 LP / Special ability: Charge. Right before the first assault, the vrölek charges towards you wildly, making the earth tremble. Roll a dice to determine if your enemy runs over you. If the result is a 5 or 6, it has been a successful attack, but you still have the chance to avoid this charge by rolling another dice. If you then roll a 6, you'll be able to fully avoid the charge. There isn't a damage location roll for a charge: if struck you take the full impact of 2d6+3 irrespective of your armor, as they are useless items before the overwhelming strength of the vrölek.

→ If you defeat this real beast: 286
→ If the vrölek defeats you, go to section 258, but don't lose this page or forget that you are in section 360.

361

Thanks to the extraordinary combat you've fought to kill the monstrosity, you win 1 experience point and regain 40 life points (with a limit of 100). But your new victory is now a thing of the past, as you must quickly keep on moving. You leave the corpse of that monster behind and head deeper down the corridor, calling Eddmont's name endlessly, who finally answers from the end of the dungeon, shaking his hands through the bars of his cell. You immediately call for the elves behind you, and they gather to help set the prisoner free, but you now realise that one of your companions is missing.

"We couldn't do anything for him," says Kúdinar with great sadness. "One of these beasts ripped off his head!"

You all understand that you don't have the time to mourn him, so you quickly put the keys you've found to good use and open Eddmont's cell, finally freeing him from his prison. To your surprise, the cousin of the King of Verinfes is just a boy, a teenager who shows clear signs of having suffered brutal torture. You now have just one more requirement in your misson: escape this hell, which is unlikely to be an easy task, as another group of enemies now enters the corridor. Get your weapon ready once again to deliver death and destruction... Keep on reading.

→ Go to section 315.

362

You leave your position behind the tree and run to the fence, hidden within the shadows of the night. Once there, you move stealthily to your left, trying to find a place where you can enter unnoticed. You walk cautiously for a long stretch where the fence runs in a straight line, but you don't seem to be in luck, as there's nothing here that draws your attention. But then, to your surprise, something crashes into the fence directly on the opposite side of your position, making the planks of the fence shake violently. You clearly hear the growls of some kind of beast, which agitatedly snorts and scratches at the fence while it smells the area, obviously alerted by your presence. You keep on moving at a fast pace, but the unseen creature on the other side follows you without hesitation, growing ever more agitated as scratches more intensely on the fence...

You then spot something that you can put to use, as right by the fence is a tall tree with a thick trunk, its branches spreading over the barrier. This tree could aid you to cross to the other side, even if that forces you to fight the creature that waits for you there. However, that is one of your missions: to kill any monstrosity that bars your way...

→ If you are willing to jump the fence using the tree: 348
→ If you decide to look for a more discreet way to get in, and now move away from the fence to try and mislead the creature before trying a different direction: 276

363

After having chosen the worst possible way forward, you resume walking, sinking deeper and deeper into the water, until it rises up to your chest. The smell is offensively nauseating, and your feet are stuck within gluey mud, making your movement slow and very laborious. Nonetheless, you continue on cautiously, almost without a sound, as you don't know what you may find ahead in this silent tunnel. Thankfully, you soon reach a set of stairs that lead you to a higher corridor, finally escaping the nauseating water. After having rested for some moments to squeeze at your soaking clothes, you resume walking until you round a corner, where you are surprised to find a guard stationed. He is a dreadful opponent holding a long rapier, which he now raises and points at you.

"Who the hell are you? Tell me the watchword!" he exclaims with a hostile attitude.

Unable to give him a coherent answer, as you didn't expect anybody to ask for a watchword, you hesitate for a moment, giving your opponent time enough to realise that you are an intruder. Without delay, the guard attacks. Give it your best effort to escape with your life...

◘ **Hireling at Krénator's service:** Rapier (SK). Damage: 1d6+4 / SK 5 / LP: 27 / Armor: Hardened leather breastplate (C). Action area: trunk (values 2, 3 and 4). Protection: 3 LP. Hardened leather armbands and greaves (A) (G). Action area: arms and legs. Protection: 2 LP / Special ability: Skillful swordsman. Your enemy is a fencing master, a veteran fighter who is very hard to beat. Given his mastery with the rapier, he cannot roll a 1 or 2. Re-roll any dice that gives these results.

→ If you can defeat this tough enemy: 377

→ If your enemy makes you bite the dust, go to section 277, but don't lose this page or forget you are in section 363.

364

Determined, you choose the tunnel to your right and immediately enter, keen to unveil the secrets hidden beyond. It immediately descends abruptly and you find it rather difficult just to maintain your balance, as it is a very steep slope and the ground becomes damper, making your footing difficult. You finally stumble on this unsteady surface and crash into the stone wall. What happens then leaves you breathless, terrified...

■ Roll for Perception (PER) with a difficulty of 6. Roll a dice and add the value of your PER attribute to the value of the dice. If the total is 6 or higher, you have succeeded in your roll.

→ If you are successful, go to section 389.
→ If you've failed, go to section 303.

Terrible is the life of the one who wants to unveil the mysteries of Urowen. You read this phrase, carved into the hard stone, when you introduce the last of the tiles. Another door, that you hadn't noticed before, opens a couple of steps to your left; a hatch similar to the one that concealed the mysterious panel.

Nervously, you think of great hidden treasures, as after you have discovered the relationship between the Code of Vorduarán and the mystery of the letters, you don't doubt that this is the work of the duÿmor alchemists. These unsociable and private dwarves, who spent their lonely life trying to unveil the mysteries of Urowen, left behind hidden secrets in these mines, as this phrase seems to prove... But you quickly set aside all of these thoughts to concentrate on the here and now, as you have a lever before you to operate. Immediately upon shifting the lever, a loud crack is heard from behind your back, as another trap opens at ground level, hidden until then by a covering of thick mud. You set your lamp on the ground and use both hands to raise a heavy tile – a perfectly carved stone plate that fits perfectly in its resting place. What you discover then leaves you breathless, as a metallic box lies within a small cubicle. You lift the heavy box with effort, and inside find the following items:

- A small bag containing several golden zaifas; very rare and highly valued all over Urowen. There is no doubt that they are coins created by the duÿmor alchemists, probably from less valued materials. If we exchange their value to common zaifas, that is to say, to the usual zaifas, these golden coins may be worth 200 zaifas.

- A pair of metallic glooming greaves wrapped in a black cloth. Action area: legs. Protection: 2 LP. Furthermore, these are magical greaves, as they've been forged by the duÿmors alchemists following a secret, painstaking process that has imbued them with the following attribute: Any time the greaves have protected you from an enemy's blow, the 2 LP that have protected you from damage will be inflicted on your enemy, who loses 2 LP regardless of their armor. Example: Your legs are struck by a blow with total damage of 5 (already deduct 1 point due to the location). The greaves give you protection for 2 LP, so you would only lose 3 LP. In addition, your enemy loses 2 LP, no matter how powerful they are or what armor is worn.

- An enchanted net. Instructions: throw the net on an enemy just before combat. The net will be damaged as soon as you throw it, as they will attempt to free themselves using their weapon. Therefore, you will only be able to use the net once. To throw it, roll a dice before the first opposed attack roll. If you roll a 5 or 6, you have successfully captured your opponent. If you roll a value from 1 to 4, your throw has failed, but you retain the net for use in a future combat. If you successfully capture your enemy, you will limit their movement during the combat, so they now deduct 2 points from the value rolled in all of their opposed attacks. In addition, this magical net inflicts damage to your opponent, who will lose 1 LP at the beginning of every combat round.

- Write down the zaifas, the greaves and the net on your character file. Remember that these coins do not fill a slot in your leather bag. As for the greaves, if you get rid of the ones you were wearing and equip this new pair, they also won't fill a slot. The net does fill a slot in your leather bag, so if you want to keep it and you have filled your bag to its maximum capacity, you will have to leave behind another item.

- After this great find, your mind once again focuses on the objective that brought you here; to obtain the roots of alédoras that will set you free from the curse of the witch. You eagerly resume your quest. Keep on reading.

→ Go to section 257.

366

This was a devastating, mortal trap... and you have seen it in operation first hand. You've suffered such severe injuries that you are literally skewered by these spears; you can hardly move and your strength rapidly fails. You bleed to death... Nobody could have predicted such a bitter end, completely alone in the darkness, unable to ask for help...

You have come really far, much farther than many would have expected, but a cruel trick of destiny has led you to an unhappy ending... Such is life and death in the relentless Lands of Urowen, a highly dangerous place, where you never know what each new estrio may bring. Keep on reading.

→ Go to section 400.

You immediately look in the direction that the toothless old man is pointing at, where you see a group of men by the entrance, standing around a warrior who wears a wonderful coat of mail.

"Which one's Toljröm? The one in the coat...?" you ask impatiently.

"Oh, no! That's his master, Bors of Raidyón. Toljröm is the one with a patch over his eye. He's unmistakable!"

Surprised, you look carefully at your objective: a middle-aged man, short and extremely wiry, almost cadaverous you could suggest, even sickly. His thinning hair is grey and, as the old man said, an eye-catching black patch makes him quite unmistakable.

"Thanks a lot for your help, my friend! Here you are, another coin to have another drink! You've earned it!"

Grateful, the old man takes the zaifa from you and promptly leaves, more than happy to have another beer. Once on your own, you carefully appraise Toljröm, who now follows his master to an empty table, where Bors of Raidyón sits with the four hirelings who entered with him. Toljröm seems to now be released from his obligations, as you have the impression that he is not invited to sit at a table with people more important than him. That circumstance creates the opportunity for you to approach your target, who walks towards the bar, clearly about to down a drink or two.

"Excuse me! Could you help?" you ask Toljröm after subtly placing yourself beside him.

"What do you want?" he answers rudely.

"I'm new in the city. I've come searching for my fortune, and I'm looking for someone who may be able to help... but firstly let me buy you a drink!"

This last phrase seems to gain Toljröm's full attention. He relaxes his grumpy face and manages a faint smile, as he willingly accepts one of the jars the waitress now serves you (delete 2 zaifas from your character file).

"You look like a decent warrior," Toljröm tells you finally. "If you came here to seek your fortune, there's always room for a good sword in Wastmur. You won't have any trouble in finding someone to hire you and, if you want to join Krénator's army, you only have to enlist. From what I know, even if the job's risky, they pay well – and in gold."

"I noticed that you entered with a knight. Do you think he may want to hire me?"

"It could be; I'd have to ask him. Although it's likely that he doesn't need your services right now. We've just come back from a long journey and he only wants to rest..."

Right then, the shouts of a man near to you interrupts your conversation.

"Who dares to fight Görlok? Is there a brave man in the room?"

"Here he goes again! Damned bastard!" says Toljröm after hearing those words. "God, I'd love to humiliate that bastard before all of these people!"

"What's going on?" you ask him, suddenly interested.

"Görlok, the one over there, is challenging anybody to a drinking competition. He has never been defeated, and that's why he pays double of what you've bet against him. I would give anything to see him humiliated. He once defeated me... I was so drunk that I fell to the ground almost unconscious, and the only thing that bastard did, aside from laugh, was to pee on my face. Yeah, that he did! He pissed on me before everybody in this room! Son of a bitch!"

Unexpectedly, you now have a clear opportunity to win Toljröm's respect and trust, as you have no doubt that if you defeat Görlok, that's what will occur. You now look intently at the man who would be your opponent, a huge, fat man; a giant with a rosy face, and no doubt a tough opponent in a drinking game. You don't know if you'll be able to defeat such a beast, but if you do, things could progress much easier for you...

→ If you are willing to face Görlok: 391

→ If you'd rather forget about the contest and attempt to gain Toljröm's trust by other means: 254

368

If you are playing this section as an alternative ending after having played another option from section 381, you can go back to the warehouse of the elves at section 292 to get properly equipped, taking new armor and filling your leather bag again (don't forget that you are in section 368 so that you can come back here directly once finished).

Also, as a special hint before you play this section, it is strongly recommended that you do not modify your original character file from this moment on. Instead, record your life points, objects in your leather bag, etc. on a separate sheet of paper. This way, as if it was a videogame, you will be able to come back to this section and restart it with your character file as it is now, right before facing such a risky and dangerous task...

Once you've chosen your mission, Dhaliara takes yourself and the four elves that will travel with you to an isolated place to give you some more details and specific information related to the tasks you'll have to fulfil. According to what she tells you, the place you have to go to is in the northern section of the town, near the harbor, which is marked on a small map she now hands you. It is a huge building, a kind of mansion, where some of the most prominent subordinates of Krénator usually lodge when they come to the city. According to the reports from your spies, the cousin of the King of Verinfes, Eddmont, is locked up inside, where he's being tortured to extract valuable information. Dhaliara doesn't really know much more about this place, aside from the fact that it is always highly protected and fiercely guarded, so the only way to enter is by using brute force. That is why Kúdinar, the group's sorcerer who destructively opened the way for you at the Tower of the Drum, is one of the elves that will go with you on this mission, as he will be responsible for blasting down the doors. From that moment on, you'll have to head to the underground dungeons, killing any enemy that tries to block your way. Once you rescue Eddmont, you'll have to quickly escape with him.

- Because of your bravery in accepting this mission, you gain 3 experience points to help improve your character file before this dangerous mission.

- Dhaliara gives each of you a powerful potion that automatically increases your life points to 100. The effects of this potion last for a full estrio, so you drink it right away. From this moment on, and until you are told otherwise, your base life points are 100. Write this down on your character file (or, as has been indicated, on a separate sheet of paper).

- The she-elf also provides you with some legendary weapons imbued with great and terrible powers. You take the following weapon. Write it down on your character file.

- **Sàgrast Scepter:** A legendary crosier able to change shape during combat, adapting itself to the attributes of the warrior who's holding it and to the weaknesses of their opponent to inflict as much damage as possible (SK, STR or MAG). Damage: 1d6+6. Special attributes: Extremely handy. Given the easy movement that the Sàgrast Scepter allows, you won't roll a 1 as long as you hold it. Re-roll any dice that give 1 as a result / Critical damage: when you wound your opponent, if you roll a 5 in a damage roll (damage: 1d6+6), not only have you inflicted 11 damage points, but you have also delivered a serious injury. Therefore, at the beginning of each subsequent combat round, your enemy loses 1 life point due to bleeding. He loses this life point right before every opposed attack roll / Bonebreaker. When you wound your enemy during combat, if you roll a 6 in your damage roll (damage: 1d6+6), not only have you have inflicted 12 damage points, but you have also broken a bone. Therefore, from that moment on, your enemy will deduct 1 point from all opposed attack rolls. If you break a second bone, they will deduct 2 points, and so on / Lock on target. When you wound an enemy, if you roll a 6 in a damage location roll, not only is this attack aiming at their head, but thanks to the power of the scepter, from that moment on all of your attacks will aim at their head, receiving the 3 additional damage points (and you won't need to roll for damage location during that combat).

Aside from all what she has already told you, Dhaliara doesn't have any more information about that place, so everything is in your hands now. The estrio passes calmly, as everyone studiously prepares in the best possible way to face the dangerous challenges waiting that night. Estrion is falling when Dhaliara gathers you all again to address you.

"Good luck to all of you, my companions and friends, as we part ways again. You know what you must do! Fulfill your missions as best you can. I hope to see all of you on the ship in the harbor. Neuköulos kan, sínfulas dänder ànfer!"

After hearing her words, you leave the room in small groups, slipping out of the building through different doors and windows to go unnoticed. When it is your turn, you leave the hiding place of the elves by a rear door, and you move into the alleyways of Wastmur, which are already in shadow, as the night is close. You head to the northern area of the city and wait for the darkness to lord over the Lands of Urowen. Keep on reading.

→ Go to section 267.

369

You run wildly towards the exit, making your way through a riotous crowd that is fighting and insulting each other without restraint; you are forced to punch nearby troublemakers more than once. But luckily, nobody seems to really focus on you, and you reach the exit largely trouble-free. You immediately step outside and then keep on running, desperate to hide from your persecutors in the dark alleys of Wastmur.

→ Go to section 273.

370

When you finally regain consciousness, you find that you are lying on the floor, on your own and with a terrible headache. ↓ Not only have you lost a third of your zaifas (round up any fraction), but you also lose 1 experience point. With wounded pride you go back to the common room to try and recover before heading off again.

→ Go back to section 335 and choose another option.

371

After checking the position of the guards, you wait for the right moment to expose yourself again, although you move against the wall, hidden within its shadow. You reach a small window from where you can see the inside of the building. From what is visible through this opening, there is just a thick, lighted candle on top of a small table; everything seems to be calm with nobody inside. You decide to enter, finding yourself in some kind of guardroom, as you can see some rough swords placed in an armory. You also discover what are undoubtedly instruments of torment, such as clamps, belts, strings and masks full of skewers, nippers and saws of different sizes, thumbscrews, gags, and several very odd instruments that you are unable to identify. A chilling thought then comes to your mind, as it is likely that all of these instruments will be employed on you if you're discovered. This thought creates a lump in your throat, as the objective of the mission is to discover something else about the origin of the alleged never-ending gold of Krénator, but this place seems to be more of a jail than a warehouse for riches. However, there's no turning back, so you cautiously move on...

Nothing else draws your attention after an examination of the room, so you pursue your quest by following a narrow spiral staircase that leads down to some kind of basement. Small oil lamps placed in slots in the wall thankfully light these stairs, as you would not feel overly comfortable traversing them in total darkness. After having walked about twenty steps you suddenly bump into someone who seems to have materialised from nowhere; you hadn't heard a single step before your unexpected meeting.

Standing face to face, you now look at a horrible, nightmarish creature. Not entirely human, his body is grotesque and deformed; a hunchback with dark skin that is covered with black fur much like an animal. His massive hands are terribly disproportionate in relation to his body size, and they end in long, sharp claws... But worst of all is his chilling face, with a deformed, flat nose and two long fangs that protrude from his lips. Your strange, infuriated enemy now launches a brutal attack: get ready to defend your life...

◻ **Jailer, deformed monstrosity:** Fangs and claws, whip with five chains of sharp stars (SK). Damage: 1d6+4 / SK 4 / LP: 27 / Armor: thick skin and fur. Action area: whole body (values 1 to 6). Protection: 3 LP / Special ability: Lethal swipe. If your opponent rolls a 6 in a damage roll, he has struck you with his claws and then violently shaken you, inflicting serious injuries. Therefore, at the beginning of each subsequent combat round, you lose 2 life points due to the bleeding. You lose these life points right before each opposed attack roll / Whip grip. When this monstrosity wounds you, if he rolled a 1 or 5 for damage location, in addition to the damage delivered, he has also caught one limb with his whip. Therefore (in addition to the usual damage of the blow), you must also deduct 1 point from your next opposed attack roll. Both special abilities (Lethal swipe and Whip grip) can be activated at the same time in the same round, meaning that the jailer catches you with his whip while striking with the claws of his other hand.

→ If you kill this enemy: 290
→ If the jailer defeats you: 236

372

Somewhat disappointed, you head all the way back, but you do feel glad to still be alive. It would have been absurd to risk your life for nothing, as it's quite possible that the cave is empty, and you wouldn't have found anything of note. You manage a smile while you think about it, you've come very far and you're alive, so you walk back to Wastmur with a sense of satisfaction. Keep on reading. → Go to section 293.

373

After a long and epic battle, you finally kill that terrifying beast. ↑ Because of your great exploit, you win 1 experience point, as it isn't easy to face such a lethal, sinister creature. After calming down and regaining a little breath, you look around and realise that you haven't yet drawn the attention of any sentinel. Keep on reading. → Go to section 317.

374

You move stealthily towards the cave's entrance, and the first thing that draws your attention is the fact that the thick surrounding vegetation suddenly disappears, giving way to rough terrain that has clearly been burnt. All around you are the remnants of burnt trees, standing or lying on blackened land; this may be a clear sign indicating the presence of a dragon in the area. If there is a dragon out here, you will hardly have any chance to escape, but you gave your word to the elves, so you proceed to the entrance of the cavern, nervous yet determined. Your fear becomes even greater when you see many broken animal bones at the entrance, their white colouring making a grotesque contrast with the blackness all around them...

Now is the time to use the ring that Dhaliara gave you, as the cavern is intimidatingly dark. Following her instructions, you place the ring on your finger and wish for light; the ring's gem immediately glows, casting suitable light ahead. This display of power gives you renewed spirits, so you start walking cautiously into the cavern, following a turn ahead. Suddenly, you see something in front of you that makes your skin crawl, as here crouches a huge creature, looking at you intently. You have never seen nor heard about such a remarkable creature, as it is a beast that reminds you of a dragon, yet it isn't. Its serpentine body is flat and slim, with a massive snout and a mouth full of long, sharp fangs. A long and powerful tail defines this terrible beast, whose body appears to be covered with endless bony scales, each one as hard as steel. But there's something else that draws your attention: a thick chain pinned to the wall seems to retain the creature with some kind of harness that holds its legs and body. You don't have time to notice anything else before the monster advances...

◘ **Giant reptile, unknown species:** Fangs (STR). Damage: 1d6+5 / STR 6 / LP: 34 / Armor: Thick scales and skin. Action area: whole body (values 1 to 6). Protection: 4 LP / Special ability: Grip. If this reptile rolls a 6 in a damage roll, it has caught you in its massive jaws and attempts to break your bones. Due to such a brutal attack, any breastplate that you're wearing will suffer the consequences (regardless of the result of the damage location, that will be used, as usual, to determine the LP you lose). This piece of armor will now protect 1 life point less (modify your character file). If the reptile catches you more than once, these points will stack until the breastplate grants 0 protection. In that case, it will be useless and you must delete it from your character file / Special ability for you: given that the reptile is chained, you can try to avoid its attacks by moving away. Therefore, when you lose an opposed attack roll and you're going to take a damage roll, you'll be allowed to roll a dice. If you get a 5 or 6, you avoid your enemy's blow. If you are a minstrel, you will avoid the blow if you get a 4, 5 or 6.

→ If you finally kill this monster: 310
→ If the massive beast kills you: 296

375

Completely unable to avoid them, you can't help but see how the massive jaws of the sea snake close around your body, right before violently raising you far above the boat. The pain that you feel is indescribable and several of your bones immediately break under the impressive pressure of your opponent's powerful grip. You scream in pain for help, but it's useless, as your fate has already been decided. Luckily, your torment is short, because after crushing you even harder within its jaws, you literally burst your guts, and the giant snake swiftly gulps you down. While your life's last heartbeats fade away, you briefly see that everything around you darkens as you move deeper into the stomach of the beast, where gastric juices will soon start to digest you... You have come very far, much farther that many would have expected, but a cruel trick of destiny has led you to a shocking end... Such is life and death in the relentless Lands of Urowen, a highly dangerous place, where you never know what each new estrio may bring.

Keep on reading.

→ Go to section 400.

376

You had to make a great effort to defeat the High Fire Elemental, a really powerful opponent, and very hard to defeat. ↑ Because of your success, you gain 2 experience points to help you improve your character file. Remember that the maximum value that any attribute may reach because of experience points (EP) is 6. In addition, as a reward for your latest victory, you regain 30 life points (with a limit of 100).

But now time flies and there must be new enemies already running towards your position to attack, alerted by what has happened. Therefore, you hurriedly search the furniture here and find a bunch of keys that you believe may open the cells in the dungeon. With renewed spirits you resume running along these passageways, but you suddenly have to make a decision, as there are two possible ways to proceed. You quickly decide to divide your forces to try and locate the cousin of the King of Verinfes as soon as possible...

→ If you decide to follow the corridor to your left: 299
→ If you'd rather take the corridor to your right: 306

377

Simply superb! You are undoubtedly becoming a real master of hand-to-hand combat. ↑ Because of that, and because of your defeat of such a terrible opponent, you win 3 experience points to help you improve your character file. Keep it up and you'll soon become a genuine 'Hero of Urowen'.

After regaining your breath from the gruesome fight, you now relax and notice a great door with iron bars blocking this tunnel. You look carefully at the rough lock and immediately return to where the corpse of your enemy lies, searching for the required key. You soon find a ring with keys, and one of them allows you to move to the other side of the tunnel.

You keep on following a long, narrow corridor until you find a staircase leading to an upper floor. Since entering this basement area, you have the impression that you have walked quite a long distance in these gloomy passageways, even thinking that you may now be outside the city's walls. However, such details are not going to help you, so you keep on walking up the stairs to a cellar full of kegs. You can tell by signs on the floor that there has been a lot of movement here recently, as if many kegs had been dragged across the floor...

Intrigued, you keep on searching, even opening one of the kegs, which only contains a spiced wine. Right then, something catches your attention, as you see a glimmering in a nearby corner: a half-buried small grain of gold. Prior to this you hadn't found a single trace of Krénator's store of gold. With renewed spirits for having finally found some of the precious metal, you store your finding and keep on exploring the building, now ascending another staircase heading to a floor above.

You are immediately surprised by what you find here, as it would appear that you are in the home of an artisan or farmer. It is a humble home, as you can see only kitchen tools and several blankets on the straw-covered floor; no sign of any inhabitants. You open another door, expecting it to lead to another room, but you instead step into a small barn where you are astonished to see a carriage, apparently ready to leave, as two black horses are harnessed to it, waiting to set off. As in the previous room, nobody is anywhere to be seen, so you immediately approach the carriage and open the rear hatch: it is loaded with several large chests, locked with sturdy padlocks.

Right then you hear a loud crack, as the door in front of the horses begins to slowly open.

"Who's there? Show yourself, you bastard!" barks a hoarse voice.

These words make your blood run cold, as you have clearly been discovered, and now can only face your destiny. You quietly move away from the carriage to discover who it is that has found you here. You can't help but feel intimidated, as your opponent is a real duÿmor, and you would bet that he is one of the fiercest of his race, judging by his appearance. You would never have imagined that you would face a duÿmor, that old, strange race also known as the Dwarfs of the Depths, whose main characteristic is their black skin. As far as you know, they only live in the innermost and most unattainable caverns of the Úreher Mountains, where nobody knows what they do to survive...

Cutting off any further contemplation, you look closely at your opponent: an admirable duÿmor, almost as burly as two dwarfs; a real giant of his race. He has extraordinary muscles and a really fierce appearance. His face is disturbing, and the wild gaze given to you under frizzy, bristly hair daubed with some kind of grease or oil, is massively intimidating. He has a thick, braided beard, where you can see many golden rings; these are similar to the thickness of the ring worn in his nose. He wears formidable armor: a reinforced coat of mail with greaves and armbands, and a sinister, strangely-shaped helmet that he holds in one hand. This impressive appearance is completed by an enormous warhammer that you can see protruding from behind his back, with one side of the head curving down to form a long and lethal spike.

"Well, well, I'm afraid you've chosen a bad moment to poke around in here!"

That's all the dwarf says as he rapidly puts his helmet on and grabs his warhammer before attacking. Intimidated and fearing for your life, you get ready for the impending fight...

* Author's note: in order to defeat this toughest of enemies, don't hesitate to use everything that you have in your leather bag, because if you are defeated, know that there are destinies worse than death.

▫ **Duÿmor, high-ranking officer:** Warhammer (STR). Damage: 1d6+6 / STR 5 / LP: 38 / Armor: Reinforced helmet (H). Action area: head. Protection: 4 LP. Coat of mail (C). Action area: trunk (values 2, 3 and 4). Protection: 5 LP. Reinforced armbands and greaves (A) (G). Action area: arms and legs. Protection: 3 LP / Special ability: Extremely tough. This enemy has outstanding endurance. Whenever he rolls a 6 in any type of roll, he regains 1 life point (with a maximum of 38) / War veteran. This enemy is a skilled warrior, a master with a warhammer. Therefore, he cannot roll a 1. Re-roll any dice that show 1 as a result. / Duÿmor rage. If his LP drop below 20, the duÿmor rage will activate, increasing his STR from 5 to 6.

→ If you are victorious in this titanic battle: 399
→ If this intimidating duÿmor defeats you: 214

378

An Elemental is a very difficult enemy to defeat, regardless of whether it is a Water, Fire, Air or, like in this case, an Earth Elemental, it is an enemy that brutally punishes you for making any small mistake... You haven't been a worthy opponent this time, and that's why you are in this difficult situation. Because of the serious injuries that the Elemental has inflicted, you permanently lose 1 base life point, due to the severe physical repercussions you'll have after this fight. Remember that you permanently lose this life point, so you now have to modify your character file. Every time you are defeated by the Elemental you will lose another base life point, so if you are defeated several times, it would then be advisable to go back to a previous base camp and resume your game from that point, knowing in advance of the difficult enemies you will have to face in the Tower of the Drum.

→ Now, if you feel ready, go back to section 272 and kill that monstrosity created by dark, arcane forces capable of controlling the power of nature.

379

Despite all your efforts to defeat your enemy, you couldn't help but lose... Right then you are lying on the floor, unarmed and completely battered, at death's door. Short of breath, you see how Bors of Raidyón now hammers his axe onto the head of the opponent who defeated you and then immediately stands above you, frowning down with a gaze full of hate. Not only have you killed several of his trusted men, but you have also attempted to humiliate him. Such an outrage can have only one punishment, as for someone like Bors of Raidyón, a mercenary used to killing in cool blood, the lives of people like yourself are completely worthless.

That is why you watch on in horror as your enemy raises his battleaxe over his head and immediately aims it at your exposed neck...

Suddenly, you are plunged into total darkness, falling into nothingness, while the floor of 'The Sword in Flames' drinks your blood, which now pours out from the huge wound where your crudely severed head was detached from the rest of your body.

You have come very far, much farther that many would have expected, but a cruel trick of destiny has led you to a really disturbing end... Such is life and death in the relentless Lands of Urowen, a highly dangerous place, where you never know what each new estrio may bring. Keep on reading.

→ Go to section 400.

380

This enemy has crushed you, humiliating you so terribly... and you won't be able to continue your adventures unless you defeat him. ↓ As a penalty for having been defeated you must choose one of these options before fighting him again: lose 1 experience point, delete 1 item from your character file or permanently lose 1 protection point from one piece of armor, as it has been severely damaged during the fight. Choose one of these options, modify your character file, and then go back to the section where you were to fight this enemy again.

381
Base camp

You now head to a big room, where all the elves sit around a table at the request of Dhaliara. It is Dhaliara herself who takes the floor after your arrival.

"My friends... you all know the reasons that have brought us here. After many estrios researching and gathering information, the elves of the snow who were hidden here have given us the information needed to conduct our assault tonight. We mustn't delay, as every estrio we stay in this dangerous city we risk discovery. That is why we must take action, and soon. I think it will be best if we assign the different missions in order to achieve all of their objectives at the same time, before raising suspicion. If we do it this way, the alarm will sound, but if we are lucky we will have achieved all of our objectives before their surveillance is strengthened, and by then we will be far away. Our mode of operation will be as follows.

Firstly: we will distribute the missions. Secondly: we will all proceed at the same time, when the night comes. Thirdly: we will gather at the ship in the harbor. As soon as the last of us arrives, we will set sail and flee from this place. If any of you are in trouble and can't make it back on time, know that we will wait for you until Estrion rises. Then, to our great regret, we will set sail leaving any stragglers behind, and they will have to flee using their own means. Unfortunately, we won't know where you are at that point, so trying to help would be very dangerous for the rest of us. Do you all agree? Any questions?"

A deathly silence descends over the room then, as all of the elves, some with serious, frowning faces, are aware of the terrible dangers they'll likely face. To the last of them they would prefer their own death rather than betray or endanger the rest of the group.

"Fine, I would not have expected any less from you," Dhaliara says. "I know you are all impatient to get ready, so we will distribute the missions right away. This is what we have to do. We must try to distribute them the best possible way..."

- Here are the different objectives that the elves of the snow have to fulfill in the city of Wastmur. Choose just one of them, as you will only play one mission this time. Once you have started playing it, you won't be allowed to come back to this section, as the other members of your team will be trying to achieve the other objectives. Please note that in all of these missions you will have to proceed unnoticed, although that will not be an easy task. Of course, you are still completely free to kill any enemy you find. Your future will depend on your choice...

→ According to our information, on the outskirts of the western area of the city, there is a great ranch where some of the creatures made by Krénator are apparently held. It is told that the wizard there is cross-breeding humans and some of the most dangerous animals in Urowen through magical means, and that he would already have created a number of powerful monstrosities to be put to use in war. Objectives: gather more information and kill as many of these beasts as you can find. Section 397.

→ The armies of Krénator grow more powerful every estrio, as the wizard is constantly hiring mercenaries thanks to gold shipments that seem to be infinite and whose origin is unknown. Objectives: gather as much information as possible on the origin of the gold and then steal as much as possible. Section 343.

→ It is said that one of the dragons that has been seen lately in the skies of Urowen has its lair in a cave on the outskirts of the city. Objectives:

check if this is true and, if it is, gather as much information as possible about the alleged dragon. Section 323.

→ Information received suggests that a traitor who has travelled from Verinfes with important information is going to sell it to our enemies. Apparently, the traitor has been seen in a tavern called 'The Sword in Flames'. Objectives: find the traitor, named Toljröm, gather information about what he has already spoken of in Wastmur, and kill him. Section 314.

→ Hardcore version. Only for advanced and extremely powerful characters, given how difficult and dangerous this gory mission will be. Do not choose this mission if you don't have at least 5 (6 is strongly recommended) in STR, SK or MAG. This hardcore version is designed to be played either now, or better still, replayed at the end of the game, once you've finished the book. As in many videogames, once you have finished your adventures in Urowen, you can come back to this section and play an extra or alternative ending. You could then come back here and play this option, as if it was an extra level of your original game or an unlocked level. To do so, if you don't choose this option right now, you can write down section 381 on your character file, indicating that once you have finished your game, you will then be able to undertake a difficult alternative ending.

When you play your chosen section, it is strongly recommended that you do not modify your character file from this moment on. Instead of doing so, it is more advisable to write down your attributes, life points, objects in your leather bag, etc, on a separate sheet of paper. That way, as if it was a videogame, in case luck turns its back on you, you'll be able to come back to this section and play it again with your character file in its original state, right before accepting the most risky and dangerous mission, that goes as follows...

Given how dangerous this mission is, you won't travel alone, instead you will be in a squad with four elves to increase your chances of success. Objectives: assault a strongly protected mansion where an important political prisoner is held and must be released. He is the cousin of the King of Verinfes, named Eddmont, who is being tortured for information. An exorbitant ransom has been asked to set him free. Section 368.

382

After a really tough fight you finally defeat your enemy, leaving his corpse on the ground of this dark alley. You seem to be safe again, so nothing now stands between you and the ship of the elves; you want to get there as soon as possible to be able to relax after this tough mission that you have fulfilled. You head directly towards the harbor to flee from this damned city, as you no longer wish to spend another minute in its filthy streets.

→ Go to section 293.

383

After searching for some time, you finally discover a small trapdoor in a corner of the floor, hidden until that moment under a pile of hay. It really isn't what you had expected, as everything suggested that if there was a doorway to be found, it would lead upstairs. When you open the trapdoor all you see is a dark, narrow tunnel heading down via a wooden staircase to the basement. At the bottom you can see a faint glow, undoubtedly coming from a source of light.

→ If you decide to go down the tunnel, using the staircase: 295
→ If you'd rather forget about this passageway, as you think it is better to leave the building and head to the other door you saw previously: 269

384

After a long and extremely epic fight, you finally defeat the terrifying beast. ↑ Because of your exploit, you win 1 experience point, as it isn't easy to face such a lethal and sinister creature. When you calm down a little and regain your breath, you move on in the direction indicated on Dhaliara's map, keen to find the entrance to the cavern. You reach a kind of ravine that blocks your way, so you decide to go through the upper area. Here is thick vegetation, which subsequently makes progress more difficult, but you get through little by little until you discover a flat path that gently descends to the huge entrance of a cave. The cavern! You have undoubtedly been lucky to find this place, as it is far more hidden than what you would have thought from what Dhaliara told you. However, this is just the beginning of your mission and danger may be waiting in any place, and if the legend of the dragon is true, it might already be stalking you. Keep on reading.

→ Go to section 374.

385

Despite your desperate attacks, the savage dip has been too tough for you, as all of the legends told about those beasts now seem to be true. Their fierceness and the fear that they instil are such that very few ever escape from their jaws. ↓ As a penalty for having lost the combat, you lose 1 base life point because of the severe physical effects its bites have caused. Delete it from your character file, remembering that it is lost for the rest of the game. If you come back to this section again you will lose another base life point, and so on. Now, take courage and stand up again to face such a sinister creature.

→ Go back to section 348 and kill that beast.

386

Great performance, totally divine! ↑ Not only do you win 2 experience points for having escaped with your life, but you also regain 40 life points (with a maximum limit of 100). After leaving the corpses of your enemies behind, you keep on moving through the mansion, until finally locating a narrow staircase heading down to the basement, where, according to your information, you will find the dungeons. You quickly descend, but the welcome you receive is not the one that you would have preferred. Make your best effort to save your life... Keep on reading.

→ Go to section 289.

387

Although you have fought bravely, you were finally defeated by a great opponent who, with a final, devastating blow makes you bite the dust, unconscious...

When you finally regain consciousness, having lost track of time, you realise in horror that you are in a cold, smelly dungeon, filled with the disgusting droppings of its previous occupant. This cell is extremely small, so much so that a man lying on the floor could touch both ends with hands and feet. The walls are made of thick stone, and a dirty pallet covers the floor. Everything is very dark, as the only source of visible light seems to come from a torch placed on the outside wall, although you can't see it from inside your cell.

Terrified, and with a terrible headache, you shift nearer to the bars that block your way. A huge rat, as fat as a rabbit, crosses the door of your cell as you do so, making you gulp. Right then you remember your belongings, which are nowhere to be seen. You have lost all of your weapons and armor, as you are now only dressed in a rough robe that reminds you of a disused bag.

A noise from the corridor draws your attention, as somebody seems to be approaching. You immediately try to manoeuvre your head between the bars to try and take a look, but it is a hopeless attempt, and only when they stop in front of you, can you see the person who has approached.

"Back, you bastard!" shouts an extremely fat man with a thick beard and a sinister smile showing rotten teeth. "What did you think you were going to find here? Stupid fool!"

"Where am I? Let me out!"

"Out? Oh, you will get out, but I can assure you that when you do you would have preferred that we left you here!"

"What do you mean?"

"You should have guessed it by now, as you will soon become one of those creatures you came to kill! Yes, yes... I can already see it in your face that everything is much clearer now... You are in the dungeons of Krénator, and you're going to be one of his experiments! Who knows, you might become really powerful, or become one of those terrible and sickly monstrosities... But I can tell you one thing... you'll never be the same! Enjoy your last moments, as we will soon take you out of here. Eat this," he says, throwing a stale loaf of bread at you. "We don't want you to starve!"

After saying these words, the jailer turns his back and immediately moves out of sight, leaving you in terrible anguish because of your ghastly, uncertain future. There are destinies much worse than death, and it would seem that this time luck has turned its back on you.

You have come very far, much farther that many would have expected, but a cruel trick of destiny has led you to a really disturbing end... Such is life and death in the relentless Lands of Urowen, a highly dangerous place, where you never know what each new estrio may bring. Keep on reading.

→ Go to section 400.

388

Despite all your efforts to escape, it has been hopeless – useless... Right then you are lying on the ground, unarmed and knocked down, at death's door. Short of breath, you look up at the terrible enemy towering above you, a merciless man and an extremely powerful adversary. Not only you have killed several of his trusted men, but you have also attempted to humiliate him. Such an outrage can have only one punishment, as for someone like Bors of Raidyón, a mercenary used to killing in cool blood, the lives of people like yourself are completely worthless. That is why you watch on in horror as your enemy raises his battleaxe over his head and immediately aims it at your exposed neck...

Suddenly, you are plunged into total darkness, falling into nothingness, while the floor of 'The Sword in Flames' drinks your blood, which now pours out from the huge wound where your crudely severed head was detached from the rest of your body.

You have come very far, much farther that many would have expected, but a cruel trick of destiny has led you to a really disturbing end... Such is life and death in the relentless Lands of Urowen, a highly dangerous place, where you never know what each new estrio may bring. Keep on reading.

→ Go to section 400.

389

To your astonished eyes, the ground beneath your feet begins to crumble, as it isn't the solid bedrock you thought it to be. You stand on a trap now activated, opening a wooden gate that hid a deep well with sharp upward-facing spears at the bottom. Fortunately, you've been able to react very quickly and have successfully jumped to the other side of the abyss. Here you land on solid ground, safe and sound and without a single scratch. You've been really lucky this time, but be really careful from now on, as danger may be waiting for you where you least expect it.

You regain your breath and calm yourself a little, as you know that it was a near disaster. When you have recovered you keep on moving.

→ Go to section 329.

390
Base camp

* **Author's note:** The end is now close, and although you've had multiple choices to choose from throughout the book, from this point on, the decisions you make will be vitally important for your future. There are over twenty different endings to be found: some of them good, but several are rather horrible, the kind of ending you would never wish to find. That is

why you must carefully consider the upcoming decisions you will have to make, as they will be crucial for your future in the dangerous Lands of Urowen. Good luck, traveller!

During your journey to the city of Wastmur, you get to know your new companions better: a group of elves of the snow, come from the distant Iced City of Krindaslon, under Dhaliara's command. Dhaliara herself asks to speak with you alone, shortly before reaching your destination.

"You fought well in the tower," Dhaliara says, "and you fulfilled the mission Brádoc gave to you, but peace is still far from Urowen. A terrible war is about to start. The followers of Zorbrak are stronger and it won't be long before they claim our lands. No doubt the death of the amazon will complicate their plans, but there are still many more enemies to defeat. As Brádoc hired you in Verinfes, my small group fulfills similar tasks. We are just an advance party of the armies of the free peoples. Our mission is to infiltrate and kill specific enemies, like Marok-häi, leaders in the ranks of our enemies, to try and deliver as much damage as possible. That task is waiting for us in Wastmur, a city under the rule of the mercenaries of Krénator, the enemies of all our peoples. I must admit that your help would be really useful, and that's why I now ask you to join us. As I've told you, we have several missions to fulfill in Wastmur, all of them extremely risky and dangerous. Keep in mind that we are fighting for peace in Urowen, for the freedom of our peoples, who are threatened more and more every estrio by the followers of the Dragon God. Of course, you are free to choose your path, but I would certainly appreciate your help. If you stay with us, we will give you weapons and equipment to face the difficult missions we have to complete. If you decide not to come with us, you will disembark out of town, where you will not be in any danger. You'll be allowed to take one of our boats to safely reach the coast. So what do you think? Can I count on you or do we part ways here?"

→ If you are willing to keep on fighting for your people with Dhaliara: 292
→ If you are tired of risking your life and decide to continue on your own: 350

391

"I will face him," you state to a rather surprised Toljröm.
"Are you sure?"
"I am. Let's see what I've got!"

"Oh, great – great! Defeat that bastard and I will be the first to salute you!" Thereupon, Toljröm raises his voice and starts to loudly cry out to the crowded room. "We have a volunteer! My new friend here wants to face Görlok! Come on everyone, let's support the foreigner!"

All gazes fix on you at once. You are led to a wide table where you take a seat at one end, facing the huge Görlok, who sits at the opposite end. The moment of truth is near. Now you must decide how many zaifas to bet, and then the game will begin...

- You'll now compete against Görlok, each of you drinking jar after jar until one can't continue. You can bet as many zaifas as you want as there's no limit. Görlok will bet as many zaifas as you do, and the winner will keep his opponent's zaifas. In your case, if you win, you'll get double. So, if you bet 30 zaifas and win, you'll get back your 30 and receive 60 zaifas from your opponent. If you lose, say goodbye to your money.

- The game proceeds as follows: double your base life points. Your opponent, given that he has 27 life points, starts with 54 points. Then, roll one dice for yourself and another for your opponent. This dice represents the first jar of wine. The points that each of you receive on this dice represent the life points that you lose. Both dice are rolled at the same time and the results are compared once rolled. The first competitor to lose all of their life points is the loser. If both of you reach 0 life points in the same round, count negative scores and the one with the lowest score will be the loser (for instance, -1 wins over -3). If there is a draw even when in negative numbers (for instance, both of you score -1 in the same round), roll again until the tie is broken.

→ If you defeat Görlok: 265
→ If you are defeated: 279

392

Despite all your efforts it has been a hopeless struggle, useless... Right then you are lying on the ground, unarmed and knocked down, at death's door. Short of breath, you look up at your merciless and powerful enemy. Terrified, you watch on in horror as he raises his scimitars over his head and then immediately plunges them into your chest... Suddenly, you are in total darkness, falling into complete nothingness.

You have come very far, much farther than many would have expected, but a cruel trick of destiny has led you to a disturbing end... Such is life and death in the relentless Lands of Urowen, a highly dangerous place, where you never know what each new estrio may bring. Keep on reading. → Go to section 400.

393

Taken by surprise, you see a huge cave bear coming out of the thick vegetation ahead. It runs directly towards you, its massive jaws wide open full of white foam, with the clear intention to attack. You can't do anything to avoid this tough fight to the death...

◘ **Cave bear:** Claws and fangs (STR). Damage: 1d6+5 / STR 6 / LP: 36 / Armor: Thick fur and skin. Action area: whole body (values 1 to 6). Protection: 4 LP / Special ability: Lethal swipe. If the bear rolls a 6 in a damage roll, it has pierced your flesh with its claws, and then violently shaken you, inflicting serious wounds. Therefore, at the beginning of each subsequent combat round you lose 3 life points due to blood loss. You lose these life points right before each opposed attack roll.

→ If you defeat this monster: 286
→ If the bear defeats you, go to section 258, but don't lose this page or forget that you are in section 393.

394

Both you and your companions have been skilled and determined, bravely fighting enemies who desperately defended their position. ↑ Because of that, you win 2 experience points for your magnificent performance. In addition, you regain 50 life points (with a maximum limit of 100) thanks to a short rest. But you don't have time to waste and now run further into the mansion, looking for a staircase that will lead you to the dungeons. That is your only thought as you hastily move on, but you are then assaulted by enemies that you would never have expected. → Go to section 281 and get your weapon ready...

395

After searching absolutely everywhere for a very long time, nothing of interest draws your attention. You begin to get nervous, knowing that you are wasting precious time, so you decide to head to the stone building with a small window that would allow you to peep inside. You cautiously make your way out and, after closing the door, go back to the carriage again. Keep on reading. → Go to section 371.

396

Despite your desperate defense, the black tiger has been too tough to defeat, and you are finally at its mercy. ↓ As a penalty for having lost this fight, you lose 1 base life point due to the terrible physical consequences of the tiger's many bites. Delete it from your character file, and remember that you've lost this base life point for the remainder of the game. If you come back to this section again, you will lose another base life point, and so on. Take courage and face the sinister creature again. → Go back to section 244 and kill that beast.

397

Once you have chosen your mission, Dhaliara gives you some more details, specific information related to the objectives you must achieve. According to her information, the remote location you have to travel to is marked on the small map that she now hands you. It is a large, fenced tract of land. She doesn't know anything else useful about this sinister place, so you'll have to find a way to sneak in unnoticed. Once there, your mission will be to gather all possible information: buildings, inhabitants, whatever else you find in the farm... Additionally, your second objective will be to kill any beast that you find in your way, and it is said that they can be highly dangerous.

Everything is in your hands now. The estrio passes calmly, as everyone studiously prepares in the best possible way to face the dangerous challenges waiting that night. Estrion is falling when Dhaliara gathers you all again to address you.

"Good luck to all of you, my companions and friends, as we part ways again. You know what you must do! Fulfill your missions as best you can. I hope to see all of you on the ship in the harbor. Neuköulos kan, sínfulas dänder ànfer!"

After hearing her words, you leave the room in small groups, slipping out of the building through different doors and windows to go unnoticed. When it is your turn, you leave the hiding place of the elves by a rear door, and you move into the alleyways of Wastmur, which are already in shadow, as the night is close. You walk towards the western area of the city and then wait until darkness has fallen upon the Lands of Urowen. Only then do you decide to leave the last buildings behind and walk along a twisting path, following the instructions on the map. Fortunately, you don't have to walk too far, as you soon find an iron gate blocking your path.

You immediately hide yourself behind the trunk of a nearby tree, looking carefully about you. You can see that there is a gate and a tall, wooden fence surrounding the area, which disappears into the distance on both sides of the entrance. You can't see anything else from your position and, after considering your options, you decide that it is too risky to attempt to sneak in by climbing the gate. That is why you think it is safer to follow the fence in one direction to find a better place from which to sneak into the farm.

→ If you choose to follow the fence to your left: 362
→ If you'd rather go to the right: 276

398

You only have a single thought after all of the combats you've fought: escape with your life from the hell in which the tavern has turned into, a mortal trap full of deadly enemies. Quickly, you make your way to the exit through a crowd that fights and insults each other without pause; you are forced to punch nearby troublemakers more than once. After finally reaching the door you immediately run for safety, hiding from your persecutors in the dark alleyways of the city of Wastmur.

→ Go to section 273.

399

As soon as you defeat the duÿmor, your first thought is to escape, as you have the impression that the dwarf with the carriage wasn't going to be alone for much longer, and that reinforcements will arrive soon... The carriage!

You look again at the carriage, as it might be useful for escaping this place. You climb onto the seat and whip the horses, who immediately move forward. As soon as you get out of the building, you look around to see if there is anybody about, but it is a dark night and everything appears calm and quiet. Apparently now out of immediate danger, you force the horses to move faster, keen to be far from that place when the corpse of the dwarf is eventually discovered.

You don't travel for too long before checking that, as you had suspected, you are on the outskirts, outside the city's walls. You now have the opportunity to escape, but suddenly come to a halt in a darkened alleyway, as you can't stop wondering what the chests in the carriage contain. You use a small lever found in the carriage to open the sturdy padlock on one of the chests. When you open it, you can't help but smile broadly, as the chest is full of large, shiny gold ingots. You immediately count how many chests there are in the carriage – four of them – so you have incredible wealth onboard. There's no doubt that the duÿmor you killed was waiting for reinforcments, ready to transport the gold in the middle of the night to an unknown destination; thankfully, you've upset his plans. This thought makes you hurry, as having discovered exactly what it is that you have stolen, your enemies will surely become aware of the robbery soon and immediately start a frantic investigation.

No one can deny that you have exceeded the objectives of Dhaliara's mission, as not only have you discovered the gold that Krénator is using to pay for his army of hirelings, but you have also been able to take a considerable portion with you. Then, a new idea starts to form in your mind, as you have to make a choice. Let's see what you are willing to do...

→ If, as you promised, you decide to return to the harbor to meet the elves, keep on reading at section 293. In this case, you will give the gold to Dhaliara, who is in command, and that wealth will be used to bear the costs of the imminent war against your enemies, the followers of Zorbrak, the Dragon God.

→ If your honor can be bought by the gold you have stolen, and you choose to leave Wastmur, keeping all of that wealth for yourself to live a good life, far from war, go to section 248.

400

«The life of every hero can become legend and make him immortal».

Famous proverb written by Neithel of Flitzgar in the
'Sinqua Çalendor' or 'Desolation Codex'.

* Author's note: with these introductory words you started your adventure long ago. It is true that you have outlived much since then, travelling many estrios and fighting in many combats, and you have taken many great risks... you have encountered many dangerous enemies and also made some new friends. You have enjoyed an exciting life in the dangerous Lands of Urowen, an adventure full of emotions and events to remember. For all of these reasons, regardless of which ending you have experienced, I hereby sincerely compliment you for having reached this section, which concludes your game with an author's note. I hope with all of my heart that you have enjoyed the adventure, and that you have found pleasure in the emotion of finding the many surprises waiting for you along the way. I also hope that when time goes by, you remember this book with the same devotion I experienced when writing it for you. However, I now challenge you to play it again, as I'm sure that you have left many secrets behind. It's up to you to start this endless journey again. And if you're still willing to discover more, I invite you to resume the adventure with the novels based in the Lands of Urowen, the trilogy 'The Manuscripts of Neithel'. Learn more about these books at my website: www.david-velasco.net

Once again... thank you, traveller! Thanks for exploring the limits of this wonderful world!

* Your help in promoting this gamebook is essential. Comments on social networks, blogs etc., are very important. Therefore, I ask that you tell all of your adventurous friends about my gamebook, and importantly, write reviews about this book on Amazon and elsewhere, using the hashtag #heroesofurowen.

For my part, as always, I will be waiting with open arms via my website, or on various social networks, where you can share experiences with myself and other readers. All forms of contact are open, and now they are more interactive than ever (Facebook, Twitter, Instagram, e-mail...), I've now added direct communication through WhatsApp or Skype so that you can feel even closer to me than ever, no matter where you are in the world.

Additionally, any submissons will be most welcome. Send me your drawings of characters, illustrations of enemies and creatures, weapons, photographs with the book, stories based on 'Heroes of Urowen'... Everything you wish to share will be welcomed enthusiastically. I wait to hear from you!

More information...

Website and social networks:
www.david-velasco.net/english

E-mail: info@david-velasco.net
WhatsApp: +34 654 890 508
Skype: david-velasco-morales

Biography

David Velasco

(Malaga, Spain) After graduating in Journalism at his hometown's university, David Velasco worked in prominent media and television roles, in management and writing positions, without ever losing his vocation as a writer. Between 2008 and 2014 he served as an editor, which allowed him to understand the world of books. He is the author of 'The Neithel's Manuscripts saga', which boasts three books that have achieved huge success in his native country: 'Sabine Vashanka, the Sorceress' (vol. I), 'The Kingdom of a Hundred Moons' (vol. II) and 'The Revenge of the King without a Throne' (vol. III).

David Velasco also published an interactive gamebook in 2012, titled 'Heroes of Urowen' (a bestseller in Spain), with which he took a new direction in his literary career. The author used a great deal of experience to create this work, applying more than fifteen years as a tireless Dungeon Master, and a habitual consumer of console and computer games, to create this fantasy adventure. The last project that surprised readers was 'Krynea, the Ninth Rune', a spectacular novel based on the video game Krynea, which has further consolidated his reputation as a skilled storyteller of great imagination.

Now David Velasco returns with Anunnaki Files, much more than a novel or a gamebook.